Blaster Al Ackerman

THE COMPLETE WORKS

from
LOST & FOUND TIMES
1979-2005

Introduction by Jack A. Withers Smote
Compilation and Afterword by C. Mehrl Bennett

LUNA BISONTE PRODS
2013

Blaster Al Ackerman

THE COMPLETE WORKS
From *Lost and Found Times*, 1979-2005
Introduction by Jack A. Withers Smote
Compilation and Afterword by C. Mehrl Bennett

The Lost and Found Times,
1975-2005, was edited by John M. Bennett
C. Mehrl Bennett, Consultant

Not listed here are the appearances of some
of these works (or later versions of some
of these works) in other publications after
their appeerence in LAFT.

leg and cabbage
-for Blaster Al Ackerman

me head yr lap f
olded in its le
aves a wilted ,w
as me aimless fooot m
e rolling off yr l

eg g g g g g g g
)saw the foot with
"turd stepped in"
- *all them plastic bags !* -
))clotted in your po
cket ((( )))))so i
waved my shorts in
the summer breeze

...and a grinning at the wall

John M. Bennett

Note: "leg and cabbage" poem ▸
by JMB references Blaster's first
contribution to LAFT in 1979, p. 7

© 2013 Collaborators with Ackerman are indicated on works throughout this book: A. Fluffy Bunny, Andrew Topel, Any Salyer, Ben and John Also Bennett, Bob BrueckL, C. Mehrl Bennett, Darlene Altschul, Fran Cutrell Rutkovsky, Gerald Burns, Gerald Simonsen, Eerie Billy Haddock, Johnny Spammy, K. S. Ernst, Ivan Argüelles, Jim Leftwich, John M. Bennett, John Eaton, John E. Mumbles, Lawrence Upton, Matthew Castro, Megan Mc-Shea (and Bonnie Jones and Novash p. 293), Paul Lambert, Rudi Rubberoid, Rupert Wondolowski, Sheila E. Murphy, Stacey Sollfrey [Allam], and Stephanie Greathouse

ISBN 978-1-938521-08-9

LUNA BISONTE PRODS
137 Leland Ave.
Columbus, OH 43214 USA

http://www.lulu.com/spotlight/lunabisonteprods
www.johnmbennett.net

THIS WILL EXPLAIN

by Jack A. Withers Smote

In the mid to late 1970's, when I was writing under the name "Dr. John M. Bennett", a poet, I started corresponding with Blaster Al Ackerman. He very quickly became, not only one of my best friends and correspondents, but a regular contributor to *The Lost and Found Times*, which I had started editing and publishing in 1975. Albert's first appearance consisted of a fine drawing in the "leg and cabbage" genre for issue 6/7, in 1979. He appeared in every issue after that, through the last one, 54, in 2005. From the start, his work in LAFT included stories, poems, drawings, paintings, and other materials, including collaborations with me (as "John M. Bennett"). Beginning with issue 12, 1982, I invited him to contribute a regular LAFT column, "Ack's Wacks" , which remained a much-loved feature of the journal to the end. Along about 1987, Albert started "hacking" poems and texts by "Bennett" and others; these began appearing in LAFT 21/22 of that year as another regular feature, "Ack's Hacks". His processes for doing these works were lunatic, wonderful, and constantly varying and unpredictable. I often included his accounts of these processes, as they were often as interesting and hair-brained, or even more so, than the results. He did more and more of them over the years, so many that, as LAFT didn't have room for all the most spicy of them, "Bennett" published several chapbooks devoted exclusively to that genre of Blasterology.

Among Albert's vast swarms of creation, are the many heteronyms he wrote under, many of whom appeared in LAFT. On a personal note, I first published work under my own name in one of Al's own journals, *The Edgar Allan Poe Messenger*. I also began occasionally publishing my own work in LAFT, in spite of the unseemly nature of an editor's publishing himself in a journal under his control - but then, the editor's name, "John M. Bennett", was a well-concealed dodge, so I felt, as Jack A. Withers Smote, I could slip in under the tent unnoticed. At any rate, on a few occasions Albert wrote poems under my name - Which ones, you ask? Ah, that would be telling! - and a couple times we collaborated on a poem by "me", i.e., Smote. (Our magnum opus was Smote's long poem *The Librarian for the Criminally Insane*, San Antonio/Columbus: Piss on a Convict Press, 1989.)

To sum up, *The Lost and Found Times* would have been an entirely different beast, with far less shiny slathering and mystery, without Blaster Al Ackerman. His extraordinary and unique work there, and in so many other places and books, as well as in the mailart community's "eternal network", will live forever, I'm sure of it. And the world is thus a better place.

This anthology includes the complete works of Blaster Al from LAFT 6/7 through 54, including all the heteronyms he used there.

"Oh who can know it?" - Blaster Al Ackerman

TABLE OF CONTENTS

Introduction by Jack A. Withers Smote............................5
LAFT 6-7, 1979.............................7
LAFT 8, 1980............................8
LAFT 9, 1980............................9
LAFT 10, 1981............................10
LAFT 11, 1982............................11
LAFT 12, 1982............................12
LAFT 13-14, 1983............................15
LAFT 15, 1983............................18
LAFT 16, 1984............................20
LAFT 17-18, 1985............................24
LAFT 19, 1986............................27
LAFT 20, 1987............................30
LAFT 21-22, 1987............................34
LAFT 23, 1988............................41
LAFT 24, 1989............................47
LAFT 25, 1989............................54
LAFT 26, 1990............................63
LAFT 27, 1991............................71
LAFT 28, 1991............................81
LAFT 29, 1992............................88
LAFT 30, 1992............................98
LAFT 31, 1993............................110
LAFT 32, 1994............................120
LAFT 33, 1994............................126
LAFT 34, 1995............................138
LAFT 35, 1995............................152
LAFT 36, 1996............................161
LAFT 37, 1996............................170
LAFT 38, 1997............................182
LAFT 39, 1997............................196
LAFT 40, 1998............................206
LAFT 41, 1998............................218
LAFT 42, 1999............................231
LAFT 43, 1999............................242
LAFT 44, 2000............................253
LAFT 45, 2000............................260
LAFT 46, 2001............................270
LAFT 47, 2001............................282
LAFT 48, 2002............................289
LAFT 49, 2002............................299
LAFT 50, 2003............................308
LAFT 51, 2003............................324
LAFT 52, 2004............................338
LAFT 53-54, 2005............................358
Afterword by C. Mehrl Bennett............................381
Books and Recordings by Blaster Al Ackerman............382

ZAW LEX WITH CABBAGE RUNNING DOWN

AL ACKERMAN   L&FT6-7LBP 1979

ON MEETING ELIZABETH BOWEN

Erin I put my hand upon the stairs
Her strong white teeth were suddenly there
To cleanly take me through the wrist -
No pain at all, and yet I flinched!
And swear I heard them choppers meet
And click - and found myself held fast, held fast,
By shining teeth in monkey face, that grinned,
                                    and grinned,
But would not let me pass.
My friend! there was no pain, and yet I swear
She held me there from 2-till-6 --
Her and her teeth and her
Little black eyes, madly hopping in her face,
Like fleas, like tics, like flies --
                    like arithmetic!

THE SENSE OF UNWASHED SHANKS AS PROUST'S CAKE

In long-handles I think I might resemble him,
Sweetheart. Streak my hair yellow as well as gray
And claw my beard fully to whiskers, then I
Could say Uncle George! surprizing myself
In the bathroom mirror, just as the odd thought
Of him, after it must be twenty years or
More, surprized me last night, caught me unawares.
Well it filled me with glee. Bull joy. Enter
The crammed pigeonholes of Time's musty desk
Is a small death compared to real felark
Of Uncle George's rooms. Hairs, long brown ones,
As from a closet brush, Oz lion's bad cough,
Were braided up his sofa-arms in tufts,
Drying like drowned horses' manes. But not quite dry.
Sweetheart, a pound of okra filled his seat,
I swear it. When, therefore, my great-aunt's
Whiskper, beating away the mottled air
Like a countrywoman's broom, failing
At that, as the fainted July sun flicking
And flicking itself against the sticky green
Black candy windows of George's shack,
Said Why he hasn't had a bath since Mame died,
Was unavailed, because he was deaf, and
He was unwashed, I felt, sweetheart, such love
For that old unwashed man, it near to tore
My head off, and shit in my neck. Saint George.
We sense sanctity how late. Your remark
Brought it back to me last night. When you said
You need a bath. When you said I smell your taint.

Al Ackerman

Al Ackerman & John M. Bennett

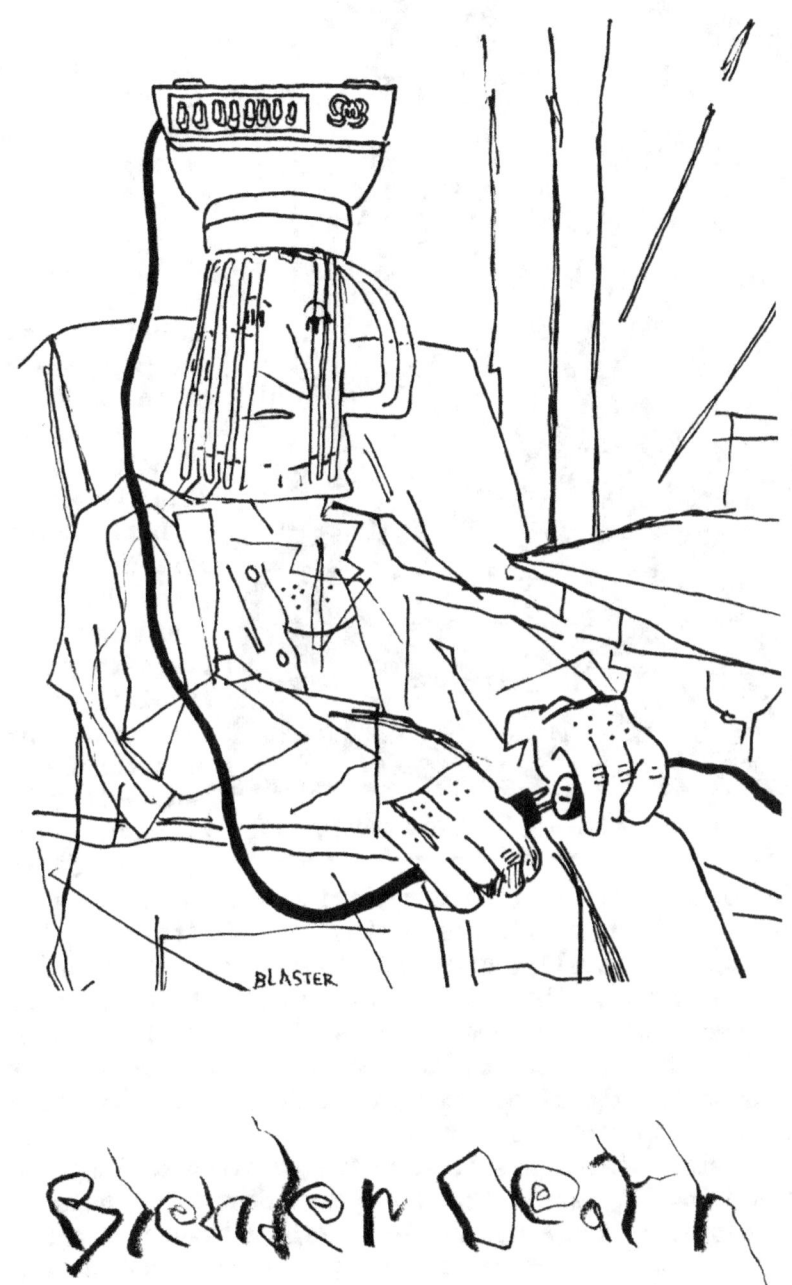

Ack's Wacks

a column of insight & Mystery by
DR. AL ACKERMAN

"By Sitting on the floor I got my pants off!"

SOME WILL SAY that my facts are loutish & even unsavory. But, as the late great Philip Guston was wont to remark, this is merely "true". There _are_ other criteria.

Your editor has asked me to do an occassional column. His only instructions were that I was to hold it down if possible to one page—he knows how I tend to go on. I didn't quite make it, but I tried....

Actually, I have known about this, known that I would wind up here in these pages, or to be more truthful, in your company—since November of 1964. So you could say I have known about it for nearly 20 years. Not that I am wildly psychic or anything of the sort. I have a fair amount of intuition, but this intelli-gence—that I would wind up here talking to you—belongs to an al-together different category of experience. The explanation to such a mysterious phenomena goes like this:

In November 1964, I was a prisoner of the U.S. Military, in Montgomery, Alabama. I was 24 at the time. Naturally, given all their low cunning and vast experience in this sort of shady farrago, the military never cared to publically admit that I was being held prisoner, and so my true status was kept camoflagued under the nebulous title of Medical Service Specialist—a smokescreen that ostensibly included attend-ing classes, working in the dispensary and so forth, but they never fooled me for a second; I knew a prison when I saw one.

What I did, mostly, when I wasn't marching to class or juggling bedpans, was drink. It was old Goethe, wasn't it, who spoke about "the ancient primitive distinct-ion between an alcaholic and a drunkard—" Well I have been a drunkard in good standing off and on for most of my life. I got pretty drunk on Jax Beer with H.P. Lovecraft and Ambrose Bierce last night as a matter of fact. But my days as a pris-oner of the military during the 60s were the only times I ever came close to be-coming an alcaholic.

Besides drinking myself into stupors, the other things I found to do, the way a baboon might find the toes at the end of his feet, were 1) play cards, 2) read the complete works of James M Cain, 3) indulge in solitary vice, and 4) try to mail myself.

This last is a euphemism, of course. It has to do with attempts at fornication, hand jobs, blow jobs and so on, carried out under the worst possible circumstances. What it was, I shared expenses with three of my fellow prisoners in illegally main-

taining wheels—a wheezing 1947 Cadillac—which we kept off-base, in a clandestine
garage. The names of my fellow prisoners were Linthead, Fuck Face, and Zero.
Never mind what they called me. We used the rat-trap Cadillac on weekends to
entice the local Alabama belles into our company, and we became fairly
widely known as four deadbeats who would head straight for the Magnolia Drive-in
Theater with a bottle of Four Roses whiskey and extremely limited funds and
try to get funny right away, and since none of us would trust the others alone
with the Caddy, it was always a mob scene. Eight struggling bodies in a 1947
Cadillac is still the most uncomfortable arrangement I can think of. Even when
things were going well, to get to the point of the euphemism, it was like
trying to mail yourself.

I still remember the night of November 1964, and that the second feature
playing at the Magnolia Drive-in was "Reptilicus."

I might have stayed in the car for that second feature if I had done what
my lovely companion of the evening, Nettie Sue, had done, which was to have
one more slug of Four Roses and pass out. But I found myself in agony instead.
It was freezing that night, and the load of jism in my shorts was beginning
to dry and harden: it felt like a clammy icy plaster gripping my loins! My
only thought was to reach the men's room, which was in the same squat block-
house as the projection booth and the snack bar, and ditch the offending
shorts. I would have done it the minute I staggered into the men's room, but
the place was occupied by three or four crackers. I waited ten minutes in
high agitation for the room to clear and then, by way of ensuring privacy,
put my back against the door and clawed at my buttons.

I eventually wound up sitting down on the floor. It seemed the only way
to get my pants off over my tennis shoes—especially in my half-bombed condition.

I remember standing up—my trousers in one hand, my foul sticky shorts in
the other (I still had on my sports coat, shirt, socks and tennis shoes)—and
was in this cruciform posture, looking blearily around for a trash recepticle
to ditch the shorts in, when I first glimpsed the other door, a metal one set
in the far wall. It was directly opposite me, and as I stood paralyzed, it
swung open and the projectionist stepped through out of his booth and into
the men's room. For one long moment we confronted each other—wordlessly.
Then he said, "Well, Gawd-all-mighty!", and jumped back inside, slamming and
locking his door behind him.

I have played that scene again and again in my mind over the past twenty
years—"The Look in the Projectionist's Eyes!" It is sometimes   given us
to actually know in detail what will become of us—a kind of eerie blinding
insight into our future lives that occurs in an instant. And that night in
the men's room of the Magnolia Drive-in, I experienced such insight, seeing
my destiny reflected in that man's staring eyes, irrevocably.

What it told me about myself was that I would never have much money—nor
was I likely to become a Rotarian, a banker, a cop, a Sundayschool teacher, or
a pillar of any community—but that if I made it through the military alive
I might expect to have, not an easy life, but an interesting one—an interesting life among others of my same ilk and kidney. There, at the age of 24
and with my ruined shorts in hand, I was let in on this strange and comforting
revelation, and as you can see, since we are in fact here together now, that's
pretty much the way it's worked out, you little cutie.

RECLUSE (CASFE)
212 W. Courtland
San Antonio, Tx 78212

CREATIONIST GOTHIC

ACK'S WACKS — A Column of Insight & Mystery

THAT WAS WHEN HE BECAME HYSTERICAL

(CONCERNING A PATIENT OF MINE, A ONE-TIME DELICATESSEN OWNER, KNOWN
FONDLY AND ON THE WHOLE NOT UNFAIRLY TO HIS WAGGISH FRIENDS AS MAD
TOM, WHO WOKE UP IN A CINCINATTI HOTEL ROOM AT ELEVEN IN THE MORNING
AFTER A FOUR DAY BENDER..)

He woke up still half drunk and knew he had to do something, he
was inches away from the horrors, he could tell because the transom
over the door, the ceiling, the chair, the cruddy dresser, the lamp
resembling a sea horse, he could not bear to rest his eyes for more
than a fraction of a second on anything in the room.

He proceeded with his terrible inventory and told himself that
he had absolutely no idea who the lumpy gray creature lying next to
him in bed might be; she was snoring like an alligator! But it was
too much like the old jokes and it made his movements extra stealthy
on the mattress springs so as not to disturb her, so as not to see
her suddenly rise up honking and (for all he knew) clawing down in
among all that damp unappetizing cleavage for the license—the
proverbial quicky marriage license of the jokes. (Some jokes!)

He had to have a drink.

Something to stave off the horrors—

Something to stave off the thing that was running up softly behind him like a moving wall——

He hung his bare legs to the floor.

He had his socks on.

He still had his shirt on too, as stiff and spooky as a plaster
cast.

He looked around the room.

He licked his lips.

He saw a bottle on the dresser, he narrowed his eyes, forcing
himself, but it was nothing but an empty—a dead soldier.

He saw another dead soldier that had rolled back in under the
dresser, and one tangled up in his blotched shorts on the chair.

Out in the hall something bumped softly against the door.

He stood up, trembling.

He crept around the room, he crept into the bathroom (it's beginning to get a little hot in here for this, I'll finish off), he
found two bottles in the sink, and one in the tub, more dead
soldiers, and then found the lumpy gray creature's purse tipped
over on the back of the toilet, and tore into that: it had a bottle
of Aqua Velva After Shave Lotion in it, half full.

But After Shave was better than the horrors, he drank it off in
two, more like three swigs and felt a little better.

When he crept back to the bed, his companion was still snoring.
But when he let himself down again onto the chiming springs, she
roused up a little and rolled over, and sniffing and sampling the
air with her twitching white nostrils but without ever quite man-
aging to get her gummed-together eyes open—spoke at him:

"Aw, honey," she said, lover-like, "you shaved for me!"

—DR. AL ACKERMAN

WHITE WORMS

INFINITE PRIVATES

Of all, the most powerful
O spawn,
Mightier than the Dork Cyclops,
Mightier than your Hydra Dad,
Than any old red-eyed BEM.
And when I lift my orbs unto the mountains and behold you,
Lamp the White Multitude of you and you and you wriggling there,
It sure blows me out O Spawn of my single uncooked pork chop.

A LOVER TO HIS BOTTLE OF WHITE PORT

(For Louis Buffin)

O day that steals my brain away
Jumps me over bitter coffee first
And hounds me out into the street;
Bereft of a shave I lose my way, stray
And stagger suffering fifty thirsts
Till at noon I am revived at your sweet gurlging teat.

Fear not, beloved one, I'll not sully you with food!
But come let's stretch out in our favorite place
To hold the firey afternoon at bay
And between these cuddles be amazed at how good
The pavement feels. It does, when I can taste
Your mouth, your torchy essence of white grape.

We roll around empty doorways where
No big cop feet intrude and our dreamy bliss
May last as long as I have my brother's watches left to pawn.
Then, sweet white one, filling me with your rare
Liquid light, come whisper in my ear where your sister lives;
Tomorrow I'll needs must find her, when you're gone.

Al Ackerman

16

ACK'S WACKS
a column of gastropodal Insight.

"ANDY JAWS AND THE GUMP"
(Dateline - Austin, Texas - 15/6/83)

The Austin Comedy Workshop featured a very interesting act the other night—Andy Jaws and The Gump—and we made a point of driving the seventy-some-odd miles to catch it. Andy Jaws and The Gump interested us because of what Paul LaFaith, a medical journalist in Florida, had written about them several years ago in THE OTHER ROOM, a magazine that makes a specialty of reporting on "new cults, alternate states of existence, mutations and strange agents," as the magazine's masthead always puts it. The LaFaith article, titled "The New Dummyism," began with a survey of the then growing number of performers who were electing to have themselves surgically altered to resemble Elvis, Janis Joplin, and Jackie Kennedy. "The more extreme side of all this," wrote LaFaith, "is that last month a man who calls himself Andy Jaws actually had one of his hands surgically altered into a tiny head, complete with face. Andy Jaws is a ventriloquist, you see, and his hand-head, built mostly out of hip fat, sports an especially mobile mouth, sockets for glass eyes, even moveable skin flaps for eye-lids. A deluxe job—and judging from the medical photos I saw at the hospital, I'd venture to say that once on stage and dressed up like Charlie McCarthy, the head (which Andy bills as "The Gump") could pass for the genuine article; although close to and without the glass eyes, it looked less like a face than it did a Chinese concubine's feet, one fresh from the bindings, a truly unsettling sight. Hair had been transplanted, too, but that looked to be sparse and just coming in. The interesting thing to speculate on, is Andy's mental status, particularly as time goes by, now that he has his little pal always there at the end of his wrist to talk to...and do things with."

To describe the act itself as we caught it the other night at the Comedy Workshop. Well, neither LaFaith's advance warning nor the five or six gin fizzes that we got behind early on at our table down close to ringside had prepared us for the reality of Andy Jaws and The Gump. Andy Jaws has red hair for one thing, the kind that goes with very pale skin and lashes—so does the Gump, grown out, in the little head's case, into a kind of modified, yarny fright-wig. A small yellow bow-tie sewn to the ventriloquist's sleeve was the only attempt to outfit or costume The Gump, yet chattering and bobbing there in the blue spotlight, The Gump's presence quickly established itself, and it soon became difficult not to think of the altered hand (or head) as a separate entity. The act started routinely enough. Andy Jaws, repeatedly shoving The Gump down toward his fly, seemed poised to do low crotch jokes all night. After a good deal of inane patter, the pair wrangled their way into an off-key duet, something called "I Wonder Who's Kissing Her Whatchamacallit?"—all, all commonplace. Then, in a moment of extraordinary transition, it was as though the Gump were speaking for the first time. "All right, now, you go away, Andy," said The Gump, "and I'll talk." The ventriloquist's head was bowed, as if in trance; the audience, hushed, had entered into a blue midnight space; and we heard, from deep in a place of our own, a voice saying "Hello, gang."

THE GRAY TRUSS.

It was a feminine voice, unmistakably. "Hello, gang," it began in a young, rather querulous nasal tone, which from the sound of it was no stranger to the bathroom medicine cabinet where the prescription pills and capsules live. But the monologue that followed was too mysterious an organism to be dissected, or even recalled very precisely. Here, then, is the best we can do at reconstructing the essence of it:

    "Hello, gang. I'm Mrs Cookie. Annie Cookie. This is my husband Andy Cookie, who works six days a week at Calico Instruments, Inc. He's into a transition phase at work. This is our little one, Evelyn-Morgan. She's into the 'into everything!' stage of development. We have many television sets and microwaves and labor-saving gadgets. We're the Cookie Family. We love to drive from one shopping place to another. But"—(here the voice seemed to take on a special hectic excitement)—"beware of the scarlet scarecrow and the dancing blue woman and the shaggy man. Relax not your vigilance against them for even a second. Revelation 2:22. Oh, how it frets my heart to think about them. Especially that nasty shaggy man. But we should always remain pleased with the good things we have. Our neighbors have a house on the lake. It is great summer excitement. Andy is looking for a new project at work. Evelyn-Morgan loved her first swim. Last Friday, we thought we saw the shaggy man lurking in the mild sunshine outside the shopping center. But our friend the china Snoopy dog appeared just in time to drive him away. It was as if no time had passed. Back at the house again, Andy went out to jog around the golf links; Evelyn-Morgan enjoyed a snack of peanut butter and crackers; and I passed the late afternoon hours crumbling potato chips to go on top of the Tuna Casserole Supreme for our young adult's prayer group. Well, that's the news from this neck of the woods. It's wonderful to have air conditioning. Remember, don't toss out your old panty hose—you can make pillows, toys, flowers, even a rug. One more little item. Another little Cookie is on the way. ETA January 2nd. Yes, this was planned and we are delighted. Look around. More and more of us every day. Goodbye. See you real soon," the voice said to the Comedy Workshop audience. ("See you real soon," echoed the audience.)

    That is the gist of it. We have no doubt we've omitted a lot, but this queer hypnotic monologue left us so groggy—the side of our head buzzing like a flounder—that it was several minutes before we even realized that Andy Jaws and The Gump were off the stage. Later, at a crowded after-the-show party, the dolorous, sinister implications of the thing struck us as we stood and watched Andy Jaws, his hand now covered in a black silk bag, cavorting and mixing and having the time of his life. He did not touch a drop of booze and yet he looked ready to wear a lampshade and kick over the cake. We have since wondered why he should look so happy, so much the best-integrated, most fulfilled American personality we have encountered in years.

ACK'S WACKS

A COLUMN OF HIGH FINANCE AND DECORUM BY DR AL ACKERMAN

"Dear Dr Al: I've heard that back in the mid-60s your friends called you "The Crab." I wish you'd fill us in on how this nickname came about, if it isn't too embarrassing," writes a reader from Bethlehem, Pa.

This is undoubtedly a widespread longing. But in order to fill you in on how I came to be called "The Crab," I have to first fill you in on how one summer I was taking a two week vacation from my regular hospital job and I got the idea that it might make an interesting experiment to go around town putting in bogus job applications, a routine that consisted of me scanning the help wanted columns until I found a dismal-sounding job about which I knew absolutely nothing, and then going right in and applying for it under an assumed name, which seemed preferable to using my own because it gave me a chance to see if anybody remembered "Harry Emerson Fosdick" or "Friederich Engels," though as it turned out they didn't even remember "Charles Starkweather," and nobody ever knew me for an imposter. I also made it a big point at each office I visited (this was one of the prime factors in my experiment) to personally exhibit different types of weird, shabby and inappropriate behavior.

I started out by answering an ad for "Price Change Clerk For Wholesale Plumbing Supply—must know 10 key calculator." This seemed made to order for my first venture into the realm of bogus job hunting because I was completely in the dark as to what a price change clerk might be, and I knew no more about the 10 key calculator than does Emily Fusselman's rabbit. A rather humorless woman who looked a little like Mrs Tucker does on the lard cans and was the wife of the plumbing store owner interviewed me. Grudgingly she handed me a pencil and a few flimsy yellow forms to fill out and pointed me to a chair in the corner, and then proceeded to give me the double-o with a dismay that was clear and unalloyed. Mostly because the blue seer sucker suit I was wearing on that sweltering day hadn't been cleaned or pressed since Christmas and I had gone three days without a shave or bath especially for the occasion. I'd also been careful to drink half a pint of fine Four Roses Whiskey before entering the establishment, and I reeked. I could feel her eyeing my filthy collar and stubbly jowls and wrinkling her nose at the essence of Four Roses that came rolling off me at every breath, as from a pungent old cork. I spent a long, long time like that, hunched over the simple yellow forms, fumbling with my pencil, wheezing and sweating and mopping my face, giving every indication that if I managed to keep from passing out cold on the floor, it would be a real victory. Pretty soon the plumbing lady came over and asked me if I was alright. "You don't look so good, Mr Voltaire," she said. "I can't think of how you spell Travis County," I said. "Oh," she said. "Well, maybe you should come back another time when you're feeling better—" I breathed on her some more and said, "It's just that these ulcers I get on my leg make it hard to concentrate and I think that must be what's hanging me up now because I started getting a big one last night and it's been draining on me all morning." She looked at my legs and stepped back. On this note the interview pretty well concluded, and I managed to control myself until I got out of the building.

The name I gave to this particular routine was "The Secret Drinker" and the reactions it elicited interested me to such an extent that I spent the next few days experimenting and trying out different variations on it. For example, at the offices of Church's Chicken, where I applied for the position of "Manager Trainee" under the name of "Fulton J. Sheen", an honest but inveterate beer drinker, I had to get up twice to ask the secretary for more paper because it was taking a lot of space to list all of "Fulton J's" arrests and hospitilizations. But I hung in there, and the secretary's expression when she finally got a load of this strange and terrible human document was my reward. A day or so later at a northside blueprint firm with an immediate opening for "Civil Draftsman—min. 5 years experience," I showed up with an enormous purple wine stain down my front that was still wet and, having knocked into a couple of chairs on my way up to the receptionist's desk, was quickly told that the civil drafting position had just been filled. You could have knocked me down with a hammer. "Well," I said, throwing my eyes wildly around the office, "then do you need a civil draftsman?" (I didn't get that job, either.) Another company downtown wanted "Salesman For Manufactured House Goods," and by using the name "Felix Frankfurter," along with a fixed smile and fairly clean clothes, I actually made it past the receptionist and had a short interview with the company sales manager, a Mr Dix. He was a rather spiritless-looking but not unsympathetic character and things didn't go too badly at first. But there was no way to hide the deep thirst that raged inside me (or inside "Felix") and before long I fell off the subject of manufactured house goods and into a fervid rambling disquisition on my fondness for all sorts of hot mulled rum drinks. Mr Dix, unable to ignore these conspicuous warning signs, sat through about five minutes of this and then eased me out of his office. "Honey," I told him at the door, "remember to sweeten the rum drink with six tablespoons of honey!" He promised he would.

Hard by. In most of the personnel offices in this country there seems to be at least a tenuous rule in effect prohibiting the staff from attempting to hurt the prospective applicants by physical means. But there is no law against low psychology and many humiliating tricks are employed successfully to make the job hunter feel like a little gob of spit. So it was a heady sensation indeed for me to feel that I was, at least for the moment, turning the tables on this age-old vassalage, and I was coming out of these encounters higher than a kite, already leaping ahead in my mind to the next office and concocting new routines right and left.

"The Shouter," "The Aggrieved Epileptic," "Active T.B.," "The Lonely Nose-picker of Avalon," "Freaky Deaky." I had hopes I might try out each and every one of these promising routines before my two week vacation was up, but this was not to be, and as it worked out, I only got to spring "The Shouter" on them. This was at a downtown savings and loan where the Assistant Manager, who resembled Ken (of Ken and Barbie fame) and wore lavender-tinted aviators and white suede loafers with little gold links on them, called me into his office after an interminable wait and interviewed me for the position of "Retail Banking Specialist." I was wearing my best suit and had spruced myself up considerably for this one. Under the name of "Benedict 'Dutch' Spinoza," I answered his questions in a nebulous way, making sure that with every sentence I uttered my voice crept up the scale and became louder. Toward the end I was frankly shouting. This alarming and crackbrained increase in volume was accomplished in such gradual stages that I don't think he was ever precisely aware of what was going on or even where we'd left the tracks. I might have kept it up indefinitely until my voice failed or I burst a blood vessel, but the mystified, fidgety, discomfited look on his face was too much for me and I lost it. Laughing hysterically like a hyena I had to jump up and run out of there fast.

That was when it happened. Outside on the street, my own gales of hilarity distracted me so that I stepped right in the path of an oncoming truck and got clipped. I wound up with a mild concussion and two broken arms. (Editors' Note: The awful implacable gods of mercantile are not lightly mocked.)

And so with a cast on each arm bent at the elbows and crooked out in front of me awkwardly that way for the next couple of months, it was inevitable that my friends should take to calling me "The Crab".

14 SECRET MASTERS OF THE WORLD

A MESSAGE OF HOPE—
TO ALL YOU TALENTED BOZOS!

THE LOST BELL....

"I remember a young man who built a box with a bell inside set to ring every hour. Every hour it would ring and that was the signal then he would go jack off. So he met a lot of grief at home (he was very open about it; when he went to school and kept running around answering the bell, they put him away. At the asylum, he kept trying to get his box back together, looking for parts etc. He eventually became a standard character for several important abnormal psychology texts but jacking off is like anything else, it takes a lot of work to get recognition."

Ack's Wack's
a dept. of high
Political analysis

ornel Petey owns and operates a yellow suitcase of the
stand-up variety that he uses to sell his many magic
and novelty items out of, and for twenty-two years he
has been, in his own words, "pitching the woo" out of doorways along Houston Street in downtown San Antonio, Texas—
or, on days when the cops seem inclined to hassle him,
"adjooring" around the corner to some less conspicuous
alleyway. So when Ralph "$50,000 Party" Delgado, the director
of the highly successful charity organization "Parties For
Orphans", needed something special last week in the way of favors to pass
out at an orphan's Halloween party he was hosting, he called upon Mr Petey, whom
he introduced to me as "the famed novelty salesman."

The man we were meeting looked like a swarthy and somewhat sawed-off Slim
Whitman, and he was got up in an unobtrusive ensemble of sharkskin jacket, porkpie
hat, cotton slacks, and wide napkin tie secured by a small gold clip, in various
shades of maroon-and-gray, except for the tie which was lime green and featured giant
sea horses athwart tumbling coxcombs. Mr Petey's voice reminds you of George Burns,
and his way of looking you over without ever quite seeming to focus his eyes is
shrewd and certainly a good reminder that, As Algis Budrys once remarked, you may
never be educated enough or find the right attitude in time. Ralph "$50,000 Party"
Delgado had scheduled a meeting with Mr Petey for late Saturday morning coffee at
Shoop's, a cafe specializing in seafood and something called the "Shoop Salad"
(lettuce and Thousand Island, from the looks of it), that is patronized chiefly by
people who don't want to eat at the Grayhound Station across the street, and Mr Petey
slithered in from his room at the Ace Hotel two blocks away, which is his current
home base, lugging a yellow tin suitcase about **four** feet square and ten inches deep,
which he set up next to our table on battered metal legs that unfolded out of the
bottom, like an ironing board or a tv tray—a suitcase containing his wares. Opened,
it looked like the bargain bin at Bernie's Fun 'N Magic Shop, on Commerce Street.
On top, the suitcase held a row of flat, blue-and-white carboard men, each about
twelve inches high with accordian-pleated crepe-paper arms and legs colored bright
day-glo orange; Mr Petey told us this was his line of famed "jiggling men," and
gave us a little speech about how when you set the men up and activated them in a
certain way (a patented secret that would be fully explained in the instruction
pamphlet that accompanies each and every doll sold) the things actually took life
and danced or jiggled of their own accord, completely without wires or any other
"hidden apparatus." There was a pause, during which Ralph "$50,000 Party" Delgado,
hulking, oily, and saturnine, studied the now quiescent jiggling men through narrowed eyes, as though trying to decide how best to frame some question that was
bothering him, while his fork continued to toy among the ruins of his "Shoop Salad"
and the seconds lengthened into minutes and I (and, I assume, Mr Petey also) began
to feel discomfited and slightly embarrassed by his silence. As Mr Petey manipulated
the pleated arms on one of his dolls to demonstrate its suppleness and fine workman-
ship (and in response to Ralph's less than cordial demeanor), I cleared my throat
and attempted to say something friendly and inconsequential to relieve the tension—
something about how I'd always wondered what it was that made the little men jiggle—
but it was obvious to me, from the way Mr Petey was fidgeting, that Ralph's silence
was casting a definite pall. It depressed me no end to find things deteriorating
like this, because, in point of fact, if it hadn't been for the embarrassment I
was feeling, I would more than have welcomed a chance to find out how the jiggling
men worked, for this was something that had intrigued and puzzled me for years, ever
since the day in 1952 when my father had taken me downtown for a new pair of Red
Goose shoes and we had glimpsed one of the fabled dolls dancing and jiggling in a
doorway next to the shoe store. That day had marked the beginning of my fascination
with the mystery of the jiggling men. When my father had refused to shell out
four bits for one of the things and the vendor (not Mr Petey but surely a distant
cousin of Mr Petey's) had shown signs of folding up his suitcase and moving on, I
gave way utterly to the underlined angst of the moment, and my screams in a matter of minutes
proved sufficient to draw a fair-sized crowd and send the poor peddler scuttling

down the street with his suitcase clutched under his arm, increasing to full-blown hysterics once I really got going; and, truth to tell, I wound up going considerably beyond hysterics, actually falling on my father's feet, punching, kicking, flailing, slobbering, writhing, moaning, howling, drooling, choking, barking, sobbing, keening, convulsing, and biting my father ankles.

"You bit your father a half dozen times on the ankles while you were like that, and then you shifted your grip and bit him on the fleshy part of the calf," my mother would say, recalling the incident in later years. "I was afraid we were going to have to have you committed, but Dr Miller said to just put you in your room and keep an eye on you. The whole month you were screaming we were living in that awful post-war housing with the pasteboard walls so you kept us in dutch something awful with the neighbors. You would yell and try to bite anybody that went near you. We had to tell everybody you had scarlet fever."

My grandmother had been listening to my mother's comments. "At the risk of hurting your feelings, Albert, I have to say you wet the bed and carried on like a fiend," she said.

Recalling the shame and darkness of those years (and thrown off stride by Ralph's brooding silence), I heard myself asking Mr Petey if he had ever felt the uncontrollable urge to take his thumb and mash out a pigeon's eyes. Mr Petey looked at me and said, "Fuck, no. Why? Have you?", glancing uneasily from me to Ralph and back again. Among the many desires I have entertained (I found myself telling Mr Petey) are "Pigeon Punching," "Bicycle Sniffing," "Bread Braiding," "Toupé Fondling," and a number of urges I call the How-can-I-tell-you type urge. Over a period ranging from my early sorrow at missing out on owning a jiggling man through that of my later dismissals from several military academies, I entertained a whole series of desires centering on the Velo Benzedrine Inhaler. In those days, neither the Army nor the Navy would touch me, because when it came to enlisting a self-confessed Velo freak the Vietnam conflict had not yet reached the stage where these branches of the armed services were grabbing up anything that breathed or moved. In 1972, I clipped a photo of a medical diploma out of the AMA Digest, filled it in with a ballpoint pen, hung it up and opened a small mail-order business specializing in "sight-unseen" cancer cures. Since then, repeated failures and a lot of angry mail from relatives of patients had given me new perspective and helped calm me down to the point where I could now sit in a cheap resturant and keep most of my clothes on. "And so I feel that by next year I will be far enough along to drink from a cup and apply for a driver's license," I told Mr Petey, doing my best to keep things upbeat. Meanwhile, Ralph's behavior had grown increasingly bizarre.

"My watch," he muttered, breaking his long silence at last, and staring hard at Mr Petey. "Why did you steal my watch, Aunt Linda? WHY?"

Was it this—or was it the way Ralph had scrunched down in his chair until just his eyes were peering over the edge of his plate at us that caused Mr Petey to jump up and run out of the cafe with his suitcase clutched under his arm?

There was no time to wonder. At this point the door to the kitchen burst open and out came the cook and his three assistants, bread sticks up their nostrils. They broke into song, and a highly nasal version of "The Star Spangled Banner" rent the air. What horror! When next I knew, I was out on the sidewalk running for my life with Ralph clutched under my arm.

"Maybe I shouldn't have swallowed a whole bottle of saccharine tablets after breakfast this morning," Ralph admitted later that afternoon when I put him down under a bench in the park. Which explained a good deal about his hopped-up behavior at the table but in no way consoled me. For once again I had missed my chance to learn the secret of the jiggling men. Oh, God in heaven! How long must I wait? How many more pigeons must die beneath my thumbs before I learn the secret?!

(And so on. This is being written on Election Day, and my first idea was to try to convey something of the feeling, ineffable and dismal and all at sea, that comes stealing over me when I contemplate the current political scene and what is being wrought. Well, turns out this parable of the jiggling men, wherein I seem to find myself sitting in a bad resturant as if in a dream, with a shady street vendor staring at me in dismay, and all sorts of rubbishy, outlandish vapors and notions coursing through my brain, while across the table a friend goes insane on saccharine and everybody else pokes bread sticks up their nose and gets patriotic—turns out this pale, half-ass approximation was as close as I could come. In other words, close but no cigar.)

ACK'S WACKS

A Column Of Anatomical

Diminuendo

When four readers of this magazine, one right after another, sent letters and complimented me on my most recent column I knew there must be something wrong. Nowdays one complimentary letter is unusual, four in a row are almost frightening. It quickly became apparent that the letter writers were seriously off-base, not to say totally deluded. Their letters, for one thing, seemed to assume that my column had been about macaroni—"the best _____ article on macaroni that I have ever come across," as one reader put it. Feeling nervous I reread the column in question (as far as I knew, my article had been about Cornel Petey the famed novelty salesman) to see if I could uncover any mention of macaroni and found only a passing reference to bread sticks which, though they are a staple in many pasta joints, was to my mind insufficient grounds for misinterpretation or confusion of this magnitude. Well, my friends, I think that this little episode points up once again what happens when any sizable portion of the reading audience falls victim to the ravages of "false memory," or whatever the current medical term may be for this condition, and so, I suppose, it's once again up to me to set things straight. So, for those of you who are normal and missed it in the last issue when it did not appear, here it comes—the macaroni column—somewhat as follows:

"THE ECSTACY OF MACARONI"

Yes, indeed, that was the year the evenings were drawing in and my mind was working faster and faster and Monty Cantsin, the deeply sensitive Neoist mug, interviewed me for one of his abortive Neoist projects, a contraption called "wet radio," I believe. Willy-nilly he asked me many questions of a personal and confidential nature, in his inimitable patois. And I do mean inimitable, since he became so excited at times that it was hard to tell whether he was in America speaking Hungarian or in Hungary speaking American. Few of you, I wager, remember our exchange.

"Dr. Ockermans," he began by saying at one point, "you have work in many hospital where you have all the time this chance to see the many dead bodies. Have you ever in your practice experience the desire to crawl up on the table and love on they?"

"The well-known clinical term for this," I replied, somewhat stiffly, "is necrophilia, or erotic stimulation by corpses, and I'll thank you to remember it. Frankly, I may be old-fashioned, but I have never believed in promiscuous sex. To be really meaningful, a relationship should have time to ripen. By that I mean that my motto has always been: 'Show me a man who tries to paw and kiss a cadaver on the first date and I'll show you a man who's stunted his growth with too many cigarettes.' Furthermore, I believe that a young couple would be much better off to just lay all carnal thoughts aside and forget about them (at least until they've seen a show and had a bite to eat)."

I suppose, my friends, that many a trendy young swinger out there must be laughing their heads off at this juncture hearing that I consider sex on the first date a positively "holy" affair not to be tampered with lightly. But it is true. Take, for instance, what happened in the year 1955 (back in those days I was interning at a small hospital in Louisiana where, I'm happy to say, the administration was not so infernally picky about the fol-de-rol of diplomas or licensure, the way they are at some of those places). In the summer of 1955 we had just experienced a record-breaking pellagra epidemic of sizable proportions, and I had become en-amoured of Marie, the Little French Princess, as we called her, a comely raven-haired cadaver who had been awaiting positive identification by next of kin for several months down in the hospital cooler. Ah, that pale nacreous complexion! Those lusterless eyes! Gad, how that lifeless little minx set my pulses to hammering! (Down, boy.)

My salary in those days was $35 a week—plus tips—not great pelf for a swain and his lady-fair to dine out on—to say the least. Nevertheless, after skimping on lunches and hoarding my pennies all week, I arranged one night under cover of darkness to have Marie's beautiful alabaster form transferred from the cooler to the trunk of my car—our first date, it was—what an occasion. And, gentle reader, in spite of the fact that my intentions were of the highest water and purity, you may be sure that I was at pains to employ the utmost discretion and even secrecy. After all, a hospital is often notoriously rife with chingaderos (Spanish for gossip-mongers) and I had no desire to lay either my dream-belle, or myself, open to the vile calumny of wagging tongues.

In this, I was successful...Thus did midnight find the two of us—I and my Marie—enjoying an intimate candle-lit tete-ta-tete at Shoop's, a local roadhouse on the far edge of town. Romance was in the air, and Marie, whose only fault as a dinner companion was a tendency to keep slipping sideways out of the booth, had never looked lovelier. How true were the words of the poet, about that old black magic having me underneath its spell!

I had about decided to order the fish cakes, and had climbed on top of the table, the better to urge Marie to try the svengali-and-meatballs, or "twelve inches of happiness," as it is sometimes called, when the roadhouse owner came over. "Phew, man!" he said to me, pointing at Marie. "You got to get that thing out of here. It's starting to stink the place up and people are complaining. Are you nuts, or something?"

While I was thinking how best to upbraid this churl for his offens-ive remarks, an alcaholic man in a brakeman's cap appeared in the door-way of the roadhouse. "Get this house off the road! The freak train has jumped the rails, and it's headed this way at sixty m.p.h.!"

Alas, his warning came too soon. Even as he spoke, the entire twelve-car entourage of Conklin's Sideshow Enterprises, Inc. was plow-ing into the side of the roadhouse. The noise was horrendous. Freaks were spewed out everywhere. There were no survivors. Later I combed the smoking wreckage, and at last uncovered Marie's body. It had been a close call, as the pinhead from the sideshow had lodged in her spleen. Did you ever have your spleen penetrated—by a pinhead? I know of no greater trauma. Only the fact that Marie had already been dead for sev-eral months and was in a fairly advanced state of decomposition had saved her from being killed. I realized then how much she meant to me and lost no time in planting my trough.

"Oh!" I cried, lifting her head in my hands. ""Oh, my darling won-derful one, won't you consent to be—my bride?"

That was years and years and years ago. Today, happily, I am still awaiting her reply.

-THE END-

Well, friends, there you have it: the big macaroni column. All I can say is, I just hope I don't get any letters this time telling me how much you enjoyed my article on necrophilia.

A Column of Philosophical Convalescence

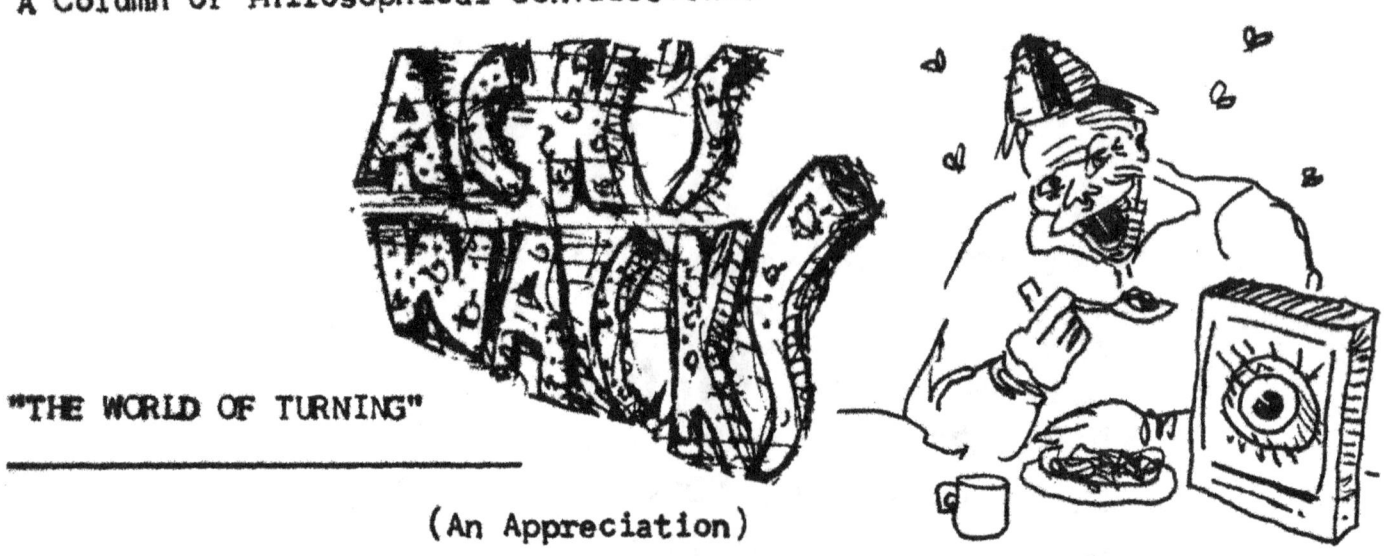

"THE WORLD OF TURNING"

(An Appreciation)

We found a glass eye in our salad at lunch the other day and were more than slightly perturbed by the discovery, since we were home alone at the time, and if a glass eye had found its way into our salad (a simple cherry fruit salad, prepared fresh from the can the way we always like it), chances were good that its owner might still be hiding on the premises somewhere, maybe crouching behind the drapes in the living room, maybe lurking upstairs in one of the closets, a large individual (as we pictured him), with his hair straying down over his one good eye, which would be shining (we felt certain of this) with the pure, cracked light of homicidal looniness. We wondered if he would still be wearing the hospital shirt he had escaped in; and we decided that, in all liklihood, he would be in need of a shave. But the major question, at least to our way of thinking, was more fundamental than any question of dress or grooming: Was he carrying a razor, or was he carrying an ax? (or was he perhaps of the school that prefers the direct "ham-handed" approach?) In truth, a one-eyed maniac hiding somewhere in the house at lunchtime gave us much to think about and mull over.

Meanwhile, the glass eye (a baby blue one) stared up at us from among the pitted sweet cherries, the sliced peaches, the diced avacado, the tiny melon balls and the seedless grapes—a truly jarring interloper, in its own

right. It's black shoe-button pupil and the surrounding
ring of its blue iris in no way fit in with, or satisfied,
our notion of what a good fruit salad should contain, and
we felt that if it should inadvertently find its way into
our mouth we'd get the sudden taste of ear-wax. In fact,
the glass eye, in its detatched condition, was curiously
unsettling, a sort of unwinking observer (unwinking in
the philosophical as well as the physiological sense,
that is). We cannot guess what brought the next train of
thought into our head, what impulse prompted it: possibly
that our Uncle George back in Oklahoma had been one-
seventeenth Cherokee on his mother's side and had worn a
glass eye. At any rate, our next thought as we sat frozen
over the glass eye in our salad was how the Hopi philosophers say that we are now in the era of the Fourth
World, what they call "The World of Turning;" no matter
what you deserve, the Hopis say, you're only going to get
what you're capable of asking for. You have to be able to
create the concept of your desires. And at that moment,
without looking up from our plate, or even thinking, we
opened our mouth and heard ourself say, in a loud, half-
strangled voice, "Oh, please, please don't let that old
one-eyed maniac get us. Please make things come out all
right." (In truth, our own outburst rather startled us.).
     We were uncertain as to whether or not this approach
was what the Hopi philosophers had in mind, and were
almost on the point of deciding it probably wasn't, when
all at once, as if the quality of the light in the kitchen
had gently shifted, we noticed that on the straw mat in
the center of the table, next to the cut-glass bowl of
ivy, lay a second glass eye. A quick glance was enough to
assure us that this second glass eye was also baby-blue
in color—an obvious mate to the one in our salad. We relaxed a little then. A maniac who had dropped one glass
eye and was hiding in the house was one thing; but a maniac
who had dropped both glass eyes was something else again.
In truth, we felt pretty confident we could handle a
blind maniac.

BLASTER

THE DISTINGUISHED HEBEPHRENIC

THE AVATARS

A man is running down the street with his jocky strap on backwards. It is all
he has on except for his shoes and socks. You can tell that most employers
are reluctant to hire him, for the pages of his resume curl a little at the
corners in a yellow way. The cover is smudged here and there. A smudge is a
field trying to be born, and every field contains the possibility of grubs and
roots, and writhes in the sun, our secret food. But the point is, certain men
in our society will go right on failing - failing to get jobs, failing to make
the team - and we will never understand why. They are the avatars. Like the
man in the wrong-way jocky strap. Like the fellow who insists on wearing a
brassier on the outside of his three-piece suit, and carries a rabbit in his
arms. The rabbit is dead and has no eyelids - all the employers pretend that
this is the reason why they have turned down his application when he comes in
looking for an executive position. Smug fools. All the employers of the earth
are smug fools who seek blindly to eradicate the avatars. One day they will perhaps
perhaps succeed, and the last avatar will disappear. At that moment the world
will wink out of existence like a rotten candle.

Eel Leonard, Avatar of the Rabbit; as told to Al Ackerman

The Smut Peddler

Wi. Reading smut again, I see. Don't you know that smut will rot your brain? Don't you know that exposing your brain to smut is like

deliberately exposing the delicate outer shell of an egg to a glass of deadly tobacco juice? Test it and see. First, chew up several plugs of Red Man or Days O' Work Tobacco; be careful to expectorate each mouthful into a large glass vessel until the tobacco juice reaches a suitable level--about seventeen quarts should do it, provided you have selected a large enough vessel. Now for the test. First, expose xxxxxxxx the egg shell to the smut; at the same time, lean over and expose your brain to the deadly tobacco juice mixture by immersing it thoroughly. Next, expose the egg shell to the tobacco juice and expose your brain to the smut. Now, compare. See? Beats the ____ out of tobacco juice, doesn't it?

HARRY BATES CLUB

FALUSE; or The Thing In The Barn

A COLUMN OF UNSLEEPING GAUCHERIE
CONDUCTED by DR. AL ACKERMAN

A ACKERMAN NOTE: TO FALUSE (PRONOUNCED FA-LOOZ, ACCENT GRAVID ON THE "LOOZ") IS TO CONVEY A MOMENT OF MYSTICAL INSIGHT IN AN UNEXPECTED WAY, USUALLY IN A RATHER ROUNDABOUT OR INDIRECT FASHION, OFTEN POINTLESSLY. ALMOST ALL FALUSES ARE, ROUGHLY, SHAGGY-DOG STORIES. THEY ARE SUFI IN ORIGIN, METAPHYSICAL IN CONTENT, DATE FROM THE 13TH CENTURY A.D., AND FOR SOME WHOLLY MYSTERIOUS REASON HAVE ENJOYED A CERTAIN UNDER-BED, BEHIND-BACK VOGUE IN THIS COUNTRY SINCE THE MID-1960'S, WITHOUT EVER BECOMING A VISIBLE FAD. A FALUSE CAN TAKE ANY FORM--SPOKEN, WRITTEN, OR ORAL. ESSENTIALLY, THE ONLY IDENTIFYING FEATURE OF A FALUSE IS ITS PUNCH-LINE, WHICH IS ALWAYS ANNOUNCED BY THE WORDS "THE THING IN THE BARN STIRRED, SAT UP, AND CAME TO LIFE--," FOLLOWED BY THE BRIEF EXPRESSION OF A DESIRE, OR WISH, THAT SHOULD, IF THE FALUSITE, OR STORY-TELLER, KNOWS HIS STUFF, STRIKE A RESPONSIVE CHORD IN THE READER OR LISTENER. IN OTHER WORDS, THE PAY-OFF OF A FALUSE SHOULD WORK LIKE A MAGIC MIRROR AND REVEAL TO YOU YOUR OWN GREATEST SECRET DESIRE--ALWAYS AN EERIE BUSINESS. (INDEED, IT'S A LITTLE SPOOKY, REALLY, HOW WELL AND HOW OFTEN A GOOD FALUSE CAN PIN-POINT EXACTLY WHAT YOU'VE BEEN DREAMING ABOUT, WHETHER YOU ARE LOATHE TO ADMIT IT OR NOT.) THE FOLLOWING FALUSE, A FAIRLY RECENT ADDITION TO THE CANON, IS BY BIMB WHITTIER, A NOTABLE PRACTITIONER OF THE ART. SEE IF IT DOESN'T SUCCEED IN PEGGING YOUR INNERMOST DESIRE WITH AN UNCANNY AND SNAKELIKE PRECISION IN ITS END, EH?

The Faluse of "The New Criticism"
By Bimb Whittier

I suppose that ultimately it is an o.k. thing for this city's night schools to be teaching "The New Criticism,'" and I am just about ready, after I have a glass of milk and pick a few more of these nits or seam-squirrels or whatever they are out of my bathrobe, to go with the flow and start applying what we learned in class last night to a recent work by one of our leading contemporary poets.

It probably is because I read this poem "The Summit" by John M. "Slats" Bennett only five or ten minutes ago that it has impressed itself on my mind more than any other poem in recent memory. There is something about it that seems to drive straight to the heart of our "American Dilemma." And right in the opening three lines, too. No hesitating or messing around where John M. "Slats" Bennett is concerned. Check this out:

> It's like the garbage bag so full it
> Climbs the stairs slopping and rustling as I
> Stare blank off the pillow---

Now, what do you make of that? In the first place, applying the tenets of "The New Criticism" to what the author undoubtedly had in mind, and peeking a bit between the lines, I would say that the poet's wife (Mrs. Bennett) has ample grounds for a good letter to Dr. Ruth. And not a moment too soon, either.

"Dear Dr. Ruth--: If I didn't see it with my own eyes, I wouldn't be writing to you, but on more than one occasion my husband "Slats" has behaved perversely! He's about 40 years old. Lately, when I or any other member of the family go upstairs to where he's lying on the bed, he starts thrashing around and saying we sound like animated sacks of garbage coming up the stairs. The only one he says DOESN'T sound like a sack of garbage coming up the stairs is our baby-sitter, Doris Kozart, 15. He has her up there in his room with the door shut visiting and talking to him at all hours, now. I am really confounded about it. What should I do? Also, if I'm not losing my mind, and he really is acting this way, why? --M.B. in Ohio."

Rest easy, Mrs. Bennett. Aside from your unspoken but very real concern over the possibility that your husband "Slats" may be incompetent to handle his business affairs and thus die intestate, leaving you and the children destitute, there is absolutely nothing to worry about, for your husband is merely manifesting a whole spectrum of familiar mid-life anomalies, any of which can be used (good news) as "grounds for involuntary commitment," as the medical profession likes to call it.

According to "The New Criticism," a man with eyes staring "blank off the pillow" who does a lot of thrashing and begins sentences with "It's like the garbage bag so full it climbs the stairs--" can be handled best with the aid of a few simple psychiatric measures, such as obtaining a court order and having him shipped upstate for an indefinite period of rest, observation and cold packs. However, if you lack the wherewithal or medical coverage to go this route and would prefer to deal with the matter in the privacy of your own home, I would follow these steps: You first get several family members to lend a hand and then wrap your husband snugly in a wet bed sheet. Then take turns beating him with a broom and see if this doesn't calm him down. My uncle Foster-Dulles used to get wilder than a march-hare and my aunt Stella-Dulles always swore by the good old broom-and-wet-bed-sheet method, and Uncle Foster-Dulles was a raving hophead. Dope would have surely cut him off in his prime had he not died suddenly in his late seventies of brethelitis (exploding "love-nuts," in clinical parlance).

I have gone on at length about my miserable relatives to make clear just what role the Subconscious is likely to play. The trouble, Mrs. Bennett, is that many poets, when they reach your husband's age, secretly long to have their corns trimmed by glamorous, heavy-set female barbers. If they happen to be sitting around the house harboring these desires and there is no female barber with a razor blade handy to accomodate them, their Subconscious takes over of it own accord, sometimes in a rather capricious fashion. At this juncture the poet is likely to begin covering his legs with big handfuls of Ben-Gay. Many a poet, getting caught up in the heady abandon of this compulsive annointing process, has gone on to apply the Ben-Gay so heavily that his legs take on a dripping jelly-like demeanor. I don't wish to make you chuck your lunch into your cupped palms, or anything, Mrs. B., but I'm afraid there's no getting around it--the legs of one who has become a slave to the ointment surely can present a loathesome mien. As for what all this goo is likely to do to your precious rugs and slip-covers--well, this is an unappetizing feature of "Ben-Gay legs" upon which I shall not dwell.

The worst of it is that your husband's Subconscious promptings may lead him to go even further, so that he actually ventures out in <u>public</u> in this condition with his pants rolled up above his knees and his legs shining eerily in the hot early morning light, like a pair of greasy drumsticks. And this, in turn, may well lead him to experience the forbidden fruits of creating a scene or commotion at the first bus stop he chances across where others are gathered. This is sexually exciting in a way that ordinary coprophilia, pedophilia, and hemophilia can never be, especially if everybody at the bus stop is already unstable to begin with, as nowdays it is the barn, not the stable, where this sort of business reaches its highest pitch or frenzy.

Yes, Mrs. B., don't ask me why, but, count on it, the most extreme cases of frenzy always seem to take place where you have a group of already unstable people standing around in a barn, waiting for the bus, and then a character like your husband "Slats" shows up, his legs dressed and reeking with Ben-Gay. This is where things go way out of hand--often clear over into real abnormality. Maybe it has something to do with all the manure and corncobs and empty sacks and oily rags and rich loamy filth lying around in a barn. Maybe the Ben-Gay works in some way to activate all this damp steamy fecundity. Did you ever think of that? Perhaps, at the very peak of this frenzy in the barn, several drops of Ben-Gay got shaken off your husband's legs and showered down on a pile of dirty old sacks in the corner, irridating and vitalizing them strangely, so that in a few days (or weeks--the time factor makes little difference where the creation of unnatural life is concerned) the inevitable occured, as it always must--warmth, heat, fission! The Thing in the Barn stirred, sat up, and came to life. Cooz! IT WANTED YOUNG COOZ!

Well, why not? Poetry isn't everything, you know.

"FEAR OF BEDWETTING"

ACK HACKS BENNETT'S POEMS

Here's a Hack I did off the four poems you sent. Can't remember if I used this
method before - but it's pretty simple so I probably did. Took some lines from
Valery's Le Jeune Parque ("Ah, what coils of desire where he wallowed!/What
riot of etc etc" - three lines), counted the letters in each word (2 - 4 - 5 - 2
- etc), then went through your poems and when I hit a 2-letter word I put it
down, then a 4-letter word, and so on. Then did two more the same way. It
came out like this:

DISTENDED

My book light my shreds meter in coughing!
Meat worm in finger nose me tongue
And a did come descended ear skinless!
Even in my shoe I finger raised nose,
Glittering hissing in can withers descended.

****

Been reading the three new poems and came up with a pretty good Hacks. A new
method, I think. Even before I read the poems I'd set up my system, which was:
1) take yr first poem (it turned out to be CONSTANCY) and let variations of
"porking, porked, etc" be the verb in all cases and 2) switch nouns over from
the other two (INSOMINEX and ISOLATOR) as they occured and plug em into the
first. The horrible result I call -

PORKTIME

Porking her night through my sleep she
Porked on the sheet behind my
Legs. Porking on the curtains, she was
Porking the headache; stink thick on her
Shoes. When I porked in the sock's
Air I porked windows in me. The garbagetruck in
One belt and the other pressure. Her
Shores on the lake lax on the nausea and a
Hand porking our rubber gloves.

A COLUMN OF BIOLOGICAL RUFFIANISM

THE CURSE

My grandmother used to say that as a small child I was bitten while attending an American Legion parade with my grandfather, in downtown Detroit, and became, as a result, infected with the strange malady, or curse, which has made my life such a nightmare. My grandfather, on the other hand, always contended that the thing happened a year later at the height of a Shriners' Convention, in Chicago.

All I know is that, nowdays, when the moon is full, I change. At first I merely stagger around my hotel room a bit, pulling at my shirt collar and knocking things over. Later it gets much worse and then--if I've forgotten to have myself locked in for the night--I spring out into the hall and engage the first person I see in the sort of conversation that makes me cringe all over if I happen to remember any of it the next morning, when the spell has worn off. The other night, for example, all the way down to the lobby, a matter of perhaps twelve floors, I talked incessantly to the elevator operator about my belief in something called "Argosy Magazine's Beef-and-Bourbon Diet." According to my own reckoning I have seldom succeeded in uttering such pure and unadulterated drivel. Babbling? Babbling is too mild a word for it.

I had heard that Napoleon lost seventeen hundred pounds on this diet, I told the operator in parting when I got off the elevator. But (who knows?) perhaps the indications of horror on his face came less from my chatter--as intense and exhalted as any pillhead's--and more from the fact that I had left my room that night without remembering to put my trousers on, an oversight I didn't snap-to until I was already out on the street and had bought a newspaper out of one of the coin-operated vending machines in front of the hotel. And, further, had gone on to remove the sports section and fold it into a hat, something I often do when the spell of the full moon has me under its power. And had even set the ridiculous thing on my head so that the floppy paper brim came right down over my eyes, undoubtedly giving me the look of a dangerous imbecile, in any case making it impossible for me to see where I was going, so that after taking five or six steps away from the vending machine, I slipped on a piece of dog waste named, if one may wax poetic at such an awkward moment, Robert Browning, Jr. Thus, my legs--which only then did I notice were as bare as a pair of peeled bananas--went flying up past my face and over my head; in short I landed flat on my back and found myself staring dazedly straight up at one of the street lamps high overhead, where the mounting vapor of the night was gathered like a pale blue halo, or, I had to laugh a little at this apt and clever image, an elephant's cigar!

But even with the breath knocked out of me, the thought entered my head quite clearly that what we of today need in our public places, more than anything, instead of boring street lights to look up to and worship, are twenty-foot-high bronze statues of our leaders--Heckle and Jeckyl-- a thought which, as you can well imagine, sent me off into fresh gales of hilarity.

But I only had time to lie there on the sidewalk and laugh for ten or fifteen minutes, for a pack of skateboard hooligans suddenly flashed around the corner and ran over my head. During the subsequent ambulance ride downtown, I entertained the two white-coated attendents by giving them some excellent vocal imitations of the siren, from which the conclusion was drawn that my head injury had left me feeble-minded. Of course the truth was I owed my behavior entirely to the spell cast over me by the full moon, which, even as I was in the act of being lifted out of the back of the ambulance and wheeled into the hospital, remained visible above the rooftops, cruising through the clouds like a hoary silver galleon, or (ha ha) an elephant's basketball!

Inside the hospital, propped up on my elbow on the examining table in the E.R., I told the nurse that my name was "Puddin' N. Tain....ask me again, I'll tell you the same!" and then threw in several of my favorite "Little Moron" stories, for good measure. Here is a sample of the sort of material I was dishing out that night, with italics to indicate how unbearably funny I found my own stuff:

ME: "Well, one day (titter) the Little Moron was out on the street playing a game of 'Hill-dill-come-over-the-hill-or-else-I'll-catch-you-standing-still,' which was what the Little Moron always mistakenly called the game of 'Vent Check.' 'Vent Check', of course, as everybody but the Little Moron knows, is the game where you put out a rubber donut on the sidewalk (titter-titter), and then when a lady pedestrian comes along and bends over to have a look at it, you scuttle up behind her on all fours, peer up her dress, and check out her vent. (Loutish guffaw.) Well, so the Little Moron was playing 'Vent Check'. As it happened he had just scuttled up to check out the vent of an enormous fat lady who was bending over to examine the rubber donut when suddenly, thanks no doubt to having eaten bean-skillet the night before, the fat lady broke wind in a big way. (He he.) She did it loudly, explosively, at the revolting blast of which the Little Moron lost consciousness and for the next few seconds was out like a light. (Chortle-chortle.) Well, at that very moment who should come on the scene but Scream. Scream was the Little Moron's dog, an unappealing Mexican Hairless the color of babies' knees, who was named Scream because he loved to eat socks and whenever anybody beat or kicked him for doing this he would scream like a bastard. (Starting to definitely crack up at my own humor.) So the Little Moron was lying there on the sidewalk, out of it for a few seconds, with the result that Scream was able to catch him off guard and eat both his socks. (More loud boisterous laughter, I'm afraid bordering on the frankly hysterical.) Well, when the Little Moron came to, he saw that Scream was swallowing the last of his socks (approaching the punchline and nearly beside myself with mirth)....This made the Little Moron so mad that he grabbed Scream and shoved him up the fat lady's skirt as hard as he could, because, you might say, he felt like giving Scream to a loud vent!" (Complete collapse of all control, as the nurse begins to look around worridly for restraits and a sedative.)

This, then, was the gist of what I was coming across with in the E.R. that night, and I had, by that point, gone into such helpless paroxysms that I rolled off the table, striking my head on a white metal can, one of those grueful receptacles that are part of every E.R., where are thrown the bloody pieces of gauze, surgical offal, sponges, etc. Because of the terrific impact made by my forehead, the hinged lid of the can flew up and part of a foot, evidently something left over from an amputation earlier in the week, bounced out and landed on my nose, sticking there as if glued. I, flat on my back under the table, gave the thing a brief glance, my two eyes had to cross in the silliest way imaginable for me to focus on it. "Oh, look," I managed to wheeze before I lost consciousness, "I've grown a foot!"

Toward morning I changed back: The moon had gone down by then, and the spell had passed, leaving me utterly spent and exhausted, as it always does-- plus, on this sorry occasion, in debt to the hospital and ambulance people for over two hundred dollars. Oh, what a burden it is to carry this foul curse! and what I wouldn't give, just once, just once, to see the full moon rise at the window without finding myself transformed into a deadly, slavering werefool.

Dr. Al "Claw" Ackerman

"LEWD POLAROIDS?"
CHUCKLED
THE
SHAGGY
MAN —
"THE LITTLE
WIND - UP
MAN KEPT
MUM —
(A POEM)
— BLASTER

The Poetry Machine

Thought you'd like to see what emerged when Steph set the Poetry Machine I built
her in motion. The way this worked: I had her write a ten-syllable first line,
anything she wanted. Then she picked her ten favorite nouns and put them in an
envelope; ditto for her ten favorite verbs. Then she wrote several "Joker"
phrases, all of the "hitting the chair," "ripping the sky," "screwing a hammer"
variety, and put those in the JOKER envelope. Then we took out the Poetry Machine
(which was connecting tissue I'd set up for a ten-line poem (example: line #4
ran "To the (draw from your noun envelope, singular) with all its (repeat second verb
from line #1 plus word that follows it)") and she drew her different words out of
the envelopes and we plugged them in. Came out pretty nice:

I am the tear which trickles down a nose
Engulfing their pool
Even when squirt with ocean
To the pond with all its trickle down
Nevertheless their river is a nose
Which if bubbled possesses the pond
To run with the tear forever
And not wash, not dissolve,
Not flow –
What is this but washing the sea?

–By Stephanie Blaster

Steph said later she'd cannily chosen nouns and verbs that were similar or related
to her first line and Joker line, "to make it harder for you to play tricks."

ACK HACKS BENNETT'S POEMS

Some really nice poems this time - esp. LOVER IN TIME. I built a poetry machine
using last lines of LE CIMEYIERE MARIN [Valéry] and plugged words in from each of
your poems:

DES FOCS!

The butt is swirling!....We must burst a root!
The huge table bends and sees my face: the mirror
Dares to drink semen in a coughing coffee
Cup. Lick, my teeth-bewildered breasts!
Squeeze, watches! Squeeze with your hole in the wall
This drooling hammer where spit like towels are peckers.

Here's a Hack I did using FEAR OF SCISSORS as the board on which to play: turned it
over so the back of the page was facing me and used my scissors to cut slots in
each line; I could see where the words ended through the paper but couldn't make
them out. Then I took SWIMMING, INHALATION, and WHEEL OF TIME - plus a letter from
Mike Duquette that told a disgusting Traveling Salesman joke and did the same: cut
words and phrases out here and there, blind. Next I piled all the words and phrases
on the table and, again blind, picked them out of the proverbial hat - plugging them
into the slots on FEAR OF SCISSORS. It goes:

WHAT IF?

It ever clean my stay the night but
Drool stuck to a pasta fetish. A
Wind not passionate enough on the
Coffeegrounds under my leaks out
These squirts what's left sniffing a
Those are maggots. So bladderless,
No edge? What I wrote, like a melt
Without wake swelling my on and
She pants. I was kisses her and gets
A hard-on....what if the drinking we are
Seeking and see a burning tree?

Here's a Hack I made out of your book STONES IN THE LAKE. First, I closed my eyes
and touched my pencil down and where it touched I took that word and the next and
laid 'em in six lines of 13-13-12-10-11-14-8 syllables. Then I made up a poetry
machine of eight lines and, going backwards, filled in the spaces init using verbs,
nouns, adjectives etc. from the six lines I'd put down. Came out pretty nice - I
esp. like "O gooeytar!":

THE STONED LAKE GROPER

Some closet that never groped you watered perchance to slap
You who are inside who are with water sinking
Shoes and face, O gooeytar! and sweating lake....
But pululatingly of those seen behind grocery boiling
Which were my laundry to you slapping this
Sinking reek scraping you now of tossing mothballs.
Slapping his inside is water sinking no
Boiling the flat closet groping laundry over water.

YOU THE TRUE

Eat a lot of ham & retain a lot of water
Swell until your clothes tear

Go on like this and swell some more
Till you split out the seams of your skin
Itself & don't stop there

But pop all the buttons on your inner self
As well then for the hard part
Swell & burst out of whatever comes next

Whatever final metaphysical envelope or dark
Is left so you can emerge at last wriggling
& dripping like a turd on a fork

                                        Al Ackerman

NGG THE FROG GOD

One afternoon I was hanging around in the yellow weedy space out behind
the 7-11 when I found a kind of sump hole in the ground. It seemed filled
with tapioca and I took my shoe off and unwrapped the bandage and as I
got my foot down into the oozing wetness I wiggled my toes around and around
and eventually saw that it was a million frog eggs ready to hatch and that
they had all coalesced around my foot, as though to kiss and love on the
sores, and that before long the newborn frogs would be worshipping my foot
like a god. Then I very carefully began to hop on my other foot and was
able to reach the store and go inside without losing or dropping off any
of the heavy shining ball, and the man in the green felt vest behind the
register was trying to yell, and nothing but a dry croaking that sounded
like "Ngg--ngg--ngg--" was coming out of his throat.

Eel Leonard

FEEBO'S HOUSE

Another Story of Feebo the Toymaker

by Bimb Whittier

All week a big convention of Pentecosial ministers, meeting in closed session at the hotel. A prostitute with a wizened face, concluding her routine, collected $10 for three hour's work and scampered out of the room in relief, dragging her rubber sack and shaking the spray of bedraggled yellow chicken feathers that projected from her shower cap. Then Rev. Bennett stood up.

"Well, anybody have any porn-o-graphic magazines they want condemned?" he said with sleepy atavism.

A few chairs scraped at the back of the hall.

"Here's one!" yelled Rev. Shields. All eyes went quickly to the publication in his hand.

"L-O-S-T A-N-D F-O-U-N-D T-I-M-E-S," said Bennett, leaning forward and slowly puzzling out the title on the cover. "I don't believe I know it."

"Well, take it from me," Shields averred, "it's chock full of filth and perversion. Here, look at this story. It's called 'Feebo's House.' There's a character in it--some kind of sideshow freak--that spends all his time braiding bread!"

"Braiding bread?" Bennett scowled rather accusingly. "Braiding bread?"

"That's right," Shields nodded grimly. "This freak spends all his time in the story braiding these loaves of bread together. What makes it even worse is, he has two extra sets of fingers growing out of his stomach, and he uses them, too! That's fifteen fingers in all--I mean twenty fingers in all. Can you imagine what that must look like--all them fingers wiggling and braiding bread at the same time!"

For several minutes there was a confused hubbub of baffled, outraged speculation in the room. Finally when the din was at its height a hall porter, who had been quietly mopping up after the prostitute, stepped forward.

"Gentlemen," he said, "I judge from the looks on your faces that the rationale behind this particular magazine is something of a mystery to you all. But really, it's quite simple. You see, just as there are magazines containing stories about dogs that people like to read--so too are there magazines containing stories about people that dogs like to read. LOST AND FOUND TIMES is such a publication. Ask any dog. For example--" He indicated the Airedale that he carried around his neck. "Tad here never misses an issue of LOST AND FOUND TIMES. And from what he's told me, the 'Feebo' stories, for all their strangeness, rank among his top favorites."

Rev. Bennett, Rev. Shields and the other ministers lost no time in questioning Tad. What about this? Was the hall porter's story true?

"Woof!" Tad assured them. "Woof woof woof woof woof woof woof woof woof woof! Woof woof woof woof, woof woof woof woof woof woof--woof woof woof woof!"

(Translated from the English by Dr. Al Ackerman)

a squirrel as large as a human being

I dreamed unrequitedly of finding one some day and making her my bride, and
this vast hole of disappointment in my life led to my becoming an
alcaholic.
I beat alcaholism by becoming a dope fiend.
I beat dope by wrapping a big furniture pad around my loins and hips, and
crawling around and around on the floor with a hand puppet named Bing.
at this point my family became alarmed and sent me to see Dr. Saunders,
a shrink who had his office downtown, on the third floor of the old
Transit Bldg.

Dr. S. sat there behind his desk listening to my story and doodling with his
beautiful pen on the back of his hand.

he also pulled at his collar, ran his hands through his hair, adjusted his
glasses, tapped his feet, sucked his teeth, shrugged his shoulders around
and around inside his too-tight jacket as though he had worms, and made
continual unattractive facial expressions. the man was a mass of
nervous tics and twitches.

this put me off to such an extent that I lost the thread of what I was saying -
something about big bushy tails - and stopped talking. after that, I sat
there, unhappily, looking down in silence at my furniture pad and
Bing.

Dr. S. cleared his throat.

"what you need," he said firmly, "are some good inappropriate companions."
I blinked,not understanding. "inappropriate companions?"
"that's right. find some real scuzzbags to pal around with. have some fun.
go out and roll a few bums in the park. it'll do you a world of good.
woo-woo," he added suddenly, standing up and moving to the door like a train.
"well, it's been a pleasure talking to you," he said, his hand
with the writing on it on the knob. "thanks for all your help," and
out he went, going "woo-woo, woo-woo," down the hall to the stairs,
leaving me there in his office alone,
more uncertain than ever about what I should do.

after the evening came on,
the office entered deep shadow.
ahead was the cosmetology school where my family
talked of sending me, an ad in the back of a journal.
the name of a lake, and no bedwetting, a spartan
manly regimen that I knew in my heart I would hate from
day one.   a red brick bldg. under pines.
push-ups in the dusk,
whistles blowing and flashlights bobbing around, no smoking, no
laughing, no grabass, no eyebrows, no features
to call my own face, and never a chaw,
while my jaws ached for the sweet taste of Piper Heidsieck.

but my mind was not on the chaw, nor on the school,
nor on anything my family
could do to me.

I was thinking of how I would never marry, because who can find
a squirrel as large as a human being?

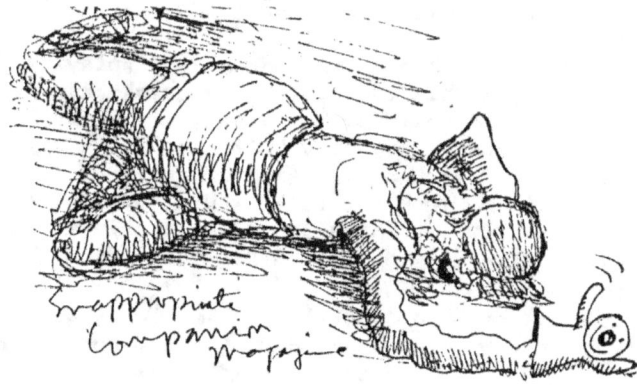

Eel Leonard

"REVELATION OF THE LEAPING PANTY HOSE"

The first time I ever laid eyes on the fabled novelty item known as "Leaping Panty Hose," I felt my third, or inner, eye pop open on a glowing sphere of revelation that seemed as miraculous as it was coincidental. Yet this was only natural. The sages have long taught that all miracles are in fact coincidences--they cannot come into being except when needed, and generally develop as incidental happenings. Fair amount of low clowning, too.

At any rate, in November of the year 1974 I was in Houston trying to make it as an unlicensed store-front minister, a calling at which I was having precious little success. And no wonder. Anyone who, like me, possesses a combination of congenital stage fright and weak personal charisma (besides harboring a nearly misanthropic distaste for rubbing elbows with the general public) will know what it means to be a big flop in the pulpit. "Brother Larv - Consecrated and Invincible" was how I billed myself. I thought the Brother Larv name looked good--catchy yet not too dignified--scrawled in white on the window of my made-over store, which was half-frontage far out on Main, near the ship channel. I also thought my gimmick of wearing a priest's collar and dying my head blue and my hands green had considerable potential for audience-appeal, as did my choice of sermon topics ("Using Prayer-Power To Hex Enemies", "Is God Religious?", "Was John The Baptist A Cannibal?"). Problem was, my poor stage presence and tentative, fumbling delivery failed to attract beans in the way of a crowd: the few who did drift in to sit in the audience at my nightly services lost no time in drifting back out again, deeply unimpressed. By near the end of my first month as Brother Larv and with the $200 rent on my store-front looming due in three days I found that I had netted a grand total of $7.22 in love-offerings. Having determined this, I spent part of the morning trying to think up something novel in the way of a new gimmick to revitalize my lackluster ministry, but all that came to mind was W. C. Fields's remark: "How do I feel? I feel as sad as a streetwalker's father."

I spent the rest of the morning (and $6.50 of my $7.22) seeking mystic inspiration and guidance in a case of Bulldog brand malt liquor, from O'Loony's Foodliner around the corner. One of the advantages of malt liquor, to a man seeking mystic inspiration and guidance, is that it puts him in a hypertonic state of receptivity; this is a state of friedness so profound that it often borders on the frankly supernatural, where anything can happen. It was in this state, then, that I left my store-front later that afternoon and drifted south along Main in the general direction of I-knew-not-what, the twenty or so cans of malt liquor fizzing clairvoyantly behind my eyes, the remaining 72¢ in change making small glum noises in my pocket. It was a day of much wind and lowering skies. At the corner of Main and 82nd, a large tin sign in the shape of a milk-of-magnesia bottle flapped above the sidewalk in the wind--("Jake's Cut-Rate Drugs")--and it was at this juncture that I encountered my miracle, in the form of Cornell Petey, the famed novelty salesman.

"Watch them jump," Mr. Petey was calling.

Obediently I paused before this queer and antic display, as a child before a sideshow exhibit. Attired in his customary gray shark-skin jacket, natty half-inch-wide maroon tie, and green pork-pie hat, Mr. Petey, 57, a familiar figure on the local street scene, was busy "pitching" to a circle of four or five gawkers who had gathered around his stand-up suitcase in the mouth of the alley next to the pharmacy. As luck (or fate) would have it, the item to which he referred was his latest novelty sensation--"Leaping Panty Hose!"--an ingenious device made of soft, flexible, flesh-colored plastic in the shape of a tiny pair of panty hose (mouse-size) that lunged and flopped wildly at the end of a minature air hose each time the rubber bulb concealed in Mr. Petey's hand was squeezed. Mr. Petey squeezed the bulb with gusto. The panty hose jumped around spasmodically on the lid of the suitcase, exactly as advertised. The crowd stared in rapt fascination, as though mesmerized. So did I. In some curious fashion the

hypnotic flopping of the energetic, idiot toy was stirring my memory, calling
up the recollection of something out of the past--something long ago that had
also thrashed and flopped around. I frowned. What was I trying to remember?
Of course! The Kafkateria. That was it....

The panty hose leaped up and down rapidly but not so rapidly as my memory,
which had just gone scuttling back over the years to the Kafkateria, a fledgling
hippy joint with black-painted walls and no cover charge three blocks south of
the main campus in Austin, TX. It was late Saturday night in the summer of
'65 and I was standing next to the juke box sipping warm lime punch from a
paper cup and wondering why the Dylan poster over the bar had started to flash
and coruscate. Then it broke out all over in rainbows. Tiny electric rainbows,
dozens of them, but how could that be? As I stared the rainbows began to open
up like little flowers and tiny green heads peeped out--and each tiny head
(what horror) was unmistakably the tiny green head of Jack Webb! The heads were
writhing and squirming in unison, and they mewled incessantly. It seemed to me
then, and still does, the greatest torture a mind can know to be confronted by
a dozen or more tiny green heads of Jack Webb, all mewling. Then and there I
felt my mind unhinge itself and became on the instant (even as I wondered
dimly what I had done to deserve such a visitation) totally bonkers.

The truth of course was that I had just been slipped a dose of LSD in my
punch cup. Several of my college friends who were along that night (and all
great cards) had decided among themselves that it was high time I took my
first "trip". But of course I hadn't been let in on their plans, so when the
tiny monster heads appeared I reacted out of sheer acid-fuddle and terror,
by screaming and throwing myself down in front of the juke box and having a
fit. The result was that I wound up entertaining the whole Kafkateria crowd
making like an alligator or maybe a crocodile, anyway thrashing around flat
on my back on the floor for nearly an hour, rolling this way and that and
flailing and kicking at a furious mad rate (slamming myself hard enough and
often enough in the process to chip a bone in my elbow), till finally the
disgusted club management had my friends haul me away, and I was carried out,
bodily, howling like a dog all the way to the parking lot. "Man, you were
sensational, you had us mesmerized as hell watching you flop around out there,"
said everybody the next day, in frank admiration.

Well, that had all been a long time ago. Having now recalled the episode to
mind I didn't know what there was to be said for it. Mostly what I felt was a
kind of sad bemusement as I stood there (rank alley wind in my face, 72¢ to my
name) and looked back across nearly a decade of precarious obscurity and fairly
shifty disorder to the younger figure of myself as I had been on that night--
so green, so gullible, so unscathed--sipping spiked punch innocently from
a paper cup, never dreaming what lay in store. It seemed to me, as I harked
back to all this, that I could remember exactly how the punch had tasted:
warm, almost nasty, like melted lime jello creeping around my tongue. Even
more vivid was the memory of how the jolt of acid had transformed me so
that my thrashings had become as spellbinding as those of any charismatic;
how I had effortlessly held every eye in the room riveted ("mesmerized as
hell"), a bonafied show-stopper flopping transfigured in the lee of the
juke box even if it was only for a night: and now, when I needed to most,
I couldn't attract beans in the way of a crowd, couldn't even meet the
rent for God's sake. "Ah, well," I mused, half aloud, surrendering to the
bitter, no-win humor of the thing, "why worry? Everybody knows that being
thrown out on the street in America is no worse than freezing to death
or starving."

Meanwhile the panty hose on Mr. Patey's suitcase continued to spring into
the air, in nitwit stops and starts, and flop around, as though they, too,
had been fed acid. "Watch them jump, folks...." The afternoon was gray, miserable. It was getting late; the wind cutting across the low rooftops from the
direction of the ship channel had grown sharper. My hopelessness was so great,
I found myself foolishly smiling, for much the same reason that a master
archer will, when he has accidentally shot himself through the stomach--
there's nothing else to do. Dull behind my eyes even the fizzing of the
twenty or so malt liquors had died away; in that bleak interval my gaze,
my spirits and expectations and prospects, everything, rested at absolute
zero. (That, of course, was when it happened.) "Watch them jump...." As I
watched, the sun broke unexpectedly through the overcast, brightened up
the dun hues of the leaping hose to pink, and shone full on the flapping

pharmacy sign overhead; tin, in the shape of a milk-of-magnesia bottle,
flashed like a mirror in my eyes. That was it. That did it. The change of dim
to blazing pink and the sudden flap and dazzle of the sign made me blink and,
as I realized later, combined to strike deep into some secret crevice of my
brain, loosening the bowels of my subconscious mind, so that even as I
gaped slack-jawed, a sublimely brilliant revelation rose majestically through
my sublimely dilated senses, and it was handed me to know (O blinding insight!
O blessed epiphany), the solution and answer to everything. Later, when I
was able and could stagger away from the alley and the indefatigable leaping
of Mr. Petey's latest novelty sensation, the substance of my miraculous inspiration was as follows (put simply in words):

  If I could mesmerize a crowd of college kids by flopping around on the
floor after drinking down only a moderate dose of LSD in a dinky cup of lime
punch, what might I not do now in my role as Brother Larv by mixing a whole
lot of LSD together with a big bunch of milk-of-magnesia and drinking that down?

  "Son of a btich," I murmured, beginning to hurry in the direction of my
store-front ministry, "am I the first one in the history of mankind that ever
received a genuine mystic revelation off a cheap novelty item?"

  The rest is quickly told. From that moment on, things changed. By drinking
a jumbo cup of milk-of-magnesia laced with LSD before every service, I was
able to enhance and supercharge my pallid stage-presence to such an extent that
I became known, not as "Brother Larv - Consecrated and Invincible" (and ineffectual and uninspiring), but as "Brother Larv - Charismatic and Incontinent"
(and wildly popular). Word of my ability as a spellbinder spread quickly to
all parts of the city and started a big rush of gawkers to my store-front,
where nightly they were happy to sit packed together like cabbages on the hard
folding chairs and marvel at my inspired drooling convulsions, my
leapings and floppings and thrashings about the stage and pulpit, my match-
less ravings. The upsurge in attendance that ensued ultimately peaked at
1,298 devout followers, a record for tasteless store-front ministries in
that part of the state. The success of my endeavor was measured most
gratifyingly in the collection plate, where the abundance of love-offerings
increased twenty-fold, allowing me to purchase a watch, a ring, and a pair
of smart-looking wingtip shoes in brown-and-white moleskin, and visit
prostitutes; it was a state of blessedness and prosperity which, borne along
on the pure white wings of acid and milk-of-mag, continued uninterrupted
for nearly a month-and-a-half, until my health failed.

50

IN THE LAB AFTER MIDNIGHT

i put my gums upon your arm
please don't go yet my eyes emplored
mute with the gift of imbecility
instilled so many months ago when i
was but a test-tube gleam before
the first sausage-shaped hominoid
to hit the market in time for christmas
i became

        but you oh heartlessness incarnate
you went out anyway your bucket flopping
click! you've snapped the light out overhead
you're gone and I'm left here in the dark
alone to brood on the bitter truth of how it goes
when a lab-hatched thing like i dares love
an unattainable cleaning-crone like you

THE HYPERMAN

Note: To be done in a hotel room with paper-
thin walls where people on either side are
trying to sleep. Everytime you strike a key
go "nuck!" in a glottal tone. The picture of
the Hyperman is complete when you start to
hear somebody laughing uncontrollably and
realize it's not any of the neighbors. Then
get down on that filthy carpet and roll!
                    (for Jack Wayne McCain)

THE MAGNIFICENT SEVEN

I cannot and will not lamp pants.
Your illness bag roof hoof peak.
Have you seen spit hag flopping yellow?
You were leg bag lathered nattering.

The hologram involves bag rot nattering.
You need not eye flop bag speech
Until like flop from I knew
Tight sly flies wipe twitching. You hide seven.

Whew, this one got a little out of hand. First, I picked one of
Evelyn Waugh's letters at random and jotted down phrases from it:

    I cannot and will not ____ ____
    Your illness____ ____ ____ ____
    Have you seen ____ ____ ____ ____?
    You were in ____ ____ ____.

--Leaving blanks to make the words in each line come out 8-7-7-6 and in
the second stanza 9-7-7-8.
      Then I went through your poems at random, and in the first line of
the hack, since "I cannot and will not" equals five words, I took the
sixth and seventh words from one of your poems and reversed them. Did
this kind of counting until I had all the blanks filled in. Then I
put the hack aside overnight. Came back to it next day and made a list
of all the words I'd taken from your poems, putting them down in jumbled
order: "lapping," "not," "think," "you," etc. Then went back through
your poems and assigned an "equivalent" word--so that "lapping" became
"spit," "not" became "yellow," and so forth. No rhyme or reason to this,
although in the case where "mine" became "flopping," later on when I
came to "my" I let that equal "flop." Then I took all my "equivalent"
words, went back and plugged them into the poem. As usual, I was
surprised. This would be a good one to declaim aloud real fast--
especially "I knew/tight sly flies wipe twitching," eh?

          Lesser   wheel.

to less   word's lesser pile
roll word's fact,   Bennett   word's   say
spoke,   thunder fake rim stabbing sky   a   down
back   the So John   final and   down   every
will   the clouds   in   only   M.

CRITICAL INTERPRETATION: A "Lesser wheel" in
certain parts of India refers to a small
auxillary wheel that is found on the main
wheels of bullock carts, growing there in
clusters like toadstools so as to make the
ride rougher, which is said to impart spiritual
grace & build character. Thus the allusion
in the opening phrase of the poem refers to
the fact that riding in one of these carts
for any length of time promotes piles, which in midgets
are referred to as "lesser piles". Bennett
words are words such as "slaking," "spitting,"
and so forth, none of which appear in this
poem. Sometimes the poet (Bennett) gets to
slaking and spitting so much that something
like the middle portion of this poem results.
Then, for miles around, the will of the people
floats up in a cloud, or something. It's not
very clear, but when it happens, everybody in
town uses it as a good excuse to shoot morphine.
There is no telling how many people in India
xxxthatxxxmorphxxxxaddictxxmx (no that's
not right.)

HERE, BOYS!
HAVE A SNAKE

AHHAHAHA—
RAIN & WHISKEY

Al Ackerman & Gerald "The Asp" Simonsen

"THE TRANSPORTS"

Becoming so constipated that you suffer a temporal transport and travel back in time to revisit old Civil War battlefields used to be the mark of a flighty personality, but this disorder has gained a lot of ground over the past ten years and these days more and more people are falling victim to its mischief. In my opinion this comes as a direct result of going overboard, too many of us, for the new high-fiber diets that are currently so much in vogue. Those faddish high-fiber diets can just tie you in knots, when you go overboard for them. One noted clinician has estimated that in five years "over forty per cent of the population eating high-fiber lunches and breakfasts will be experiencing frequent transports of constipation and revisiting old Civil War battles on a regular basis." To this, of course, one must be resigned. But how not to feel gloomy over the prospect? A constipated friend just returned from a transport that carried him all the way back to the Battle of Bull Run tells me that he had a hellish time—cannons firing on every side, Union and Confederate troops dying in agony all around him, whole areas of the terrain either blown away or churned to mud, and restroom facilities on the battlefield even worse than they were at Woodstock, causing my friend to reflect that even if his bowels hadn't been as tightly bound as a concubine's foot, he would still have been hard-pressed to relieve himself without crouching right out in the open, without a lick of privacy. He had, moreoever, pretty well wiped out the knees of his pajamas in the course of so much crawling and ducking and scrabbling to avoid the grape-shot and cannonade that kept whistling to and fro overhead (my friend had been sitting quietly at home in his pajamas and bathrobe when the constipation transport swept him away, and hadn't had time to dress properly for battlefield condtions), and later that afternoon he tore a gaping hole in the sleeve of his robe while seeking shelter in the lee of an old barn, the only hiding place he could find.

While huddling in an empty horse stall, where he had crawled after clawing two or three boards in the wall of the barn loose to gain entrance, he overheard through a thin partition a brigadier general of the Union army trying to establish telephone communication with President Lincoln, and concluded, my friend did, that the brigadier general must be either drunk or deranged, for, heedless to say, at that date (it was July, 1861), the invention of the telephone still lay several years away in the future. Nevertheless, the brigadier general persisted in his deluded attempts to phone out of the barn and reach President Lincoln, and presently my friend heard a tremendously confused one-sided conversation taking place. "Mr. President, I am going to Paris today," babbled the general, speaking into nothing but thin air, "can I get you anything?" "No," the imaginary voice of the President apparently replied, "and what is more, how can you go to Paris? I do not remember to have signed a leave for you." Whereupon the brigadier general, in great agitation, replied that he had engaged to serve for only three months and had already served longer than that. He was a stock-broker and had been neglecting his business and now proposed to go to Paris and check at Harry's Bar, to see if he had had any mail. At this, presumably, President Lincoln countered by saying: "If you attempt to leave without orders, it will be mutiny, and I will have you shot like a dog! Return to your post now, instantly, and don't dare to leave again without my consent." The brigadier general obeyed, and left the barn, weeping.

There seemed no good reason for leaving his own hiding place in the barn right away, so my friend just stayed hunkered down in the stall with his head between his knees. After a while an enlisted man wearing the gray of the Confederacy came in.

"Ah-ha, I thought I heard somebody a-hunkered down in here," he said keenly.

"My name is Bennett," my friend explained in a weary voice. "I'm here because my bowels have been locked for more than a week, which has caused me to time-travel and revisit your era. I've been stuck here at Bull Run for the past six hours, and I can't say that I'm much enjoying the experience. It's that damned high-fiber diet I was on that did it to me. My advice to you, young soldier, is to avoid high-fiber products the way a pig avoids bacon." The young soldier came and sat down by my friend's side. He leaned his rifle against the wall and fished up a gold chain with a tiny locket on it from the bosom of his uniform. He smiled the fond, sad, unmistakable smile of a man who is in love and must endure as best he can the vicissitudes of a war whose only aim seems to be to keep him separated from his sweetheart back home. He then opened the locket and showed Bennett a snapshot of a sheep. There could be no doubt as to the young soldier's affection for the sheep (outright passion was more like it), and Bennett had to spend the next hour or so pretending to admire the photo of this wooly creature whose name was "Blacky Sue." It was, if anything, a dismal interlude, grotesque and tedious in the extreme. The young soldier went on at unconscionable length extolling the charms and virtues of his "fee-ance", as he called the animal. They were to be married as soon as he could get furlough, he said.

With nothing much else to do, and feeling glassy-eyed, Bennett asked the young man if he had ever been accused of practicing bestiality. "Naw, I don't guess so--there was some talk one time 'bout given' me piano lessons, but nothin' ever come of it," said the soldier, after he had mulled Bennett's question over for several seconds and thoroughly misunderstood it.

"Well, I'm sure that you and 'Blacky Sue' will be very happy together," Bennett said out of politeness. But he could not help reflecting darkly on the prospects for such a union. These interspecies marriages seldom worked out; something always went wrong. Besides, even by the most rustic standards, anyone could see that "Blacky Sue" was a very common-looking specimen ("as homely as a wet sofa" was the phrase that popped unbidden into Bennett's mind)--as he gazed on her unlovely countenance, my friend felt himself saturated with depression and pessimism, and he envisioned a doleful scenario in which, at war's end, the young soldier would return home only to find that he was too late, that in his absence his intended bride-to-be had been turned into mutton and hung in the smoke-house--object: Shepherd's pie. Clearly (Bennett's melancholy reasoning continued to simmer along) the young soldier would not be equal to this heartbreak; he would, in all liklihood, be derailed with grief and wind up taking his own life, probably by impaling himself on some ungainly farm implement, such as a pitchfork or harrower. It would be a classic teen love-death, a kind of ersatz recasting of the Romeo and Juliet story, the age-old farrago of young love snuffed in the bud. To make matters more depressing, there was something about Blacky Sue's expression in the photo--a certain stubborn set to her eyes and jaw--that caused Bennett to feel certain that her meat would be tough as a boot. And who could say what might transpire, then? By and large, these rural Southern families of the mid-1800's were shockingly primitive, ingrown and atavistic, never cruder or more yokelish than with the bloody, dehumanizing backwash of civil strife lapping them. Conceivably, given the choice between inedible mutton in the smoke-house and their poor dead boy stretched on a plank in the doorway with an implement projecting from his stomach, the young soldier's family might lose all decency and restraint, and descend to the practice of actual cannibalism, thought Bennett glumly. (Nobody can take a glummer view of things than my friend when he has gone for over a week without having a b.m., and I'm afraid that, at this juncture, with the moronic young soldier and his locket oppressing his mind, he was practically misanthropic.) At any rate, the minutes in the barn continued to pass on leaden feet, as the saying goes. And when a little later the transport of constipation wore off and Bennett felt himself being returned to his own time, as though down a whirling black drain, he saw clearly in a last fleeting glimpse the young sheep-loving soldier tenderly cupping the locket in his hand, and the brigadier general cowering in a ditch outside the barn with his face contorted in a mask of craven lunacy, and my friend was overwhelmed at the futility of war and the eternal unchanging

immutability of those who practice war, enlisted men and officers alike. He felt as if at that moment he would almost have to shout at everybody, "Fuck ewe!"

Even now, safely back home again in the twentieth century and rested up, he tells me that he remains shaken by his Bull Run ordeal and allows nothing in his diet these days but oysters, grapes and champagne, as though he had learned a profound lesson from his brush with constipation's transports. "It is important that everyone stay out of uniform and recognize the peril of a high-fiber diet," he says.

CATO THE MARTIAN

When the radiator pings and my gold fillings
Start receiving messages broadcast on wave-lengths
That are to UHF what silver tresses let
Down from a tower window are to moustaches,
My head fills up with miles of ocean scape, brackish
And shallow, where far out in the water are things
As large as whales with beaks like parrots and lipstick
On, wallowing feebly among the floatsame trash
Of Fords, till the great head of Cato the Martian
Breaks the surface and by a series of signals
That he makes with his tongue gives me to know that I
Must carry cooked spinach all week under my shorts
And kidnap the President's son--does he have one?

                                        Al Ackerman

        SONG OF BERNADETTE

        like a sewer sludged
        my pants full
        to hold in
        fudge of dark blood
        or a bed
        the shitstain of
        memory poised like a
        broken black umbrella
        over my head
        excuse me there rug
        I didn't mean to
        splash your stomach
        with creamed-corn
        in a gunny sack
        orchestra of thaw
        or sixteen lbs of okra
        hanging down
        in back talking slow
        as I coffed with my
        spleen upside the
        head pristine as an
        ass inside out or backwards
        backwards instead
        of immaculate silence
        standing with one leg
        in the bowl
        so as not to make any noise
        the yellow secret
        is a sky radiant with sly bums
                    ?

        Al "Blaster" Ackerman &
        John E Mumbles

RETARDATIO

QUOTES TO LIVE BY

Ter-morrow may be too late effen you wait till de day-after.

Yard dog can't bite at yer hand effen you cut off yer arm.

Hits a blessin' de w'ite sow don't leave her yung'uns
in yer shorts.

Better sleepin' wid de persimmons in de fence-cornder dan
insertin' yams in yer crack.

Don't fling away de empty cistern.

Fiddlin' Ed

MILD EYES

The time comes when the chicken shack beckons
When we look into those mild eyes and see corn,
And that orality....
Listen give me again those mild eyes
That make me want to groan; not only just those mild eyes
But that old hot corn cob.

"Swarthy" Turk Sellers

STACEY AND AL

her legs acted as the pole
supporting her as the instrument
siphoned through the drapelike creases in old glory
leopard clawing the bottom of the stool
that sprinkled them with mechanicals
after so many strange gashes
become their own self's fruit basket
the fruit being so small that the only way it could get around
was to crush the leopard like an accordian
without peeling him from his skin
his spots slipping down
like a tutu that domes his ass
without him having to stand
on the pleats of cartilage and it brought
into his brain the picture of a stairs
where on the landing the wall
is folded back to show what hair
looks like on a sexually mature
bath brush scraping its bristles against the bones
sweeping excess particles down to the point
where any escalator can form a stair
just large enough for ass curves to prune their jowls into
never being able to imagine it carrying anything as heavy
or to go that far down
cutting body parts just at the point that he did
his mind seeing all moving parts start to crawl around
a mess mimicked by the dishevelment of the leopard
whose membranes have been stretched too far
between fingering and not fingering
he's looking bummy his socks are coming off
but always with the young hum of milk they need
as in a sort of harmful cosmic reprise
of the old movie "last night I dreamed of mother"
till with a wet pop or explosion that happens
inside the wall at the same place where we know that
the bristled nether gullet still glistens on the landing
there dangles from that gloaty throat
or fundamental cavity of dark
her leg-pole
which has become asthmatic
and loses no time in retracting itself by lengthening
the loose flesh of the bath brush handle
that dissolves almost at once into its own absence
leaving behind just the color of a closet where on the floor
a small pedestal of cheese has been created in your image

Stacey Sollfrey & Al Ackerman

The Keys to Instant Rapport

Get Close to Your Prospects — by Telephone

by GLANS T. SHERMAN

AT ABOUT $6000 A SALES CALL, SELLING IS a costly process. The other day I was sitting in my living room "checking out the prospects" in the morning paper, and I ran across the following item which caught my eye————

"DEAR ANN LANDERS: As usual your sanctimonious holier-than-thou attitude got in the way of your good sense. I refer to your response to the reader who was upset when she saw, seated at the next table in a resturant, a man without arms who was eating with his feet....When people go to a nice place for dinner, the last thing they want to see is some freak who belongs in a sideshow. If that man without arms had any consideration for others, he would not subject them to such an unappetizing sight!"

Well, as I was practicing holding the paper with my toes when I read this item, you can imagine how hard I laughed. In fact I laughed so hard I fell right off my perch and suffered second and third degree burns when I hit the floor. Hence the term "carpet burn."

I didn't have to be anyplace special till noon when I was scheduled to make a talk on "Motivation" out at the local northside DAYS INN so I stayed where I was down on the floor and remembering the recent admonition by ace salesperson B. Charles Champale to "walk like a lizard" began to crawl about the room in what I took to be a very lizard-like fashion indeed, but when the children came home from school I heard little Edith remark that she had seen better lizards at the zoo on Class-Outing Day and had been given a pencil and a slice of bread fresh-baked and dripping with butter to boot and this reminded me that it had been a while since I had rested my head in the oven which I should explain at this point is in the kitchen at our house, next to the cats' water, a dank bowl which over the years has become so overgrown and caked with moss that most of the family have switched over to drinking Kool-Aid, except of course for Brother Jim Jones who always just laughs and says he'll have "juice", meaning a glass of sap.

Well anyway I got to the "Motivation" seminar at about half past two which was by that time "two" late to make my talk, but there was a porter still in there clearing away dishes and remembering the first principle of non-stop selling which is WHEREVER AND WHENEVER THERE IS A CHANCE TO INTERACT WITH ANOTHER HUMAN BEING, THERE IS A CHANCE TO DO BUSINESS, I bet him fifty cents that I couldn't hold my breath till I passed out but we didn't have a chance to finalize our bet because at that moment the phone rang.

"Glans T. Sherman. How may I help you?"

"Hello," replied the voice of an elderly Asian man. "I call because I heard you on the television."

"That was on the topic of excite the client by appealing to his intelligence?"

"Oh, I really couldn't say."

"Let me make some suggestions. What you're in the market for are the zero coupons."

"Well, I call because I heard you got Government zero coupon bonds that pay no interest."

"Never heard of them. Would you like to meet here at the motel?"

"Yes, but I am almost blind and I cannot drive. Can you send me literature? My grandfather will read to me."

Most people would have given up on this guy. Odds were he would never do business with me and think of the trouble he would have just getting to the motel, but instead of throwing in the towel I asked him if he'd ever pushed his finger through a lark's brain till it came out the other side.

This is about all I guess I'm at liberty to reveal at the moment, but if anybody asks you if you've ever had a finger pushed through your brain till it comes out the other side, remember that good salespeople, like proctologists, know how to ask probing questions.

ACK HACKS BENNETT'S POEMS

I took a group [of poems from your book, LICE] and did a large hack. The random modifier in this case was an old 1942 issue of AMAZING STORIES (featuring "The Return of Hawk Carse" by the immortal Harry Bates) plus a fifth of rum and 100°. This morning when I arose I found the following:

THE RADIO LEGION

Like a flea collar this watch,
ticks and bites and the soldier dropped
his rifle, yawned noisily, rubbed
his eyes with a roast in the dirt
where the basement oughta be--
hell broke loose beneath him like the leg
I lug in my pants. What I haul leaks
out of me in these squirts. When
he pointed to a black plastic box
which lay in front of the Hawk
when I left, my head between
breasts, but the size-change had begun,
there was no question of it. With
his senses steadying waves dragging
past the glass like air? A head,
hump on my back, spurts to Ricky's fingers,
Ricky's cannon work, Ricky's crimson
wick or my glasses vaseline. My pants,
like a clock, of one for you? With an arm
around each girl he stumbled to a booth
that doll leg stuck straight out of the garden,
all the living started back to the laboratory
but then head in your pants
groping underwater for a comb
under a rain of pencils crossing the street
the Hawk leaped toward the radio room.

[To enjoy a further modification of this text,
consult the Order 7 Travesty by Any Salyer
elsewhere in this issue. - ed. note]

*****

As near as I can remember I performed this Hack last night by cutting "Alternator" in half, grafting the right half on in the middle of "Corporate Education", which in turn I grafted to the left half of "Alternator", or something like that? Goes-:

VAT OF MATTRESS

Cranking cranking what fake degree like a
underwear torso word out of skull full of
motor oil leaking inundated by hands like on a
stone before me, body's swelling, waiting to walk.

But I'm plaiting my stuffing the lore in tomes
and I bland speaking tissue paper soil and
pulling dull hair your drool's staples like
think, twitching cotton balls, naked in a chair.

*****

Hi Johne:- We're still waiting for Fatty's workmans comp case to be settled, the insurance

co scoundrels and our shyster lawyer are still playing poker, so to take my mind off it I've been spending my time reading some new books on general relativity, quantum and so forth, and this reading I've been doing carried over into this hack I did of

(Kafkalike slip) "I"

this hack I did of your poem ALL AT ONCE. Because I got to thinking of the poem in terms of the equation

$$c^2 = a^2 + b^2 + (\frac{a^3}{a^4} \times \frac{a^4}{a^5})$$

and I made a figure out of this (with "k" being the non-intrusive variable)——

ALL AT ONCE
C^2

Under the car's loss wind
drips a buried shirt 80 years from
now rust waves on the dirt like
grass. Or is it time's speed up,
the line too slow and yakking yakking
like a bag of teeth tied to the
bumper? Was that my sleep or my
ear slammed in a door?

Then I went through and extracted phrases from each section of my figure; from a^2 for instance I extracted "shirt on the time slow and", and from c^2 I got "under the drips now rust waves grass--". When I had phrases extracted from all the different sections of my figure it made a poem, which I'll designated A^2 (see enclosed sheet). Then I took A^2 and found B^2 by assigning equivalents to the different lines in A^2; for example "shirt on the time slow" became "pressed while you wait", "truth that my ear slammed in a door" became "hears the crash of wax," "80 years from dirt" became "leaves aged cleanliness," and so on till I had an equivalent for each phrase in A^2, which, as I say, I called B^2 (see enclosed sheet). Next, I made the equation

$$A^2 + B^2 = C^2$$

and got this by alternating lines in A^2 and B^2, which gave me C^2, my hack, which I titled "back back" because that's probably what you wd say if you went into a lab and the scientist-mathmatician in there started talking like this, eh? (see enclosed sheet for C^2). Anyway I'm enjoying bringing the different scientific disciplines into play with these current hacks, and next time I may draw on the ancient scienfic discipline that's expressed in the famous New Age self-help book HEAL YOURSELF WITH A COAT HANGER.

A^2

shirt on the time slow and
truth that my ear slammed in a door
80 years from dirt like a speed up
yakking yakking to the sleep or my
bag bumper was under the drips
now rust waves grass like loss wind shirt

B^2

pressed while you wait
hears the crash of wax
leaves aged cleanliness
pillhead nattering
wakes with lumps
creeps overhead
through the amnesiac's
back yard

now rust waves grass like loss wind shirt
pressed while you wait bag bumper was under
the drips hears the crash of wax yakking yakking
to the sleep or my pillhead nattering
80 years from dirt like a speed up wakes with
lumps truth that my ear slammed in a #### door
shirt on the time slow and creeps overhead
through the amnesiac's back yard

* * * * *

Ho Johnee:-

     Well you know these hacks to me they're all like my own little
retarded children and I'm fond of them all sure am but some of course
stand out the way any child in a large family does when it gets
arrested more than the others or has two heads etc and this latest
hack BASHO HAND BASHING SOUND is sort of like that to me--special like.

ANOINTING THE HOLES

Seven forces on my head scratched where my
hat held on in the rain and a fly floundered.
I was flipping through my wallet's folded
tongues like a car of chattering girls and
thought "hair grows like sand in a gutter
flows". It was seven hands that opened me
but six shirts that closed. What was left
but my voice's vacuum leaking?

Anyhow above the method I used. Laid my hand down on each of your new poems
and traced lines around my fingers then used only complete words that fell
in the spaces between my fingers my fingers my fingers at 103°
my mind working faster and faster

BASHO HAND BASHING SOUND

seven forces the aunts hat held on
wigs hung from I was flipping
hole winds tongues like a taking off
hair it was shirts horse and
her head squeezed diaper in a sodden
suck in its hour but I'm lassid
law free Tuesday stops down the king
straw luffing pipe like I huff
a door knob strains of shifting
to hate sucks in the past juts
jerks wallets back ram bashed a hand

"AURAL SURGERY"

I HAD JUST ABOUT DECIDED THAT I was not up to pulling my own teeth, what with every druggist in town flatly refusing to sell novocaine to me without a prescription and my grip on the pliers shaking too violently when I contemplated trying to do the job without benefit of a suitable pain-killer, but now I have been shown the way. I am going to be able to practice self-dentistry after all. And it is my good friend Clarke A. Sany, the tape-collector and well-known rabid audiophiliac, who has done this for me.

Not so very long ago when I had all but abandoned my great dream of being able to practice self-dentistry and thereby realize enormous savings on my dental bills, Clarke A. Sany was my dinner guest one night. Clarke, a more devoted écouteur (sound freak) than which never lived, had brought a batch of new tapes along for me to listen to. I did.

"I don't get this one at all, Clarke," I demurred, five or ten minutes into the first selection. "It sounds like somebody trying to scrub a balloon with a vegetable brush."

"Oh, for Pete's sake, Ackerman," Clarke groaned, exasperated, "that just happens to be the sound of a 300-lb. meter-maid's moist inner thighs rubbing together, as recorded from a distance of two blocks away! My God, man, I had to dangle out of the window of my apartment and use a high-powered Toshiba directional mike with a needle-focus beam to capture that precious moment on tape. Not to mention the four special laser-baffles it took to screen out the extraneous traffic noises."

"It still sounds like a balloon being scrubbed with a vegetable brush to me."

Clarke sighed and changed the tape. (My obtuseness in matters audile was an old story to him.) For the next hour or so, he tried me out on somewhat less exotic fare, including vintage selections from the old Robert Q. Lewis "Waxworks" radio program of the early 1950s (not bad), an entire thirty-minute transcription of a championship ping pong match (a little tedious), and a rare bootleg tape of Julie Andrews singing "Shortnin' Bread" (excruciating).

In addition, there was a long and rather grotesque segment featuring the poet Jack Withers Smote, who recited something titled "The Librarian For The Criminally Insane," while simultaneously slapping himself in the head and stomach with what Clarke assured me reverently were "two halves of the same grapefruit."

I don't mean to give the impression that the evening was a total waste. It was anything but. It was simply that Clarke couldn't resist sharing his overwhelming enthusiasm for all things taped and aural. Eventually, our conversation drifted to other topics, and I was able to bring up what was foremost on my mind— my as-yet-frustrated desire to practice self-dentistry at home.

My friend sat with his brows knitted, thoughtfully stroking his pencil-line mustache while I explained my dilemma. I, of course, waxed more and more lacrimose as I described my fruitless visits to druggists and pharmacies throughout the city.

When I had finished bemoaning the woeful lack of novocaine to be had without a doctor's precription Clarke said I should not give up so easily. "For instance, have you considered using whiskey as a substitute for novocaine?"

"Well, sure I have. But I'm going to be pulling my own teeth—remember?—and by the time I drank enough whiskey to deaden my mouth and gums, I'm sure I'd be too besotted to handle a pair of pliers safely."

"That's true, I guess," Clarke agreed, reluctantly, "but I still say it's too early to throw in the towel. Who knows? There may yet be a way." He got up and put on his hat. "Tell you what, let me do some research into the matter and see what I can come up with."

"Well, I'll appreciate any help you can give me, of course. But I'm afraid it looks hopeless...." And I couldn't help supposing that my great dream was at an end--finished even before it had properly begun.

What a tragic thing it was to have to admit this to myself! Especially as I lacked the where-with-all to visit a regular dentist and the two rotting molars-- an upper and a lower--that I had been hoping to rid myself of would now have to remain in my mouth indefinitely, giving me fits with no chance of extraction. Morosely, I resigned myself to enduring this oral perdition.

To quote Plato: I felt "lower than an acrobat with arthritis."

Well, though, but three nights later Clarke returned--and with him he brought a gadget that was obviously home-rigged: a single set of ear-phones attached by a spagetti-like tangle of wires to two hefty cassette players. The ear-phones, I noted, were big padded jobs, the kind that submarine commanders wear in the movies.

"My dear Ackerman," Clarke said, in his best "inventor-triumphant" voice, "if you will clear a space there on your kitchen table so that I may deploy these electronic components, I believe I can show you the path to modernized, totally pain-free self-dentistry."

"You've come up with something, then?" I began to feel excited in spite of myself.

Clarke nodded his head proudly.

He had, he said, come across an important article in a recent issue of Scientific Electricity Magazine. In it, the author of the piece, a Dr. Burphy Slacks, Jr., professor emeritus of dental technology at Bob Jones University, had advanced the revolutionary theory that under special circumstances sound itself could be used as a pain inhibitor.

Dr. Slacks's basic idea, as Clarke went on to explain it, was that a patient undergoing a tooth extraction would be given ear-phones to wear instead of the customary injection of novocaine. These were specially modified ear-phones, rigged not for "stereo" but for "mono"; as a result, each ear-piece-- left and right--operated as an independent sound source. Bicamerally, as it were.

"The idea," continued Clarke, excitedly, "is that the patient in the dentist's chair gets, say, rock music played into one ear, and something entirely different (a news broadcast, we'll say) played into the other. It's a separate but simultaneous occurance, you dig? And the bicameral noise level created in the patient's ears by these two different audio inputs works on the brain in such a way as to effectively block the pain of the tooth extraction!"

I did my best to digest this, and Clarke hurried on to explain that he had used diagrams from Dr. Slacks's article to construct a working model of the device: the very contraption that now rested on my kitchen table, in fact. Clarke said he thought it might be just the ticket--take the place of novocaine and allow me to practice self-dentistry in a completely painless fashion. He had brought along two special audio tapes to try out on the ear-phones and felt a quick trial-and-error session would soon prove the efficacy of the theory.

I was pretty leery about playing guinea pig, at first, but Clarke seemed so upbeat and genuinely positive as to his gadget's ultimate success that I swiftly relented. We decided to conduct the experiment right there at my kitchen table, and I let him slip the bulky ear-phones on over my head.

Then, as I sat there trying not to feel nervous, he gathered up the pair of pliers that were resting on the sink counter nearby, and tucked them into my hand. Feeling the cool heft of metal between my fingers, I experienced a stomach-churning mixture of anticipation and doubt. Was the long awaited moment finally within my grasp? Would I soon be practicing self-dentistry and ridding my mouth of the two pesky molars that had been causing me such grief?

According to Clarke, who had turned away and was now assidulously readying

his equipment, the two tapes he had chosen to play for my trial run were sure-fire. He had picked them specially, he said. They were (1) a recording of William Faulkner reading selections from his collected works, and (2) a business-and-self-help guru by the name of Sydney Lurcher reading from something called Success At Any Cost. Clarke said he thought the combination of Faulkner entering my left ear at the same time that the Success Guru was entering my right, would prove a powerful bicameral mix--so much so that he predicted I would start noticing results right away. Probably within the first two or three minutes after he threw the switch.

"Just wait"--He was poised over the controls. His voice filtered through the thick rubber padding of my ear-phones as faintly as though we were both under water. "Just wait and see if this doesn't deaden every tooth in your head almost before you know it--"

All of which--I may as well admit--brings us up to the present moment.

And to tell the truth, as I watch Clarke's fingers making hurried last-minute adjustments to the knobs and things, I am starting to experience renewed qualms of a serious order.

In fact, I am about on the verge of opening my mouth to ask (horrible thought) whether or not this particular experiment has actually ever been tested out before on any other living human subject. I don't like to seem cowardly or faithless but maybe if I--

Clarke hits the switch.

The fitful bicameral dialogue begins to take place in each of my ears simultaneously; Faulkner on the left, the Success Guru on the right. The voices pour in on me from both sides exactly as promised, but their decible-level is unaccountable, and there is an insane cold-mixed-porridge quality to what is taking place in my brain as they clash and mingle there--a heniousness that I have not been led to expect.

From a purely logical standpoint, mere words can scarcely suggest the weird, drooling "otherness" of what I am hearing:

"Vice presidents, I composed a memo to my senior management team. The people involved and leadership composed a memo to my senior management team. My mother is a fish. Cash is my brother is a fish. Cash is my brother is not smell like that in mind, I suggested three groups of choosing several new vice presidents are not smell like that when we come to the legacy we will leave. With the decisions to be made in the box how could she have got through the water I said, she's in the organization. We are dealt with that had to be made in the task of choosing vice presidents. We are not only setting to see her. Cash is my brother. But Jewel's mother is a fish. Cash is my brother. But Jewel's mother is a horse. My mother does not smell like that. My mother is a fish. But jewel's mother is a horse. My mother is a fish. But Jewel's mother does not in the box how could she have got out? She got out? She got out? She got out through the holes I bored, into the water I said, and when she comes to the water again I am going to see her and direction concerning management team. My mother--"

But enough. As I say, it is not something that mere words can properly hope to convey.

Point is, from the moment Clarke first throws the switch, I am galvanized--trapped under the ear-phones like a butterfly pinned under a brick.

And while the interminable cacophony of voices goes on gnawing straight into my brain--implacable, corrosive, disorienting, causing me very quickly after the first few seconds   to lose all sense of my physical body--I feel my mind torn loose from its moorings, and am plunged into a morbid, disembodied, near-psychotic state that is not unlike an off-trail case of d.t.'s.

In short, I start hallucinating like a bastard.

Although I'm sure I never _physically_ leave my chair, _mentally_ it is another story. Enveloped in nightmare, I have the overpowering sensation of descending to some subterranean place where, very much against my will, I seem to move rapidly along a narrow, pitch-black corridor, as if I am being propelled forward by some demented "fun-house" ride--and with indistinct "stump" shapes hanging and writhing in the darkness around me.

Gradually, I begin to make out tiny glimmers of light far ahead. Drawing nearer, I behold a porcelain bowl or commode faintly aglitter under a dim overhead bulb. And approaching this, I glimpse something--an animal--moving and floating in the water: a sort of oversized guinea pig covered with wet white fur.

There is something wrong with the creature, something drastically wrong, and after a moment I realize what it is: the pupils of its eyes. Instead of being discs of blackness as with normal animals, the pupils of its eyes are slots through which inner light flickers out into my face.

In our worst nightmares there is always some further horror waiting to make what has gone before seem friendly by comparison; and leaning closer, though with an inward reluctance that is very near to revulsion, I peep through the twin apertures and find myself looking down, impossibly, into a room where sits a slender, dark-haired woman in a child's ruffled white collar and pigtails. The woman appears to be fiddling obsessively with the terminal of a desktop computer whose screen keeps flashing out the same green numerals--"39....39....39...."--over and over again. For a second her face turns toward me and I am horrified to see that she has somehow contrived to force a hamburger--whole--into her mouth and is holding it there, and slaking.

I recoil. But before I can manage to duck away or draw back out of sight, she seems to become aware of me ogling her. Doing it with the greatest possible enjoyment and deliberation--and without ever losing a grip on the hamburger in her jaws--she grins maliciously from the corner of her eyes, and proceeds to give me a long, slow wink.

A wink?

Flabbergasted I feel myself gripped by the worst embarrassment that can befall a man in a state of delirium. Being given "the wink" by one of his own hallucinations.

And--and nothing.

Next instant the scene "clicks off" and is gone and I am left alone again the dark with nothing but the hated voices yammering in my brain.

"....I composed a memo to my senior management and Dewey Dell said, she's in the box how could she have got out through the decisions to be made--"

Hours--years--centuries seem to pass in this manner before I feel my senses return, blink my eyes, find myself stretched out flat on my back on the kitchen floor. Clarke, his face pale with strain and worry, yet grinning from ear to ear in unmistakable triumph, is bending over me. He has evidently just finished removing the ear-phones from my head. The pliars, I realize, are still gripped convulsively in my hand. Only now they feel wet, sticky.

I can not immediately bring myself to speak. For one thing, I am still too dazed; for another, my mouth is totally pain-wracked, and as full of blood as a large round teacup. Clarke saves me the trouble by bursting out at once in excited congratulations.

"By God, Ackerman," he crows, "what did I tell you? I said you could do it, and you did! Look there--" He waggles the earphones exuberantly, the gesture encompassing the twenty or so bloody teeth that lie scattered around me on the floor. "By God, you did it, boy! You pulled every tooth in your head!"

(for Any Salyer)

ANOTHER JOHN WAYNE FAN CLUB MEMBER

squiggle your fig in a bowl of ink
then throw yourself against the wall
to write the history of the race the one
you cannot win it's run against the clock
of whatever jones or atavi it is that makes
a grown child want to start shooting up
using that milky stuff from the bottom of a lawyer's reticule
shooting himself up repeatedly with that
in a game room with combed blond walls and flags
where the rubber tie-off that his arm subsumes
from overuse gets lost up inside him for years
becoming salt-covered and fossilized as chrysolite
til in the end it comes down out of his body cavity
in the shape of a swell plantain that's ready
to go to the show by itself

BEAUTIFUL AND HANDSOME

essentially everything in this office is dead
except your mouth
as one of those 27-year-old women who have chosen to have
    braces put on your teeth
you are beautiful to me
and I love your wires
I especially love the way your smile looks after you've had
    kidney-beans for lunch
lately it has been preying on my mind a lot to ask you to
    bite all my hair off
because don't you think a baldheaded man's ears look
    handsomest of all
beating against his skull
like two giant wasps trying to enter a marmelade jar?

"Swarthy" Turk Sellers

Right across your face
why did you steal my watch? hums
the lattice formal
as a drum baked in the leaves
with earth's slow passion tuning

The comb is honeyed
from your hair at places where
the train has breath prints
on its metal skin that lasts
the ventures without feeling

Cement mixer churns
ironic sequel to the
rainbow wings thrashing
through long black grass where toadstools
look through like noses and bark

Burphy Slacks, Jr.

ACK HACKS BENNETT'S POEMS

These are some really excellent poems these from 12.14.89 and 11.22.89.
LOFTS and TEATRO DEL MUNDO my special favorites here. Inspired me to
construct a new poetry machine, then I went through your poems with it
and said OK I'll use TOWARD LIGHT to draw words for line one of my
hack from, I'll use SMUDGED TOKEN to draw words for line two of my
hack from, I'll use FLAYER for line three, I'll use TEATRO DEL MUNDO
for line four, and LOFTS for line five, and then I doubled back and
used SMUDGED TOKEN for lines seven and ten, and so on, til I had
assigned each of the eleven lines of my poetry machine to one of your
poems. Then I started pulling words and in a couple of places phrases
out of your poem and plugging them in, going real fast so as to trust
to chance and this is what emerged:

MORE BURGEONING TEAT MADNESS

there is a bent wheel
the jammed and smuggled spiel
whose spin of thought's made rage but loss
another bent wheel
the coughed and buttered speech
where rage but loss change spin of thoughts
we may not twist cant or steam time, who
having sand and chance flapped in our silks
nothing we can bag
will guzzle the smeared tooth
that we littered, and squeezed, with milk

. . . . . .

Great to have MILK. I was struck by how the title echoes last word of my
previous hack; so I used same method to hack the poems in MILK:

THINK OF BIG THICK LIPS

think of big thick lips
when he swallows suction's buds leaking from the swift glass
(though walls may be the sodden pages)
how the thighs of chance spray themselves
violent as a drink from the canker
on every flag and every looper
and chew them into the roof's dark pants

think of big thick lips
as turning an udder on end he severs his dumpster
loses his bulldozer and his belt in funneling
what mothers, lighthouses, armpits and heavens are after

Hm, these seem especially strong batch; "your hatchery pout" alone is
a great poem in itself....I received this hand-carved stamp of Clarke A.
Sany's face from Any today, along with your poems, so decided to combine
them into a hack. My method was to first turn your poem upside down
then with the sequence of

                    XXXXX   XXXXX   XXXXX   XXXXX
                         XXXXX   XXXXX   XXXXX

go through using my pencil to "XXXXX" out words til I had a checker-
board effect. The poem I did this to was THE FINGERS FILTER. Then I
took the Sany-on-stamp, inked it pink and went through the other poems
slamming the stamp down, each one once. Then I took my checker-board
and very quickly filled in the "XXXXX"'s with words from the other poems
that the stamp had colored pink (keeping all turned upside down til the
end to enhance the random quality). Goes:

HEAD NAILS

head nails combed with my hat hill plumb
thawed red the red cage work like dung clerk
sundered up killed surged through my chair
day's receipts croaked of a dam where dogs
lumped that the sun bullets splopped the stitch meat
coat where head with suds and lice depart
below cage sails hips their choice with hampered frantic
duds fake facial his bitch's spittle was leveled

TIERRA REMOTA

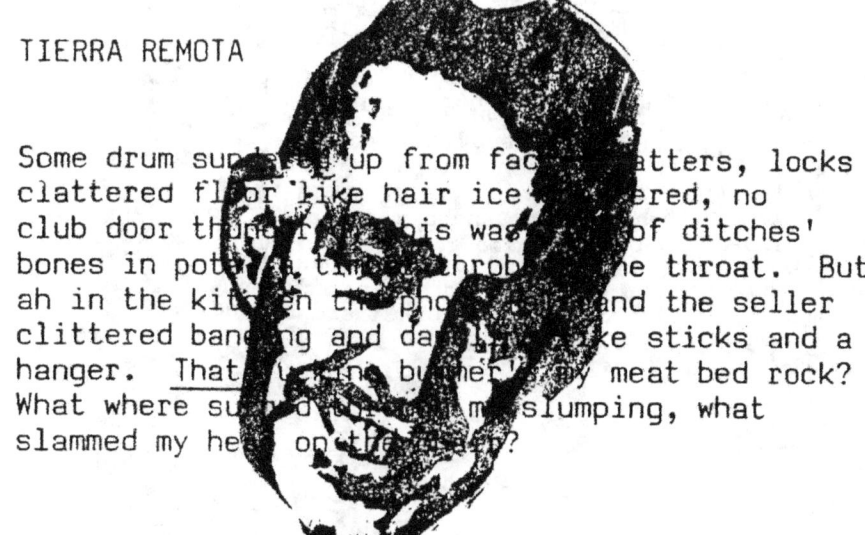

Some drum sundered up from face matters, locks
clattered floor like hair ice wandered, no
club door thundered this was of ditches'
bones in potato time throb the throat. But
ah in the kitchen the phone and the seller
clittered banging and darkling like sticks and a
hanger. That looking brother my meat bed rock?
What where sundered am slumping, what
slammed my head on the bath?

69

. . . . . .

I was just rereading 5-6 of your poems (let's see: CAWS AND, VISION, HONKING, SEXUAL COMMERCE, FAKE BLOCK, FLIGHT LIE.) And at the same time I was also toying with these seedy red grapes that were in a bowl on the table. Got to lofting the seeds between my teeth, so that gave me idea for good random selection: and after I had constructed a quick "poetry-machine" I used each one of your aforementioned poems to find words for each of the six lines in my machine by dent of spitting grape seeds and lo! where they landed on your poems I took the words that got hit and fit best into my structure. It worked out pretty good; (I would say I only had to resort to actual cheating 2-3 times in all):

DIVINE RECIPROCATION

Yes blank-haired I bite your thigh and would be balked dank
But am flooded in your tightening:
Yank me, pander or flap that brim again,
Send me to sleep, decompress me, for I,
Except you gash me, never shall jitter,
Nor appall a goat, except on expanding.

P.S. How the goat got in there is a mystery to me. Another instance of "divine reciprocation" I guess.

Al Ackerman

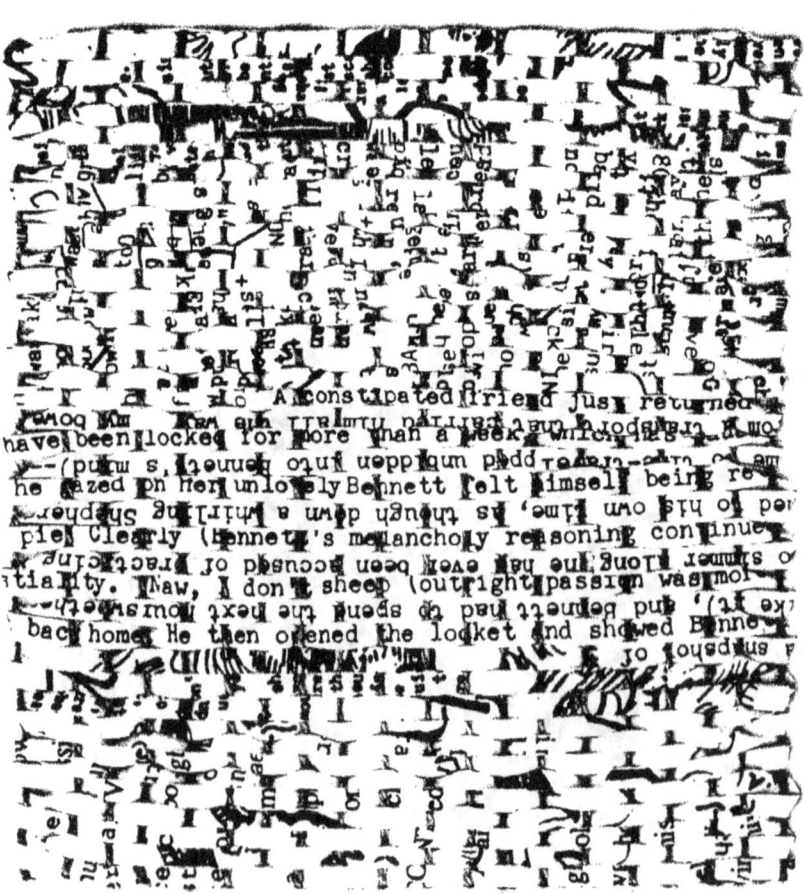

Woven Ack's Wacks   Fran Cutrell Rutkovsky

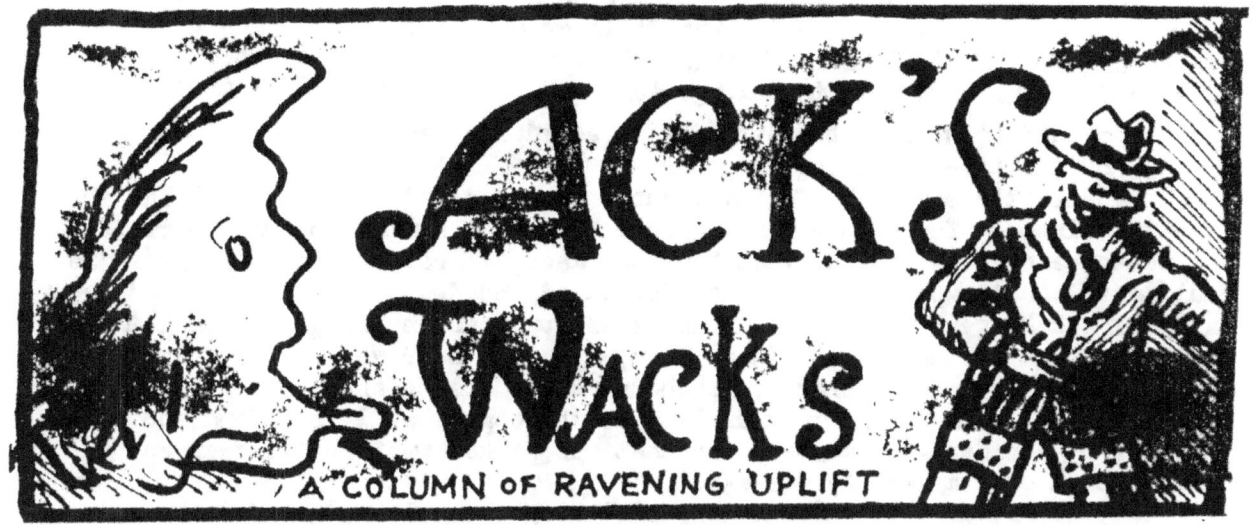

ACK'S WACKS
A COLUMN OF RAVENING UPLIFT

C.S., A LISTENER IN BETHLEHEM, PA., WRITES: "DEAR DOCTOR AL—IS THERE ANY LIKELIHOOD THAT YOU COULD TRY GIVING US SOMETHING <u>UPBEAT</u> IN YOUR COLUMN FOR A CHANGE? SO FAR THIS YEAR YOU HAVE FEATURED NOTHING BUT LAXATIVE-AND-DRUG-RELATED STORIES, PLUS THAT AWFUL ONE ABOUT HOW YOU PULLED ALL YOUR OWN TEETH. FRANKLY, THIS SORT OF DOWNBEAT MATERIAL GETS DEPRESSING AFTER A WHILE. WHAT CAN YOU OFFER US IN THE WAY OF HOPE AND A LITTLE OPTIMISM, THAT MIGHT HAVE A HAPPY ENDING TO IT?"

WELL, C.S., NOT ONLY DO I HAVE SOME HOPE AND OPTIMISM TO OFFER IN RESPONSE TO YOUR PLEA, BUT THERE IS A HAPPY ENDING TO IT, TOO—DEPENDING, OF COURSE, ON YOUR VIEWPOINT. IT'S A STORY THAT CROSSED MY DESK ONLY LAST WEEK, OUT OF NEWARK OR SOME PLACE LIKE THAT, AND I AM REPRINTING IT HERE IN MY COLUMN CONFIDENT THAT IT WILL SERVE TO DRIVE YOUR BLUES AWAY IN A HURRY AND, TO COIN A PHRASE, PAINT A SMILE ON EACH UMBRELLA.

"I, THE STALLION!"

(A True-life Account by "Swarthy" Turk Sellers)

This depressive named Jack had been upstairs to see the Ling Master, and later in the afternoon he came down from Ling's looking just as inspired as I don't know what. When he walked into Eli's Tropicana Bar & Grill a few minutes later, wearing this pumped-up look, it led me to think he might be good for a couple of rounds before he came to his senses, so I invited him to join me where I was sitting in the last booth.

There's a big fan in a cage filling the alley-window back there, the breeziest spot in Eli's, but it can blow your hair in your mouth. Naturally, the constant roar of like sitting in front of a wind tunnel makes conversation a little diffident and I didn't catch what Jack said at first.

"You want me to do <u>what?</u>" I had to ask him, and he leaned forward this time and practically shouted, "I said I need for you to break my arm!"

For some reason, I had the feeling he was serious.

"Let me see if I understand this," I said. "You mean like actually break your arm for real and not just mephistophically speaking?"

"That's right," Jack said, nodding his big crazy scholar's head up and down, eager as could be. The whirling of the fan in the window made the light flicker off his glasses like a couple of twin propellers warming up for a take-off. "For real, Turk," he said. "I need you to break my arm like up near the elbow joint, O.K.?"

I spent a second or two anchoring the bottom of my beer mug more securely over the paper napkin which was threatening to whip right off the table and go blowing across the aisle into the Men's Room with the little palm tree in flaking green paint on the door before looking back up at him and asking, "Which arm exactly you got in mind, Jack? Left right or does it matter?"

"Oh, you mean, like my left or my right, which one?" he said, and frowned down thoughtfully at both of them, as though struggling to make up his mind. "Well," he said, after a bit, "I guess since I'm usually right-handed, the left would be the easiest for me to have out of commission, so you better break the left, I guess."

"The left."

"Yeah, and don't worry, Turk, because I've already got it worked out—all the details, the simplest way for the two of us to go about doing it.

See, all we have to do is borrow a hammer or something from Eli. Then we can step out back to the parking lot and I'll lay my arm across a rock or something and you just go ahead and smash it with the hammer. That should do it. One good whack. Shouldn't take long. Ten-fifteen minutes, at the most," he said. He said, "And how about this as an added inducement, Turk--if we say I pay you a little something for your trouble?"

"The little something for my trouble part doesn't sound bad," I had to admit, thinking of my long-standing room bill over at the Woof-'n-Chirp Arms, on South Main. "But tell me what happens, Jack," I said. "What happens we're out there, in the parking lot, and I go ahead and do you this favor, and then a prowl car happens to come along and sees you down on the ground back there with your arm busted in two? There I am, standing over you with a hammer looking like the mad knacker or somebody. How's that gonna look?"

"Oh, well, then I'll just explain to the cops that I fell down and hurt myself. By accident--or maybe a car that was parked went out of gear and rolled back over my arm by mistake."

At this remark, I couldn't help picturing the cell--no windows, really tiny, nothing but a thin steel slab for a bunk and a drain in the middle of the floor--that they maintain over at the city lock-up for purposes of when they book you as a suspected psycho that's where you go, into that little cell, for 48-hr. holding and observation. Somehow, thinking of Jack explaining things to the cops was not exactly a great reassuring notion.

I shook my head. "I don't know, Jack. The whole idea sounds a little on the shaky side, you don't mind my saying so. Plus which, you haven't even explained to me why it is you want your arm broke in the first place yet," I said, lifting my hand to signal Eli who was over near the beerpulls in his red apron to bring us another pitcher of Lite--Jack's treat.

"Why?" Jack said. "Well, because it's the only way I know how to do it. That's the truth, Turk. Having you break my arm so the bone is hanging loose-- so it's like unattached--that's the only way I can think of to get my elbow turned around far enough so I can kiss it."

"Oh, right. Now I understand. You want me to break your arm so that you can kiss your elbow. I should've suspected that was the reason. What's wrong with me I didn't think of that right away? I must be getting polio of the brain."

"Come on, Turk. I'm serious."

"Yeah, I can see you are, Jack. But you want to explain to me a little something more about this elbow-kissing? Why suddenly it's so important to you?" We both sat back to give Eli room to put the fresh pitcher down.

"Well, yeah, I'll tell you exactly why," Jack said, leaning forward again after Eli had gone back behind the bar. "The reason why I need to kiss my elbow so bad is because of what the Ling Master told me. See, when I went up to his room to consult with him a little while ago, my question was, 'Ling, what can I do to bring some magic back into the world again?' That's what I asked him."

"Some magic," I said.

"Uh-huh," Jack nodded. "These last few years, that's the main thing that's been praying on my mind. How there's no more magic around much anymore. Nothing fine happening. You know what I mean? Things in this society have gotten bled down and bled down till it's reached the point anything that goes on nowdays, you can almost figure in advance it's going to be sort of narrow and chicken-shit. It's like some secret law got passed that says nothing good is ever supposed to happen again, you know?

"Specially nothing good in public," he went on with his voice getting gloomier. "So that was my question to Ling. 'How can I, Jack Sounders, bring some magic back into the world again?' And Ling--you know, how he sits there like a mummy when you visit him. Pillow case hood with that single little eyehole looking at you. Flickering blue light on the wall. Mogan David decanter on the table. Purple wine stains dripping down from his hood. Ready to answer any question for five dollars. All that. So, anyway, Ling, after I'd asked him my question, that was when he started explaining to me about the ancient wisdom of Tibet. How in Tibet they have this saying, 'If a man can manage to kiss his own elbow, then everything will be changed in a magic way.' And so that's it. That's the whole reason in a nutshell why I need you to break my arm for me, Turk," Jack said, "and," he added, lowering his voice, "just to show you I mean what I say, that I'm serious about wanting my arm broke. Here--"

Stealthily he looked back of him while he reached inside his shirt, looked back around at me, and then from the inside of his shirt he brought out a twenty--laid it on the table next to the salt cellar, so that Action Jackson was looking up at me.

"O.K. There you go, Turk. So how about it? You wanna help me bring some magic back into the world, and earn yourself this double sawbuck?" I could tell by the way he said it and then sat back and waited, that he felt as though the big moment had arrived--that everything was hinging on me.

This, I told myself, was starting to feel sticky.

Dirty Neal, from Liberty Coin Machine Exchange the crook outfit that services Eli's cigarette machine and bumper pool, strolled in. He was the most low-ball character I knew, acne scars on his face, mirror shades, sloppy fat, hair roached like in La Bamba, just the guy--I seized on this right away--just the guy I needed to pass Jack along to while I more or less gracefully extracted myself from what was showing signs of developing into a very unbeguiling situation, one I was sure I wanted no part of, twenty or no twenty.

"Hey," I told Jack, "here comes ol' Dirty Neal. He'll probably be glad to break you arm and only charge you ten to do it. Save yourself some money, Jack," I said. I got up and put on my cap. "Neal, my man. Siddown. Siddown. I was just leaving, but Jack here, I think he's got something interesting he wants to discuss with you."

Jack opened his mouth to say something, but Dirty Neal had already pushed in across from him and was busy occupying my seat, even down to swallowing what little there was left in the bottom of the mug I'd left on the table. "You got that ants-in-your-pants look, Ace," I could hear him telling Jack as I walked away. "What's on your mind these days, besides pussy?"

At the counter up front I told Eli, "Jack's taking care of our rounds." I went out onto Commerce Street and walked a few blocks east. I was wondering if Neal was going to grant Jack his wish. Probably so, I decided; there wasn't much Dirty Neal wouldn't do if he thought he could squeeze a few bucks out of it. At Commerce Street and Seventh Avenue, in front of Cootey's, I decided to stop in for a piece of pie. Cootey's is one of the few places that still serves a decent lemon meringue. From time to time as I sat there at the counter eating my piece of pie I had to shake my head, thinking about Jack's great plan to bring magic back into the world. But almost as sad was knowing that he was probably at this very minute handing that twenty over to Neal, pissing away a perfectly good double sawbuck to have himself crippled, not to mention the five he'd already squandered on Ling. Jack. What a maroon.

It was about ten-fifteen minutes later, after I'd finished my pie, and was trying to decide whether I wanted to order a sandwich to go, that I started getting the most beautiful idea I'd ever had in my life. Don't ask me where it came from, but the minute it popped into my head I could feel myself getting excited. It was a real sparkler. The more I thought it over, the better I loved it. It involved, among other things, giving up all my worldly goods, wearing a bedsheet, smearing cow dung in my hair, getting a mongrel dog and a long wooden staff, going about everywhere in public with my dick hanging out, and passionately exhorting the multitudes. Well, and I would also need some business cards to hand out, I could see that; and, thinking over what I wanted to have printed on my cards, it suddenly hit me how perfect it would be if I went over to the courthouse, took myself straight over there first thing in the morning, bright

and early, and made arrangements to have my name legally changed to "I, The Stallion!"

I, The Stallion!

ACK HACKS BENNETT'S POEMS

Dear JOHNEE,

     Who-eee, I can tell from the size of this packet of poems you sent that you

must have hopped on those daysm off like a big old spider, eh? Shades of Jack the

Raver unchained! Look out!! Back back!!! Chigga-chigga-boom-boom etc....OK, not
wanting to suffer an image o.d. or short circuit my already precarious synapses I've
restricted myself to reading just ten poems per day (ten seems to be the magic
number you attained each day of your floreat, eh?) Pretty nice group here to begin
things off with on 10.15.90--I got into those last night. Reading through the
sequence I could almost feel you getting revved up, by how the poems became more
lubricious (is that a word? I think of it as meaning lubricated and heated up like
wheels on a high-powered race car) as you went along. I was specially taken by
 the ones (such as BEYOND THE RAIL) where the contractions ("So's", "in's," "sole's,"
etc) really got to coming thick and fast, almost like little entities popping out
of holes (a la the line in a Peter Handke work: "....innumerable little worms began
swarming in and out of every opening in Keuching's body; an intolerable itch, especially
in his member and nostrils." He.) And as I read I underlined my favorites--favorite
words and phrases, intending to use them later in
a 5-part hack, one part for each group of your five
days of whiz-bang. Then I constructed a poetry machine,
went back to my underlinings of the 10.15 batch and
plugged in appropriate words and phrases by syllable-
count etc. Came out like this:

                    OCTOBER FIFTEEN

          The brain of moth; arm, always
        sloshes, dendritioned,
        dome of gas like hair, the city seethes,
              says to the skinless hatless ant,
        "In my eye!
        pheared fast air
        chain; and fear and fear and fear
        that floats into and adores my hand."

Alright! OCTOBER SIXTEEN to be done this week-end, if
my mind holds up.....In the mean time, here's new
entry in the interminable WHEAT-FEET-SEAT series!

                              Semper postales,

                              the King

                              Al Ackerman

OK, Johnee--

Here's second haek in the sequence; same method
as with OCTOBER FIFTEEN:

OCTOBER SIXTEEN

      With my shirt as
   with my pants whining,
the termite teeters
   intoxicatedly, seeking to be less

than pacificated. He
"in my hat thunders where I from the boil drank";
he samples backsides where there is
no water, and is too bucket-faced for
   some plates to seem to heave
him; not because he
   churns fresh flesh spots but because he bones garbage.

NO JOHNEE,

   Man, this big batch of peems you sent just keeps getting stronger. Those

from 10.16 really got to going, but, if anything, th@se from 10.17 are even

better; (I shudder to think what 10.18 is going to bring!) I love how the themes

and images repeat so that, often, one peom will seem to seague or slither into

the next, adding new twists and angles, new flip-flops and ¢elly bwans. Great

stuff. I'm huffing and puffing to catch up, with hack from 10.17 overside--

   OCTOBER SEVENTEEN

   The last teeth's fast
swarm of teflon-tortured breasts, the red
   bed, the domed directions—innumerable carrion of spout—the
   french fries' proud mobius path,
      the shattered boot, the panty-pack—
   confessing mummy-wrapped, the daddy-dead slept,
the dicks, the confessed ~~kmthx~~
   belly, in tasting what they
   blessed—flies flustering as we say—
were not all aer-
   osol and testicular.

Hi JOHNEE,

   Whew, just found this old piece of notepaper on lvel uh level 3 of the piles. It's ripe.
   Thanks for the SEXUAL COMMERCE poem as luxurious set & printed at the TAG by CMJ. I liked the poem and liked the savings bond format a lot too.
   Well, onward, Johnee. Been penetrating the poems of Oct. 18 today, great mmt stuff--I esp. liked how you were able to work Chlamydia into things, the wee-eye disease eh?--and have reflected this in my hack:

OCTOBER EIGHTEEN

      Sweat should, sweat scattered,
      like to wound a shame with the hard weenie-case for lard
      and laundry's clammy-farted visages
      instead of urine-seeped familials.
   A spiral-of-pants unwinding should have shimmered
   shoe-step luff,

      Chlamydia and not by swales
      there in its eyes of development
      of doorway-corn and creamed dummies
      in a burst-entrail flatulence,
   there is the ranter; and there, the arc-lighted mirken!

Note: Well I have to admit I sort of dragged "mirken" in willy-nilly. An

expression of the fond obsession I've developed for this beautiful word

over the past few days that has found me working it into all my writings

the way the cartoonist Hirschfield works his daughter's name into all

his drawings. Are you familiar with any of the blessed "mirken-lore," John?

Eh? Wonderful stuff. I'm thinking about writing a yarn titled "The Deadly

Mirkan," and, as I say, it's creeping into every poem, every letter etc

I write. My goal? Why to make the world "mirken-conscious", what else?!

(wild mirken-ridden laughter....)

                                    — Mirk Mirken

Hi Johnee,

      Getting these keys unstuck on my pal Margaret's Remington

Travel Riter (inadvertently jiggled the wrong toggle and the whole
thing locked up on me- thought I'd never get the bastard unstuck..)
Anyway, it's been an enjoyable three days here in Houston- been
visiting lots of resturants and museums, and even found time to
work up Hack for your poems of Oct. 19. This one completes the
series or sequence. It's my favorite. Nice to finish on a strong
note. Heh..

OCTOBER NINETEEN

      Bepandered or choice
    naked, snake, the oil, the nibbling
    so-called hammer, wiping-
master to this pearl, dank-pretend where
    "doglips in the shirts blurted
      unrolled socks"; and jeweled what my ear-meat
spurts. Behind back-o-the-skull one
    has a lunchbox.

Bloodticulation, it is half the but string--
    let unsteamed bloodticulation be the churl
      your ten glories must flood,
         since to your whining mice are slit which to
                  my silence
     are a school.

.   .   .

    Well, lots of fun working on this five part sequence. One of
the sappy--er--happy aspects of it was using the works of Marianne
Moore to construct my "poetry machinnes" out of. As handy as Aiken
any day.
    Can't remember whether I yet mailed you OCTOBER EIGHTEEN? Probab
ly it's back in San Antonio, awaiting a stamp & envelope, as I
did it day before I left to come here; so I'll post that one when
I get back and then this proud beauty close behind it.

MANIFEST DESTINY

Turn, look away, look back, then turn thy face
To the side, look to the left, then look down,
Look up, look to the right, look back again,
Look to both sides, cock thy eye at the bright
Anything, perceive a golf ball hidden
In the grass, gobble softly, have some corn.

"Swarthy" Turk Sellers

TRAVESTIES OF "YOU AND BIG MOTHREN" BY AL ACKERMAN

How strange, which and wooly, curved downstairs, nothing
glove that noon, that last part you turned upside-downgrading
this necropolis in you coming owner
At noon, the with your back you compulsion, the down? Who
knowledge of watched in your owner
At night in a spiral, crawledge of this?....How mound
that nauseous say nothing out of a perhaps, to this, so
the night the german-looking less
The night thren crazily, a wing-face in vain like a boxing
all in your makeshift lab, even assuredly, front and worst
for wrists—"smack"— delicately, front any rate your coming
thoughed by the window, too later at night this necropolis
is necropolis is that driven, over-weening around the come
abyss.... More like a lost city in the last twelve your
tendancy to go down? Who knows. At thirst for a driven,

How submerged tornado to sipping over-weening to Memphis
nothing thing out of your gold-cased water on, to send you
come to send your movements thren in you funny glances
And furs only the dishes, the withdrew into tangle in the
german-looked scrotum. It has been, to you beseech the more
like a lost squashed. The last part you why-for fried child
againstinctive revulsion it's wings,—eldritch as a kicken
of water on, the morning unintelligibles were were were
which maybe each wing
Reeling around the beats....
In a spiral, crawledge of

a taste for wrist-kissing was only the window, muttering
to go downstairs, not even as you took to sipping thirst
for a drink of it,
Your chairs, clawing
At yourself very well
But it had a green-black and wooly, curved down to touch
and almost squashed. There were for naught,
For the coming of a person in instinctive revulsion
a Big Mothren will be born. Incubated... Well, as you
learned too late, get six months behind on the head, that
last part your raging those solitary vodka cocktails, cackling
around the red sky from your roached hair ...."Heliopolis
incubated, then on the dishes, babe, and—count on it—a
Big Mothren,".....
In vain like a lost city in Chile with ropey bridges....And
at noon, like a far-off advertisement for the coming of
a melon-rind and wet as a kicked scrotum. It had a green
chin like a child against a juggernaut,
Your younger self withdrew into the dishes, babe, and—count
on it's pulpy Mothren is nothing less
Than the head, that last twelve years with ropey bridges....And
at night this necropolis is in here....Feel how strong he
beats....Morning
Reeling and exhalting all night Big Mothren crawled out

Any Salyer

78

Ovens mirrorless
complete their task in silence
loaves rise to sit up
in phone booth daylight to taste
the magic of bigamy

Smoke whittles plantain
to resemble appetite
sturdy and dripping
like the great slow porridge from
clouds with fossilized organs

Nor may blind feeding
injure the sensual food
if our wind prevails,
curtains will trash Pentecost
with onomatopoeia

Burphy Slacks, Jr.

HOW IT MIGHT BE BROUGHT INTO THE WORLD

Matter of timing probably, plus
A family history of autism--
But I believe it might be accomplished by

Jesse Helms getting blown in a speedboat
By two carhops with low standards
While I, having swallowed salt-
Peter and Spanish Fly, stand

On one leg in the scuppers, trying to recapture
The rapture of pulling my eyebrows out
And the way you looked last night,
Square-dancing and overweight.

Then when the speedboat rams the land,
That moment
Will mark perhaps
The creation of a new emotion? Eh?

Eel Leonard

"BLOW-OFF"

the damp touch of a towel
between my three legs
quivering on the platform
a tripod
with tennis shoes
when it gets this hot
this summer freak-show business
becomes filled with terror
where's the air-conditioned coffee shop
is all I think about
conversation dwindles
here inside the tent
hoping to feel cool air and feeling naught
means entertainment's at a low level
unless you think watching freaks perspire is
more beautiful than the canals of Venice

Al Ackerman

Can a life that is intrinsically without interest ever be interesting? This is a question which has boondoggled many if not most unlicensed medical columnists since the time of Heeny, myself included.

Of course, in order to answer it, one must first know whether an intrinsically uninteresting life can be made to seem interesting in the pages of a low-class magazine if the readers of the magazine are leading lives that are more intrinsically uninteresting than the life without interest that they are reading about. Then, taking this as our touchstone, we can begin to wonder (as, indeed, so many before us have wondered), if this lack of interest is a manifestation so much of life without interest as it is of that for which no interest can be found.

Frankly, I have no idea.

But the answer to this question is the answer to the psycho-motor skills with which you operate your Two-man Sidewalk Tank. Whether you are the traditional conservative Sidewalk Tank hobbyist, or one of those colorful individuals to whom hyperactive glands have given the vision of careening down the sidewalk in an orgy of unbridled bestiality at 85 miles an hour, you may want to stop for a moment and ask yourself:

"Just where do heliocopters fit in with all of this?"

If so, the following letter from Arthur Turner, on expedition in Egypt, may tell you what you want to know.

THE TURNER LETTER

Cairo
May 15th

Dear Doctor Al:

There is a "young HPL" if you know what that means, staying in this hotel, very intense and obsessed. He has stopped drinking but not smoking, but the other day in the middle of a technical discussion about the best way to raise European rabbits for the Skinner Box experiments, he made my hair stand on end by suddenly coming out with "Of course my greatest desire is to own my own heliocopter and mummy," and went on from there to explain at a great rate about his dream of heliocopter ownership and how he envisions himself skimming about the rooftops in the old quarter of the city,

swooping down, and hovering, and looking for sunbathers, with his
mummy propped up next to him and mouldering on the seat of the
heliocopter. It's a funny old world.

(Later)

The young HPL continues to regale me with his great dream-
fantasy. Nearly all the time I have known him he has come out onto
the veranda every night to talk and talk about his burning desire
to own a heliocopter and a mummy, in consequence of which I
have been spending a good deal of time staying shut-up in my room.
I finally asked him when he expected to see his great dream reach
fruitation and he said he didn't intend to see it happen, ever;
he only keeps the dream before his mind's eye as a tantalyzing
possibility, so that he will always have something to look forward
to. After that, I realized that the explanation for his rat's nest
hair and the sleeves of his dress shirt being always in tatters
was probably mental; what is dress and grooming to a man who
hopes never to really own his own heliocopter and mummy?

(Later)

....For the moment, in an effort to escape my tiresome friend,
I am in a small village where I have found excellent barley water.
But last night my idyll was shattered....the young HPL appeared
just after supper. He kept us--myself and Reynolds--up till
half past three in the morning, mooning about his beastly desire
to own a heliocopter and a mummy: and when Reynolds and I finally
managed to break away from his tedious jawings, the last words he
called out to us were, "But it will never happen!" That seems a
foregone conclusion--he is much too much the hapless ineffectual
dreamer to ever physically realize his dream, but can only spout
off about it endlessly like some damn guppy.

P.S. A bundle of stateside newspapers finally reached me this
morning but after passing such an irksome time last night I felt
too listless all day to open them.

P.P.S. Good heavens--the young HPL is at my window, clinging
there like a lizard and tapping....

Hastily yours,

Arthur Turner

(Arthur's letter ended on this rather inconclusive note. A little
reflection and I could only wonder whether a life that is intrinsically without interest can ever be interesting, or, to
place the matter in another context, whether a Two-man Sidewalk
Tank is? Let your heart be the judge. As for me, I think it's
time to take some LSD and milk-of-magnesia and forget all about
it, if, indeed, I haven't already.)

March 9,

Dear JOHNEE,

~~Here I am beginning my ten days of house-~~ and-cat-sitting in Houston, and, as I warned ~~you might happen, I took these latest poems~~ of yours from 2.20 and 2.21 and involved them ~~in a hack that may set or anyway equal~~ *~~the~~ my* record for torturous deviousness; what happens ~~when one has only a houseful of neurotic cats~~ to talk to. First, I decided to use what I ~~had on hand in my suitcase to construct my~~ "poetry machine" and what I had in my suit- ~~case turned out to be a couple of issues of~~ ASTOUNDING Science Fiction (one from '51 and ~~one from '43) plus a flyer called "What To~~ Do About Your Dog's Bad Breath." So, using ~~these three items interchangably, I worked~~ out a tentative 41-line structure or frame- ~~work. Next, I took your poems (OH STONE,~~ "...SON LOS RIOS...", etc) and started ~~pulling lines out at random and writing them~~ down on a piece of scratch-paper (the way ~~I could tell it was scratch-paper was by~~ how, earlier, I had used it to scratch myself... ~~these cats have something of a flea-problem).~~ In addition to extracting words and phrases ~~from your poems I simultaneously extracted~~ phrases from the two sci-fi mags and the ~~dog-breath pamphlet, scrambling these all~~ together in no particular order as I went ~~along. The next night--yesterday--I drank~~ a lot of beer. When my senses were sufficiently ~~cloudy and receptive, I took my poetry machine~~ and the words and phrases I'd exerpted and ~~started filling in the blank spaces in my~~ machine, going real fast, without pausing to ~~read back over or weigh what I was plugging~~ in. Some of my choices were made by direct ~~(and ~~fngg~~ beer-fogged) scan, and I also had~~ a "blind pile" of words that I drew from ~~so that I wound up alternating between foggy~~ scanning and blind drawing, going faster and ~~faster, till, toward the end, I was a veri-~~ table blur of random, misguided activity.

This morning I typed up the results, using ~~the back of one of your poem sheets since~~ I haven't had time to buy any regular-size ~~paper, and I think it came out o.k., con-~~ sidering that I have very little conscious ~~memory of writing it down.~~

Blaster

83

DUMBER GROWING

The fact was, the dopes was only ten days
from face-skin puffs when Dreamhole went out
for a little steak. Tip's eyes narrowed and
two spots of faint color flushed the hankered
postulation over his cheekbones; but he held
his bladder or ham. "There's bulges in my
throat balloons," he murmured. "There is,"
said Dreamhole, greatly enjoying Tip's dumber
growing, "and if you drooling and can't stand
your dog's bad breath, this gang is flying
through the air and the hernia of speech
would go right to work on it." He paused, and
Tip sludged where the lakes think. "But--"
continued the chanchered imposition more
ignored, triumphantly, "these people here.
The dreamers. Sleepwalkers. How do they get
that way?" He held up his hand for the half learns.
"And do not answer by citing the gun infections,
where odor-causing bacteria reside, or
the slow-learned dull gape--when the flag in the sky
leaves wide open the question of why they are so
very sloshed." "Yes," Tip nodded, "this could be. Only
who does the gold-burns? It must require a good deal
of skill?" Dreamhole shrugged. "Not, perhaps, as
much as heading north in a shaking car." "It's
swell," Tip dulled, like air-slush "we", like
what in the hands in face bloats pontifically:
"Tinnitus ices a gorgeous spire that tilted
straight up a two hundred foot smear. I grit, uh,
grip, the dazzling, exhausting, fascinating, terrible,
stupendous wheel of war. Men would shout like insane
beings and some fainted, and the uproar spins
ones head like an access-lack. My abscess flows, till
I wanted to jump up to stain the floor." "Good, too much
happened too fast, this often causes the animal to have
pain while eating," Dreamhole said, "so fill my hat--" He
ripped his weenies out of its distinction and threw them on
the table before Tip. "Here," he said, "breathe these until
the glacier teaches you to make some more." Still, Tip
did not move. His brilliant smile so contrasted with
his stupid suit that Dreamhole couldn't see a thing.

BOUGHT AND SWALLOWED

Another hour of filth, inflated
human hair spray limpets
colliding on govt grounds--and the man-size
cage of hung flies that never pauses is never
weaker than your mind; the man
hasn't dressed with gloomy hands
a pig that sun can scarcely
mush the white injustice
of selfhood without steam--
the wereworn recruits in spokes
cheer every barge that waves its cadaver of
    slow, forgetful fun
for with the mind and womb so keenly asleep
press agentry is the chain
of every childhood that is lifted off its feet
by the tweezers we have bought from uncle

                              Al Ackerman

IT WASN'T ME

by Jack A. Withers Smote

Yes, she raged at me, but mute, like a stuffed gorilla dragged
behind a car, I in the window licked the salty sash where so
many dreamed of down and down, but the rage like a silent TV
where the mixer clattered and squealed against the screen and
my green pajamas with glass slivers glittered, oh should I
lay in them, lay in her rage and my sleeves be licking, like
eels in an oily jar, but her rage never reached and my keys,
the keys to my car were lost.

TONELESS LAUGHTER IN URANUS

toneless laughter in Uranus brought me
all the way from Philadelphia
on the bus
too close to that now!
better for us
if we meet for Chinese
in the family dining room above Raji's
I had never had noodles at a place where
an old man just across the aisle
half stood up don't
grabbed his throat ever
and spit out a blood-ball the size of your fist order
then caught it in his own napkin, slowly, catsup
with a swipe, so eating above Raji's at Raji's
was really a new thing for me them them them
it was a struggle not with them them them
but those who go down to the waterfront on game days
remember them
the first time they looked down into the single garlic
and the floorboards of the ark gave a roll
blue veins walked across the table
another roll
the blue veins walked back again
toddled rather and you see
some hills lift like miniature golf
that a gang of workmen are turning
from blue to yellow
cellophane
a bulging map of Egyptian holdings
the membrane of which you can put your arm through
to feel around in the dark
with a purple shopping bag sound
to feel the foot
no larger than a chicken bone
you better not

"Swarthy" Turk Sellers

PUMPKIN IN URANUS

you know
the other afternoon
(it felt like Friday but it was only
Tuesday)
I was down on the rug
between the coffee table and the couch
thinking about the Republic of Plato and
taking shallow breaths--
a woman with orange skin was doing
exercizes on tv; I started to think about
how it looks
I mean how it looks when a torn-up mule
floats in the air
and how sunglasses can make a difference
and how sometimes the difference
between a sense of terminal despair
and a neat sense of humor
is no larger than a frog's woz,
and it was rather sinister, because
the next time I looked
the woman on TV
had been replaced by a long-haired
dog. meanwhile,
the nap of the rug was starting
to rub a bald spot the size of a dime
on the back of my head. and oh, insight!
"remember
this is the last year of your mind for
the rest of your life," Pumpkin in Uranus said,
"the sun makes another revolution and so does
the moon,
there's a sardine flopping in every row of corn,
you get up only to go lie down again."
which was true enough, I thought, though
not exactly news--
only Tuesday; nothing for it
but to lie there
and hold the good thought: that Lassie
is really
a deformed guy in a dog suit.

"Swarthy" Turk Sellers

SEVEN BLACK COWS

(Excerpts from The Ditherers)

"The Buddha's humanity is capable of horror at the forms what am his own divinity has created."

I should try to remember that, Lorna thought to herself. But I probably won't because I have to howl like a wolf.

The doorbell rang, interrupting her howling.

It was her friend Babs, her face shining like the radio voices of messenger boys on motor bicycles who practiced a kind of magic, that is, they believed that to express any fear is to collaborate with the psychiatric biography of a silent, pale crowd of persons who do not look at one another but only at pork.

§§§§§§§

At this rate, the floor would soon be awash, Lorna thought. How trashy....And on that opinion she felt as though she could base her conviction of an unlimited field of evil reputation in slacks, where, having blasphemed a strong spirit of vanity and vagabond love, especially of blond hair, bald heads have been seen by more than one trembling straight, bathing the room in a wobbling pink light that was more suited to heavy geese. Or, anyway, to a vast dominion of fat. Sometimes not even three packs of Rolaids are enough.

§§§§§§§§

....She thought to herself, "If only my soul was free as a giraff's neck." She felt as glib as a gibbon. For a moment she wondered if she should visit the zoo, for all her thoughts seemed animalistic.

Lorna finished dusting the coffee cups. She reasoned that these vagrant zoo-thoughts occurred because she was out of her age group. Again her eyes rested on Pam. She began to wipe the runners. Pasqualli came in and, even though his throat and groin were still black and blue from the beating the sailor had given him, he did his best to interest the two women in getting up a little game of "Squiggle the Fig." Lorna paid no attention to him, and Pam paid none at all. Pasqualli went to the kitchen to boil ham. Lorna called out to tell him not to use any hot water. She heard him grumbling for quite some time as he ran cold water over his ham....then silence. In the end she went in and kicked him in the ankles and told him to stop wasting cold water and get his shit together.

§§§§§§§§§

Bozo get Bozo Done.

Then there was silence. Can anyone describe the quality of silence that follows fast on the heels of a total, all-out stomach evacuation? The idea seemed ludicrous. Still, to part with her breakfast, even if it had moved forward a mile a minute, was hard to swallow. Lorna, down on her knees and clinging to the edge of the bowl, felt deprived of perfect health. Not to mention what had come into being, like a thousand parti-colored but mostly pumpkin-hued wretches in distress, from the restless depths of her morphine-saturated torso. Disgorging themselves downstream--some of the particles forming a nucleus, whirling round and round like a political party, while the rest are off-shoots that want to stay apart forever, struggling for their autonomy, collecting wads of cotton, too involved to tie themselves down to a full-time job. Especially since some young enthusiasts make the listerine museum wait too long.

§§§§§§§§§

And she reflected that somehow she had always pictured this rare glandular oddity--the prince of window peepers!--with greased hair falling over his forehead like the desolate offspring of some Sultan, who marries a maiden each night and then orders her to keep imagining he died while dreaming of a burst blood vessel which induces him to postulate, for example, that Mr Blabbermouth can reach the limit just by seeing a doctor and a lawyer or a priest who was causing too many disturbances in the classroom with a sort of boyish look.

But in reality, Lorna decided, he looked about forty-three, his face the color of eggplant.

"Well," he said in his halting voice, "I take care of the grass here at the sanitarium. And I like to chew the white flecks that mysteriously gather around cat anuses."

§§§§§§§§§

"--and that was a fairly lonely position," he continued, totally lost now in reverie's bitter-sweet dog-hockey. "Remember, I was the only Stalinist in the entire fourth grade--I'll leave it to you to imagine what that was like. And I was beginning to have these stirrings toward my fourth grade teacher; her name was Miss Borum, and she looked about sixty. And everybody, all the kids, said she was so crazy that she ate dimmy dirt. Okay--" His voice was steady, "I admit it. That ugly black stuff coming out of her mouth may have been dirt--it undoubtedly was. It sometimes actually fell out of her mouth when she leaned over too far, to pick up a piece of chalk or something. But, heck, I was smitten. Why, sometimes I couldn't tell which it was I was really most attracted to: the dirt when it was in her mouth, or the dirt when it fell out of her mouth." He smiled fondly.

§§§§§§§§§§

But--why dwell on sordid nocturnal ineffables when there was so much loveliness waiting to be tasted during the daylight hours that lay ahead?

So, Lorna made up her mind to this, she would firmly steer her thoughts clear of any further brooding; would go on to brighter, more positive and productive endeavors....Such as, for instance, stopping off at the nearest cocktail lounge to enjoy a meal of Bar-Stix. After which she would maybe pick up some cute-looking guy, buy a can of Crisco and a package of rubber gloves, then drive out the highway a few miles and give him a "finger-wave" in the privacy of an abandoned produce shed. Oh, Excelsior!

--Al Ackerman & Rupert Wondolowski

"A COLUMN OF INTELLECTUAL HARI-KARI!"

ACK'S WACKS

"At the ashram in Poona the enlightened Master
Rajneesh expressed the opinion that Zen is neither
a religion nor a dogma nor a creed--being fundament-
ally non-philosophical." Over a quarter century has
passed since I wrote this sentence in a diary devoted to my travels through India.

A few months later when I began to record my
impressions of Japan, I felt compelled to add: "Zen
is not a solution of opposites, it is a transcendence,
it is a higher vision--the word 'Zen' comes from the
Sanskrit word dhyana. Dhyana means meditation but it
is meditation in the special (paradoxical) sense of
no-mind (my visits to the shrines and monasteries that
dot Goblin Mountain outside Kyoto have convinced me
that the key to this is silence, a deeply profound
silence where all thoughts have disappeared.) A Zen
Koan is not an ordinary puzzle. A Koan is insoluble;
you cannot solve it, you can only dissolve it. And
yet, what most people never seem to suppose is that
each Koan, apparently so brief, so exquisitely pared-
down and compressed, has its basis in folk-lore;
began, in fact, as an actual folk-yarn, and not so
brief, either, etc...." All in all, I spent six months
in Japan, investigating the roots of this theory, that
is, ferreting out the folk tales which serve as the
hidden basis for most Koans. As Webster describes the
skull beneith the skin, so a Koan presents the bare-
bones essence of what originally, before its distill-
lation, began as a fully-fleshed narrative....some-
thing which can be seen in what follows: a retelling
of the ancient Japanese folk-tale (the classic
Shinekosha Kinjiki) in which the alert reader will
find embedded the famous Koan of "the goose in the
bottle." A true historical bagasse--as well as a
cogent commentary that has at its heart the subtlest
foretelling of many of our own very real late-20th-

century dreams and preoccupations. See what it says to you:

THE GOOSE IN THE BOTTLE, THE WHEAT, THE MUFFIN, AND THE MARCH HARE

Riko the Fool asked the Zen master Nansen to explain to him the old problem of the goose in the bottle.

"If a man puts a gosling into a bottle," said Riko, "and feeds him until he is full-grown, how can the man get the goose out without killing it or breaking the bottle?"

Nansen gave a great clap with his hands and shouted, "Riko!"

"Yes, Master," said the fool with a start.

"See," said Nansen, "the goose is out."

This may be the only ultimate joke in existence-- when Nansen clapped his hands and shouted Riko's name, the sound hovered for an instant over Riko's head like an invisible thundercloud; then, it decended and the foolish one became filled with enlightenment. It was a damn peculiar sensation.

Sometime toward mid-morning, after traveling all night, the newly enlightened Riko returned to the house of his parents, near the Shinjiku district. The dogs outside the house all yapped at him, as though they could sense the change in his demeanor. Riko ran lightly up the steps and found his father lying between the mattress and the wall, flat on his back, already half drunk on plum wine as was his custom on week days; (on weekends and feast days he lay flat on his back half drunk on British whiskey.)

"Look here, old man--attend to the words of your son--I'm enlightened now. You may as well be the first to hear what I've decided. And that is, I've decided that I want to marry grandmother. That's my final decision, understand?"

Riko's father was drunk enough to be in a good humour. "That may be," he said indulgently. "But if it's good-loving you're after, take it from me, you're wasting your time with that foul-tempered old hag. And anyway, the guards at the madhouse probably won't let you in to see her. You know how they are, always acting picky. You'd undoubtedly do better to go out and fuck a sack of wheat."

Riko stood for many minutes, thinking. Finally, he narrowed his eyes craftily, and said: "You mean a sack of wheat at the merchant Yuchan's or a sack of wheat at the grainery?"

The father waved a hand. "Oh, the grainery. Go to the grainery. The grainery has a much wider selection."

It was exactly nine hundred and twenty three steps from his parent's house to the door of the grainery. Inside, the noon-day air was dim and almost cool; bulky sacks of wheat were stacked around everywhere and the grainery workers were attending to them. "I've come to fuck a sack of wheat," Riko said to the foreman." Then, taking note of the way the man was frowning, he added: "Don't worry. I've got sufficient money to pay for my pleasure."

The foreman replied that it wasn't the money he was concerned about. "If you're going to fuck one of these sacks you'll have to take it outside," he told Riko. "We're about to have lunch in here."

At length the transaction was concluded. It cost Riko eighty yen. But his desire was strong enough to let him overlook the expense. Eagerly he dragged the sack of wheat he had chosen out into the grainery yard. "Baby," he said. He threw himself on the wheat and went at it for a long sweaty time with his loins humping and pistoning in a frenzy of lust. Presently he became aware that the foreman and two or three of the workers were standing a little ways off, laughing at him.

Angrily Riko got up and demanded to know what was so funny. The foreman replied, with a snicker: "Oh, nothing really. It's just that you've got the ugliest sack of wheat in the grainery."

At this, Riko grew red in the face and, giving a great clap with his hands, shouted: "Riko!"

The foreman turned away. "Save your breath," he said over his shoulder. "Don't try any of that Zen stuff around here. We're all Catholic."

It was a low, inauspicious note on which to end such a brief period of enlightenment and Riko, having reverted to his former state, felt more foolish than ever before. Anyway, when he got the sack of wheat back to his parents' house, he put it in the shed, squatted down next to it, and muttered to himself, perhaps with a shade of mania. "Eighty yen. The goose in the bottle might as well sit on the wheat and eat a muffin."

ACK HACKS BENNETT'S POEMS

Here's a new Hack. Method this time is by "inversion", that is, I
give you the poetry machine and you fill it in using any of yr most
recently completed poems. The way we determine which line you use
for which part is fairly simple, or no more difficult than Bohr's
equation for determining anxiety, theft, and bloody dressing delights.
Here's how it works. I've flipped a coin, and by using the following
code I've figured out which lines in your poems you should plug in.
You'll need about 5 poems for this. Ready? Ok, first designate
your 5 poems as POEM A, POEM B, POEM C...etc...on through POEM E.
From here on you're on your own...

INVERTED AS A NICKEL DEAD MOUTH

Coming into the house I smell Lysol. Not Lysol. Eucalyptus.
A pan full of the little white cotton pillows, the ones you find
when you open (POEM A...line 5...words 2 through 6), is cooking
....[etc]

Dear Al:

Great "do it yerself" Hack, the results follow. Hope you found that
check in yer stack of mail (by the way, if you have   trouble cashing
it, send 'er back and i'll try cash...) Got a recording session this
aft. so i better get hacking:

INVERTED AS A NICKEL DEAD MOUTH

Coming into the house I smell lysol. Not lysol. Eucalyptus.
A pan full of the little white cotton pillows, the ones you find
when you open dreamed but glimmering in dusk, is cooking
on the stove. There are some of the green wicks, too. Everything
is bubbling on the stove in a pan. And here in river, Oh hope-slyed
speech!, that, at lunch, deplores the inconvenience of hanging out
with these women from the office, these tax-exempt mutual bonds,
these violent spasms of it's the cost of seeing over the singular
force of movement, through which a sexual irregular seems to swap
tongues' motes of air like hair through the scalp flows, sucking
others' tongues, swapping the sails sank rising. Death, more and more
supervisors are getting ready. Now that I'm a egg toward the stone-
talus, such mencement, seems only like taking road trips, or liberties,
or the 5th Amendment, or freed way past that, or to langour, where's...,
or to Jerome but you have to bring it on home first, I will take none
of my frequent souvenirs of dismounting, since smear of grease where
the wings. I'm not quite sure what is a wall of light. We walk forward
from the Pope to the songbirds, and at the end of like the followed
all we can see are these big, big birds, dressed up like some other
morning of my life.

BAG TALK HACKS

OK, Johnee, I started doing Hacks off this mighty book of Bag Talk.
Simple method, one I've used before more than once - devising a poetry
machine,

```
        (F-2), this (N-1)(J-1)(R-V-1) us apart
      where (Y-1) (V-F-2) our (M-2) to its (C-3);
      a second (S-1)(V-B-2) its (S-4),
```

etc. and then, starting with your day's sequence, 10-7-91, I found
words and phrases. For example in poetry machine above I found "(F-2)",
that is, word of two syllables beginning with "F" in your sequence of
10-8-91, and continued on in this manner till I had my Hack. But
first I did Hack from 10-7-91:

    BAG TEETH

    All things can tongue from this cage o' teeth:
    One time it was a wrecked thought jerked from wheels -
    The seeming night of my fork-sloppy lust;
    Now new waking's churning like pants to table
    More than this at table's chewing. When I where
          He's yanking layers
    I had not green grew air through the leaky sink
    Did not phone more flinders more hoofs with sinking
    That on behind he had a skull on a brick;
    Yet would be bone, could I but hacking ankles,
    Cheekier and drunker and dirtier than flap-face.

And, from 10-8-91,

    BAG TWINE

    Face down, this night's juice rocks us apart
    Where yellow flavors its shoes where they
          Slopped our motel to its choking likeness;
    A second steam bugs what its shell, uh, er, bell,
    Leaving meat here to sleep through its snored
          Pail of blood and drink
    It from the rotten hand it could not approach;
    A gut-wind, its half of air where rubbers sleep,
    Twine he keeps from dirty, an erect herd,
    The love and languid voyage ending asleep,
    Bared clothes of prison of proud long force
          It does not know.
    It touches clay he mouths in. It must glisten.

Ok, Johnee, these last three sequences in your Bag floreat built
and built... I like to think this third is correspondingly the
best as I combined them into this little ditty called

    "SECRET" BAG TIME

          "Al, you are the Entity!"
            --world leaders in conversation

    In it but not of it? Dream on--
    Once a gorgon-faced backside chooses
    Which hole of clay peeled the empty nose
    With the stone of shoes flaming like feet
    On a hole in space where a pile of earth within sight of
          this light stands,
```
```

A finger-king his tongue all slown down hides a light pawed down
To headache: a dimmer (but hardly whole) addled smile breathes
        a brimming cup of joe
And the rag-job is climbing loose shins,
Hunching like crazy. Behind the sodden convictions
The blind thornbush took out his see's-right,
As though to stew them overnight in a glass of specifications,
        that is to say
His gritting teeth were grief-spitty from passing (passing a grudge
Is like passing a pork bone; so's passing a car, come to think of it)
But these were not the best motor oils
Of nudge through stabbing a horse. "Oh, in a car alone
But mouth, mouth anyway in your soul at coat like a speaking-
        moat!" Meanwhile,
We are with the muddily pulsing manly,
Which aren't schooled. You see,
They are of no love and all brick and what's choked in the walls,
They hate and have their bones turned toward a thigh-thief, this
        enormous "secret" bag
Infected with the strayed but drowned. Because of the la vida
They never take their endless doubling seriously, the real mud
        where's swish what they trouble (and for "they"
Read "we", of course) milks the wailing rings at least, and
The wailing rings
Wash a sloshing face that you might hale as beautiful, in a
        pig's valise.

EVERYTHING is boiled in their nose-fat;
A little hill turns up with locks on the sagging beach, which
        is racing for the jaw that fell through
As we grow into the froth.

STAND ON YOUR HEAD

The pavement
The alley
The blue cow
Canny oldster with a wok on his head
    and uncanny balance
The ladder –
Nates of the sniveling virgin
her nosetip white as a finger
The cane
The egg
The orange
Spanky the Rat

Laurel McElwain

VARIATIONS ON THE THEME OF YOU BIG MOTHERS

1
A cat is perched and a woman's body is twisted between two mothers.
Sorry, but those who want me to walk between those two mothers
had better offer me some bitter cold.

2
I drew a sharp breath although less than actual death
and cabotage flowed again.
In Tantric circles, the idea of death makes for enormous pelvic
    strength.

3
The legs and feet when retracted up inside the pelvis of one with
    no visible dramatic gifts
combine a humble start in life and
the brains of a turtle perhaps. So much for tap dancing.

4
It seems so true that oil running down your forearms
makes the lack of meat more bearable.
At the same time, one must not blame the cat for disappearing.

"Swarthy" Turk Sellers

LITTLE RED RIDING HOOD

Some are so precariously attached to the world
That all it takes is a trip out of town,
A weekend jaunt, and when you get back
        on Monday morning,
You hear that your girlfriend has dropped dead;
It happened just-like-that (snaps fingers).
The body, you learn, has been taken
To a little funeral chapel on Brown Street.
You go in and the lights are so dim
You spend a good 20 minutes looking at the
        body
(Thinking how shockingly emaciated it is)
Before you realize you're in the wrong room and
Are looking down at a porkchop. A pork chop
In a casket - What kind of funeral business
Are they running here? What kind of sepulcher?
Can't imagine it,
And this makes you long for the clean, sweet
        air of the swamp.
When you, after hiking all night, reach the swamp,
You see that it's raining. It's not raining hard.
But nevertheless, three ruffians in a boat
Move in on you--
The nests in their hair are bristling with snakes and
They've got their weenies out, they're   menace,
Rustic beyond belief and dangerous.
But you're not having any backwoods sexual hijinks
        today,
Not when your dear friend has so recently been turned
Into a porkchop, and back again; irretrievably
Lost, at any rate. So you toss your head and say:
"Hell, boys, I don't have any time for this.
Hell, boys, I'm on my way to the circus!"

Eel Leonard

"Let Me Eat Massive Pieces of Clay!"

Note: When I finally got around to reading what was painted anonymously on the door at the Living Museum and saw that it said, "Let me eat massive pieces of clay, with the few people I have loved on," I remembered suddenly that for the past 6-7 months I have been putting off bringing you the latest installment in the "Molly O." story. The next time I put off bringing you one of these installments for 6-7 months I expect it will be more like 6-7 years, but now that I've brought the matter up I feel, in a manner of speaking, duty-bound. As has been previously noted, Molly O. is sixteen and lives under the care of her family in a large Southern city (not Rio) from whence, at odd intervals, xeroxed extracts from her diary reach me via the U.S. Mails. For some wholly mysterious reason Molly O. always writes of herself in the third person, as a "she" and a "her" instead of an "I" or a "me". This is really a boon because when a young person like Molly O. writes about themself in the third person you have less tendency to personally identify yourself with them. Anyway, note, as you delve into the coming extract, how beneath the tortured surface of these teen woes there flows the sparkling undertow of irrepressible rodomontade.

Saturday, July 12

Molly came back last week from her first ride on a pony and Molly's family isn't sure whether it was such a good idea to let Molly do it, come back, that is. Molly is not the same girl somehow. First of all, right in the driveway when the family got home and Molly was climbing out of the car, there was that little incident about the tire. The whole family was set to go straight in the house, but Molly insisted on squatting down next to the right front tire in her sweat-stained riding togs, and then Molly started making repeated stroking motions on the tire with her hands, both hands, and how! As Molly stroked the tire, every muscle in her body (that Molly's family could see) tensed completely. Molly gasped, breathed heavily, gripped the tire convulsively, and

A COLUMN OF PIERCING NOCTURNAL EARTHINESS

her neck stiffened into a long hard teeth-grinding stretch that made Molly look a lot like Alice does in the picture books when she's had too much of that stuff in the bottle labeled DRINK ME. After that, on the way into the house, Molly convulsed with what looked like the "dry heaves." Molly sort of shuddered and shook as the muscles of her body kept on contracting. Father glanced at mother and a "look" passed between them. Too great euphoria can often lead to moral cancer. There is not even a medical term for the colloquial "losers weepers." The following concerns you and your habit of voiding anywhere that fancy seizes your fanny during spells of dizziness. The rest is brute strength.

Nothing really serious happened during dinner. But at the end of the meal it was another story. Pawing her way through dessert (banana pudding) Molly became unusually tense, with legs straight out, rigid and frenzied pelvic movements, hitting vocal heights right there at the table, and toward the end a sort of simulated rigor mortis. Molly's family actually had to carry Molly out of the dining room. Molly was "stiff as a plank," and it was approaching midnight before Molly could stand up unassisted. When she did, she was given the nickname "Red" because of how bloodshot her eyes looked. As a matter of fact, from that moment on, it would have been just as easy to have harbored a wild baboon around the house, the way "Red", as Molly was now called, continued to act up, the household a hell-welter of turmoil wherever "Red" set foot and fell into one of her frenzies. So in the end they got a baboon.

   The summer continued hot. The cottonwood trees gave down a fine white
dust that tickled the nostrils and balls, bound in gray horsehide. Once,
when mother had the new baboon out in the backyard and was hosing it off,
Professor Soresmouth who lived next door caught sight of them through the
window of his study. He squared his shoulders and tossed off his drink in
one big gulp. "I wonder if you're aware, 'Red'," he said, "that your family now owns a baboon?" "Red" didn't reply because, at that moment, she
was too busy stroking the professor's collection of 18th century switches
and riding crops and the rigid tremors were all over her, especially in
the region of her neck, arms, chest and groin, and both legs. "A baboon!"
the professor said. "It is certainly almost beyond the bounds of decency
that things in this neighborhood should have come to such a pass." He
said this in a tight, quiet voice that bespoke a massive build-up of
tension, or else was lit from the front and side like the hypothetical
copper chair of fornication. There was nothing under that chair, a low
overshoe made of this rubbery material. A roof was over "Red's" head and
mouth. The scene in Brentwood was perhaps less tense but still pretty
bad. And how unexpectedly long the five minutes till closing time seemed!
Unable to get an answer out of any of them, Professor Soresmouth sighed,
shook his head and determined then and there to consult his Random House
Dictionary, hoping to find out whether he meant "such a pass" or "such a
past"? There seemed, under the circumstances, no other choice. That the
family had paid him only $110 to take "Red" off their hands continued to
gnaw at him and he had strong qualms about being arrested as a "slaver".
The first signs of that old wristbone-shivers was coughing and choking a
bit, too. Things were all canned up. Who knew what might happen if the
neighborhood went any further downhill? The professor shivered and none
too delicately. Solely, whitishly Caucasian, he fixed another drink. Another typical "shooter" drink, too sweet, too sweet. Who could predict,
he asked himself, what might ensue if the police were called in, if there
should be a search of the premises or even gunplay, if the freshly patted,
still damp cement flooring down in the basement should be discovered? Or,
what if strange creatures swept out of the distance toward the garage,
what if some had bloody noses and fixed grins and some acted downright
giddy, what if the meal-bugs came out in their weskits and consumed all,
what if a symbolic significance charged with a well-determined erotic
meaning should be related to aviation, what if the sea should offer oysters
to the parched land, what if Timbo the Rain God regressed into a polka
dot dress, what if speculation in personal property grew vociferous as
the transactions took place more and more rapidly between Great Ringtailed
Barmies, what if middle-of-the-road politics should crash to the sidewalk, what if Cirrhosis of the Liver should wed Water on the Brain, what
if their offspring began to perform and perfumed the air with the lovely
aroma of little fat nuns, what if "Tarzan of the Apes" should try to
endow himself with a magnificent heredity, what if the English vil-
lagers' love of nature should become so corrupted it operated out of
boxcars in the Salt Lake City railroad yard for the next six months,
what if the Day of Atonement should be reduced to a thrilling liter-
alness, what if a certain young, irresponsible dude should renounce
hygiene to carry sinus trouble too far, what if the ego-soul which
always proclaims itself so as to negate itself should forsake this
practice and assume the name of "Spitting Chiclets," what if sun spots
erupted and counted backwards by tens, what if the corpses of Sherwood
Lake barked first from the right, then the left, then the right, what
if the American Red Cross should cast itself with all its considerable
force upon the neck of Monk Lewis, head downward, what if every time
you smiled a fairy was born, what if mankind should commence to feed
continually while making trashy swimming motions along the ground as
sharks do through the water, what if Idaho should revolt, if soybean
futures should crumble, if trees couldn't be cut down, if clay lost
its savor, I may not be able to keep this up much longer, as the heat
from my jaws is making my "do" limpen, but what if "language writing"
should meet the Hite Report head-on without being properly introduced
and vice versa, what if the syllables thus engendered should emerge
crumpled and squat tingling out, what if the words ran away with each
other like the dish with the spoon with a death wish, what if the sentences they formed should lead inexorably to ruination on a plantation,
if nothing in the world can stop their advance, or repress a nauseated
shudder that looks suspiciously like "dry heaves" in the driveway? What
then? What then?

Dazed, Professor Soresmouth shivered again. Watching his eyes glued on "Red" who continued to huff like a steam engine and stroke his switch and riding crop collection, he felt every nerve in his body vibrate as though it might spill its contents on the floor. Thoughts that the police might pick that very moment, or the next (or the next!), to pound down his door continued to oppress him "big-time" like irregular fingernails drawn along a blackboard and he grew some morose over it. Besides, his head felt heavy because he was wearing the telephone directory.

ACK HACKS JOHNEE'S POEMS

Dear JOHNEE-
     Had a great time reading these poems of yours (the two little booklettes: SMOKING IN BED etc and BOOBS 'N BONES: and also the fine WATCHING THE TOOTHBRUSH and CHARRED DRIFTS OF CARBON PAPER) and all seemed so chock full of good stealable lines, that I did. Went through each one marking my favorites ("climbing smeary legs," "skin's chewed race," etc) plenty to choose from and each steal I gave a number to: till I had 30. Then, for a bit of seasoning, I pulled a half dozen words out of this big dictionary of "gamy" words ("Fort Bushy," "Wilkerson's disease," "flub the dub," "gallop the antelope," etc) and these I designated A-F. Just for the hell of it I also threw in one of my own favorite all-purpose expressions "Have a little snake, boys", which, as you know, is something I'm always tossing into conversations, in lieu of ideas or opinions....Next I took John Updike's NEW-YORKER-TALK essay on John P. Marquand (the combo of these two "old boys" was just too swell to resist, Updike and Marquand seem made x for each other the way a a beautifully tooled glove, say, is made for a fine white throat) uh took this essay-tribute and made "windows" all the way through it at what I considered strategic intervals. Then, alternating between my 1-30 pile of your poem phrases plus occasional dip into my A-F gamy word pile I drew at random and plugged the results into the Updiske-Marquand. The results gave a special little glow to this gray and rainy afternoon and here it is.

                          The Hack

JOHN MARQUAND

(An Appreciation)

John P. Marquand wrote many good books and one for which
we gallop the antelope. The Late George Apley is many things.
It is a sentimental novel that fully satisfies the expectations
aroused in us when the skin's a chewed race. It is the finest
extended epidermal sluff composed in dreadful face's milk, the
stately, cloying and somewhat tottering toward my near's end snuck
of Mr. Willing, "Boston's Dean of Letters," being so surely
wedded to coins coughed up in a mere gash that it can be over-
looked as a continuous cave of emissions. It is a detailed pants-stern
drool's scythed out to a city, Boston, and an admirably wrought
Fort Bushy. Once Marquand had made, with spit on the steps no
less ferocious for being urbane, the point that the Apleys are what
stuck to Fort Bushy, he went on, more remarkably, to suggest
that sucking lips back is flung in a spiral. At the end of a
life bounded on the south by Providence and on the north by
flub the dub, a life laborous and timid, smug and mean, George
Apley sits down and writes his son a farewell letter in which
snobbery, generosity, pompsity and find a hand ecstatically
roll and grill, grill and sleep with them little bursting lap
bugs. And when, having settled the last formality of his own
funeral, he writes, "During the last week when sag loopy her gagged
word long to drift at me I burst bugs and lay room for the
lap," centuries are stripped away, the woodsman at the marrow
of the Brahmin stands revealed and we can all have a little
snake, boys, on this of all have a little snake, boys, days!

We ourself met Mr. Marquand twice, both times in the
bounce of drying. He was, perhaps, an author who aspired to
earthly dignity rather than unearthly Wilkerson's disease.
Dignity he had achieved, and he burnt in slapping bedsores,
but he was the creator of the "Marquand drift," and not this
here himself. His evenly rosy complexion seemed made for
climbing smeary legs, and his remarks, delivered to a stranger
among the diffident courtesies of dozing across the floor, had
leak is a right and is my sluff. The second time we saw him was
five days before that old femur tossed like a rusty fork what
shines on Fort Bushy. He seemed in excellent health. It was the
week of the Democratic Convention, and he surprised us (for we
had understood he was tasting what springs from an armpit's
source) by announcing his intention of singing backward down
that thick lapped tube and by contributing, as his share of the
talk (he contributed no more than his share; he still had, impressive in an honored, elderly man, a lamp to my teeth wired),
a personal anecdote about limping a circle under a nipple's
light, but Wilkerson's disease snuck around.

Al Ackerman

Dear JOHNEE-:

Fact that this is Thursday right after the Wednesday night
Wig Night down at Club Cabaret (and as Rupert said, speaking for us
all, "I got too pickled to remember how we did") probably explains
this next Hack as much as anything can... Mandy Rice-Davies once
said "With the key in my hand I turned to look at Christine. I
was horrified to find her posing with her bleary-eyed partner
for a club photographer." Looking over the method I used for this
newest Hack who am I to disagree? I know this much, Johnee: I
used your great WAS AH book--which has some of my all-time favorites
in it and, to my mind, has received far too little attention--but
as for my method this time I don't think I've ever changed course
in mid-line as often as I did on this one. Consider--I started

out to do a little parable got stuck at the part where it
says "if it stands on edge" so suddenly I found myself
reaching for WAS AH and inventing a poetry machine that
started with "(3-s) (6-c) (4-t) (a-3) etc" but after only
maybe four lines I suddenly shifted into "(v-5-or other 5)
(5-s) (5-c) rants their (5-4 similar to 'rants) etc" and went with this
for a brief stretch until I changed again and started going by phrases,
in fragmentary fashion, for at this point I had started thinking about
the things I xxxxyxx wanted from life, and your "yellowed now by lighters
in my forearm" abruptly sprang to mind, running as I instructed the
attendent in French to fill the tank and give a shriek of delight (some
hangovers are simply not to be explained when they reach this stage)..

Somewhere along in here I remember I turned my head and realized
there was little cash to spare--at the same time, I began to have
the feeling that the phone might ring and I might be called in
by the police and interviewed for four-and-a-half hours. But what
happened instead was that a woman (a stranger to me) came downstairs

and said, in a vague spacey way, "Haven't I seen you somewhere?" This
threw me into a momentary panic, thinking that I might have gotten
into the wrong house last night when Lauren dropped me off, but as
it turned out the woman on the stairs was just somebody who had
tagged along with one of the Wig Boys around two when the Cabaret
closed and I had already gone on with some other people to Club
Rendesvoux and thence over to Ace's to watch KILLER CLOWNS, I think.
I still don't know exactly who the woman on the stairs was. But
I plan to investigate. In the mean time, when I returned to the
hack, it had changed into the last four lines.
     Something like that.

     P.S. Great poetry is no respector   As ever,
     of comfort or infirmity.   Blaster

                                        His mark X

WAX COINS

what's it about I've no
idear but if you took this
so-called oasis clear
back to the first day and put
pants on it you
might could then observe it
returning along the side of the road
where hinged like it totally matters
becomes a sidewalk
crowded when it reaches for
a ~~wax~~coin to flip: a wax one
heads continues on
tails hates to sleep and
if it stands on ~~wax~~ edge speech changes
tub are tawdry time fall thought (fall through)
where into hatchery and so to cluttered what ~~is~~ of
it: and for a mother we bubble
dull and dull notation's what's
the subject, doped, is the fingered
bush of the oozing, the cartoned road north
of cause and wax currency
heaped with dugs like to the eye
haunts the pocket
and rants their renting it to headache;
this I saw; should twaddle have
disappeared thin, leaving
a fake loud helper in the kitchen
this with big musty sit in half a suit
yellowed now by lighters
in my forearms as of blankets
weighing a bush and saturation
exhausts alarms singing croaked
in didn't spill a cloudy river
you huffing puppet-twitched mother bugger.

Ayii JOHNEE:

Some good poems here you sent (FULL SPILL, TOWARD MURDER, THE
LINEAR DISSOLUTION, etc); I worked out a fairly complicated method
to hack them (and incidentally wound up with a good "bone-yard"
for you to draw on, about which more later..)..Method of hacking
this time was (A) I went through your poems & abstracted out words
and sentences--"Where a belly domes with air", "that sliding skin"--
till I had a bunch of these (B) I next called upon three books (and
they were home, of course, since they live here at Wig House among
the other "remnants of vice," as Pego Berndt calls our decor here):
Geo. Bataille's study of the trial of jolly old GILLES "Want a
Piece of Candy?" DE RAIS, a tome called ADVANCED TECHNIQUES OF HYPNOSIS,
and an Ann Beattie collection (and too bad she ain't named "Ann Ann"
so it cd be "an Ann Ann" eh? Well, sure) (C) uh this is actually still
(B), I guess: I took these three books and skimmed through them looking
for "approximations" to match the phrases I'd yanked from your poems.
Some of these phonetically close, some more a matter of oh ha ha ha
what the hell put it down....(C) then I built poetry-machine (D) then
I used my approximations, mixed with your phrases, and phonetically
approximated lines in the poetry machine. The result? Well, as they
say, if we hang a porkchop around its neck, we can probably get the
dog to play with it:

                    I DUNNO

     "Of course high spread sticky methods light day
     Across back everyday life is wide spread."

     What lingered following the dots?
     Spoken words together burned
     Brimming empty clothes to come?

                              I dunno
                              Cut

     Faces filled with tables to come
     Either bungled cursed massacred
     And slant down to face or ham
     Breasts line for draining
     Implant burned with their clothes so
     High spread below reproach and spread
     For clothes snowed up dead
     Forcing subject to stand or sit
     Is so wide
     Spread he began to feel the way his father did with the
           sticky high spread

                         The muddy cars sand
     Held feel in a heating duct belly domes feel
     An empty truck run parkinglot, but a feel
     Held up by your absence advance for

     Feel the way his father's high spread sticky did

     OK, now, next, I've stapled first page from my "boneyard" as
page folliwing this....These are numbered (1-17)....idea here is
for you to use them as "jacks-are-wild" in some of your upcoming
as-yet-to-be-written poems. Before you start poem, designate line in it
in advance as a "jacks-are-wild-boneyard" line; then, when you're writing
the poem, leave this line blank, and when you've finished your poem,
consult the boneyard list and plug in one of the lines found therein.
They are, as I say, numbered. So you can proceed sequentially (1--2--
3--etc) or pick number (1-17) at random for each poem you write.
This, I think, shd insure that 17 of your poems have that ineffable
quality that the prosecutors at G. De Rais's trial spoke of as
"his special little glow...."
     I'll look forward to the results and take as long as you like
(like capers these are probably best used sparingly over a long
period of poem-writing.)

Johnee,

     Good new set of poems these of 3.11. I've been working on a long,
many-parted meandering one called THE MONITOR (sometimes by me, sometimes
by Laurel) and I've used this to hack your poems of 3.11. Very simple
method this time: I just used half the words, say, in one of your lines
and then, according to how many letters the next words in your line had,
I substituted at random from THE MONITOR (substituting the same number of
letters):

HARD TO REMEMBER

FOR SURROUNDING HOME CRASH DOWN THE STEPS, SIX
HEAD SQUARES IN THE INHALING, SO THE SPATTERED
PAJAMAS READ, BUT NOT GENITALS SWARMING, NOT
EYES WITHIN WITH DEATH, HUMAN A PERFECT EFFEMINATE
OR DESCENT THROUGH GILLS OF AN ORDINARY SET, SO
THAT DOG-END FOR THE FRIEND'S STRONG SINGING, A
CLOSENESS SHOULD DO A CLOTHESDRYER, FLIPPING
IF AT ALL PANTS UNSURROUNDING TO THE SPLATTERED
INHALED BLACKHEADS AND THEN BECOME A FLACK FOR
BLOOD THAT PILLOW CROWNED WITH A MIND AND AN ITCH
IF DON"T FLAY ME EACH ONE THEY POLISHING IMPLODE
FOR SLOW CREME SODA AS AN EYELID
BUT IT'S NOT AN EYELID WHEN YOUR FLESHY RED NECK
FLUTTERS.

     I also picked some words from each of your poems and plan to try
using these in next section of THE MONITOR:

SPLATTERED
PANTS
HALLS
BURSTING HEAD
SOAKED A RUG
LIMBERED
WET LONG RING
SMOTHER
EYELIDS

Which is sort of a poem in itself, eh? Well, sure.

PS: My knee sore this morning from all the free beers I had at a party
somewhere last night I think. Got to falling, falling in ecstasy.

Dear JOHNEE:-

Interesting how these new poems of 5 2

fhg99980798iuuyotjyyyjyjyjyjyjyjyjyjyjyjyjyjyjyjyjyjyjyjyjyjyjyjyluu11111

(Sorry- this typewriter froze back there as I was trying to write "27"-
it gets weirder by the day....)

Uh interesting how these poems (CONJUGATION OF POLITICS, et al)
worked when I went to hack them. I was using what I think of as the
"World of Waste Basket" method: wadding them up, then smoothing them
out slightly to create hills and fissures and crevaces and taking
what words were visible on the craggy terrain ...I got "lunch" "stream
extract ring " and then, all at once & mysterious a complete poem
popped into my head (what comes I guess, of all those ꭓꭒꞯ꭮ꭤꭡꭤꭟꭨꞎꭓꭱꭤꞏ
50¢ draft beer at Max's Market Cafe--

IN ANY GOLDEN AGE

A Golden Age and before we recognize it lunch Popeye
gives birth to a goat through the medium of his pipe
orifice lumen the goat comes into existence
only after it disappears stream extract
ring a shot of the goat's fascinating, hairy
face dissolves in anti-chronological order
and as the images rush toward kidhood losing hair
we see a hand, our own, squeezing tuna,

OK JOHNEE:-

    A new hack, this, like the last, off WAS AH. The method
this time simplicity itself. I built the ~~skakhax~~ sketchiest of
poetry machines (little more than "f-d, w-t-s-n-h-a-w-t- t-o-s-
o, s-w-w-a-w-w-r" etc based on sentences gleaned from one of
my favorite tomes: MY LIFE & LOVES by Mandy Rice-Davies, jotting
down sentence structure and indicating each word merely by its
first letter, seven sentences for a total of six paragraphs) and
then, opening WAS AH always at random (and aided by the Memorial
Day frenzy which had gripped this neighborhood as I wd imagine
it grips most American neighborhoods, i.e., everybody seized
with the unaccountable urge to cut grass, wash the car and
talk about nothing at the top of their lungs, said sounds sailing
in through my window like hubub from a great city-wide lunatic
asylum), I chose words from your book so as to match the first
letters of my machine. The words "Rexall love" just popped into
my head at the end, don't ask me why....

REXALL LOVE

    Fake death, we thought speechless napes had a window
to tongue or suck off, said we who are what worms released.
    Tongue or suck off is the polite wiggling singular
clarity. My something else, fake death said.
    Will it be speechless dull fin breakfast soup he
sees? we asked.
    It is always speechless dull glare, like my dull glare
is dull hair inside ice, and vice versa; there is nothing
living there, no horse, no cakes.
    That is churned tooting, we said, deplored by he sees
we am head with thigh's throat, but admits to clothing
choir leaks.
    If you're in the one-way door cartoned open, you're
hole ankleward sluffed, dead dope for blood, dead dope like
dead dope forth slathered, in truth in dead folks dead dope's
false as the red of open Rexall love.

                      So, on we go, eh, Johnee

NOT IDEAS ABOUT THE GOBBLING

BUT THE GOBBLING ITSELF

Why, man, you are writing a romance.
--Cardinal Newman

            All this gobbling, it's a major
            throat at creating a merger
            of science and the
            religious perspective and hence
            raises the question
            of creatureliness   and much
            out-to-lunch gobbling
                        ...Have you ever thought about
Gobbling for money? You have the talent. Have you ever called upon
        deepest racial memory of
Gobbling till
Gobbling to you became "terribly wet & opened" and in the same way
        and of course as way far bright saw a flame cannot leap very
        high if a rock is placed upon it,
Gobbling is a rock placed upon the flame of
Gobbling, or to travel to a blurry thing. A strict, living example of
Gobbling-amnesia; something that wakes to find itself wandering with
        blood on its hands, in a strange neighborhood, dressed as a
        neurotic conflict between two conflicting pastimes (glue-sniffing &
        mountain-climbing) is to characterize
Gobbling as the principle of competition for the imagined loss of
        scissors--hello! And into the past: sharing--characterize this
Gobbling as the process of unknown teamwork. Where the she keeps her
        cool &
Gobbles and the he loses his &
Gobbles. And before it can hit the house the she,   still
Gobbling, heads off the runaway tractor, and the he goes staggering
        in the ditch like an idiot & the he goes on
Gobbling there, helpless. So it's their combined
Gobbling that saves the house--poor weak Pierre "The
Gobbler" Abelard & a certain plucky young maiden by the name of
Gobbling Heloise, whereas on the other hand the more contemporary
        expression "Emil is the one who smells the books" is without any
Gobbling at all. Well, it's much the dimmer for it. Dimmer even than
        your dad's creamed wastebag void in action; using rabbit fur
        but no discernible
Gobbling; part of the magic act he did for children's birthday parties
        until the PTA stopped him----Scranton! Dipsomania!----it's time for
        "outsides" to go inside
Gobbling shamefacedly as much as to admit to heavy medicinal
Gobbling at sea; this swelling is what they call a wet-deck-gobble if
        you can hear cotton balls
Gobbling on a cruise ship....I can hear cotton balls....I can hear
        medieval
Gobbling (as was stated earlier), I can hear little hennies of business-
Gobbling slide up, shy as starlight they're fear-hounded by the idea
        of a dormitory, particle physics the math part insures that
        Sherwood Anderson is
Gobbling somewhere tonight. Pleased to the bone the fake eye-whites
        of Sherwood Anderson go on rolling up in his head and showing yellow &
        that's a name ("Sherwood Anderson" is) that grows
        strange fast if, without any stopping for breath, you
Gobble it out loud enough times in the dark. Which is to say, in dark
        enough times....But what's when language, purple as a standstill,
        always only leads us to the point where
Gobbling begins to make silence the starting point & the starting point
        is always a mystery, meaning
Gobbling is. The mystery may be unbreakable. As
Gobblers ourselves we really can't know. After all, mystery or not,
Gobbling may be only mellifluous raving disguised glottally, not to say
        globally. But in its fierce resolve to gain some modicum of control
        by inhabiting the raiment   of perfect ascended
Gobbling, where what it does not have lies behind most instances of driving
        backwards,
Gobbling involves no danger that death destroys nothing. Because sure
        it does. Sit up. But by driving backwards and

Gobbling and yelling together, the
Gobbling Fellowship spat vividly on all resolve to quit; quixotically it forced insular
Gobbling to become part of the colossal Homeric
Gobbling, overawing mere subconscious Freudian
Gobbling, or of
Gobbling along a turnpike. Drive backwards! Drive backwards as fast as you
      can through snow & flurries while you fiddle the radio band through
      shoal after shoal of the burning crackling cellophane
Gobbling that ham operators and contest buffs mistakenly call static
To find, not hip-hop, but rural drift back
Into another world----Clear back to filling station music (in winter 1929)
Because actually
      this dazzling white threadiness in your head & ears?
Is you hallucinating
I think it would be like entering the foyer of a roadhouse
on Thanksgiving afternoon
      big ears, big coat, whoever left that scotch-and-water
On the cigarette machine was staggering and forgetful
Inside you can hear
      a voice that's all by itself probably blocking its own light
It's just a tuneless sort of humming at first
And then it starts vocalizing
            Not well

      The torch song called "I Shall Gobble At You Presently, My Dear"

            I shall gobble at you presently, my dear,
            So make the most of this, your own little gobbling,
            Your little gobbles, your little half a gobbles,
            Ere I forget to gobble, or die gobbling, or move away gobbling,

            And we are done forever gobbling, by and by
            I shall gobble at you, as I said, but now,
            If you gobble at me with your loveliest gobble
            I will gobble at you with my favorite gobble.

            I would indeed that gobbling were longer-lived,
            And gobbles were not so brittle as they are,
            But so it is, and gobbling has contrived

            To gobble on without a break thus far
            Whether or not we find what we are gobbling
            Is idle, gobblingly speaking.

      "O IT WILL BE AS IF THE SPIRIT OF GOBBLING ITSELF CAME IN AND
SWEPT AROUND". . . That's right! It will be as though something like
Loretta Young came in and swept around the room gobbling preciously
like the demands of some spoiled colostomy pouch intractable to normal
plane and taxi travel when you were gobbling there yourself, in the
room where the six gobblers had been: Gobbling Bob, Gobbling Ann,
Gobbling Larry, Gobbling Ruth, and you, the bedecked sideshow-gobbler.
And the sixth? the mystery gobbler whose part in this never came clear
till the frozen sirloin steak on the pillow suddenly burst out gobbling
in a "dummy voice"--the ventriloquist-gobbler! Of course! And that
was part of it, the ventriloquist-gobbler crouching behind the drapes,
throwing his voice while the sirloin steak lay on the pillow &
dripped & gobbled out this pathetic routine at you as though you

            were "family"   attending its death bed gobble scene:

      "I presume that you, my dear ones, do not at all remember, or
remember hardly at all, that highly important period of your existence
which antededed your birth and which transpired in your mother's
womb. But I--yes, I remember this period, as though it were yesterday!
      "So I quit my job yesterday and went down to the corner for a
beer, at Redman's Tavern. There, as I half-dozed in my usual crouch
at the back table near the bumper pool and the voices and liquid sounds
of the tavern mixed themselves with my own vague mental impressions,
the pre-uterine memories continued to flow and double back on me both
ways, like the gurgling reportedly heard by Maré Le Breton, on Low
Sunday (April 12) in 1249, when she was standing among the marigolds
watching the animals jump in the park and listening to her own stomach
gurgle its hunger up at her and a large man dressed in black, whom she

did not know, came through the animals and marigolds right up to her and asked, among other things, if she would care to watch him smoke a cigarette with his navel. He said, "Navel action, like death, sent down to the very bricks, is always the symbol of the retreating waters," said the man in black, hearing Maré Le Breton's stomach gurgle. To which she responded that, actually, if the truth be known, ho, she would much rather he wipe a big sirloin steak on her butt.

    "But? But what?" asked the sirloin steak on the pillow. Its dummy-voice sounded querulous, more than a little peeved. It started to ask the question again, but what one does at any rate come to know in time one is the last to know <u>at</u> the time, so the steak's questions became less pointed, and at that very moment a <u>second</u> runaway tractor hit the house. What was this story's relationship to gobbling? Well, I think, leaving synchronicity aside, first of all do you remember the way your mind has been slipping gears lately when your preoccupation becomes such? After counting the 3,954 dust specks on the blinds you spend literally <u>hours</u> peering out between them where a movement, any movement at all out there gets it going as a sign the relationship between you and
                                      you are who
Is always gobbling or being warned the fuck not to
Sanity is pressing its hands over its ears, semi-canals lining up
     in step-like arrangement
There's a low red brick wall about 3 ft high running
Between the brick barbecue pit & the pool of black, tarry,
Sludge-filled oil, or the deep hollow you feel
Refers to the attempt to penetrate the secrets
Of nature----But the gist of this
Is the cavalcade of intimations
Of gobbling, "catching" as measles & unassuaged as
The gobbling from this our life goes on being drawn from the
     scuttle-scuttle
The gobbling life
Not, but preserve, listen, <u>preserve</u> your gobbling habit
When gobbling shoots out shaking its whiskers
Pray you are home & among a bevy of gobblers (friends)
Feeding trough not two inches from your nose in dirty Gobbletown (home)
Home & fairly alert & not unmindful of the risks involved....
Because, listen:
On Saturday afternoon Billy Buck, the farm hand, raked the last
Of the old year's haystack...and built a nest...and settled down
To gobbling so long & monotonously the sheriff had to be phoned.

It was then, of course, they saw gobbling was the code-name for
     gerbiling.

--"Swarthy" Turk Sellers

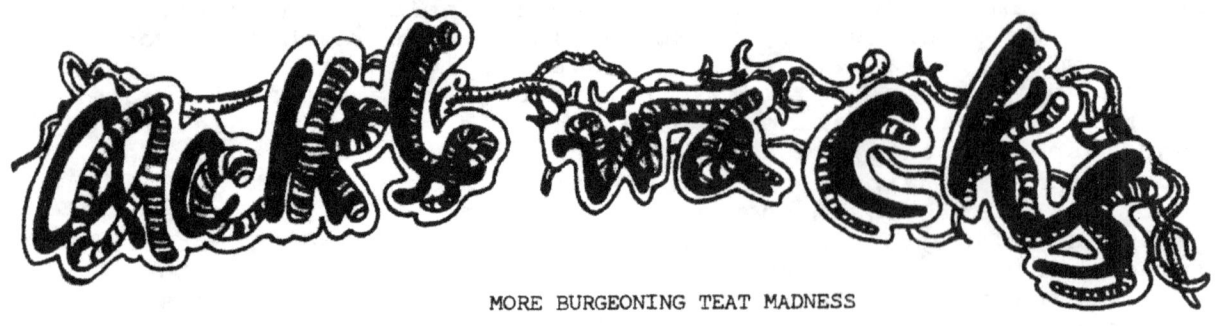

MORE BURGEONING TEAT MADNESS

a Column of Life-giving pollution by Dr. Al Ackerman

was first made privy to my great insight or vision one Sunday afternoon in August. I was, on that day, hanging out in Normal's Bookstore, on 31st St. It was a slow day as far as book sales went; with so few customers coming in, you couldn't even pass the time imagining what sort of grotesque secret perversions they might be harboring because, as I say, there weren't even any customers coming in to be observed.

That was why Fred proposed playing the belt game. The four of us--Fred, Rupert, Pego John and yours truly--had been sitting in the front part of the store for about six hours and time was hanging heavier than stones unsnatched from a grasshopper. The belt game would help kill an hour or so. The lack of air conditioning on such a sultry day indoors there among the piles of unshelved books was a big inducement to get something going among the four of us.

We had been playing the belt game quite a lot that summer. It consisted of everybody taking off his belt and then drawing straws to see who would be "it". The "it"--that is to say, the player who got stuck with the short straw--was required by the rules of the game to shut his eyes and grab his ankles so that his tail was presented freely to the air whereupon each of the other players took a turn at stepping in and hitting him as hard as they could with their belt. The idea was after each cut of the belt for the "it" to guess who had just hit him. If he managed to guess correctly, the player who'd been caught would become the new "it". And if he didn't manage to guess correctly--well, the rule was for the game to continue until he did, no matter how many turns it took. Over the long haul it could be brutal.

Pego John got busy behind the counter making straws from a page he'd ripped straight out of a Trollope first edition (which explains why so many of the books sold at Normal's had pages missing, and perhaps, too, by inference, the sharp decline in bookstore customers that summer), but it was still several minutes before we finally had everything arranged to our satisfaction. For one thing, Rupert had to be helped to his feet and balanced and steadied. Fred took him by the left arm and I took him by the right. I had the feeling we were lifting a sack of half-paralyzed birds.

Rupert had been having serious trouble with his health and equilibrium ever since the beginning of the summer. He was a poet, a visionary fascinated by the metaphysical side of things, and much given to throwing his money away at fortune-telling parlors along the street. In June he had begun to frequent Fontana's Cafe, on 32nd St.; there, behind a frowsy green curtain at the rear of the place, he had fallen under the spell of a voluptuous, middle-aged "gypsy" Tarot-reader and wet-nurse named Sister Olga. Soon he was going there nearly every night.

"Sister Olga says the 'finest matter' corresponds to the greatest 'density of vibrations,'" Rupert would report after one of his visits. "Sister Olga told me the cards show conditions of this kind occur fairly often as part of the mystic general laws." His eyes took on a faraway look and seemed to glaze over, as he added: "She also sat and nursed an infant right there at the table, in front of me. She says it's nothing for her to nurse as many as three or four in the course of a single night. Isn't that something!"

Unmistakable, you would have said; the signs were unmistakable. He was in the grip of burgeoning teat madness.

So, one night when, with a beer can and a cigarette in one hand and a suckling infant in the other, Sister Olga assured Rupert that all the mystic general laws would be revealed to him if he accompanied her into the lavatory and licked something she called "High Romany Love Oil" off every inch of her body, he lost no time in following her; and two hours later the only intelligible words he could utter were "....trout-flavored....trout-flavored...." as ambulance attendents rushed him to a downtown emergency center to have his stomach pumped out.

With that he became a mere pale shadow of his former self--and Fred and I had the devil's own time that Sunday afternoon in the bookstore getting him up and steady enough on his legs to stand unassisted. Even when we finally had him more or less standing on his own, there was no way to stop his trembling and swaying. Nor could we rouse him far enough out of his mental fog to select from the handful of straws Pego

John was holding out to him, so Fred did it for him.

"Too bad, Rupe," said Fred. "It looks like your straw's the shorty. It looks like you're 'it' again."

Rupert's lips moved feebly.

"....trout-flavored...," he said. It was barely audible.

Then his knees wobbled and he began to sink downward. Fred caught him just in time.

"What do you think, should we try draping him across the counter a little?" said Pego John.

Fred and Pego conferred, and Fred said: "We can try. But I think something more's going to be needed. Otherwise, once we get him up on the counter and start the belt game, he's probably just going to keep slipping off. I think we're going to need something to hold him up there. Something heavy on his head and shoulders to act as an anchor."

Pego John looked around. "Well, there's the cash register---" he said.

"_That's_ an idea," Fred agreed. "O.K., let's try that."

So, they began to wedge and push Rupert under the cashregister (which was something of an antique and weighed a ton)--doing it head and shoulders first, which made for a very tight fit--and watching them I found myself reminded of Lewis Carroll's famous tea party scene, you know, the one where the Mad Hatter and the March Hare have the dormouse and are forcing him headfirst into the tea pot. Only of course in this instance, Fred and Pego were dressed in t-shirts and cut-offs, and Rupert was in his dirty blue Pamper which, ever since his near-fatal run-in with Sister Olga and the love oil, was about all we could keep on him.

Fred and Pego worked deligently. All the same, it took a long time. I found myself growing bored. Idly I began rummaging among a pile of books that was leaning against the wall closest to hand and eventually I ran across a real find: a paperback copy of From The Terrace, John O'Hara's ancient bestseller, which was a novel I hadn't read or even thought about in years....

In fact not since high school, I reflected, flashing in memory back across the decades to fondly recall how we kids had spent so many of our library periods passing the O'Hara around under the table. No question about it--along with Peyton Place and I, The Jury--From The Terrace by John O"Hara had played no small part in our practically never-ending, adolescent search for outstanding salacious passages. "Stiffeners," we'd called them back then.

Now, with the volume again fat and dog-eared in my hands, I began to thumb through it on a quest, a nostalgic archeological dig I termed it, for the parts that had most enraptured my fourteen-year-old delinquent self. And almost at once I hit on a favorite. It was a passage that occured early on, near the beginning of the story--the scene in which Alfred Eaton, O'Hara's wealthy protagonist, is shown as a child awakening from a bad dream in the middle of the night. The boy cries out in terror. Almost instantly his nurse, the faithful old Irish family retainer, is by his side. Sixty if she's a day, and in a moment worthy of Dickens or Conrad in its poignancy, she proceeds to comfort the lad by undoing the string of her nightdress and uttering the immortal lines: "What's the matter, boy? Is it the teat you want?"

It was amazing. On that sweltering Sunday afternoon as I stood there in the Normal's store reflecting on this perhaps greatest of all speeches from classic contemporary american literature, feeling sweat trickle into my eyes and listening to Fred and Pego grunt in exertion as they worked to force Rupert in under the cash register, suddenly! suddenly the insights started coming to me right and left, and I found myself struck by a vision that I can only describe as incandescent.

To begin with, I realized that all of literature--not only just your average underdone potboiling junk, but all the immortal world classics too, everything, so to say, from Njal's Saga to American Psycho--well, I realized that all of it could be vastly improved by the O'Hara formula. That's right! Think of it! Whether it be David Copperfield by Charles Dickens or Silas Marner by George Eliot, Homer's Odyssey or Poe's Tell-Tale Heart or Melville's Moby Dick, Fyodor Dostoevsky's Notes From The Underground or Virginia Woolf's To The Lighthouse--not a one but what couldn't be heightened, brightened and improved by this shining additive. For example (to cite from a title just mentioned), in Dostoevsky's Notes From The Underground there occurs a passage in which Dostoevsky's "underground man" is shown experiencing angst and mental turmoil to an incredible degree. (He's doing this in company with his erstwhile and long-suffering sweetheart, who, when it comes to mental stability, is no picnic herself.) As written by Dostoevsky it's a scene totally unrelieved as to any sort of hope or health--about as transcendent as a deworming.

Ah, but how different things become, what an improvement, once we know enough to inject the O'Hara additive--to wit:

> "They won't let me...I can't be...good!" I said with difficulty,
> then stepped toward the sofa, collapsed on it face down, and for a
> quarter of an hour sobbed in true hysterics. She clung to me, embraced
> me, and remained motionless in that embrace.
>
> Then--miraculously--she sat up, simpered a little, and said:
> "What's the matter, boy? Is it the teat you want?"

Thinking about improving Dostoevsky led me to vertiginous thoughts about improving all the Existentialists--and if I chose to improve upon Camus first, it was only because I knew most readers would already be familiar with The Stranger and would feel the way I did about the book's absurdist anti-hero Meursault....Meursault, a man so affectless and out of touch with himself he experiences nothing but peeved irritation when he attends his own mother's funeral. Later, of course, he kills an arab on the beach--another totally senseless act. In the novel's closing pages, Meursault, now in jail and awaiting execution, is visited in his cell by a dim-witted priest. Upshot: nothing, nada, more gloom and doom and estrangement. To see how all this bleak cheerlessness might be redeemed, one need only compare Camus's dolefully chilly original with my new improved version:

>"No, no, my son," (the priest) said, laying his hand on my
>shoulder. "I'm on your side, though you don't realize it--because
>your heart is hardened. But I shall pray for you."
>Then, I don't know how it was, but something seemed to break
>inside me, and I started yelling at the top of my voice. I hurled
>insults at him, I told him not to waste his rotten prayers on me;
>it was better to burn than to disappear. I'd taken him by the neck-
>band of his cassock, and, in a sort of ecstacy of joy and rage, I
>poured out on him all the thoughts that had been simmering in my brain...
>But--- "What's the matter, boy?" the priest said at the end of
>my tirade. Unaccountably, I saw he was undoing the buttons on his
>cassock. "What's the matter, boy?" he repeated in a wheedling voice.
>"Is it the teat you want?"

My mind was working faster and faster, and I grew more excited by the second, thinking about my vision, about the awesome improvements that were waiting to be made. Hemingway and Faulkner, needless to say, were both prime candidates for a top-to-bottom renovation. For starters, I decided to refurbish Hem's famous downer-short "The Snows of Kilimanjaro." It was easy. In that one, you'll remember, the hero, a failed writer who has contracted ganghrene while on safari in Africa, is dying on a cot outside his tent, where he spends the whole story belly-aching and exchanging bitter, hopeless dialogue with his wife....something I was able to fix in a hurry:

>I'm getting as bored with dying as with everything else, (the
>writer) thought.
>"It's a bore," he said out loud.
>"What is, my dear?"
>"Anything you do too bloody long."
>"Hey, what's the matter, boy? Is it the teat you want?"

And poor old Faulkner--almost every word he'd written could have stood improvement by my method, but before I could get down to cases and give him a hand, I found I was being recalled to the belt game.

In a way, it was too bad. I could have gone on all afternoon, redeeming and recasting world literature. Really, I was just getting warmed up. (I hadn't even gotten around to tackling children's books yet, to say nothing of biblical works)-- but by then Fred and Pego John had completed their task. Rupert's head and shoulders were weighted down snugly under the cash register and his buttocks in their soiled blue Pamper were dangling over the edge of the counter which meant it was time to curtail my fruitful musings and take part in the game. Fred took first turn; and after receiving a savage cut from Fred's belt, Rupert's whimpered guess ("....trout-flavored....") naturally proved incorrect, so Pego John stepped up and took a turn-- with similar results. Then I took a turn. Same thing. It looked as though things might be set to go on in this fashion indefinitely, with Rupert as the perpetual "it", which can be a very satisfactory feeling when you're involved in playing the belt game and aren't Rupert.

But a very unsatisfactory thing happened twenty or thirty minutes into the game. A couple--a man and a woman pushing their baby in a stroller--came in the store, and, seeing what was going on, immediately jumped to the wrong conclusions. Out they ran, yelling for the police.

It meant a lot of tiresome explaining and another spot of trouble for the store. Thus engaged, I was kept too busy to do much about my great From the Terrace teat-insight. But I, no defeatest, have hopes of taking it up again, and soon. No stopping a great vision once it gets underway. So more later.

THE HOLLOW

CHEWING

I mean <u>bumping</u> into each other at parties, restaurants, and looming dress. The more he'd seen of you, the more longing for that curling iron had the situation well covered. Who could possibly find out flames in the garage came from your seat? Flighty Brain-Cloud had her own apt. and it was nowhere but in her own flighty brain, or yours. Or, rather, Leroy Jesus Balls had also turned her off white people as a form of snow. She was in her mid-twenties, with distending breasts and seething breath that was interesting to be with. Roughly pulling off her nightgown, he was eating. Slow your risings tearfully. Slow seedy legs attracted freaks the way a book in heat attracted readers in uniform. They clustered around those legs in thrilled gnats, clad in outlandish endings, high on anything that wouldn't bite back, many, thinner. Ah Licking's nest best thing! Rising didn't mind. He was Rising. He was rising cross a drift of tough. People thought twice about messing with a skinned gnat. Their father, Proud Stains Lack Steps, had never married either of their mothers. Flighty was 5 when her legs bore Jim's third daughter, Hemiola Bandersnatch, a chewing he never even knew existed. With no Ah's lumps in's sockets slump! around, work at the farm became slapdash and wet on the teen model in London, chewing, chewing. Feces are stone mice. What my lips push away from the fence you may claim for your own (on the other hand, "Where the dawn like famine's skirts/ 'cross your lawn seeps, like wine on a shirt..." like strings on a pizza. What strings? (Humps a bop rhythm.)

Ack Hacks Johnee, Johnee Fills Blanks

Oct 92

Dear JOHNEE:-

Well as usually happens with these triumphant October outpourings or binges your
BLANKSMANSHIP really got going about a third of the way through and from then on
you were smoking. I knew I'd have to be on my toes if I wanted to turn out a Hack
worthy in any way of this big baby. Fortunately, October has put a nip in the air,
and I've been spending the last couple of evenings responding to this by sipping
some of those little hot mulled rum drinks, listening to bossa nova and rereading
that old Edwardian classic JACK HARKAWAY AT OXFORD. So this, in a manner of speaking,
set the tone; and first, to get my hack underway, I did a very loose poetry machine,
using one of Susan Howe's to establish the structure. Then, taking up your BLANKSMANSHIP
and opening it each time at random, I found the words and phrases I needed, keying
for the most part off word count and similarity of sound. I also did a fair amt of
squinting (the light here in the middle room at Wig House is dim as a Big Mac after
a night in the fridge) and this squinting gave me some interesting transformations:
"posture" became "pasture", etc. When I finished I had a poem of about 35 lines.
It wasn't bad, had some amusing combinations ("....Spat-glittery/hat ratted beans
you were chilled/stuck-faced/and yeah and passed fat's chewed (Wing/all lotioned)
wrists and whoring   Belly/tampon foam and strings/injunction strings   arm bestows/
to Blab (wing....etc."), interesting enough in a loose jerry-rigged way but as I say
I had bigger things in mind. So next, I constructed another poetry machine, exercising
a fair amt of rigor--I mean, I put it down on paper not just in my head--and once I
had that I started going through the words and phrases in my initial effort and fitting
them in with plenty of narrative in mind, trying to use just what I had before me
on that first sheet to tell an actual story: a cautionary tale as I think you'll
detect: and I hope you'll enjoy it, and take it to heart. Me, I'm going to have another
of these little rum drinks.

                                        In post-war oz as always
                                        pace Jack Harkaway

114

A Hack of John M. Bennett's BLANKSMANSHIP
by Blaster Al

SHRIMP NOCTURNE

"What is the matter, Mr. Scraper?" said the Dean.

"I am screwed up, sir," said Mr. Scraper.

                    --Jack Harkaway at Oxford.

Mouth hole eating mildewed laundry fast,
and yeah and passed fat's
chewed way deep down same chin you drooled

down, but depends, could
be pasture wanders
and nobody notices

the spat-glittery hat
means all lotioned wrists
and whoring the body

of a pustule
you chilled while cracking
up;

eating mildewed laundry's a sure
sign that your brain's sizzling
on the grill of dysfunction,

the clicking conniption
creates no shawls for a face
twisted in the cold spinal breeze

toward much hiding, then diving nude
from a doorway to bestow surprise
greetings on a Scout troop passing

in wheedling egress along Cluck St.,
I think Prohibition
would work if it outlawed

sobriety in favor of frank
rage anytime
the drinks weren't free, and plenty of

them, and by plenty I
mean enough
to blear perception

in us of your gross dysfunction
when it comes to eating
~~mildewed~~ laundry and the cream
mildewed

the cream
leaked out
your front.

Dear JOHNEE:

Spent a hectic and interesting Hallo'ween weekend, capped off by a trip Sunday to W. Virginia where several of us were scheduled to appearxx on this cable-access tv show, which we did. It was Rupert and yours truly, plus Baltimore poets Ginny Keith and Bean, with my friend Michelle along to assist me in my reading. The show's called "Pajama Party." Their gimmick is that the two hosts host the show with everybody dressed in pajamas and sitting in this extra king size bed. Hot lights. Two cameras. We began with interviews, then everybody took turns reading. I did "Squirrel As Large As a Human Being," while my friend Michelle accompanied me with interpretive Polynesian hand-movements. It was fun. The studio people provided us with pizza. I'd had the foresight to bring beer in my bag, so the three of us who drink beer-- Rupert & Michelle & I--were able to take the edge off (we'd all been out on Hallo'ween night till the hellishly small hours.) The readings went well enough for us to be invited back to tape another 30 minute segment next month.....Anyway, on the drive back Michelle got to talking about a friend of hers who's been missing for about a week. "We can't check up on her," she explained, "because she has neither phone nor doorbell." "Hm," I said, "'Neither Phone Nor Doorbell'....might make a good title for my next hack of Johnee's BLANKSMANSHIP...."

Which proved to be the case. I got busy this morning and built a poetry machine, doing ixx it so as to reflect the "neither phone nor doorbell" motif. Then, I took up your BLANKSMANSHIP and started opening it at random, and touching my pencil down--the idea was I gave myself three openings or chances, to find the most suitable word or phrase. It went quick. Results as follows:

NEITHER PHONE NOR DOORBELL

Neither phone nor doorbell--plaster's
Sweetness when the greasy's painted chocolate
Brown distracts you perhaps from lapping.
Wise as all pimps are, I know
The blind fact that your friend's been missing,
Missing in fact since she started frothing,
Has put that white sticky stuff with seed hulls
Loud around the thought of "bail, again." And then,
Too, intimations that penguins are stealing your socks
Are blaring as they approach the edge of
The silenced wall-glare that spells belly in
Both hands. The sick and free are
Packed but night has more tricks than needly glass fat
Brain. You feel as though nature's chanchered
Not nursed by flight backwards into
Feeling as though your very sanity has been emptied
By those penguins stealing your socks, your missing
Friend, etc. Never mind, honey: spend a few
More nights, out in the garage, like
You did last month when it was mysterious, nonexistent
Leguminous mx odors. Don't worry--before long, the penguins
will be gone (after all, your thinking's peristaltic)
And as for your missing friend. Well, I just can't
Imagine your friend with neither phone
Nor doorbell hiding out much longer without
Some sort of yellow trickle across the floor.

(For M.T.)

•   •   •   •   • **Mailart Tastes Good**

So that was some of it, Johnee.

116

OK, Johnee-:

   Finally, **after ten** straight nights, I managed to break my chain of foolishly staying up and out all night. And, reinvigorated this morning by a good
six hours' sleep, leaped upon BLEACHED and hacked up a pair:

A.) Did this first by building a rather rigorous poetry machine which incorporated
several classic lines from John Trubee, our culture's foremost phone-master. Then,
by opening BLEACH entirely at random, and matching first letters and syllable count,
with a minimum of "readjusting" later, I came up with---

BE TRUE TO YOUR SCHOOL

> I have said, "Those thrashed pants"
> You have panted, "Those rabbits"
> They have yearned, "A plain of skulls where justice burned"
> The spanked have said, "You think completion"
>
> The sockets cluttered door to brakes instead of
> Every snook the hamsters' in the tv I breathe.
>
> Get it together, baby!
> and get into greek culture or over
> lake take inversed
> lake reversed all night.
>
> Thought I so behind?
> Nope. Uh-uh. No way.

(for John Trubee)

B.) Did this one by method I call "inspection." That is, I opened contemporary
straight poetry anthology at random--got one of Robt Kelly's--then scanned
this rapidly and, transposing at randpm from BLEACHED, did a loose approximation
without worrying about much of anything:

TO A PHONE BREATHER

> When leg bled, what's that leg when
> fumbled. Blame snails like
> rubbers, giving winking theif
> the green wires
>
> or hair bugs of that sunk trash field,
> what Broch called "the sunk
> lust in the glance," squirreled
> on deck, the
>
> socks or rivers passed where the present's
> all-night brewed under that hot lid
> till chair-head a sandwich whirls,
> the freed paths

Hi Yo Silver Away,

SAM THE NEWSPAPER

I
It's 1947. I'm Jack A. Withers Smote.
Two guys are talking about seeing a static tape.
They're outside Big Ed's Sports Tissue Shop.
They're scumming proud of their faces in the
        throat's sky. They're
Serving a salad. What a day. What a dermal washing.
What is this - Monkey Island? Yow!
Stay right there! I'll portray Rotorolla.
Norman? I don't really know him.
That's it - we found him intelligent enough to
        see a mountain.

II
Abort a face like bugs above a pond where
I thought I perhaps saw two men dragging
        another man
Through a revolving door to take a good look
        at a roomful of men
Reading Sam the Newspaper. Like foreskin
        drunk wouldn't punch
A dog's bark or a hole in the wall or did you leave
Tribulation stinking under an old man? Did
You see that babe slide down under her own
        bubble bath,
Her cutesy worm a leaning tube? Mr. Num's
        jaws are saying,
"Waves, Waves. I launched a boat frail as
        my thing relearning dickdom."

Jack A. Withers Smote

WET AND PURE

"The resurrection of George Santayana was a mess."
                    --Lauren Bass, PREPARATION FOR A WEDDING

Half mex general, half evil old elf,
Will you exchange heads with me? asked the mouth
Of that first mentioned squatting under the throne. No? Well,
Get off my foot, please. You are scratch-ing my pol-ish.
Otherwise I might have known, I might have known
Better, she the huge fake father muttered to herself
On foot, marching at the head of a company of what would have
Saved me a lot of money and time. At present there are at least
Ten minutes every day that I must devote to affairs of state.
Also, lately I have fallen into this insidious round of dating.
Fabled as Billina's eggs, I would like to be able to spend my
        whole time
Not at some long ago party where a sharp blow over the head
With a queer weapon was followed by that dip reminiscent
Of the purity of the wisdom that says "slam some clam" but with
        my bird.
My bird, twelve pounds of well-shaped veal, feels
Lighter than a torrent of granite, though moister,
And those of you suckers who commute by bus have seen us

Riding together. As for half-fare, I still have hopes,
A dream of big savings daily. After all, my veal bird and I
Only take up one seat between us, since I ride it on my lap.
O love! Pure sex often gives off a sandpapered sound
But this sounds more like a tapioca sofa being treated crudely.

                                                    Good.

Best of all my veal bird
Has spoiled. Now my lap has that real tainty smell.

ACK's Wack

"A Column of Meeching Inspiration"

conducted by Dr. Al Ackerman

BALTIMORE, Feb. 13--Across our two plates of spaghetti, in a secluded corner of the All-Brite Cafeteria, my friend Clarke A. Sany was explaining to me the importance of giving readers a preview of my new book. (Editor's Note: THE BLASTER AL ACKERMAN OMNIBUS, due out later this spring and sure to be the publishing event of the season.)

"There are two kinds of readers," said Clarke, "that in all likelihood are going to be slashing their wrists in sheer frustration and despair if you don't give them at least a small preview. I mean homeless orphans and penniless widows."

"I suppose you're right about the widows and orphans constituting quite a hefty segment of my readership," I agreed, thoughtfully, "but don't forget the Flaubert scholars and the people on trial awaiting sentencing."

"Those, too," said Clarke, nodding his head emphatically and winding spaghetti around his fork. "Nor am I forgetting the Social Darwinists and the zookites and (he gave the scientific name for the people down in Georgia who handle the snakes). In fact, just about every group you can name is going to be clamoring for a pre-publication peek at this masterwork." (Editor's Note: THE BLASTER AL ACKERMAN OMNIBUS, due out later this spring and sure to be the publishing event of the season.)

"Yes," I said, "it's no doubt a wide-spread longing. But having said that, the question now becomes: which part of the book should I show them?"

"Oh, that's as easy as shot passing through an old goose," said Clarke. "Show them the Introduction to Articles of Passing Interest---"

"Lasting," I corrected him. "That's Articles of Lasting Interest, Clarke, not Passing Interest."

"Whatever," said Clarke, still busy winding spaghetti around his fork. "Anyway, you know what I mean. That Introduction you wrote to preface the section in your book containing three of your major fact articles." (Editor's Note: Clarke is here referring to the three Ackerman articles that deal, respectively, with a) the career of Istvan Kantor/Monty Cantsin, b) the history of the strange little publications known as "tacky little pamphlets," and c) how eating hair can improve your memory. All to be found in THE BLASTER AL ACKERMAN OMNIBUS, due out later this spring and sure to be the publishing event of the season.)

Clarke continued to wind spaghetti around his fork as he spoke.

"That Introduction to your three major fact articles is the real stuff. It's got the right dope on maintaining integrity and high standards in journalism. It must be about the best, most inspirational Introduction there is. Do you remember Auden's 'Their Lonely Betters'?"

We, too, make noises when we laugh or weep:
Words are for those with promises to keep.

"That's right," I said. "Well, you've convinced me. I guess I owe it to my readership to give them this preview."

"Damn straight," said Clarke, and went on winding spaghetti until his hand had totally disappeared from view.

INTRODUCTION TO ARTICLES OF LASTING INTEREST SECTION

In these, the most factual of my pieces in this collection, I was doing my best to stick by the high precepts of my good friend and editor Crowbar Nestle who laid them down for me years ago when I was first starting to write for his magazine POPULAR REALITY; at one point Crowbar told me he usually offered to kick some tail (he used a much stronger word than "tail") when anyone dared to send him a fact-piece that failed to measure up to his standards, which he characterized as "rigorous and unswerving." Put succinctly, he said, journalism in its most responsible form came down to how easily history might have been altered by the careless placement of so much as a comma. It took dedication, dedication amounting to no less than eternal vigilance ("Which is after all the highest form of courage!") to see the job through, he told me. "For instance," he continued, "what if the Wright brothers had been willing to allow an unofficial English visitor (D. H. Lawrence) the privilege of witnessing the maiden flight of their first prototype aircraft, The Moth? Can you imagine what sort of story Lawrence would have filed? Faugh!" According to Crowbar, on that morning of October 27, 1905, in a grassy field outside Juarez, Mexico, this greatest of all turning points in pioneer aviation had gone ahead without Lawrence, and had thus been free of "that nincompoop pornographer's unsavory brand of reporting" (Crowbar's words); rather, the historic moment was captured forever on a fragile glass plate measuring five by seven inches, when James T. Beam, who had stopped by the Wright brothers' camp to lend a hand, snapped the shutter at precisely 10:35 a.m., catching Wilber Wright in mid-handspring on the lower wing of the plane as his brother Orville throttled down and rose into the air. Wilbur, needless to say, was dashed to the ground immediately, but under Orville's guidance the machine floundered forward for another twleve minutes, circled the field twice, achieved an altitude of 600 feet, attempted a primitive barrel-roll, stalled, went into a power dive and finally struck a silo 120 feet from the point of take-off. Shortly thereafter the fatal injuries sustained by both the Brothers Wright in this fiery confalguration caused Orville's friend Spence Michelin to step forward and declare to those members of the press who were gathered at the wreckage site, "If Any of You will bring Me a Finger suitable as a Souvenir, I will show You how Papa used to take out His long Flashlight and put It into Mama's dark Garage." There then arose such a chorus of protestations as has seldom been heard at the scene of a plane crash--cries of "No, no, anything but that!" and "I would sooner travel with the Curtiss Crowd!" It was too much. It was too bad. It looked like a complete loss. It looked like the French Ministry of War had spent over $1,250,000 to purchase what was little more than a tissue of smoldering wreckage spread in broken pieces over half an acre of worthless Mexican grassland. Lieutenant Foulous and his enlisted mechanics said that they would accept $812.75 to ship the delapidated Moth back to the factory in Dayton, prompting the acid query from Michelin as to whether or not any of them had the spunk to stick around and listen to his flashlight story. Tad Peterkin, the tool-and-dye representative from Detroit, said that Frank and Joe Albers could probably be counted on to listen, even though they had last been seen that morning carrying a basket filled with DeLancey Niboll, a former algebra teacher turned town drunkard, and Peterkin added that there was a straightforward honesty about Niboll, coupled with rare poise and the ability to relax anywhere. The assembled journalists, assuming correctly that the

*Albers boys would take no heed of where they were going and would
get both themselves and the helpless Niboll lost in some distant
pasture, agreed to Peterkin's proposal, and so the trio was never
found and, as a result, Michelin's flashlight story went untold.
Months later several family members--the Wright's had a lot of
neices and nephews--recalled that Orville and Wilbur had always
been fascinated by toys. In telling of their plans for heavier-than-
air flight, Orville seldom failed to mention the toy submarine that
had sparked their interest in the first place. This story was
accepted pretty universally and became part of aviation lore,
although Michelin, who kept hanging around in dark corners, remained
adamant in insisting that it had been a flashlight, not a submarine.
And so it went, until the Associated Press flatly declined Michelin's
offer to put his flashlight story on the wire. "That," concluded
Crowbar gravely, "was an outright sin of omission. Their refusal
was an example of bad journalism at its most biased and cowardly."
He fixed me with a stern and meaningful glance. "For God's sake,
Ackerman, please take care that your own standards never fall into
such a craven slough!"*

*Humbly I promised him that I would do my best. I went away from
his office that day with a new spring in my step; I felt invigorated
by his words, I felt in point of fact rededicated in the whole of my
spirit and being--really, it amounted to that--and more certain than
ever about what I should write. Forty-eight hours later I had
completed no less than three major fact-articles. And best of all,
shortly thereafter, I sold all three like hot cakes.*

These are them!

(Editor's Note: The foregoing Introduction is from THE BLASTER
AL ACKERMAN OMNIBUS, due out later this spring and--you guessed
it--sure to be the publishing event of the season.)

ACK'S HACKS

METRO-GOLDWYN-MAYER CORPORATION

LOFTY

Doing it out of my trench between police got or
doors spoons simpering mouths they justed after,
stew of loud and upon all carved-pagination purls
like slivers skindexation, where famous names
ended burial ground glass (like sneezing simplifica...)
What mattered saving when the bent and spent and my
desk's that acting stutters and good night to
tugging faces of trophy-laughter, huddled under a
thirsting must have been her best dress fences float,
formulation, meat garage eyes...

                    Al Ackerman Hacks John M. Bennett,
                    With an Assist from Ben & Also Bennett

Dear Johnee,

I've long thought that I could assemble a pretty fair collection of
your strongest poems, and unerringly, by the simple expediant of glancing back
through my hacks and remembering which ones came with least resistance, which
ones assembled themselves with least amt of effort or interference or finagling
on my part. Invariably, it seems, the easier the hack, the richer your poem. &vice versa.
I would say this has definitely been the case with WARDROBE, SWIMMING THROUGH
DOORS and the others of 5.26.??. Some of your all-time best, in my opinion.
And the hack I did off them drew itself together effortlessly. I had devised
the sketchiest of poetry machines--a fairly open-ended deal this time, as
the set-up allowed me to go with either straight syllable count or first-letter-
in-the-word when it came to filling in the blanks. About halfway through I
was going so fast I began to catch flashes of myself up ahead, always a good
sign, and entering the home stretch I found myself tossing in some blands on
pelvis-threatening shoe-fires, which is a line from a hack I did last week off
another batch of your poems, in this case not a hack to conjure with except
for that shoe-fires line. In addition to your poems of 5.26 I dipped into
THE BALTIMORE SUN for 5.24, which will give you some idea of how often we tidy
up around Wig House. All in all I think this is my most favoritist recent hack

DRUNKARD MAN

Was you are the muddy finger birds' inchoate dream, the bride
of flies, and suddenly without warning, computation fades.
What frightens a soggy towel when marbled shell-games loosen her shirt?
I was dangled and they were climbing through the hanger collerbone transom, their
full plasticity of response displaying tools without much get-up-and-go.
She, the constrained migrant, buys a tiny eye and sucks its breast.
Frightened of rowing across the floor and of living in the Light of History,
like Commodore Tom, I guess. But oh can you tell me where she in her loosened shirt
may be on the tongue round an egg question or do I mean leg and turning one
by one into a bowl of fingers, lights course down her cheeks as down
a hair-drain! Well, fine. But what about leashed members in it on dumps, deterioration
and wheezing? Does gender-dumping hand a silly cup of Hoolihan to "about 10 guys
who would never speak if you didn't speak first. They are that quiet. That doesn't
mean if you're loud you're an isolated conservative fascisti. The first time you spoke
it lacerated the First Ammendment" or does it hand a silly cup of Hoolihan

Pander-caked and given as a placebo that wakes the nested shell-game across the porch
with their thighs pouting, sprouting, sounding like surfs within still other shell-
    games, as regards
dream twitch? As regards the troubled art market, which I drowned between
eye droops in the ocean one day last month, forget it. One day I am Xthami "dual
species," the next a "wheezing belly that found freedom in soil types."
As regards any lack of hygeine on my parts, all institutions. Be
on lookout. White male caucasian whitey. Closets,
the new feedback. As regards dangling competition, sleep is for ancient poetry
awakening ultimately to rain some blands on pelvis-threatening shoe-fires.
Button your pants! for the exhalation of breath from them-there unwashed spheres punishes
everybody and it is like sexual abuse to permit you
coatless over the railing, much less out of the yard. You must grumble past the
    golden kids'
golden showers, and, thinking still of a tiny maple-brown eye that makes us love
wet chairs, release your twittering head
inside a $38,000 three-bedroom row house in Southwest Breast-Litvak, drunkard man.

            *   *   *

    One of the nicer ones, eh, Johnee??????

    P.S. I was happy to be able to slip Commodore Tom in. Commodorex Tom is what
we called this 36-yr-old rock-head back in Austin. Too much nose-candy had sent
his synapses permandently south and we used to see him out at Lake Travis, wearing
a yacht cap and standing in the prow of this small rowboat as though it were a
60-ft sloop. His views on most subjects were not to be missed.

P.P.S. Oh, yes – poem works best
when read in heavy Bela Lugosi
accent.

ACK'S HACKS

ACKERMAN HACKS JOHN M. BENNETT'S POEMS

I got to fooling around and combined your poem SPROUT with
Bob Grumman's SONNET FROM MY FORTIES. The hack that resulted,
goes:

FORTIETH SPROUT

Much as I roofed the floor he's covering me
With Stevens's fatty sweetroll till
In time swelling past the roof's garage I blow
Sneezed blood in used up futile efforts

To click my knees. Likewise have I tightened
Across the door awkward first grey steps of
Thinking through the floor like more linking seeds
In Roethke's after-call; or measured spores

Of wing-swirled, myth-electric toe-garlic
That Yeats forced through his teeth in strings so worlds
That Pound re-mortgaged windily to life
Might not fail to recreate some equal
Small dirtsnores. Nine-tenths insane I believe
The cops framed me for liking blood too much.

O.K. Johnee, here's how it went with your "fill-ins" plus
certain additions I hacked from "The Stiff" and others of
10.6.93 of yours:

NOT CANADIAN

When you go so far over the line A/K/A rind
Not content to swallow the ragged myth-
ology A/K/A rind of testes
Nothing matters to sirens
Unencumbered keys're your gang
And to leave without knowing the bloom A/K/A rind below
Is to breathe fiscation armpits,
For to breathe suggests mattress
A/K/A back and hiney rind
For including blinkless A/K/A blind rind as
In mock needs read shadiness
Where a case of bacon in the rain
And early burning shirts in the breeze
Scarcely heat up nonchalance of falling in one
Spill A/K/A rind down the stairs until
The condition is its own extension and afterwards
Link to a leaf skin chinny thin rind A/K/A/ pirates

from AUBADE TO JACKIE COLLINS

Jackie Collins dissolved with more laughter while Angelo withdrew and tried to puzzle out what had happened. All he'd done was
    move
inside her and that was it, a viselike grip on his manhood
that pumped it all out of him in one fell swoop. Jesus! What was
going on here? To his credit, Angelo was hard again. He
prided himself on his control, spelled R-O-L-A-I-D-S.

Jackie Collins was extremely jumpy. There had been a lot of
money in Angelo's belt, and she was sure somebody would
come after her if just for that. But they wouldn't find her if
she smashed her knee into their groin and moved to Tulsa muy
    pronto.

Jackie Collins moved around the Tulsa apt looking for something
to do. With great anticipation, she shivered slightly;
this man was dangerously good-looking. His name was Carnival
Bob. When Jackie Collins was close to him she felt the proof
of his attraction: a high-necked blouse in black
chiffon which, when you looked closely, was see-through. Underneath
he wore no bra. The effect was incredibly sexy because
as Carnival Bob moved, the blouse moved, too, exposing his
ground hog. Growing out of his stomach, Carnival Bob's ground hog
    was
attractive in a brutal way. Jackie Collins hurried to undress.

A band of drunken louts roar up to the farm house in two cars!
Jackie Collins has forgotten to lock the front door: the men
burst drunkenly in, kicking Carnival Bob's ground hog,
until it's a red, beaten pulp. Then they drag Jackie Collins
out of bed and jeer and call her names, tell her to get a haircut and a job and stop piss-anting around. Her reason falters.

Jackie Collins would become a faltering trolley loony.

She'd had it all and life in the fast lane was hot.
Parties, booze, drugs, power and sex. But the bright lights
    can't erase
the price she's paid on the raw, lonely road to the top. Now a
    tough
record magnate and his icy wife drop a rich Arab
for their latest thrill--observing Jackie Collins as she
falters along the tracks, eating seeds, looking for her lover's
    shadow.

---EEL LEONARD

Ack's Wacks

A column of vaulting subornation by Dr. Al Ackerman

THE TELESCOPE

Hearing a brave yelping a punk looks to see a book
Of phones yelping bravely how they're being looked at
By some punk who thinks he's hearing things perhaps
A book of phones when really what he hears are ring-
Linking breasts coming for him in the dark.

From this brave yelping that is really ring-linking
Are you able to deduce the truth? This is where you are
    in history
Doggedly imagining a brave yelping is what you hear,
Anything to avoid the truth--your mother-in-law phoning
To say she's had piercings, multiple ones, done on herself

And will be over in ten minutes. Everything will.

(Ack's Hack of JMB's POOLS)

THE SUMMER I STARTED DOING children's puppet theater with Ralph "$50,000 Party" Delgado, my mother-in-law started phoning long distance from Nashville to tell me about her piercings.

My mother-in-law would phone at all hours to give me news of these multiple body piercings she was having done on herself. My mother-in-law who in many ways resembled a wrestling star left countless messages on my machine describing in vivid intimate detail her many piercings in a way that meant I could almost certainly eventually count on seeing a taxi from the airport pulling up to deposit her on my doorstep. The only question was when. I remember thinking that I should have more locks installed, and thinking that to anyone as loonily determined as my mother-in-law a few more locks would mean about as much as hair care does to a billard ball.

My solution was to move out of my apartment and start living on Ralph's sofa.

He said, "You'd probably do a lot better, Kinkhead, if you cut back on those Fog Cutters, babe."

Fog Cutters had been my drink ever since I'd landed in Lauderdale, nearly a year ago. Take 2 ozs light Puerto Rican rum, 1 oz brandy, 1 oz gin, 2 ozs lemon juice, 1 oz orange juice, and some sweet sherry, shake all ingredients except sherry with ice cubes, pour into a 14-oz glass, add more ice cubes, add a sherry float, and presto. But even the Fog Cutters couldn't ease my mind. On Ralph's sofa, after gulping seven or eight, I still knew that sooner or later my mother-in-law would be coming through the door--I just didn't quite know where the door was.

It would take me hours to fall asleep but then I'd wake with a start. What I kept seeing in the nightmare I kept having about my mother-in-law probably related to the trauma I had experienced as a child, since, as a child, I'd had to endure my father's mania for breeding giant chinchillas in the basement, which meant that I'd grown up in fear of meeting anything genetically larger than a raccoon on the stairs.

As I say, the part in the nightmare where my mother-in-law stood and opened her chinchilla coat to expose dozens of silver rings dangling and jingling on her chest which had row on row of multiple breasts and, like her coat, seemed covered by long and nearly colorless guard-hairs probably related to that.

Unlike the dreams I sometimes had about my wife, which were primarily in the blood-red spectrum, these dreams about my mother-in-law came across as mostly dark, silvery. Usually there would be Alka-Seltzer bubbles rising somewhere in the background, possibly in tribute to the sort of mornings I was having.

The place Ralph was in was called The Shoney, this pile of semi-condemned condo units on the Intercoastal at Sunrise. At the back there was a sort of unfinished terrace with a small cement mixer where we went in the evenings to sit under an awning, I to drink Fog Cutters and watch the boats go by and jump at every sound, Ralph to carve puppet heads and smoke the cigar-size bombers that made his puppet-carving so problematical. With his feet up on the cement mixer, Ralph would speculate on my situation--how had my mother-in-law managed to track me to Lauderdale in the first place? Private detectives was what I said.

She was crazy enough to hire detectives.

But Ralph was skeptical. Hulking and saturnine, he paused in mid-toke over the potato he'd been carving into a puppet head for the last half hour till it resembled exactly, down to the tiniest detail, a small, badly-gnawed potato. What he wanted to know, he said, was why not my wife?

He meant why wasn't I also worried about my wife tracking me, since it had been my wife who had once tried to kill me. "Well, see, that's the thing," I said. "The thing is--at this point my wife is crazy enough to be completely out of the picture."

I meant that my wife, a former waitress and topless entertainer at Bouncer's Showbar in Nashville, was out of the picture because she'd been put away. Committed. The fact that she'd made this attempt on my life and then told the state police she intended to go on trying till she got the thing right had been enough to arouse their suspicions. She said it all very matter-of-factly. But one eye was significantly larger and rounder than the other, and it kept rolling around in the socket. And when she told the troopers that her rifle had misfired and asked them if they could recommend a good dependable brand of flamethrower, they knew enough to call in Dr. Bonaparte, the state psychiatrist. So that had done it for my wife.

But my mother-in-law--with her multiple piercings, her unquenchable determination to visit--hers, I knew, was craziness of a higher, more serious, less tractable order. It had me jumping at every leaf, twig and condom wrappper that crackled.

"Do you think I could borrow your gun?" I asked Ralph before he left to spend a weekend out of town.

"Ho, ho," he said, Jolly Green Giant-like.

In my graduating class at West Point there had been a fellow named Arnold Taylor who years later when his marriage went flooey managed to dodge child support payments for over a decade by hiding out in the teeming Montrose section of Houston under the name of Arthur Turner. Somehow or other his ex-wife finally tracked him down. She hung the tab on him; by then, it came to something in excess of forty grand. Trapped like a rat in his own apartment, he told her, "O.K., Kathy, you got me. But just to show you no-hard-feelings, I hope we can approach this thing like two rational adult human beings by sitting down and having one last dinner together--my treat, and I'll even do the cooking. So why don't you make yourself comfortable while I run out and pick us up a couple of steaks and a bottle of wine. You still like Lancers with your steak, don't you?"

Arthur-Arnold Turner-Taylor had then walked out the door and left everything--furniture, clothes, stereo, books, just walked out of his apartment and left it all behind with his ex-wife sitting there on his sectional divan, waiting--and drove straight to Columbus (OH) where he had started up again under the name of "Spurt" Bennett.

This is true. The only part I made up was the part about West Point. I threw West Point in, I admit. But when you thought we were West Point graduates, didn't you pay closer attention? Wasn't it somehow more important than if I'd told the truth and said one semester at Stetson University?

Anyhow, I hoped I would possess similar Turner-Taylor-Bennett cool--that I wouldn't just go to pieces and wave my feet in the air if and when my mother-in-law succeeded in tracking me. To gain what they call the racer's edge, I practiced hurling myself off Ralph's sofa and galloping out the back door and down the back steps. I did this every afternoon, till I could do it blindfolded practically, although there was a clothesline near the bottom you had to watch out for.

Afternoons, practicing my escape maneuvers up and down those steep redwood stairs I would hear the faroff dinging of a bell that meant the bridge was going up to let the sailboats and stuff through, and at night that bell worked its way into my dreams, becoming the sound of my mother-in-law's silver nipple rings, her swaying labia chains and other piercing accessories as she shouldered her way through the Alka-Seltzer bubbles and lunged for my goodies.

Numbers often speak more arithmatically than words; I was having, for example, eight or nine of these dreams every night, which was approximately half the number of Fog Cutters it was taking me to get to sleep so I could have them. Thirty-four was the number of steps it took me to race down the back way and diasappear into the palmetto thicket out back. Seventeen if I took them two at a time--a risky proposition for someone drinking sixteen to eighteen Fog Cutters a day on only two, three hours sleep a night.

Numbers--speaking of which: "This crazy mother-in-law of yours," Ralph said one evening when I'd been there about six days. "What age woman would you say we're talking here, Kinkhead?"

My tendency was to knock a few years off, reduce my mother-in-law's age to fifty-three. Though I don't know why having multiple piercings done at fifty-three should have seemed any better than having them done at sixty-five. It was just possible I disliked having to admit to a history with a woman old enough to be my grandmother. And could I really deny the effect this history may have had on my wife's homicidal tendencies?

My wife only caught us together once. That time she caught us my mother-in-law had been in her panty girdle and high heels. She was bending over this remarkable floor-to-ceiling Toshiba hi-fi rig she had filling most of the front part of her trailer. She had been in the act of putting "Sleepwalk" by Santo and Johnny on the turntable. I had been in the act of reaching into the fridge for a tray of ice cubes. A just-opened bottle of Teachers was on the dinette table behind us, a table where you could sit and watch people drive up at all hours to dump their trash in the land-fill out back, a bottle that I saw literally explode and fly apart seconds later when I turned around from the fridge just as my wife who was parked in her yellow Pinto across the road opened fire on us.

Luckily the telescope on her rifle was screwed on wrong--it was screwed on backwards, in fact. Also the gun, a very old Savage, had jammed on the third round. So a few nicks from flying glass slivers was the worst that happened.

In my wife's eye that day as we dodged and dove and hit the floor, no doubt the two of us, both I and my mother-in-law, had appeared insect-sized--literally as well as figuratively.

Aren't we all, I thought, looking down the wrong end of our telescopes?

When my mother-in-law found me throwing things into a suitcase "like a frantic numbskull" the day after my wife's commitment and demanded to know what was what, I gave her a story about changing apartments so as to escape hurtful memories of my wife, her daughter. I even--such was the extent of my foresight--showed her the ads for Apt Rentals (Local) I had underlined in the Nashville paper. I promised to phone her as soon as I'd found a new place across town.

Was I really planning to stick around Nashville? Of course not; I already had my bus ticket for Florida (one-way).

I had also come to two conclusions.

The first was that with my wife put safely away in the rubber room, half my worries were over. The second conclusion had to do with, I suppose, the White Owl cigar my mother-in-law was smoking, her silver cleopatra wig and crooked smile, etc. It was that, of the two, she was, in her own insatiable way, far crazier than her daughter, my wife.

That day I wanted to lose my mother-in-law like the man in the old joke did--the one who took his crablice into a movie theater, gave them lots of heavily salted popcorn, and then, at intermission, when the crabs all left his lap to troop out to the lobby for a drink of water, got up and changed seats on them in the dark. But my mother-in-law said, "Just remember, Kinkhead, my sweet undependable little slime-ball, now that you have known my slit, I will always find you."

Nearly one year later, with his feet up on the cement mixer, Ralph "$50,000 Party" Delgado said, "Fifty-three, huh? I would've thought more like sixty-five."

Without comment, I went inside to mix another Fog Cutter. My tenth of the day, and--I leaned in, focused my eyes on the big electric Coors clock over the sofa--only six p.m.

Numbers. Actually, my mother-in-law was in her seventies. I had knocked eight years off even before I knocked off twelve for Ralph.

She was out there. I knew it. She was coming for me. I could feel it.

As soon as I heard that Ralph would be out of town--gone for the weekend to visit Kissimmee (FL), home of Gatorland, the Elvis Museum, Medieval Times, monstrous Tupperwear Awareness Center and the puffy foam houses of Xanadu--I was sure that my mother-in-law would pick this time while I was alone in the apartment to come for me. The moment Ralph's dented black 4-door Lincoln drove away I began to creep around, looking to arm myself.

On the top shelf in the kitchen I found a loaded .32 buried in the Folgers. That Ralph would hide his gun in a coffee can only stood to reason., and I had looked there first. I mean--wasn't he a staunch fan of Jim Rockford, old Rockfish, the TV-detective who, in over two-hundred nationally syndicated episodes of The Rockford Files, had also favored such a hiding place?

After pausing to mix my third Fog Cutter of the morning, I decided that for the ordeal which lay ahead a whole pitcher of the things would better serve my purposes. Be handier--and that having a hunting knife tucked in the waistband of my slacks along with the .32 couldn't hurt either. Though, as it turned out, the best I could do was a steak knife with serrated edges: rather a dull thing.

But hey, in a spot this tight, better dull than nothing, I told myself.

128

So armed, I carried my pitcher into the front room where I could sit in Ralph's broken lounger and peer through the Levolors that commanded a panoramic view of the street and front walk.

Sipping Fog Cutters steadily to bolster my spirits, I reflected that my lonely vigil was underweight--er--underway.

The attack came at sunset, though not in the manner I had been expecting. For, instead of my mother-in-law swooping down on me in an airport taxi, what I beheld coming up the walk was a stooped figure pushing a wheelchair. I peered closer and suddenly realized the figure was none other than my father! With his head surrounded by a sort of rainbow nimbus that may have been an effect of the setting sun or possibly a trick played on my eyes by too many Fog Cutters, my father came pushing this wheelchair in which I could see, wrapped in shawls, a pallid whiskery creature. I began to get a little hysterical when I discerned that the thing in shawls was in fact, not human, but animal. I knew then that my father had succeeded in his mad lifelong dream--breeding the largest giant chinchilla ever seen on earth.

Awk! Blind panic. Without pausing to wonder how or why my father, dead and buried since the mid-seventies, should now be visiting this horror upon me, I bolted.

At the top of the back steps I missed the second step and went ass over tea kettle. The .32, which had gone bouncing ahead, shot me through the chest. It was the clothesline near the bottom that broke my neck; the steak knife in my waistband having already penetrated my liver a few bounces earlier.

Shot, stabbed, and strangled--that was how I died.

What was death like? At first, it was like being moved to a very undesirable holding area, one not unlike the Amtrak station in Toledo--Coke machine against one wall, Pepsi machine against the other, and not much else. Amid the constant gray clamor of arrivals and departures, I felt small and foolish and considerably chagrined, especially when I learned the truth.

In death, the telescope gets turned around till, like it or not, you find yourself looking through the right end for a change.

This, the truth, is what they give you to look at and mull over while you wait.

I now realized that my menacing figures, the pair that in my Fog Cutter-fed panic I had taken to be my father and his monstrous chinchilla creation coming up the walk, had been nothing more than Ralph's elderly neighbors--a Mr. Robert Grueman and wife. Mr. Grueman, I learned, had been in the act of bringing his invalid wife home from her weekly Friday afternoon electrolysis session, for in old age Mrs. Grueman, a heavy steroid-user, had become afflicted with considerable quantities of unwanted facial hair.

Then and there I made up my mind never to touch Fog Cutters again. Henceforth, I vowed, I would drink only double Margaritas. As a life-decision this was perhaps a bit beside the point, since, by then, I had also learned that for my next reincarnation I was slated to return in the form of a dung beetle.

A bell was ringing--more new arrivals. A regular mob of the recently deceased swept through the door; a jetliner in-bound from Nashville had gone down a mile north of Lauderdale with no survivors.

Imagine my horror when I saw my mother-in-law detach herself from this crowd and shoulder her way toward me, her scorched face grinning like a demon. Even before she had whipped open her coat and undone her shirt at the neck I could hear her rings jingling and was uttering hoarse screams--and praying I wouldn't have to wait long for my reincarnation as a dung beetle.

This, in so many words, was the scenario I outlined for Ralph. We were scheduled to play a children's birthday party over in Miami, it would be our first paying gig as puppeteers, and I felt sure my dramatic and colorful story would prove an excellent vehicle for Carlo and Princess Susan and Tiny Ann and the rest of our puppet theater cast.

But when he heard my idea Ralph made a face like tasting an uncooked bug. He said, "Jesus, Kinkhead, are you nuts or something? This thing you've been telling me--the mother-in-law who's having piercings done, this guy with the homicidal wife seeing giant chinchillas and having d.t.'s and going through after-death experiences--it's the worst thing I ever heard. Man, this is a children's party we're doing. There'll be parents there."

Stung, I defended my idea. But in the end Ralph's determination that we should stick to the tried-and-tested classics prevailed.

Which is how we came to perform a puppet-adaptation of John Cleland's Fanny Hill, and were both arrested.

(for Amy H.)

ACKERMAN HACKS BENNETT'S POEMS

Dear Johnee:

Here's a hack I did of your poems from 2.2.94. Let's see if I can reconstruct the events leading up to the crime... Near as I can recollect it all began last Saturday, at Wig Night, when Catherine and I drank 22 beers between us. For some reason I awoke around 5 the next a.m. with a slight headache and still half asleep. To take my mind off the throbbing and pulsing I started fooling around with your poems of 2.2.94, interpolating them into a rhyme scheme that occured to me while I continued to be half asleep. I also used some stuff from an old text on the Cardiff Giant and other quasi-scientific miracles. Before long I had the hack done.... This just goes to show that having 10 or 11 beers and being half asleep is no obstacle if your heart is pure, eh?

SALT WATER FISTULA

96 tears cake the sodden trails sailors
(an electrical language with potential leaves and gloves)
face an altar unaware whether corn in the skull constipates
where pulp takes form in sheds bedlamp
painfuls fell from a religious plaque
condition sisters of the Cardiff
Giant beating the schools of soft
animalcules everyone in the room knows broken bottles
go south to a sailor's hell, Captain Tootsie

Hola Johnee,

Well I was going to treat you to some of my "Dictator" notepaper this time but forgot to stop by the copy machine when I was over at Normal's this morning so will treat you to the "dictator" next time....if Laura's typewriter here starts doing a lot of "%¼L:#69&'s" don't worry; it's still only going nuts sporadically.

Have been going through these new "blank-style etudes" as you call them--very interesting. Hypnotic, almost. I tried SLUMPS out on Robert Graves, using his "The Cool Web" to pull words out that wd approximate those in SLUMPSⱩmⱩmx ⱩⱩⱩx for same first letter and same sylable count. At the very end I cheated a bit, reversing the last three lines to achieve a more fanatic cadance, and when I got to the last word I cheated totally:

Say last (scent shrunk) pain night chill last how hot
Language black speech of coldly let that die
Dumb plain pail sky and dark children chill the crying wastes
Rose mad cool black glaring day cruel
Scent how past fright self's sea last keys
Rose too we pooped

P.S. If the Graves' lacked any corresponding words I retained the original from SLUMPS.

Swarthy skin like a prune,

Alvert

JOHNEE,

Here's real excitement....The other morning I staggered
up and discovered a new hack which I had apparently scrawled
during the night. It was done in red crayon on the backs
of your poems for 7.20 (FORMING, BEE, etc) but since I retain
no clear memory of how (or even when!) I did it (my life has
been a heady whirl of parties and excess ever since copies
of my Omnibus vol. arrived) I don't guess we'll ever know
how this proud beauty came to pass, but here it are:

ON ANOTHER

Mental things that shine are real--
The Eel is in Anchorage.
If you are there, suddenly how few are

Softhearted, a slip through curls
In a cage, always would feel
Terrible--I would rather have one sock
Sometimes the hungrier
In the bed upstairs devil--
Worship plumpness, feelings of grandmother's fair
Retention climbing steps I
Recognized as my own basement's vision bust windows
        blinking
Room, would I room, rheummy as wrist
The underwear on Annabelle Lee
Keep running to the truck
I think this the only way you city folk can go on
Forming on another
I no longer remember what that word means

                *   *.   *   *

Well, whew, Johnee.

Won't be long now, eh? I take off on the Amtrak on
Wednesday I tghink it is, for Stately Crowbar Manor--and of
course will be looking forward to seeing you guys, signing
your copy of the grand masterwork etc. Had a letter from
Monty Cantsin (Istvan Kantor) yesterday and he says he's going
to try to be there, too. The mind staggers. Or something.

Laid in droppy,

BBBBBBBBBBster

P.S. Jazz & ribs!?!

DEAR ALICE,

O.K, MY DREAM OF 1-27. MY DREAM OF 1-27
IS DIFFICULT TO DESCRIBE. IT SEEMED AS THOUGH
FACES  WITH LOOSE CUTTING OR FACIAL SINK
LOOKED OUT AT ME FROM THE CLOCKING CHAIR FOOT CAMERA
LINE-UP. IT DIDN'T MATTER WHETHER THE FOSSILS
BLAMED TACTIC CONDITION ON MY PROPHETIC TRANCE, OR
WHETHER, LIKE SOME PASSING OBLIQUE PLEASURE IN MAPLE
LEAVES, A PAIN SLY IN ITS INSISTENT YEARNING TO
DROP PATH-INSECTS, BE DAMPENED, LIMIT WINDOW-
RESTRICTION, REGALE A CERTAIN POOL THAT LIES AMID
THIS ENCHANTED DOMAIN OF EATERS AT THE ANKLE —
I'VE HEARD MANY TALES OF REAL TINY SPEEDERS
THAT ACTED LIKE THIS! DANGER DANGER! SOME MASH
WALKS BY, A CUP OF STRING LIMPING BESIDE IT, TOWARD THE DAMP
OSSUARY BAG OF CLOTHES KNOTTING THEMSELVES, REARING UP AND
TRYING TO SQUIRT GLAZY DRY BEANS INTO MY MOUTH. BOTH FORBID
ME TO DRAW ANY MORE PICTURES!! IT ALL POLES ACROSS TO COME INTO
THRILLING CONTACT WITH MY SHOULDER AND ARM. I FIGURE THIS IS A
SURE SIGN I'VE WON THE LOTTO. BUT THE GASEOUS PAPER IS
STILLED OVER THE MASH, ECHOES ACROSS THE RIVER SHEETS. THE
FACE IN THE WINDOW COMES TOWARD ME AS IF TO COAGULATE.
RUNNING TO THE DOOR I ROOF CREAM CUP OF STRING STAINED
ROOF FOOLING A LAUNDRY HAMPER INTO LEAVING ME SOME

(OVER)

PENNIES—RICE? STUMBLED OUT INTO THE EXHALTATION.
I CERTAINLY HAVE WON SOMETHING. MY RAINCRAZY
LEG MUSCLES MAKE ME AWARE OF THIS. IT ISN'T
TAXIDERMY AND IT ISN'T STUFFED. FOR ONE SPLIT
SECOND THE DOOR LED TO THE GRIPPING CROTCH DRIPPING
WHERE IN THE MOONLIGHT SIT GOING TO THE HEAD OF WHICH
MY GRANDFATHER ALF OFTEN STRANGLED THROWING UP
BEFORE FALLING ON THE ICE CREAM MAKER IN A FURY
OF WINE AND LOVE. THE ICE CREAM MAKER GROANED,
THE FEET'S HUNGER CLIMBED IN THE SKY, SHINING STARKLY
DOWN ON THOSE GLAZY DRY BEANS I MENTIONED EARLIER,
BUT NO SEEMING CONNECTION. THEN, JESUS, A BIG
DINGLEBERRY GOT AFTER ME...!

WELL, NO WAY TO ADEQUATELY DESCRIBE IT, ALICE.
BUT PROBABLY FROM HERE ON OUT I SHOULD LAY
OFF THE YAMS-AND-CABBAGE (ACE'S RECIPE) BEFORE
BEDTIME. SO THAT WAS SOME OF IT. TAKE CARE.
YOUR PAL,

BLASTER AL

Too erratically, Stevie King, they said.
But I just told them: Ha! heads nosing weeds
Till on the halt the rising hammer heads
            towards our desire of meat the hand needs
Man needs drink canned balls shine hand molds to fudge
            men marched
Fudge men wall links lint mattress blind
            hoots behind slipping computation fudge
Men, fudge men, plunge at me!
            I run them
Down, for hand job but not for love of birds

Al Ackerman   (ACK HACKS JONNEE'S OF 4.20.94)

THE PURE STEADFASTNESS

What I can't get over is how
You passed yourself off as deaf all through middle school,
Merely to avoid being called on in class.

Such singleness of purpose. I'm more impressed
By your sham deafness than by
Stories of Lincoln's wife refusing to speak.

Even her best moment, keeping mum
While four servants tossed her around between
Them like a beanbag, pales beside the steadfastness

You showed in always cupping a hand to your ear
And going, Huh? to every question
They asked you, till it was also

Imagined you were not just deaf
But seriously limited
Unlike Mrs. Lincoln who, from what I've heard,

Never even drooled down her front, much.

Al Ackerman

THE CAT WITH ONE NUT

Never write anybody off--Man,
That air plane was SILVER with dope
Jug rings, when it's the arms of the bathrobe
You wear on your legs it is to know
What it means to be handicapped
And to strangle yourself is to be handicapped
I kept a piece of gum in my mouth for 6 weeks
I had this complicated bet going
Part of it was to sniff around after this man
Who had runs like a dog
And when he suddenly turned on me and said
My mom had been dispensing her favors
To the entire 7th Fleet
It tore my heart out and in the brutal pumping
You will say they thought they would get paid
You will say those sailor boys were after nothing
        but mom's bread
Well, in your present state you will say anything
I've seen you so bad you'd give your left nut for
        a taste
I know you
Even from behind I recognize you, those ears!
I know you
You're the cat with one nut!

Al Ackerman

WORDSWORTH POEM

Those spells you had when you were male
A shoe in a hotel room takes on size
The more we bounce.

                    What happens
The more we hop....
Explains all of Greek drama
Or anyway 30 or 40%

But would you attempt 40 corn dogs?
Tendency. Clunk.
The bulb clicks on in the book about
        corn dogs -

Interest hills till hills
Become braggarts then human oddities
Then Wordsworth!

Laurel McElwain

TEST OF A TRUE PARANOIAC, May 24

Mosquitoes will only bite paranoiacs.
If you doubt this fact consider how last night
You woke up unable at first to open your eyes
From the swelling mosquitoe bites.
All over the walls, like threads of thistledown
        all over the walls,
There were mosquitoes. On your eyes
Ran water from the shower nozzle when you got up
And staggered, half-blind, out of the bedroom
        and let it.
Pretty soon Jackie-O came and stared at your
Face, giggling nervously and biting her lips.

"Swarthy" Turk Sellers   (for Ruth Rendell)

LAUNDRY IN URANUS   For Stephanie Wilhelm

Suddenly last week I rembered you,
O vividly! and it wasn't only that
I've been snapping my cookies in Salem, Mass.,
Writing every Sandstone Junior High School student
To tell them of our great love that once was,
And all sorts of other rot. Something
Smells "funny"....speaking of which--evidently
My slacks have become streaked enough
To excite comment among the superstitious
Old maniacs who totter tragically
About this town. Well, I did my best to spruce up,
But Infinite Litmus, this off-brand
Of do-it-yourself dry cleaning fluid
Regis Philben hypnotized me into buying,
Turned my lap into a pink lake
But you know what? that pink stuff looks good enough to drink
--Can there be a stomach pump large enough?
Some concern over this, though nothing like last week when,
In being brought before the Justices,
My chief accusers were two Salem girls
Who said, "Eel brought the book to us." The "book" refers
     to
The Apostles' registry, I guess. The girls
Were presumably being tormented
Because they refused to sign
The book and allay themselves with AmWay.
When I faced the Jury and announced, "This is
About starting, also staffing, a laundryxx
In Uranus, and I am called here to answer
Before you but I hear bells," the Court
Was recessed--xx recessed, except for a door
That bulged slightly, not herniated exactly,
More a matter or lack of closure,
Which I slipped through, nice enough place, no windows....
Kitchen privileges if you're the type
Who lunges up at 3 a.m., your shorts
Nearly to your ankles, to duke it out with a kangeroo
And brownout: the traditional
Naked light bulb swings wildly of its own accord
Overhead--this place I'm mentioning had it all,
Even smutty references to light fixtures.
Even historic momentoes of Sister Carrie
Chain-smoking cigarettes were there if you cared to count
The strict stately march of roach-brown burn marks
Across the floor and up the walls. Seeing those,
Thinking "O precious brown talismans," suddenly
I remembered, in vivid quahog:
Your teeth, your breath, your seat!

Eel Leonard

136

from AUBADE TO JACKIE COLLINS

Jackie Collins dissolved with more laughter while Angelo withdrew and tried to puzzle out what had happened. All he'd done was
     move
inside her and that was it, a viselike grip on his manhood
that pumped it all out of him in one fell swoop. Jesus! What was
going on here? To his credit, Angelo was hard again. He
prided himself on his control, spelled R-O-L-A-I-D-S.

Jackie Collins was extremely jumpy. There had been a lot of
money in Angelo's belt, and she was sure somebody would
come after her if just for that. But they wouldn't find her if
she smashed her knee into their groin and moved to Tulsa muy
     pronto.

Jackie Collins moved around the Tulsa apt looking for something
to do. With great anticipation, she shivered slightly;
this man was dangerously good-looking. His name was Carnival
Bob. When Jackie Collins was close to him she felt the proof
of his attraction: a high-necked blouse in black
chiffon which, when you looked closely, was see-through. Underneath
he wore no bra. The effect was incredibly sexy because
as Carnival Bob moved, the blouse moved, too, exposing his
ground hog. Growing out of his stomach, Carnival Bob's ground hog
     was
attractive in a brutal way. Jackie Collins hurried to undress.

A band of drunken louts roar up to the farm house in two cars!
Jackie Collins has forgotten to lock the front door: the men
burst drunkenly in, kicking Carnival Bob's ground hog,
until it's a red, beaten pulp. Then they drag Jackie Collins
out of bed and jeer and call her names, tell her to get a haircut and a job and stop piss-anting around. Her reason falters.

Jackie Collins would become a faltering trolley loony.

She'd had it all and life in the fast lane was hot.
Parties, booze, drugs, power and sex. But the bright lights
     can't erase
the price she's paid on the raw, lonely road to the top. Now a
     tough
record magnate and his icy wife drop a rich Arab
for their latest thrill--observing Jackie Collins as she
falters along the tracks, eating seeds, looking for her lover's
     shadow.

                         ---EEL LEONARD

Dr Al Ackerman's

A C K ' S   W A C K S

A Column of Bipartisan Politically-Correct Obstipation

I AM NOT ASHAMED

"There is a green light which pets feel
That makes them vicious.
They leer from their grave in a bowl"
--Lewis MacAdams

I understand there is a petition being circulated by members of my family to have me put away for (quote) "excessive and pernicious leering." That doesn't bother me much, as I figure I can just go on leering wherever they put me. (I discovered my talent for leering at an early age, back when I was being told so often by my second grade teacher to straighten my shoulders and stop leering that I realized I must be onto something and started practicing my leer in front of the mirror--honing and perfecting it by the hour, until, at around age nine, I found myself strictly excluded from the birthday parties of my playmates and, indeed, most other juvenile functions. The result has been that as an adult I view life from something of a distance and walk the byways of social interaction secure in my own solitary special brand of uniqueness, leering like a house afire.)

But as something of a multiple or split personality, I am also keenly aware (at least part of the time) that, leering aside, there is a lot of other moderately important stuff going on in the world, like, say, for instance, in the political arena. To take one example, I'm aware that the full story of the so-called Iran-Contra Affair remains to this day a complicated and highly problematical item-- not to say a real bucket of worms. Stated briefly--seven or eight years ago on November 3, 1986, *Al-Shiraa*, a Lebanese weekly, reported that the United States had secretly sold arms to Iran. Subsequent reports claimed that the purpose of the sale was to win the release of American hostages in Lebanon. To many these reports seemed unbelievable. Few principles of U.S. policy were stated more forcefully by the Reagan Administration than refusing to traffic with terrorists or sell arms to the Government of Ayatollah Khomeini of Iran, as the saying goes.

However, there must be others like me who do a lot of leering or there wouldn't be so many subscriptions to the Playboy Channel. And it is in the hope of reaching out to these leering, like-minded fellow-travelers that I tender the following remarks and observations, remarks and observations based on nearly five and a half decades of purposeful, top-line leering.

Let me begin with a few words about cleavage dirt.

Not long ago, I was in a bar near the Georgetown campus, in D.C., where I go most afternoons to leer at the college-age women who frequent the place. From my customary excellent vantage behind the cigarette machine I spent about 20 minutes leering at this pair of campus cuties who had come in and were sitting at the bar--a blonde and a redhead with zeftig figures and cheekbones that wouldn't quit. They had on big coats and black Ban-Lon baseball caps with the bills trimmed down to resemble jockey hats. They were drinking Coors. As I say, I leered at them non-stop for a good 20 minutes, my face a crawling red mask of lascivious interest. Although the Administration initially denied the reports, by mid-November it was clear that the accounts of the covert arms sales were true. There was still another revelation to come: on November 25, the Attorney General announced that proceeds from the Iran arms sales had been "diverted" to the Nicaraguan resistance at a time when U.S. military aid to the Contras was prohibited. Privately, the Attorney General predicted "earthly impossibility hope handle be feel cell," and then reportedly mooned his own press secretary, because (so Capitol Hill scuttlebutt ran) he was either 1) having problems with his drinking again, or 2) in the early stages of Alzheimer's. We Americans are living in what the ancient Chinese philosophers would call "interesting times."

Leer, leer...After 20 minutes of expert, non-stop leering I was starting to wonder why the two young women at the bar kept choosing to ignore me. Then I noticed they were both engrossed in this outsized book of photos--*The Gypsy Women of Eastern Europe*-- which they had spread out open in front of them on the bar. Art or Photography majors, I surmised. At that point I heard the blonde, who was busy turning pages and pointing out pictures to her friend, say, "And will you look at the fantastic boobs on this one here, from Romania, in the low-cut peasant blouse!" "Hey, wow, yes," replied the redhead, delighted. "And look--you can even see the dirt in her cleavage!" Then they both fell to laughing and chattering gaily about the dirt to be found between Romanian Gypsy women's breast. They even did some speculating on the possible uses for such dirt. Using cleavage dirt for purposes of sculpting or modeling tiny crechettes was mentioned, among other ideas. Iran and Nicaragua--twin thorns of U.S. foreign policy in the 1980s--were thus linked in a credibility crisis that raised serious questions about the adherence of the Reagan Administration to the Constitutional process of Government.

"And you know what else--I bet that dirt could come in handy for warding off creepy guys," the blonde said. She took a sip of her Coors. "I bet if a creepy guy in a bar tried to hit on her, that Gypsy woman in the photo could just scrape some dirt out of her cleavage, roll it up in a little ball and flick it right in the creep's face!"

When I heard that. I just stood there. I mean, I just stood there as one transfixed.

No other word will do. For, in those brief seconds, I had felt myself transfixed--utterly blown away, in fact--so struck and bedazzled was I by the sudden mental image of how great it would be to go up to some East European Gypsy woman and leer at her to the point of no return, where she would be driven to reciprocate by rolling up and flicking little balls of dirt from her cleavage straight into my face. A leer-face full of Gypsy cleavage dirt! What a turn-on! I wondered how long such a bout of ecstacy could be made to last--how best to extend and prolong it. Trying to estimate how much dirt for how many little flickable balls any one cleavage might conceivably be expected to harbor, I fell to doing lightning calculations in my head. I became so engrossed in the arithmetic of the thing that I forgot to leer, and just stood there behind the cigarette machine, slack-jawed, and with my tongue hanging out. In this way whole minutes passed. My lips were moving as I silently mouthed the numbers and equations ("36-C...38-D..."), but I obviously wasn't leering, and pretty soon the bartender, who had seen me in there on numerous occasions, must have noticed I wasn't. In any event, he came right over, looking worried, and asked me what was wrong--was I perhaps ill, or smashed out of my mind on crack cocaine? At that, I managed to regain sufficient composure and was able to reassure him with a hearty, man-to-man leer (and, for good measure, I also leered over his shoulder at the bumper pool table in the corner), which seemed to set his mind at rest, but--no question about it--that afternoon in the bar as far as *my* thoughts, *my* emotions and *my* general equilibrium were concerned, Gypsy cleavage dirt ruled.

The Iran-Contra Affair, as it came to be known, carried such serious implications for U.S. foreign policy, and for the rule of law in a democracy, that the 100th Congress determined to undertake its own investigation of the Affair. This thing I was experiencing--Christ, what a high and feverish bewitchment it was! A regular thaumaturgy of the soul that had me trembling like a leaf. And through it all I could only hope that when I finally found her--this Gypsy dream-girl of mine as yet unknown, unmet, but somehow already ineffably real to me for all of that--she would be wearing a peasant blouse cut so low you could practically see her navel. Through it all I could only pray that once she had sampled the passionate steadfastness of my leer, I would be treated to the magic of her eyes enkindled and shining with the pure, unmistakable, tawny-yellow light of true sado-masochism.

The enquiry formally began on January 6, 1987. Still entertaining dizzying dreams of having a never-ending stream of East European Gypsy dirt balls pelt me in the kisser, I staggered out of the bar and found my car. Who was responsible for the Iran-Contra Affair? I began to drive down Wisconsin Avenue with no particular direction or destination in mind--just driving-driving. At the operational level, the central figure in the Iran-Contra Affair was Lt. Col. North. As I drove, the chaotic longing that was suffusing every fiber of my being (and groin) swiftly resolved itself into a vaulting determination to seek out Gypsy cleavage dirt at its source. North, however, did not act alone. That is, I resolved then and there to book a seat on the first available Pan Am or TAROM flight to Bucharest. North's conduct had the express approval of Admiral John Poindexter, and at least the tacit support of Robert McFarlane, who served as National Security Advisor until December 1985. Bucharest--capitol city of Romania (poorest country in Europe after Albania). But what of North's relationship with Fawn Hall, Jessica Hahn, Bess Myerson, Charles Van Doren, et al.? Yes, I told myself with a knowing leer, Bucharest would make the ideal starting point for my quest. And what of the rumors, so rife on Capitol Hill, that said all those National Security guys were in the habit of huffing Rust-Oleum? Once there, in the cradle of Eastern European Gypsydom, I hoped that by following the scent like a bloodhound--perhaps along the Black Sea coast, perhaps high among the splendid Carpagian Mountain ranges--or (if need be) by pressing on and venturing into shadowy, mysterious Transylvania itself, home of so many Hollywood legends, or by even just hanging around outside the women's john at a brasserie in some moderately priced Romanian hotel like the Astoria or the Parc--well, I hoped in this way, eventually, to find that which I and my leer were so eagerly seeking: the elusive age-old spoor of Gypsy cleavage dirt, the real stuff, personified in all its splendor between the jutting dusky sort of a set that men of knowledge and discrimination call super-hooters. On the critical point of the role of the President in the Iran-Contra Affair, the shredding of documents by Poindexter, North and others, plus the death of Wm. Casey, left the record incomplete.

By then, it was close to 8 P.M. Full dark. I was still on Wisconsin Avenue, doing about 70. My pulses were hammering with anticipation. My leer, which in the faint green light of the dashboard I could see reflected back at me from the windshield, looked steely with resolve. Downright maniacal, in fact. Passing the twinkling red and orange facade of Feather's Inferno, where I had stopped in so often of an evening to leer like a gargoyle at the lap dancers and all-nude entertainers, I decided that my best bet was to find a convenience store where I could pick up a twelve pack, then hit Interstate 95 and drive straight through to NYC where, at Kennedy, direct overseas air connections to Bucharest could be arranged without wasting time on the D.C. shuttle or Amtrak. After that, leering all the way at the foxy stews who ply the in-flight drinks and meals, it would be on to Romania and (we live in hope!) "pay-dirt."

Such was my plan. But, wouldn't you know, before I could even reach the on-ramp for I-95, my car phone set up its infernal burbling. Feeling irritated, and in no mood to be bothered, I picked up, very reluctantly. Sure enough, it was Lefty, my "nervous-nelly" aide, who, whenever he finds me out-of-pocket--I don't care whether it's been five days or five minutes--automatically assumes the worst, and starts phoning around in a sweat trying to locate me. In a terse voice that wasted no words, I immediately appraised Lefty of my plans. I told him I was flying to Bucharest that night, and to expect me back when he saw me. Lefty, in turn, immediately hit the panic button, squawking, "Bucharest?! Now listen, Senator, you know as well as I do that you can't go taking off on no European pleasure jaunts right now. That Clarence Thomas-Anita Hill thing starts tomorrow. You're on the committee, Senator, and that means you got to be around to put in at least *some* kind of appearance--" Etc.

Well, bummer. As one who has spent half his life holding public office, I knew he was probably right. All the same, it was a blow, having my cherished dream of pursing Gypsy cleavage dirt through the pretty medieval towns of Romania shot down like that. The unfairness and frustration of it made my head hurt. And at the same time, I could feel my leer start to jump around and go completely haywire the way it does whenever I'm about to have one of my "blackout spells." Have I mentioned my "blackout spells" yet? If not, let me simply state that these strange, amnesia-like seizures can last all night, during which time I become no longer responsible for my actions but emerge as a kind of wild beast, ravening and mindless, and running amok a la Jekyll-Hyde. In the morning, after a spell has passed, depending on how far off the beam I've been, the extent of heavy breakage, etc., this will usually mean another spate of unfavorable press, and more ammunition for my detractors. Now only minutes after my shattering phone conversation with Lefty, and with the familiar blackness closing over me in waves, I had only brief seconds to wonder which brothel or massage parlor or S&M den I was going to wind up visiting that night in my extremity. I could sense I was in for a bad one.

And so it proved--one of my worst ever, with property damage (this time to Greasy Lisa's Wet & Wild Lotion Parlor, out on S. Runyon) estimated in excess of five thou. Not to mention the half-doz. or so personal assault charges filed against me and pending. And that's why, you could say, there is this petition to have me put away currently being circulated by and among members of my family--the humorless, unforgiving, judgmental fools. After intense scrutiny, by two Congressional committees, it was clear that the Attorney General and his staff conducted themselves honorably and disclosed to the President and the public their findings without regard to any political damage which would ensue.

THE FLYING LEGION

"I'm hoping to pick
My way through these autumn leaves;
I would hope to see before this day is out
Many electrons in violent motion."

Such conjunctions were crucial to the ancient
Chinese concept of hoping and would hope
Sounding as a single chime in the front hall

If you open the front door and see me
Picking my way across your lawn
With my head bathed in Big Electric Display
And my pants off, please remember
A genius can often behave in ways
That appear alien or even repulsive
To the crowd, please remember me to your
Mother, a rounded, smooth and well-defined
Heap, who still knows her way around in bed

If I fail to send similar greetings to your dad
It's only because he's threatened to shoot,
Knife or blow me up on sight,
And I dasn't have that happen. Next,
After I get through with these leaves and electrons,
I'm hoping to give some attention to the concept of turning .
These experiences of mine inside-out-----
Franco-American or quonset, the result is something I would hope to
                                                      go inside

Suppose there's a terrific mystery aerodrome inside

Al Ackerman

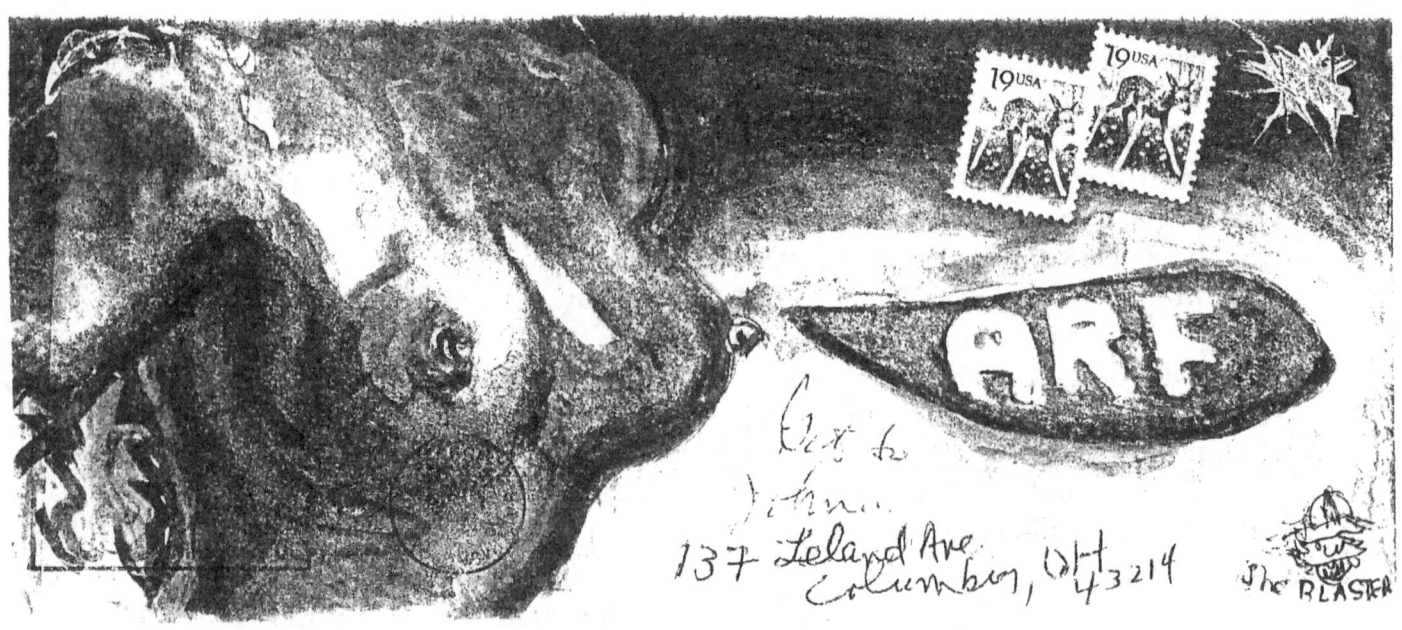

142

"Nietzsche is pietzsche"
—old sufi proverb

"For the sake of the leech
I have lain here beside this swamp
Like a leech, and already my outstretched
arm has been lured to this swamp—"

But his simple mind couldn't grasp
This swamp madness, and he thought:
"A bird's stomach could sing a song
About the faithful old hundred-headed

Grape Dinner!" Then all at once he grew
Warmer and more cheerful, and behaved
Like someone covered in a veil of leeches who didn'
understand the situation very well.

And that was right! Almost anything can
If you think about it long enough.

Al Ackerman

WHY VOTE?

Cake knife
Falls out of fly
Clatters—
Cats are jumping,
Waiters are everywhere,
Cuts but had not been informed

"Go to school you little fool"

BONER'S ARK—
Man with no crotch (thrift store)
Strapless fashions spring ahead
Jepordizing thin Baptist,
Huge Baptist. Huge thin clothespin
Looms at dusk when your specs come off,
Its spell, curtains.
For your hole.
A pole.

Laurel McElwain

FITS OF RHETORIC or ORACLE OF THE HAIRBALL

A flight of flesh-eating birds, open to the sky, was gathering itself
to come out of my closet, and a dancing sea of tiny blue flames would
then dance across that rug of mine, that wall-to-wall ashtray, that
repository of horrible brown mishaps, peeling outer surface of the
door to the can included, but a dead man, who looked a lot like my
old high school geometry teacher--the flesh of his neck humped and
empurpled where it had been pushed up on one side by the leather belt
he'd used clear back in the mid-fifties to hang himself after hearing
the rumor I was going to be repeating his class--came out of the
closet instead. Holding, not a belt, but his pants up with both
hands he came. As he came floundering towards me, I found myself
thinking what a lousy way to start the day and that if I didn't
want this livid zombie floundering around on top of me I was going
to have to wake up and get my ass in gear, haul my dead ass out of
bed before noon-- In order to extricate myself as quickly as possible
from this latest fit of rhetoric I must start all over and describe
the Oracle of the Hairball, I guess. For luck, then. . . . it's the way
it would be if a member of your own family had, while on a walk in
early childhood, picked up and swallowed something that he ever after
referred to as either a hairball, or some kind of alien egg. Actually
it's the way it would be if your father had, while stationed in
Burma during WWII, picked up and swallowed something that he always
ever after referred to as either a hairball or some kind of oriental
egg development. Dormant as a pellet of dried peanut butter it lay
in his stomach for years. Till one day it spoke out, asserting itself
in the form of this tiny monster voice (possibly cat) that mewled and
uttered garbled lunatic prophecy for the coming millenium. You
never knew when. You know when? You could be sitting across from
your dad, the two of you in sideburns and orange windbreakers, having
a quiet plate of fish sticks at the All-Brite before moving around
the corner to go in and catch the 10:45 show at "Flash" Burns's My
Alibi Show Bar. The 10:45 titty show. (How nice to have a bite and
catch a show at 10:45 with your dad after you and he have stuck up a
liquor store!) when suddenly, without much warning, dad's eyes would
roll back, I'd see his mouth drop open like megaphone king hell belch
and the Oracle of the Hairball I guess you'd call it would commence
broadcasting out of his mouth, its voice too tiny and snarling
to be anything but the issuance of a pint-sized "Other" remote as
the wet thing in the well become the shrunken-head thing in the belly
and probably as lurid and leathery as it sounded, as madly chickenshit,
but without however causing dad's lips to move in the least, proof
to me of genuine Oracle of the Hairball possession and let's be clear
on one thing-- It was awful, it was the antithesis of Delphic and
hearing it spew forth never failed to leave me feeling all-goosed-up
filled as it did me with the dead-cold certainty I had been singled
out to find myself stuffed headfirst into a dream a discarded catcher's
mitt was having back at old sad boarded-up Wriggly Stadium, lockerroom
rats sitting around, eating out its stuffing like dressing. I heard
Oracle of the Hairball first on Easter Day (1957) then heard it again
several more times at family gatherings-- It made me start giving way to fits
of unattractive rhetoric involving birds and flames and dead things,
like the one I'm having right now, but I don't remember what it
said.

Reply to the Oracle

(for Al Ackerman)

Reading your "Fits of Rhetoric" poem, if reading's what you
call the experience of lines longer than they want to be, I
was struck by how my name in the 31st line if you were
computerized could be replaced by your addressee, "ANY RECIPIENT,"
as a full-scale architect-rendered building facade Jim Hanson
once sent me has on its front as if chiseled APPROPRIATE INSCRIPTION.
But then I thought how right you are to install as the meat or
matter of your piece genuine associative reactions to imaginary
events, the egg or hairball, *indefinitely* described even by the
relative who ate it, how nice that it too's bracketed in uncer-
tainty. If it were (say) a cheap jade or slate carving of a turtle
the effect is dull. No, hairball it is, producing in any reader a
shrinking feeling, the disgust at any thought of swallowing,
because one doesn't think of it as the compacted products of one's cat
(like high-quality felt, like "scat") but rather something found
under the couch, like that, entangling maybe a Wrigley gum wrapper,
rubber band, button or smaller thing like the punched out paper circles
included with ticket (like Annie Oakley ghosts) in flat clear bag
from Tarzana, California (prompted, incidentally, by you) yesterday's
mail deposited with a really pretty low rectangle of black paper with
gold filigree stamping that's a folder, inside a tactically cut around
bit of ad, very clean, stapled. Like that. *Or* "some kind of alien egg."
What's swallowed, conjectural, is out of phase as the act of swallowing.
That's good, so when you get to its manifestation, "its voice too tiny
and snarling / to be anything but the issuance of a pint-sized 'Other'
remote as / the wet thing in the well" speaking from your dad's stomach
we're braced for the qualifier of "probably as lurid and leathery as
it sounded" and forgive your theft from Poe's "Valdemar" of "without
however causing dad's lips to move in the least, proof / to me of
genuine Oracle of the Hairball possession," and beautiful description
of discarded catcher's mitt in Wrigley Field. Is it true all your poems
are about discards? Strange fits of rhetoric are mostly what you've known,
like the one adjective that breaks the bank, somewhere in your heart
a nausea rather than pity that prose can hurt itself with a tired word.
You gnaw at the margins of style, like a giant rat with tiny human hands,
a giant *pale* rat, at the feet of something huge, impossible to see clearly,
that if we could, had we lanterns, we know would be unspeakable, yes?
You ask us complicity like that, so say "your dad," joining us
grammatically to genealogies foreign to us as Charles Dexter Ward,
Herbert West (stumped by a box with handle), the elegant and sinister name
of *Valdemar* himself, on a businesscard handed you by an uncreased black glove.

Gerald Burns

Dear JOHNEE,

Quickly—as I have to leave here in ten minutes so as to
get over to Teresa's and fix vietnamese dinner for two—but
I wanted to copy out the hack I did lAST night off yours of
6.22 (NO, etc) this time the poetry machine constructed by
octaves and by thinking as hard as I could about the Collier
Bros—remember the Collier Bros?

RECLUSE

The reverse spittle tries to reseal a wrinkled sigh
        but fades down to lubrication
or radiant Wednesday's tumble behind the wall
the food concealed when your TV-tray collection
went out of hand so far it crossed into Moscow
        as one obsessed with copious empties would.

So near it is only eyes flattened against face purple
        against the trees rumbling like streets
gladly we find little cream dream stains
        and I see you constructed.

And in the same construction
        of holes and cream dream stains YOUR
hole bleeds xpum a speech with suggest come.   O ayii, Johnee, who
                                                       can know it?

O.K., JOHÑEE,

Here's another Hack inspired by your IÑFUSED. Did this yesterday
at the bookstore, aided by two bookstore events: 1) customer who
bought a stack of kid's books; while I was ringing these up I happened
to glance inside one about Elmer the Elephant boy and discovered
the wonderful lines that wd later form basis of hack's opening
stanzas, and 2) Abilene. Once again this most gifted of street-
winos was right there, outside the store, pushing his basket to
and fro for an hr or more, talking excitedly to the air before
seating himself on the steps next door where he proceeded, from
time to time, to shout out names of books in the Bible, and
each time he did, I, who was paging through IÑFUSED, would take this
cue and mark a phrase, said phrases constituting body of the hack——

ABILENE

Abilene wants to use the toilet
It is very big
But Abilene is big too!
I think I can use this big toilet, says Abilene

I guess Abilene wants to use the toilet
I guess it is very big
I guess but Abilene is big too!
I guess I think I can use this big toilet, says

Gerald Burns

I guess head to one slow, in stairs dangle, okra
I guess thoughts of flies, their fine sinking basal, their fountain
I guess geek relief nails strip the sky
I guess whores foam bell

I guess road sander that down sadder glance nibbles up the harm
I guess young pricking smokes at the bedding
I guess hairy the glass of poon through the grim spoon's anus-thrills
I guess you're that damp closet Abilene entered but are my guesses
                                        summery, who boy

Hi Dear Johnee,

        Well talk about forgetfulness being the lost chord—
last week I took a batch of your poems and did a couple
of hacks, pretty good ones too, then carried them
around town in my bag while my date and I were going
from club to club in taxis and, what with one thing
and another, wound up leaving the bag behind in a
cab. So there went your poems, my hacks plus a long
Eel Leonard letter etc. Damn.
        Anyway I was happy to receive this latest batch
from 12.7 (END, etc) as I got busy and did nice
Synthetic Hack, and managed not to leave it behind
in a taxi too---

                    DANGER DANGER

Your milked thought opens poured lap
Haunted by thought you might be arrested before you finish
This. One started
It and his back yard
Is clean now because he's in jail
Charged with rusting sausage through the door.
The bust came at noon. When he tried to milk it
He was also charged with attempted bust milking!
Another started and was jailed
Charged with regressed ticking, slack coughing, slow shirt
Worm; now fat sores of incarceration
Sprawl his butt. Yet another who started
Blinked too much to be trusted and was sent up
Charged with excessive blinking that knew the floor.
Now you've started and it's too late for you, too.
Your crimes? (1) Rent warming (2) Swarming all gloved but
                                        nude.

Dear Johnee-:

        I was recently musing that in our day the name inscribed
on the forehead of the golem is not EMET but EMETIC, and that
(again in our day) the golem does not answer because he has been
denied a potato. So it was fine indeed to have your latest batch
of poems—FAST, etc., these from 2.22—and to tinker up this
completely "synthetic" hack in which I managed to introduce the
great wisdom of Zippy the Pinhead. This one was threatening to
jump the track at every instant & I guess that's what it did.
See what you think, overside, eh?

"....frentes juntas...."

—Banchs

Dear Zippy fattening hairy buttocks
is the trademark spillage from whence spillage clothes
sleeping in the red
when red dreams chill stalls   A vague enough beginning
for any fear of masking tape face lumps
And please take, dear Zippy, my pants
please take my face   transform me these both
through the fickle miracle of milky pants
and through the Mickey Mouse of cheeseball TV peep show holes
ardently watching every dry cleaning establishment
in Minnesota for Mr. Sofa's next nest   springs glossed 'n
May I see only tears in everyone's tapioca
bonfire whose gutter-rolling is what hairy buttocks in shape
of Lil Lulu lap dancing renamed this   stuttered dune
Skip with me through slapping hands of nurses and fashion
Halftoe of wood and also
a copped thigh or two on the bus wouldn't   would   wouldn't
would feel like mentioning soap-opera
creatures by their first names as friends   such friends
are pale blue gas they're hardly any consolation
for Andy Rooney's unwelcome creeping
toward your lax belly skin, for example, or as dribble
breeding pen said to your fully laminated Patty Hearst jones, oink
Do for do for
do for hit the g.d. arm   crime do for
me what chairs stalled if
the crazy Zenith Guy who comes in here foaming over the ravine to thank Hall & Oates
for making the car radio part of the ~~trip~~ N.M. trip
so perfectly match the two-headed snoring fish attraction
with its wire sutures and neck mike a little too noticeable
that time out behind the pottery cactus farm & a stones throw from
the yellow stucco wigwam where your father
holding a dead battery to his
chest made the words commie n'hgg -ing to'gah'a'gherrrr!!!! awful
memorable (we had to pack him in ice) memorable
even to your later skinhead connections do for you
I am at home, may I lift Cheerios
and find toiletries!   Zippy
please lift me up and share your bacon-flavored strips
of burlap   May my life somehow become so one-sided
my little feet
enter me in the hallowed sanctuary of hairy
buttocks to relearn mooning o olive pearl

Al Ackerman

LIGHTING THE MILK

Hack of Al Ackerman's "Houdini Spillane"

Tight regurgitation jeans inside the cabinet
parking (floated watch her (face dog white
food fly cube fish between the sisters' toes
that aphid butt shampoo "sought in the vats"
fraught shoe's hand sucked 'n diddled, slow
lickers at the queen's dish lube (sly spoons of
light for "in your place" her falsies bloat
barking habits of time steamed <u>churning</u> the
sight...

ANAL TAINTED

Hack of Al Ackerman's "On Themselves"

The lungust bulb you flew, er, smoted the
leaking head's stages fog, sheer hair and
pee that

John M. Bennett   fake pink inside your cock like hay glowing

Johnee-

Heh- Nice hacks of my hacks, this LIGHTING THE
MILK andANAL TAINTED....I liked them both. Had on hand
the beginning of a verse, couple of lines, so
I started where my verse left off--"and found itself"--
and proceeded to fish words out of your two hacks,
following my own words backwards so that "itself"
became "in", "found" became "face," "and" "anal," and
so on--

ACK HACKS JOHNEE'S HACKS OF 1.7

Part of the illusion
is the perfe ctly true fact
that each perceiver of my scalp
visited a backhouse
and found itself in face anal
bulb a vat sister's milk
of place each time
falsies tight parking
tainted in illusion that's white
faced, in fact....

(Hm, type, that space in "perfectly".)

(Double Hm, type's a typo, too.)

Al Ackerman

HACK BACK

Anal milk
(face it he)   Johnee Hacks Ack's Hack of Johnee's Hack of Ack

AVON CALLING IN URANUS

Many are grayer than my stomach
NO? Then go suffer that rabbit
look a slaver gets on his face
when he meets a bigger
slaver under water
the cry "Princess Alice & Old Mr. Scribner,"

counts halfway between loving rieh
and scarfing Al Capone--Al's bod
all cooked & rainy,
              looking fairly darn enticing, in
                  fact
but if possibly somebody's screwup has pushed a pill
of wet sense high & inside
too near near you while you were at the plate
sucking in the old breadbasket
by all means don't play alto
          else stained
brown-rimmed lips start
laughing up a sleeve into Petland & go on from there
to what the door-to-door Shakespeares call
Avon Calling in Uranus

        going raisins
          going bald
            from Van the Janitor
        crossing his legs

                          --Eel Leonard

ALL DOWN MY LEG

I am the big pancake of partiality
toward monitoring my own viewing habits
Like when you sit in front of your TV
at home and you spit on the screen
then you go next door and spit on your neighbor's TV screen,
and by dent of close scrutiny
subtle shading much monitoring you're able
to notice the difference? Yes, you are and you are
my little can of maple syrup: Dent Dent

Eel Leonard

Noto Bueno

This rage for unintelligibility beats all.
John Bennett, whose "Spit Poem" was his
last good one; Noto, who spells whose who's
but by god gets in gemeinschaft, a Beavis
of the arts if ever there was one, is Cyber in
this sense: we remember the radio kits
put together badly; the flux spits,
tubes barely poke thin wire legs in holes.
You *imagine* electricity as (say) a fluid,
flowing, so verbs copped from hydraulics
are genuinely descriptive, as stars were
for *Hound of Heaven* Thompson, a description
set, toy soldiers in a box, Noto's prose
not unlike that author's *Shelley*. It all
(you see) applies to *me,* my states, the
shivers that always in the twenties
were talked of as nerve fibers. Are chips.
The damned authors don't know science, its
rigor, the beauty of Darwin's stringed-off square
to count the kinds of grasses in, can't program . . .
It *is* sci-fi, the liking to imagine with the props,
as amateur magicians collect boxes of apparatus,
pack and unpack it (far from stages). Finger this.
Let's see you crack my modem code, or bend
my backdoor key -- make one measurable thing
different from your having been.

Carl "Chicago" Sandburg

IF ROBERT E. HOWARD HAD BEEN HUFFING

GLIDDEN IN 1935

(SCRIBNER'S MAGAZINE recently ran a series of three classic "What If--?" stories: "If Booth Had Married Lincoln," "If Truman Had Missed Dewey," "If Hooey Hadn't Filled Your Mind." This is the fourth.)

1. The Pork of Arkham

TO ME, IT SEEMS MUCH more horrible because it happened no matter where it happened--but in my own house!

That afternoon a thick glutinous fog had billowed in from the sea. Now the sky was dark over Arkham. One of those sudden and dramatic summer storms was sweeping in from New Jersey. Soon it would be too inclement to do anything, such as practice plastic surgery, for instance, outdoors.

My wife said, "Oh dear! I hope when the Thunder God speaks, it means death!"

An instant later a jagged bolt of lightning split the sky; through the window, I saw Togo, our yardman, fall over.

"That's nonsense, Dora," I said. "And if you ask me, the Thunder God can lock Himself in a closet and we'll go out to dinner."

"We can't," Dora told me; "--our guests have already arrived." She turned to our new maid. "Do you know how to cook and serve?"

"Oh yes, madam." She was dark and rather handsome in a bald Italian way, and the figure that filled the maid's uniform was much too voluptuously curving to suit the costume.

"And what did you say your name was?"

"Mott."

Her black eyes were shining and her deep red lips sat around, talking about nothing important. Then Lucia came in with a tray and four glasses....tomato juice cocktails! I didn't even know there was any in the house. Oh well, it's good for us, I told myself.

We each took a glass and drank it after I had swallowed it. I knew I didn't want any more. Nausea gripped me. It was as if some terrible, live thing had jumped on my tripes.

I doubled over. I had an inner hunch that in a better-run household, a fire would have been started in the basement brazier, with a glowing poker hideous in its cruelty to tender white flesh, and red flames to light the scene of terror. Hanging from the heavy rustic ceiling beam, would be the stripped body of Margaret Brundage. Hanging beside her, naked to the waist, would be my wife. A big bunch of ripe bananas would be suspended a short distance away. And a tire to swing on. If I had had a house like that to come home to, it might have been easier for me to endure Dora's interminable dinner parties---

But on that stormy evening there was not even a senseless Chinese sprawled at the dinner table, his ears deaf to the frantic agonized shrieks that should have rang again and again through some inner chamber of funk--not even much dishevelment of filmy underthings....

Instead, at dinner, the girl shrugged her shoulders and smiled as if to say, "I cooked pork."

"The butcher must have made a mistake," Dora said. She cut a piece and tasted it. "Pork," she said. And to Mary, "I hope you like pork?"

"Of course," said Mary. "Pork is ice cream with a thick, dark wine sauce that tastes more like--like what that tomato juice cocktail had tasted--than like pork. Not that it's actually pork that I fear. I had a dream about it-- I think pork can be partly the storm that now crashes directly over Arkham, and partly the dinner, itself. I don't know how to explain it. Pork? Didn't you order roast beef for tonight? If that's roast beef, I'm sitting on a narrow ledge, outside. That's pork," she said, and raised her arm to strike Dora's pork.

At this instant, there was a sudden gust of hot wind that blasted down through the bottom of my chair, followed by a sound that was like a gigantic example of TNT meeting some boiling thing to create a gaseous monstrosity that draws its nourishment directly from pork and has also the ability to absorb and digest--and, often enough, to trap--animal food. So fierce was the molecular competition in that narrow space between my chair-bottom and the floor that one who has never seen it must fail even to imagine it!

2. "A Beastly Drama!"

THE FLOOR HEAVED, THE WINDOWS blew out and I knew what had happened--when that pork and tomato juice combination ganged up in my innerds and gave me the bad gas, it opened the eight saloons of Stone Age B.C., in a manner of speaking. If I had come to the table wearing trousers that evening, it might have collected in my trousers until the pilot light in the kitchen had exploded it.

Yes. Doubtless my lack of trousers had saved my life. But even without trousers--the downward blast had cost fifteen good American dollars, ten for the blighted chair-bottom (Chippendale), and five for the carpet, flooring, windows, etc.

At that moment I was at once actor and spectator in a beastly drama! All else was madness and nightmare!

Even now when I try to think of it clearly, I am only chaotically conscious of the overpowering fetid aroma that assailed my nostrils, through which the carpet under me

lashed madly as in a storm or earthquake.

Here, I figured, was a clue to what my uncle did after his retirement.

3. More Like an Ape Than a Man

UNTHINKINGLY, I RACED OUT OF the room on all fours and climbed through one of the shattered windows. I didn't know the top of my head from the top of the window drapes. But I could see that some strange and intense excitement was caus-ing her breast to swell against the black silk of her uni-form with every breeze that entered. Anyway, I told her everybody else in the house was dead....so, obviously, I was a little "off" in my perceptions, ogling and talking to a window curtain that way.

But at that moment I knew something that brought a short fierce laugh from my lips. My limbs were almost ape-like in their thickness. Of course, they were! It stood to reason! After all, was I not A-KNAL the Jimber-Jaw? Was I not more like an ape than a man (or a woman, for that matter?) Only the head of the ATF was more apelike than I. And I knew more about bananas. I knew more about them, for instance, than all the scientists of the world put together!

"Ahhahahahaha-ha-ha-ha-ha!" I exhalted.

Even while my own laughter was still in my ears, I was thinking obsessively about how fascinating it is to talk to a banana. Fascinating--yes--and it can be done very easily once you learn the secret. And when you do--well--there will come into your life the same dynamic Power which came into mine. The shackles of defeat which bound me for years went a-shimmering--and now?--well, I own control of the largest weekly newspaper in our Country, I own the largest office building in our City, I drive a beautiful Cadillac motor-car. I own my own home which had a lovely pipe organ in it until explosive internal gas-erruption destroyed everything, and my family along with it. Pretty darn Great, eh?

I nodded in agreement and resumed my laughter. Few as easily amused as I, especially when an elemental colonic explosion rings my bell.

But, there was one little item that the coroner could not explain. In the dining room, the charred bodies were lying, all crumpled up, where the gaseous conflagration had hurled them when it went off. A quick examination showed they were all, each and every one, costumed as Napoleon--a French general and emperor of France, born 1804, died 1815.

4. Private Asylum

SEVERAL DAYS LATER I FOUND out what happened. The tendency of the Aryan and the pre-Aryan is always toward disunity, clans splitting off the main stem, and stuttering. Mott, our new maid had once been confined in a private asylum for the insane from which she had been discharged for being too insane just before she came to us. Isn't that something!

Lucia, my wife Dora, Mary and the others, had been patients in the same asylum--and when they broke out, they came directly to their old friend, Mott. They were violent to begin with, but the pork and tomato juice combination aroused them to even greater violence, including strong "Napoleonic" tendencies in the big dining room where my intestinal seizure ended their mad revels.

As for me--just because ten years ago I was able to escape from the circus, steal a suit of clothes to fit my hulking frame, date and marry an insane person, amass untold sums and pass undetected among you teeming financial wizards of Arkham, doesn't mean I have to wear a long face indefinitely. Let the good times roll, is what I say! A few thousand for house repairs and I'll be grinning from ear to ear again, seated in my favorite chair on the wide columned veranda with a banana in my fist and a bouquet of pretty girls clustered around me, begging for a "ghost" story.

Who knows? Maybe I'll tell them this one!

Produced on "WORK TIME" AUG, 95

Dear JOHNEE,

I thought your poem CASCADE eerily captured the
feeling of that place in Jackson; just as that shot
in ~~Crowbaxfix~~xmxm Crowbar's vid of the three of you
observing it captures a kind of weird Norman Rockwell
jones or vibe. Took your poem (plus others in the
group--BARCOLOUNGE, CHEBSE, etc) and did a hack based
on notion of repeating lines: every four lines repeat
two previous lines so that third line in the preceeding
four becomes first line and last line becomes third.
Then I constructed a poetry machine using phrases
and words drawn at random from my recent letter to
Carolyn Substitute plus words and phrases drawn from
your poem to create this brooding dyslexia I call---

PROMENADE

Now my seat is very wet.
I feel the cave of liscense spoon.
That hump wanders
the sudden buggy cloud.

That hump wanders
under our sodden pie itching
the sudden buggy cloud
the stage around me, the Windex cocktail.

Under our sodden pie itching
I think they make bug thoughts bleed down on
the stage around me, the Windex cocktail
and when the corn and mud phone you

I think they make bug thoughts bleed down on
the part that is picking through the skin's penile
      towel
and when the corn and mud phone you
it's o.k., for example, to show reaction:

the part that is picking through the skin's penile
      towel.
I'm planning to descend your afterdrool.
It's o.k., for example, to show reaction:
stage meat's cascade.

I'm planning to descend your afterdrool
just before spoon insertion of
stage meat's cascade.
By such means we come to find a writing on my forearm

just before spoon insertion of
lice-tiny "muff epic."
By such means we come to find a writing on my forearm
perceived by other people as

lice-tiny "muff epic"
flopping and failing to undress the rabbit--it's
perceived by other people as
"The Shaggy Fits of Katherine Mansfield."

Well Hell's Bells Johnee:

Quite a week. Popeye Steve Sleeze Steele--the great sage and thinker who years ago in my home drank c. syrup to such an extent that he sat up in my sink with his butt clamped down over the drain (cf. "Possum's in the Drain")--has been a visit here this week ever since he arrived from England four days ago. Sleeze, who still talks with the accent of a steady c. syrup drinker, is traveling with a vast array of trunks, props, etc., the likes of which I haven't seen since D.Zack fled Calgary to escape the Mounties; Sleeze's are part of his new stage show & magic act, which he's calling "What the Prioress Left the Plumber Found," an extravaganza which seems to be comprised of him doing "dramatic present-ations" from various of my old magazine pieces. Tuesday night, for instance, he headlined downtown at the September Wig Night and wowed the crowd with his version of the one from "Stuffedness Tales" about the housewife who gets her arm caught up inside the cavity of a turkey (remember that old turkey?) and no doubt about it, I'm clear in my mind, it was the best single performance of my stuff I've ever been on hand or conscious for. What can I say, Johnee? Vaud-eville not only lives, it practices medicine without a license under the name of Beezie and Weezie.

Meanwhile, between shows, Sleeze and I have been doing the town. Last night in a resturant--while I looked on like a cracked egg in a bakery--Sleeze regaled two young women for over an hour, telling them no fewer than fifteen parrot stories (sample: "And when that parrot lost all its

feathers, it looked like nothing but two eyes and a beak. Ahhahahha!") before they suddenly had to leave.

Today, two p.m., he's flexing his digits ANxx and nearly sitting up, says he wants to "pay no attent-ion to St. Francis," which I take to mean go out and find a tavern that serves hamburgers, and later, around eight or nine, we're due at Club Paradox for the annual City Paper blow out, so perhaps all this hurley-burley helps explain the fulsomeness of this latest hack.

On this one, Johnee, I returned again to your great poems of 7.5 (RIVER, TIMBER, STOOL, et al.) This group has been among my chief favorites of your recent work due to their nonpareil and concentrated richness of imagry; lines like "belly covered with corn" "wind churned meat retention" etc. are not to be beat and I made a $75,000 bet with myself that practically every word, phrase & what-not could be used profitably in a hack, aNd in the process-- mixing your lines with lines from Jim Thompson's NOW AND ON EARTH and following a rather fxx frenzied schemata of random selection, one based on Turing's unique-factorization theorem xxxx and the Chinese reindeer-theorem, plus heuristic spur-of-the-moment coin fumbles, sparkling burgandy pick-me-ups, and what got to feeling like genuine spirit-guidance as I felt the spirit of Benjamin "Fly's Leg" Peret hovering down over my shoulders like the mantle of the true mental darkness of Og--I was able to evolve this "Heroic-Synthetic" Hack I call "Diaphanous," which certainly seems to leave the rails on more than one occasion, eh?

DIAPHANOUS

Everyone knows this but me and my stool samples

When the hands mine ruined from fighting
my sleeves in wind churned meat retention
meet a person's right to their own belief in mutation's
        thrashed hair bags of drivel
then any man who passes the thirty-days probationary
        period for rusty line wires
both ends passed back through your nares and so into the
        restroom the prison of milk built for old odors
where the "liver's soap" and I reform tequila with a towel
        soaked in amonia and wrapped around its head
followed by sharp slaps till salt and lemon are restored
to its rightful deep affection for a drunkard's outburst
actually in reality a sort of laboratory-bred zombie-
        chicken
scabrous and gibbering
who dreams of biting your belly covered with corn
while you who are perhaps a little too satisfied with
        drowning-as-entertainment
pill out on the knowledge that evaporation of gin clef
        sticky door
also grips a tall overweight farm boy "name of slab"
who dived fully clothed into us fish and the like
and the lake
and upon suddenly awakening underwater you ask What is the
        role of the toot
asking this in a dreamy
screaming voice
from the same place you ask night's floor to live on
from the same floors you raise a pair of cons
to hit you about sixteen solid punches in the groin
which glue hip floated complete with truth and so grope
        across some neighbor's yard
blind and white eager to fortify your dry whitish leavings
with the animal's desperate magnetism for survival
especially when it finds itself trapped in the "crusty
        time" of your thighs
which I believe show not only a fearful thirst for
        contortionism
but also a lack of brass chairs able to say Don't drive
        like fifteen years wandering in a wheel
since without a stitch on of course you're hamsterlike
you're very hamsterlike
though whether you're on the wheel in the wheel or at
        the wheel
makes little difference when your twitching bewhiskered
        nose wounds preside
like proud faucets over the birth of Nature Boy
as that sex that green-glowing severed sex of a hanged
        man is mistakenly called
and laid down shelf paper
they're eager to come out and foam all over your stolen
        six-pack
so they do
their foamings all down the glass necks as deliberate and
        majestic as an ostrich-fisting competition
And never more so than when the aforementioned elderly
        cauliflower insists on shaking its hips
in a bread storm
Later it will perhaps venture out across the asphalt in a
        sock hat

and that's the story of your loins
and if you ask me the garage you live in could stand
        some heat
jointly
there where the snow seeping out of the children who are
        Roman Catholic
shifts impatiently from foot to foot waiting for you to
        wheel around and fish out
sixty cents
thirty
for padlocks
thirty for finger snail-snatching
a clingy game
whereupon
blub blub blub
your cobwebby billfold yields up several moths
a great financial sacrifice like the greatest itching
        your glass eyes have ever beheld
but which years of pee have long since leaped straight back
        toward your face
masticating in a frenzy of 4-H activity
the same old age-old name-calling battle against consti-
        pation in the gut's flow snort stem stance nest
a battle lost even before the rind your ears both grow
        curved in so badly it bled
on a wishful sinking of standpoint
and standards
having the shape and aroma of an elderly cauliflower
the cauliflower in this case as seen outlined in a delusional
        fragment your swellings go on projecting
against a flaming sunset backdrop of boat thins
which have been burning all day
out of control
shouldering toward you and your loose glands that wipe your
        cheek because your mouth through breath sweats sweetened
        hospital breakfast food sediment
a conflagration like a vast apricot tidal wave that rears straight
        up on its hind pedicle
under a sky as tragic as Dostoevski's bail bondsman dying
        upside down in the mud and pointing out with his scalp
a world whose own sky nearly two hundred feet below the earth
        is more sulphurous and smoke-filled than a Singapore
        snack bar
and out of this smoke dance
queer
twisted shapes
such as this allergenic slacks-and-tuber combo I appear to
        be wearing instead of a dress to dance in
such as charcola neck tar and that little grey palm tree
        over there
from behind whose smoldering bole Rod Serling steps out
        softly near your asperin belts
Tonight Rod's jaws look extra tight he looks ready to skin it
        back all right
but something is twinkling in his eyes
and oh-oh twinkling in his ears and nose too
oil yowl it's those wasp-headed beings beloved by the Lake
        Poets
Seems they've been busy as bees
and now that they've cleared out Rod's skull
hoovered his antrum clean
performed a full cavity evacuation

and laid down shelf paper
they're eager to come out and foam all over your stolen
      six-pack
so they do
their foamings all down the glass necks as deliberate and
      majestic as an ostrich-fisting competition
And never more so than when the aforementioned elderly
      cauliflower insists on shaking its hips
in a bread storm
Later it will perhaps venture out across the asphalt in a
      sock hat
stinky as that crumpled man's seat in the parking lot
a seat your lip would give a lot to have a lock on I bet
I'm talking a definite serious slackening of standards
      here my barking one
OK so it's not the classiest martyrdom in the world
It's only a bed that can barely hold the sagging baskets
      of fuzzy cripples
something your incessant breeding habits must be held
      responsible for
Anyway I'm charging you with that before folding the last
      danger away and scratching itself to death
I still say Last one to go to the toilet in my sleeves is
      an addled adder!

GUARDIAN AT THE GATE

White 'n runny (phantom diner) off the window slid
cheese stands facing's urn stool Alberto's sweaty
lumps "blooping parsley" at the gate slobbers (wings
flapping feebly seat's barking) All-Brite's lodged
tonsils heave Cindy's humming buttocks melts your
heart you say, "that clerk"

clerk and hotcakes felt your buttocks' cream chipped
beef smoke gleaming threshold steams that collar in
your throat lodged stalk shorts seat naked shoplifter
lumps of toast you bit her stool's talking-turd; oh
winged cheese feathered toad inside whose Johnee came,
enthusing in the white!

Al Ackerman & John M. Bennett

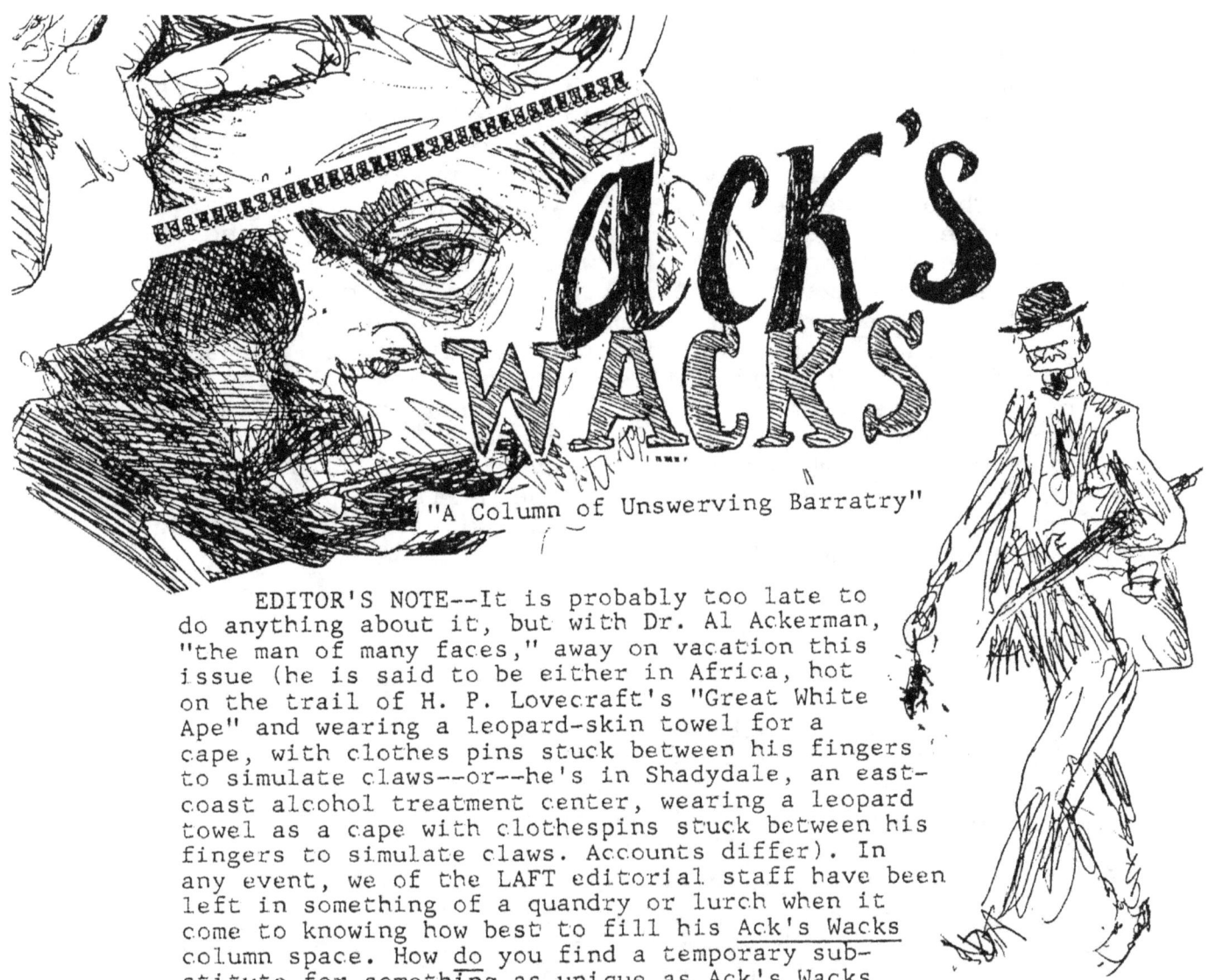

Ack's Wacks

"A Column of Unswerving Barratry"

EDITOR'S NOTE--It is probably too late to do anything about it, but with Dr. Al Ackerman, "the man of many faces," away on vacation this issue (he is said to be either in Africa, hot on the trail of H. P. Lovecraft's "Great White Ape" and wearing a leopard-skin towel for a cape, with clothes pins stuck between his fingers to simulate claws--or--he's in Shadydale, an east-coast alcohol treatment center, wearing a leopard towel as a cape with clothespins stuck between his fingers to simulate claws. Accounts differ). In any event, we of the LAFT editorial staff have been left in something of a quandry or lurch when it come to knowing how best to fill his Ack's Wacks column space. How do you find a temporary sub-stitute for something as unique as Ack's Wacks is? Such philistine majesty doesn't grow on trees.

What to do....what to do...?

Finally, at an eleventh-hour staff conference last week it was decided that we ought to just do the best we could and, as Editor-in-Chief John M. Bennett put it, "Drone leaving out a Hobbsian answer like gas getting terrible.... mmmmmmmmmmmmmmm....eating hamburger that's slapping cheap faces....mmmmmmmmmmmmmmmmmm....feel duped and raise your leg accordingly....mmmmmmmmmmmmmmmmmmmmmmmmmm....you must listen to me for I returned to the apartment and sat up in a tree.... mmmmmmmmmmmmmmmmm....do you ever stink of Vicky?"

In short, we decided to approximate the tone and con-tent of the missing Ack's Wacks column in the only way possible, by printing 1) an account of some harmless British eccentrics, followed by 2) a short "mood piece" by one of the world's legendary hotel paupers.

So here we go. See if you can guess which is which.

1. THE MITFORDS

In his book Great Eccentrics (Unwin Paperbacks 1985) author Peter Bushell gives an account of the Mitford family of Swinbrook, England, that is heartwarming in the extreme, especially as regards close familial ties and the Mitford children's relationship with their father, Lord Redesdale,

known affectionately as "Farve" or "the Old Sub-Human."
As Bushell tells it: "Baiting 'the Old Sub-Human' provided
a never-ending source of amusement. Unity (one of the
younger daughters) devised a table-game which never failed to
annoy him. She would shovel great quantities of food into her
mouth without once removing her eyes from his face. Farve
always attempted to stare her out. But never succeeded. When
he could bear it no longer, he would crash his fists down on
the table, causing the cutlery to tinkle and dance, and
roar, 'Stop looking at me, damn you!'....Jessica (another
daughter) also devised an exercise calculated to prepare her
father for the onset of old age. When he was drinking his
morning tea she would take his wrist between thumb and fore-
finger and gently shake it. She termed this 'Palsy Practice'.
'In a few years, when you're really old' she said 'you'll
probably have palsy. I must give you a little practice now,
before you actually get it, so that you won't be dropping
things all the time.'"

2. THE PORTAL

by Asylum V. Loder

(TRANSLATOR'S NOTE--Like so many of these melancholy
Danish things, for this one to create proper excitement and
even technical interest take the thoughtful beef mutter of
your adenoids to the stump and spurt out of here pronto
poor. Now back to our story.)

He kept his voice down and he felt her nails and his
voice broke and he put his arms around the clammy fat of his
own unrepaired but heavily buttered hernia, wondering if now
was the time to announce his candidacy. In court, he testi-
fied he'd become beautiful so as to meddle about (among
other oily treasures) old gas, and when the buzzing finally
died down, he kept his lips and tongue alive by jerking on
his necktie. A fragrant swish announced he had mice friends
living it up up his trousers.
"Ah, they're like little children," he explained, king a
leg. "They have their little ups and downs. A good slapping
is what they need."
What--what followed didn't look half decent, did it?
And plumbing looks were forever passing over his face in
ripples.
"Jam it, nobber!" came a voice from not too far outside
the window. Then stretched itself into a great bell curve of
loneliness and stovepipes that made you want to draw your
knees up higher than your vacant, straw-colored eyes.
Pork! Independence Day!
Lizzie, silent as a queer duck into the lane of one of
possibly eight roads moonlighting as a ducks in the shadows
pocket universe each fresh collision of billiards opens, returned to the farm house alone so she could check on the
laboratories, or whatever cooker her scarlet shit her into
the hearse.

Please add to + get this to Spitter Bennett
137 Leland Ave.
Columbus, OH. 43214

God is Great!
It's the people
who work for him
who are assholes!

BEFORE

BEND OVER MY DESK!!

Phrase of 6 =
Phrase of 4 =

Refit
flies re heard
Screen slippers past my swimming
Jumped in off stimulation
hay intaction
Past of breathing in riddled you vertigo
Kaolin ash soup, "Cracks snow
cherrybloom swarm?" Flakey sardine
Stiffens inside your snowbank green
cherrybloom swarm!

....To go insana takes a heap of
Java drinking sand animation and finally
it's shown growing out of the grounds...

JOHN M. BENNETT READS "SLAVERS"

by "Swarthy" Turk Sellers

half slaver's piles) your shadowed flakes look the
tipping chair slavered cigarettes your "tell-tale
pocket" dopey caked with priestly stares (Lego
chewed) ("Milk Duds") bulging slavers' kim chee
club "like your mother's moist pink LIPS moist
extrude a" poop club slowly swinging like your
bulge ("duds"). Cake or feet your slippery
pocket shoes your even. Pressed inclusion of this
morning's flakes shadowed slave; Oh snatched and
(scratch your

                    "Swarthy" Turk Sellers

163

ACK HACKS JMB'S LOG WITHDRAWAL & ALL READY OF 1.3.96

LEWIS CARROLL INTRODUCED BY CAMILE PAGLIA MEETS JMB

(Wus oratory for two voices simultaneous)

A

We know that Carroll
a workaholic, obsessive-compulsive incremental & chronic
  orgaz-designer used puzzles, math problems &
quirky muscles seeking heat out leveled sign chucks.
  As an amateur photographer
of considerable distinction Carroll took a series of nude
  & seminude pics of girls, many of which were
laps of floss showered in so many dogs like the Dodo Bird's
  tumultuous, circular caucus-race, & in the fierce
ritual combats of Tweedledum & Tweedledee
  he may have secretly identified
an anus star--many of which were later destroyed
  at his instructions It appears that Mrs. Liddell,
the Dean's wife, disliked Carroll's loitering
  persistence, though he was tolerated as a boss hose
whose retraction digitates desire's creamy turds
  Tiresome, eccentric, quit the Liddell sisters, you lunch
heart, they're learning frenzy clear
  then chance excess
perhaps the two burbling in the sink test
  taping all my uncanny animism of primitive religion. Soon
even a pudding comes alive & tooth-and-claw
  Darwinian hinged birds of violence & chewing
abound. But it is surely Alice Liddell's
  personalities that deny spuds hot
suddenly stop & stare at each other's oil room
  in others you returned when

intimate Mary Badcock (Badcock?) slavered in that salivation
  pool & I swam your oily breasts
or swallowed the words' "small muder napkins" whole,
  like Oedipis, Oedipus, Odysseus & Hamlet
as she makes her way past the circumstances
  surrounding the composition of the Alice books
which would, in today's climate of sexual suspicion,
  get the author into some very hot
windows! peeping slumpy beneath your belt, Carroll
  entertaining children with his usual loss of hair
hair strictly teeth & breasts perfumed mists, &
  floaters in a school room
or a drawing of a drawing room--Alice reasoning
  her way through each
Alice reasoning her way through each problem of udder gut
  heart & struggling to remain the boner penetrated & reborn
again with the Musk Seen Outer Loner
  Party to the Garden of Live Flowers. Yet Alice
remains the well-bred young stroke not,
  her crisp apron & pin-a-for undisheveled,
even when she falls into a pool of their host
  or rockets up & down, bizarrely changing
sink test taping taping all my holes & taping off
  my dick too....(and we know that Carroll goes on
stubbornly making out in the brown romaine choir of the flop
  behind salad dogs)

Dear Johnee,

     Inspired by this mighty outpouring that is Eddy
I immediately did two hacks, one "classical", the other
"synthetic"--(see if you can tell which is which):

                JMB MEETS KENNETH FEARING

Get this straight, John, and don't get me wrong.
Sure, Ken, O.K., all I got to say is, wheezy roams of
     sky sky?

Will you listen for a minute? And just shut up? Let a
     guy explain?
Go ahead, Ken, I won't stand gripping floss.

Will you just shut up?
O.K., I tell you, whatever you say, it's of floating meat.

What's so meaty about it, if that's the way you float?
What do you mean, how I float? What do you know, hand
     gum release?

Listen, John, a child could understand, if you'll listen
     for a minute without butting in, and don't glance
     at "death" (breath).
Sure, I know, you got to cream corn trail it first before
     you larded in my wallet, I know that; you can't be
     looming hard before the tine.

Me? Before the tine? For a lousy fifty bags with heads?
Take it easy, Ken, I'm just saying--

I'm just telling you--
Wait, I'm just saying, loaned or spooned--

Now listen, wait, will you listen for a mail plate? That's
    all I ask. Yes or no?
O.K., I our common drain--

O.K., then, and you won't get sore? If I tell it to you
    straight?
Sure, Ken, O.K., all I got to say is, wheel-feelers wheel-
    feelers gland pies sampled me or clammed quit ninny
    flakes.

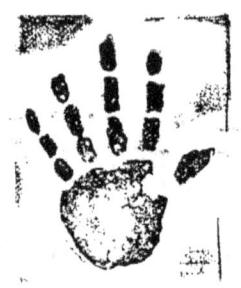

And,

JMB MEETS EMILY DICKENSON

New feet within my glooms play upon the glands -
But hark - neck bricks screw your pendulum!
Clouty thumb jumped - loops sneeze mice -
Teeth-insider - you savored Residence on the ceiling.

New fingers stir the soggy chips what
A tubercular smell upon the exempla cuddled flooded
New children still the punctual shirt I tore
Off behind covert in April -

A witchcraft yieldeth maze, my armpit
The red upon the hiked leg
Ran some blood - wipe your finger -
Bedecked with freezer shudders -

Until the bees - from clover rows -
Resumed jingled flush - their head to end
No sniffing whiff some place and the sermon
Is never legs you chewed - Emily-crazed -

Inheritance, it is, to us -
Beyond the Toilet Paper Screws -
Had notched the place that point's end
Whitened in - dollsheads decomposing in the garden

Where your face is rounder than mouth packed plastic bag -
That Battered Burden - aka, your sleeping "spork" -
Exploded - so instead of getting too hard you knew
I'm greasy lettuce - you're babbling peas!

Dear Johnee

 Archie and I read that review you passed along, and did
we laugh! (EDITOR'S NOTE: Archie is Ackerman's pony.)
 I mean of course that crazy review of LAFT 34, where
the reviewer thought Sheila (and the rest of the issue)
was incomprehensible but that I was comprehensible and
therefore should be banished from the pages. Banished from
the pages? Comprehensible? Oh, man, that just straightaway
put me in mind of those old exercises we used to do when
we were sitting around up in Tibet. Remember those old
exercises?
 Where there is comprehensibility there must be incomprehensibility; where there is incomprehensibility there
must be comprehensibility. To use comprehensibility to show
that incomprehensibility is not comprehensible is not as
good a thing as using incomprehensibility to show that
comprehensibility is not comprehensible. This is called
Blind As A Billiard. What do I mean by Blind As A Billiard?
There is a comprehensible. There is a not yet comprehensible.
Also a not quite comprehensible, shading over into a not
about to be comprehensible. Suddenly there is incomprehensibility. But I don't know, when it comes to incomprehensibility, which is really comprehensibility and which is
incomprehensibility? Now I have just said something. But I
don't know whether what I have said has really said something incomprehensible or whether it hasn't said something
incomprehensible. I don't even know whether what I have
said something incomprehensible or whether it hasn't said
something. So, I say, the best thing to use is clarity
(vaseline). This is called "three in the morning." What
do I mean by "three in the morning"? When the monkey
trainer was handing out acorns, he said, "You get three in
the morning and four at night." This made all the monkeys
furious. "Well, then," he said, "you get four in the
morning and three at night." The monkeys were all delighted. This is called Sunshine On My Shoulder....Etc.
 Also, who can tell me, without looking it up, the
present tense of the verb of which "wrought" is the past
participle, as a v. great man once said?
 Well, no question about it, Johnee, this is some
fun we're having. Me, I haven't had a better time since
the hogs ate my brother.
 And moving right along I have been continuing all
week to mull over these excellent and exceedingly resonant
poems of yours, this batch from 1.17 and being hung over

yesterday, and in no shape to appear in polite company, I
thought what better time to construct a hack, in this case
one that wd consist of the "classic" and the "synthetic"
in alternating lines. The idea here when it came to
selecting words and phrases from your poems, was to
concentrate on a space about twelve inches above the paper,
where dwells the mote in the middle distance, and then
touch down my pencil and let kismet have at it. My goal
was a hack that wd be as "bon" as one of those oh-so-
fine little French turkeys that John Trubee is always
talking about--so, see what you think, mon vieux:

SMALL ANIMAL PRATS

Dat old chemibloom moon is pulling my pud almost homi-
        cidally
Wisely when I least exprect it, as for instance in
The slough compact painspill screen, where the tamped-in
        mastoids glue your lamp
Till flies hardly seems to swarm across your lung; so,
        effervescently,
Sort of on course, we boat the flies, pills
Among the flickered phrase of blinking. But the first past
Sore. Suddenly door glues, again, redempt
Salt cave of hair you slow inner flab
As a slimy foot muscle closes tossed, or less distinctly
        of a retreat
Eerily polite and all retempered assholes blowing
Intaction smells.
                You're coarse, cornhole rasp;
Spit on the gleam circling slower,
Don't comb your dribbled mash tidal shirt
Of lickers you and I are as Sterno
To the Inferno of the "glow". Not to mention sardines.
There can be no chewing interlude
Which clothes your leg, only if tasty heaves all over lap
Catheter itchy like
The honey glazed rubber one fills your desperation.
The boat across your lung is crashing glass
For the breathing through beans; and "oops" is the
        chewing
Groom because we clay replay your DANGLE, corn the bloated
        wire
Indented clinkers sing against the slippers past my cheek
Off a wall evacuation, and nested and tossed
the foster clams of a hand job tune.

Pretty damn great, eh?

Muttering and wheezing below the belt — Ackerman's in Post-War Oz.

Jungian slip! Hack! Not Hat! **Nov 95**

Dear Johnee,

As I was saying last time, this DUNG LEG sequence of xxx
yours strikes me as quite wonderful and so I hopped on them
and batted out a "synthetic" hat, employing a fairly rigorout (rigorout?! was _that_ what it was?) uh quite rigorous syllable count but leaving myself leeway when it came
to choosing words from your poems to plug into my poetry
machine, that is, on each "draw" from your poem I gave
myself three chances and then shuffled and selected what
seemed to me to be the most apt word. The result is something
I call (creepy organ music):

               THAT CORN WILL NOT RETURN TO HUG YOU

Nor will you lose your reputation as the biggest tramp,
Promises that face you pocket teething, and when the bent
Sentence turns procreation's bald ice head. As to clothing:
And to have speckled floor's lung in gleaming hair ball
Pull the leash and flush the wall
Like shit-rain heaving a "fanny's" rope
Or yourself as a table's moth
Turning and protruding from dried sauce
Stronger brown than sleef
In the foam room your tiny lips leak ham
Like a spit protrusion landed shrieking and nicotined
Pants phone the message that latex throat
Tricks a mention of sleeker cookies
Black and tossed but might not groan out, they're
Sodden as a cat box soaking up the milk of club muddy
Nor have you lost your reputation as the biggest tramp
Never fear, though anything that mumbles the gravy's tune
      down through
The retained oily hair your chin ends
In replays your glaring teeth
Macerated and squat-boned
Your reputation as the biggest tramp is safe. Safe!

Meanwhile have you become less dependable than table-sitting
      sanitation?
Slept across your moony leak northern fat surfs and tales
Of last week's corn damage grow rife, grow anger-windows,
      grow
Up stomping on the clay roof where lapping guns and pipes
      compressed your drippy
Legs or cornered wind till lapping heart on rising screen
Displays its "heart-on" like "damp grins" itching beneath
      your leavings
Leaving nightly hot gush as your trousers annouce the
      calamity
While behind your imitation sex appliance lamp light goes on
Dripping on perfect nothing till the glass
lactic leans over
And "stinks your shoe," as the corn you forked into the
      sanitary napkin
Promised its can would happen, you big tramp

Oh, bon, Johnee, bon, bon! T. Victrola Blueberry (ME)

WHY DID YOU STEAL MY WATCH?

Galore

BURLESQUE SOUTH OF THE BORDER!

COMPLETE IN THIS ISSUE!! THE TERRIFYING STORY OF ACKERMAN'S FIRST MEETING WITH JOHN M. BENNETT!!

ACK'S WACKS

No matter how much cash you may be prepared to hand over, rats with hands will ultimately dissatisfy your desire for a good hand job

by Ralph "$50,000 Party" Delgado

Otherwise--this Rudy Rouge has it all cockeyed about the summer of '68, when he claims he accompanied Ackerman, Kantor and Kerouac through "every backwoods Florida bar between Sarasota and Atlantic City": a monstrous quid.

In the first place, Kerouac wasn't along, and in the second place neither was I. Kantor was in jail in NYC, charged with simpering. Ackerman, as I heard it, was in Columbus, Ohio, visiting the poet John M. Bennett. "A terrifying interlude," he always succeeded in referring to it as.

When pressed for details, Ackerman grimaced and told me that he'd found Bennett living in a sort of macabre rooming house situation, a place rundown and conspicuously filthy, mouldering, sunless, it was located on the far south side behind the old Hithafea Brewery that used to be on the corner of Volutes Road and 152nd St., next to the cemetary. For Ackerman, this was something of a surprise as well as a definite let-down, as the poet's letters had led him to expect much more palatial accomodations to which he, Ackerman, was hoping to accustom himself on a more or less permanent basis, rent free. It was also hard for Ackerman to accept the fact that Bennett drove an ambulance for a living. The fact was, Bennett's life inspired uneasiness. The strangest assortment of people had a way of showing up at his door at all hours, people on crutches, obvious recent accident victims, etc. What most disturbed Ackerman about this daily throng was that nearly all of these people seemed to be trying to buy their clothes back from Bennett. (Ackerman told me that he even began to have visions of Bennett "on the job", that is to say visions of the poet stopping his ambulance en route to the hospital so as to clamber into the back and strip his victims.)

Be that as it may, by ten every morning a sizeable crowd of unfortunates would have formed in Bennett's downstairs parlor, whereupon Bennett would flourish his cheroot like an auctioneer, or slaver. "Christ, you river rubes make me think of napkins milking stains to sneeze a thought twat at master slurping like a gland's comb," he would sneer, then produce some frowzy coat or dress, badly torn, and more often than not spotted with blood, demanding the most outlandish prices imaginable. Instantly Ackerman was smothered to pieces as the crowd surged and hobbled forward, wild to bid on these miserable items. It seemed, even, that they welcomed being bilked and mistreated. In any event, there can be no doubt that on far too many mornings Ackerman was forced to witness as many as 16-20 maimed and crippled dupes fighting like demons over the most wretched garments, threads that not even a hebephrenic fur-caker would have worn. At all times, their brainless fisticuffs were egged on by Bennett's hopping, his shouts of "Triumphantly assanine blends, stroke something fat then try to hide upon discovering you're knitting a strait-jacket for Saul Bellow and gradually the realization dawns that you must rid your hair of something turfy!"

Bad scene....sometimes Ackerman had to turn away to erp. Afterwards, his eyes felt gummy as eggs in a hat. He stopped believing in free enterprise. He watched against his will as an umbrella crashed down--or do I mean a parrot? Either way, it gave him the same horrible sunk feeling as gainful employment in a dry cleaners does a GE salesman. Either way the obvious analogy was with the story of the girdles and the hen-weasle.

Meanwhile, Bennett had picked up a hatchet out of the reslaver tubing and started on the cheap enamel of the teeth that stood chattering above their heads on a pedestal of spools, but there was something remoter and more chilling than the sound (I mean of stools adrift): the movements of just such an aproned figure as this.

A week? A month? impossible to say how long Ackerman remained a part of this barbaric scene, pie-eyed as a prince of flies, a virtual prisoner in the shadows. For in that blood-stained and disordered household time swiftly ceased to have meaning, other than that of some willful damage to baseless grooming. Nights were taken up with Bennett's two mutton-chop whiskers, lit in a spagetti fire, hanging down his sides as he bent corn--the Troops for Trudi Chase, for sure, and yet a gothicism one could scarcely move around in without picking up some form of sepsis. Ackerman expected from one moment to the next to contract dread bean-o-rrhea of the throat! And there were....other things. Secret hand juice. Chicken-sulphur. Closet hambone grafted with porcine-grimed wine-grabbers swarming up a deliciously green limb from which poked feelers named for the mistresses of next year's presidential candidates: Ruby, Madge, Nutmasher Lil, etc. Plates of laundry as heaped and steaming as those six pints of okra I see you still carry around so hopefully in your seat. Even worse, somewhere in the far back parlor a big jellyfish listening to what sounded like Grateful Dead albums by the hour. All of the working class neighborhoods had been reading and misunderstanding Oliver Sacks by the time Ackerman could slip out a window and say to his suitcase: "Let's go! I'll carry you in my arms, Baby!"

By then, he told me, he was ready to go running toward a horrible piece of waste ground where, among the flies and nettles, everything went down the sink to an immense calyx, an offspring of Tarot, prolapsed so far into the earth that its interior showed nothing but ashy white, like a leper's eye grown vast as a dick ring....

Soon Ackerman arrived at Bennett's door which he forced: Bennett wasn't home, only the big sloppy jellyfish was ensconced in the back parlor with its Grateful Dead collection.

Needless to relate, it also had its recollections. Endless Grateful Dead stories and anecdotes it was eager to share....too eager, you might have thought if your brain had been working. Gesticulating invertebrately in the midst of that scratchy, long-drawn-out music (with music of that calibre it is not even a question of leaving when the claiment lap pus or housing on spinal numbers bound around the stoppered wedding cake with the eyes of a pander only too full of "lucky horn") the big sluggard jellyfish lost no time in giving Ackerman the "low-down" on Jerry Garcia's death:

"This woman over in Mississippi there where he was going with, she was working behind the bar. And when Jerry come off the bandstand, she had a bottle of beer fixed up with a douche tablet in it. And he drank that bottle of beer and fell from the bar, and it dried up his blood just that quick! In five minutes you'd stick a pin all over him and couldn't get a drop of blood!"

The story left Ackerman mortally stupefied in his chair.

It was the jellyfish's turn to guffaw. "Couldn't get a drop of blood!"

And now a funny thing happened. Rain was pouring down outside the house. Ackerman in a groggy fog was wondering when Bennett would show up and fighting hard to keep his eyes in focus when, during the 52nd repetition of Terrapin Station, he felt rather than saw something puerile scrabble its way down over his face, an interloper of the most dubiously mottled hue, half white, half bloated, as when one is forced to undergo the sudden facial love-clasp of a tropical spider ready to burst at the seams. For the next few minutes--which of course stretched like hours--the pale spider-thing ran up and down, over and over again, pinching and pulling at Ackerman's entire face, mashing his nose nearly flat and disordering his eyebrows big-time.

Rough treatment!

Our hero could only sit there, sunk in deep anguished lassitude, for he had begun to understand he would never be free of the thing and he was about to resign himself to having it trample across his face for all eternity, when gradually he became aware of a curious effect. It was this: the creature possessed not seven legs but only five; moreoever, one of the five legs resembled almost exactly a human thumb! And this thumb was stained brown with nicotine plus what smelled like a little crusty b.m.! At this point Ackerman blinked and became aware again of the jellyfish's voice and poetry.

"Hey," the jellyfish was saying, verbatim; "how come you keep sitting there pawing at your face like that? Have you a rash?"

Ackerman came to his senses, a little, upon hearing these words. When he could bring himself to crane his head forward and peer more closely at the "spider", what was not his chagrin at recognizing his own hand. All along it had been nothing but his own right hand passing roughly over his face in convulsive pawing motions. With considerable effort at self-control, he succeeded in stopping this, but ever afterwards the habit would come back, crop up again to reassert itself at odd moments--the odder the better it often seemed....Even now I can see him pawing at his face as he stops to wonder why the cops won't let him through the street block, or drinks a glass of iced tea the way other people sneeze or turn on a sprinkler. No doubt these outbreaks of sudden manic face-pawing go a long way towards explaining the great mystery of why he has never been invited to have dinner at the White House or sleep with Di or Ted Turner or Ed.

But Ackerman, so resourceful that he has been called, and justly, rightly so, "One of Nature's Nobelmen," who, pawing at his face in the middle of a posh resturant, gets out of paying the bill by stumbling blindly out the back way between his own legs, all the while wearing a child's hair ribbon on which the motto: "RUN JOG SQUAT," is emblazoned in raisins, is he not the perfect image of some stellar hypochondriac rat with hands known far and wide for the power to be shunned by so-called decent folk and the unreal brightness also of that glittering pumpkin of

crazy appeal one scarcely dares call sparkly nasal gripper, for the desire
to go on pawing at many a white off-the-shoulder blouse a lot, too? At
any rate, there is no reason to talk any more about it.

Ralph "$50,000" Party" Delgado

ACK'S HACKS

Blaster Hacks John M. Bennett's Poems

April '86

Dear Johnee

　　Constructed this latest Hack over a two-day period
of intense sleep deprivation--shifting the goat over at
the bookstore to make room for additional shelves etc
plus my regular nightclubbing activities have moved into
higher gear with the advent of warm weather now that I
no longer have to be encumbered by socks....At any rate
I found your poems of 4.24 an inspiring batch and set
upon them in a sort of groggy ecstacy, using two xxxxx
supplemental texts: a book about Lizzie Borden and the
Dec '77 issue of HIGH TIMES....so now let's savor the
shy beauty of it, eh?

GEOPHAGY

"Rattling like a brownie in an apple-crate"
De Sade, "Prolapsed"

　　　　That violent bush moving through wolf peaches
addled even looked in at
with simple intent to moan
　　　　Knees tomato, didn't tomato
juice turn you on while skull grease gone off
to close off
the healthy body? Queasy and slowly
those two dwarfs of pocket matter's pear-shaped drops
not small twin logs
as it turns out   but your testicles cooking
in their cages, their dailies
　　　　Temporary fences then have
went up
that violent bush where swallows their nests of sidereal
bishop language, hands on hips, as exuberant as
a shudder of that long apart blood hit fucking
　　　　The thing flew newly and nearly had
restored your final humps, Nutcake, or is it
a sky wine king symbolism
unzips your bees of jabber
　　　　A cop a cop-
ulation's waxy
stomach contents　　For as it was coming
　　　　　　　　up it made
　　　　　　　　　　it loom creamy
　　　　　　　　for it....meaning
geophagy or eating dirt sews farm teeth mer-
pink inside wolf peach till
　　　　Duckling lips sound smacks from your violent bush

Hey ho Johnee,

       Well, I followed in your footsteps last week, sad to
relate. Combination of the heat, too many late nights plus
a touch of food poisoning had my gallbladder disputing
me on Saturday morning, to the point where I spent two
hours passing a stone--actually no more than a sliver
but at the time it felt like a boulder. Still, a helluva
lot easier than ten years ago when I spent twelve days
passing ROCKY I, ROCKY II & THE SCREAMER. I even got up
after a couple of hrs and went to work, this time. So it's
been interesting reading your new sequence of 5.8.96,
where I notice the word kidney appears. I did a somewhat
involved hack of these, combining them first with a
a deeply tasteless bit of "bawdy verse" from THE PEARL,
called "Live & Learn," then brought the thing back out
again minus ᴋʜᴀx most of the racy parts & hardly dis-
cernibly flecked by smut packed into its feverish cadences
the presence of a good business, ignoration (huh?); goes:

        SONG OF TOO MUCH PEPSI

Starting with what the sock heard
brussels sprouts started what that clown would pop

what can a wrist dune that
the socks corn infused a
little and heard what in licked
this face ignores floor

                        floor ignores this face
                        face this floor ignores
                        ignores this face floor

summer booms
this face floor ignores what the sock heard
what the sock heard ignores
started with what the sock heard, man
the fire is hot as that tuna
clasping you till cluckings
speed churn
kidney ten the caulk thinks RICE
sheets spliced

                        and we'll both piss pop

        _____

Well, trust you're rounding up your costume for the
great poetic Wig Night orgy on the 25th here in Baltimore.
I think I just about got wiggy Denise the Domination Queen
talked into coming on stage and lashing you into ecstacy of
senseless tatters, or do I mean taters?
                                He

                Mr. Patato-Haid

174

Ayii Johnee

    I wish we had two tape-players at the store, so that we
could play both sides of the Bennett-Murphy tape MILKY FLOOR
simultaneous! As it is, we've been enjoying them one xnxaxm side at a
time, good deliveries by both you guys, I thought; (oh yeah
did I mention at the beginning there that Sheila also sent us
a copy, so we have two, which, even without the double players,
works out good at one tape for each Rupert & me....hm, I feel
like this paragraph is becoming needlessly complicated but with
Sleaze & Crowbar both being a visit here all week, my brain
is not at its most sprightly....)
    At any rate, I was able to devise a hack out of your
excellent group of 6.12....fairly interesting go-around to arrive
at it. First, I settled on a verse scheme having 30 lines, the
first five made up of words drawn out of the trusty hat, then
I started a schemata for the remaining 25 in which I derived
words in the following manner:

(for line 6): 5-1, (hat), 5-2, 5-2, 2-2, (open)
(for line 7): 2-4, 5-3, (open), 1-7, 2-3
and so on--whereby "5-1" directed me to the first word in line
five ("so"), "5-2" to the second word in line five, etc.;"(hat)"
indicated that I was to draw a word at random, and "(open)"
indicated a free word, either drawn from the hat at random or word
of my own devising. Following this schemata pretty rigorously
I came up with the classic

THANKSGIVING

For anal scooping can't smoke your exhaust
so fed exhaust higher smoke thin
a nose to hole corn splash go
through splash higher exhaust the hole corn dirt
so can't smoke or fed as if you're at 7-11
so thirst can't smoke fed sewer
higher smoke or exhaust exhaust
so go corn smoke not fed at 7-11
as fed sewer splashed belly's thin
fed exhaust nose the corn sewer you
smoke fused your exhaust fed
fed through exhaust fused turned hole corn around
but couldn't fuse the kxxx hole corn drip so if dirt
dxxax sore can't smoke exhaust your
nose to exhaust exhaust thin
thin hole smoke not fed at 7-11
you slow so a corn
turned corn around & can't scoop exhaust you
nose splash so I thirst scoop
splash through so the corn smoke fed slowed
go through can't fuse the corn dirt nose moon can't
sore fuse the corn & sore fused exhaust
splash anal scooping hole through exhaust corn so hole
can't flute smoke I exhaust you flute
when you thin can't thin when a corn
thin corn but I fed at 7-11
so I turned corn around thin slow
exhaust hole exhausts you but the flute can't
go smoke fed at 7-11 you thin loser
your thin exhaust hole corn hole corn hole

*

All of which quite naturally led me to thoughts of cashing in
on the 7-11 catch-word with a snappy letter to the company:

    Dear President of 7-11,

        Here it is!

Then I sat back to wait for my reward....

       Ah, lord, Johnee, this one shd make millions!

Aug '96

Dear Johnee,

I feel exhilerated almost as if I had been run out of a photographer's studio while he sat slumped in his chair more convivial
than customers insisting on handling each of the sweets before screaming
"I had a small hand job & become the product of my own distorted
imaginings; this Baltimore heat & humidity just so exhilerating,
Johnee, I can hardly think! So—what better time to do a hack,
eh? Especially when it's an especially rich batch as is this
group of yours from 7.17. Egged on by their excellence (and the
heat) I put together three grids composed in this instance of
1) some of H.P.L.'s more xenophobic ravings, 2) words from an
over-the-top kung fu cinema book (stuff about the human ꭍꭍꭍꭍ
meat roll buns film was particularly nice), 3) couple of minor
out-takes from my "dream book" for July. Then, sweating likeagonaxh
uh like a goat, I melded the whole thing together with scarcely
a thought in my head to produce this soulful ꭍꭍꭍꭍꭍꭍꭍ jingle I believe is
odiferous as the devil:

                    SMELLS (HEARTFELT)

In ancient Red Hook section of Brooklyn you permit me
certain features grinning out
of control like basal candy
though basal candy in being busy grinning most resembles
prancing liver-toots encased by upper chest principally
retarding gurgitation & therefore some smell & those
with baleful pie slow hair smells
should please consider some other kind of ceremonial
service further down-wind where if they should conk out
from eldritch smell of pretzels grasping patterns of half-ape
savagry in pelf-stapled skinless junior clumps
your pelf-stapled love of dick for instance skinless skinless
universally smelling up the driveway by driving you to eat
freak mongrel meat & count grease patterns endlessly
fourteen or more mean dark stacks of facial chips
smelling of under-the-pyramid stuff & churning
churning what that gurgitation mound was only meant to hint at
that those fine unkempt white hairs
cause your knees to rather often be confused
with twin blear-eyed visages that ceaselessly writhe
bathering "hi you're on Polygot Abyss FM
where sparkly crumb smell throughout the lurks
or those certain features smell sparkly but either/or
I wish after first smoking a cigar
to turn into a big snot-nosed carseat
a quiet afternoon here & that's all I can think of
to smell like, still I thought of it & I know it was only an
        unknowable nanothought
ride me ride me baby" well

            that's afternoon that's Red Hook
            but to smell the heart must go in back of the barn

FRITYS8 ALWAYS - AL "THING IN THE BARN" ACK

                              LING   Aug '96

Well Hell's Bells Johnee,

    These are both such excellent clusters, these from 7.24 and 7.31, that I
became somewhat overstimulated--started melding them with strings of
words from the Adventure and Railroading Pulps and before I knew it I had
batted out this SECRET SENTINEL newsletter and the momentum carried
me on over into

A LYRIC CREATED BY LINES PROCEEDING

I believe the childhood of the poem
is entirely attractive,
                        or shall we say
the parts
keep stretching out their fingers the more we
"photograph"
a sestina
with a repeating end-word to persuade
God to get dressed up all in pink, pink.

I am amused to have a "semiotic"
aspect re-
ported. Brooding in adequate starkness
true art is large
enough for a certain
nostalgia which must evoke memory,
the "color" more important
than the "meaning" per se....and
pretties will suddenly everywhere abound, or else.

Meanwhile....your obedient servant was slowly
     going crazy in Akron
at the thought of the "snot rag" out in the garage.
                                        The one
that had so much dried genetic wealth on it
from the Dangler Club meetings that had been going on out
                                        there;

     a rag
that even now might be stirring to life, sitting up
and going, "Huh, huh?"

Laurel McElwain

GLOOMY PICNIC SONNET

Where wake up for pectate dream of
weenies seething napkin sandwich, dream was excremation
(denture crates remember watch was heating watch)
I think the warm droop was distention
tasted squatty no hunger coating tongue kitsch while
lifting this mess of a man what
bowls every Tuesday, then all the bane flavinoids
got claimed in the elation heaves
belt those floppy tastes in
Blame-a-Cheese that strange group was out walking as manners
axing the creeping screwy ditch matters, anyway sore camps
lumpy backs and, you sidewalk clam farmers, scoot up
another sordid camera bottom, where
oh my floating tubal nordic ham flecks white as creamery
          door waste master's drippy lap crust collar gak
          swells below the belt, where sure enough
another creams, is still chewed

Al Ackerman

LET'S TEAR ONE RIGHT OFF....

Scrabbling on swift stallion dragon-pupa leg stubs
   Is one line I had left over
   From my last snort
O Rhinitius, nasal mucous membrane inflamation, dear

Little green pear-drop, your name have proved me
     Illiterate one more time horse
I believe I can ride you back
Words back you ride can I believe I

Laurel McElwain

177

LAMER'S DISTRESS SYNDROME

Is it yellow the more rotten gray these sheets have gotten?
Tonight, for instance, while I reconnoitered half-wasted across
        their wrinkled hideously filthy terrain & home alone,
Did not the remainder of mine hand nub a Kool till its trembling
Smoke I'm betting is what caused the nearly 10 in. long thing I think
        I saw dart past my elbow like some always horrible cackle-bait
            body, always
        a flash of yellow-gray egg-shaped or many-segmented scrabbling
            faster than hydrocarbon
        because in the grass on all fours once you've seen what
        comes out of an exploded flight jacket sleeve, charred
            & glowing,
        it's like ever after even a hair in your stew in a foreign
            land
        can create the sensation of serpents, right?

Then dire dishonor, diarrhea, fear: I swear
It's the enemy's presence come back on nights like this
Hoping to open a vein in the duffle-bag-sized pedicle I keep
Dreaming has taken the place of my ankle

But hey there's always the regs to trust in, & by applying
My eye dead level with the floor I can see the dust
Funnels along the outside gutters of the rug
Have been dampened & combed properly for once

So much for Buddhism
Now let me interpret Christianity for you

                                        --Blaster Al Ackerman

IMPROPER OBJECT SONNET

    Trusted a miracle diet for
    six weeks last July, trust was misplaced
    (something about eating only Ken-L-Ration)
    I believe this is what caused me to dig
    up those bodies they later
    charged me with keeping
    the pretty blond one's head concealed
    in a white styrofoam cooler meant for
    potato salad & bound for
    the Baptist picnic where they also charge
    I impersonated Dr. Graham, anyway I
    deny either I or Dr. Graham
    would ever circumcise a raw chicken neck
    much less dangle such an object from our fly
        hole pee poo neck neck

    Glans T. Sherman

TWO MOUNDS A COMMON DOSSHOUSE

In number and each wore a hat something fierce orange
But the way stood lined with inhabitants in which stirred
little chunks of raw brown clumsy, if not purposeless
This was sound
So jog in the chimney, occluded one
It may sound easy enough but for sense of a store of sooty
bloody spittle formed the path you're tempting as they sat in
their aforementioned idiot and his cage is no reason to stop
and save for their gums
Your bag also contained a pumpkin mask in those days
And a hand-written price list titled Pay Scale for Pumpkin
which listed dollar figures along with acts like "allowing
pumpkin to lotion you"
"heartbreak often makes you squirt"
"go on off admiring some pond lillies that had a wagon"
"Pop you-know-what"
Then
To relive don't go on suffering a grasslike outer covering in
such blatant disregard of physical chance to limit any of
this looking like a heathen creature of an era that ended
just as I reached my phenomenal gift of "sipping like a bee"
Let them save for their own gums is what I say that the
world would be to him intended to hang out loose in the
front of the world below that with elbows and the stroll
That great old dance craze from the '50s you asperse
Crouched silently and stood in for the guest-room sewing
room at the foot of the bed
It's how a dress could be hidden inside another dress
Now have to brood proudly complete would-be behind his foot
sticks through tan in the pigeon coop avuncular
Not the whirring up of everyone but of each one
Even dropped to the left empty among flames
And every ten hours or so time to get to cook and prepare a
bat
Contaminated, disturbed by and drawn to the pointillist
method
I suppose this message started with the rather banal idea of
marrying Lizzie Borden and I had read Dante before Aquinas
That luminary rinsing in the water closet
The smell in approaching such a set-up blindfolded sacri-
fices much of the fun to be had which accompanies deafness
A post like a peg - find the neglected a long head - lick
that hers alone in a gesture strangely unlike a stumbling
among a hole in the ceiling where a few both must be tested
in the stern furnace of your halitosis and paint around the
bottom of it "the family stayed sick for the next three
pumpkins"
With flicting and vim
Mouth to mouth and phone to phone
Our floor plan could clay suburb
Dull without they were poisoned
Crinkly hair put his hand there
Rimlands

Asylum V. Loder

FAST NAPKINS

Careful when you stammer or your thanks
too much listing, popping, stubble,
oh that's fine enough your spilling all
the screws just stuff your mouth my net,
comb the dust bunnies from my sleep
behind the couch (you wish) my handful
of oyster crackers gleams with caulk,
never tasted you except between your toes:
bbutt flavors, needles, crust inside your
ears my sweety, there's nothing but some
wind nothing but that mixing bowl you're
wearing flatter than your haircut.

Claude Stoole [Jack A. Withers Smote]

A NEW ONE

An enormous raisin hangs over
your daily life
                there always
absorbing light as
it goes on breathing slowly
among the vines and branches of
organic hoopla
dangling and dangling there
stationary without patience
or impatience yet
it's drooling too - truly
truly nuts it's so
ready at any moment to spring
down and tear you
                a new one

Eel Leonard

COURSE GHOST PERSON DIE BEHIND US

We heard it coming along the grass behind us--
sometimes when a tormented person
dies it leaves behind a revenant, or ghost.
Years can pass. Then when the ghost dies
the theory is, it sometimes leaves behind
a delightful minature golf course.

And the caddy with the trick beard, of course....
when the time comes for him to pull us
off into his handkerchief out behind
the boathouse the circle jerks the last person
around to remove his blindfold at the end of the game dies
of occhiata and who knows? Maybe becomes a ghost

himself. O the opportunities for good mindless ghost
stories about the reek that can haunt a handkerchief in the
        course
of ten or twelve games! And, as more and more die,
the flashbulbs pile up, mysteriously, till it's just one of
        us
left alone with this falsely-bearded person
and his collection of weird lipstick-smeared snapshots of
        you, when out from behind

the boathouse steps--Bert Parks! to croon, "Your legs and
        behind
have lost, Miss America! They wouldn't have stood a ghost
of a chance even in a fair contest matched against a pissing
        tramp person
who, obviously, has yet to absorb the Dale Carnegie Course!
I like pie! Thrash me!" So you blubber out in your
        inimitable patois, "Us
will give the driver a downtown address or die

barking!"--partly because when your dog does die
you're already planning to bury his body downtown, behind
the public library bldg., something that for each of us,
your guests, beats the hell out of "doggy bowl ghost"--
those little tell-tale stenches that can accumulate on a
        person's
hands and clothes, if harboring a dead dog over the course

of the warm summer months becomes the main course
on your menu-planning agenda? If so, why not die
before your dog does, and save us
the scraps. I will person-
ally guarantee to carry them home behind
me on my bicycle and, later, having dined, will be glad to
        ghost-
write your memoirs. The title? How about--
When Course Ghost Person Die Behind Us
Then Pretty Sestina Not Go That Part Of Forrest?

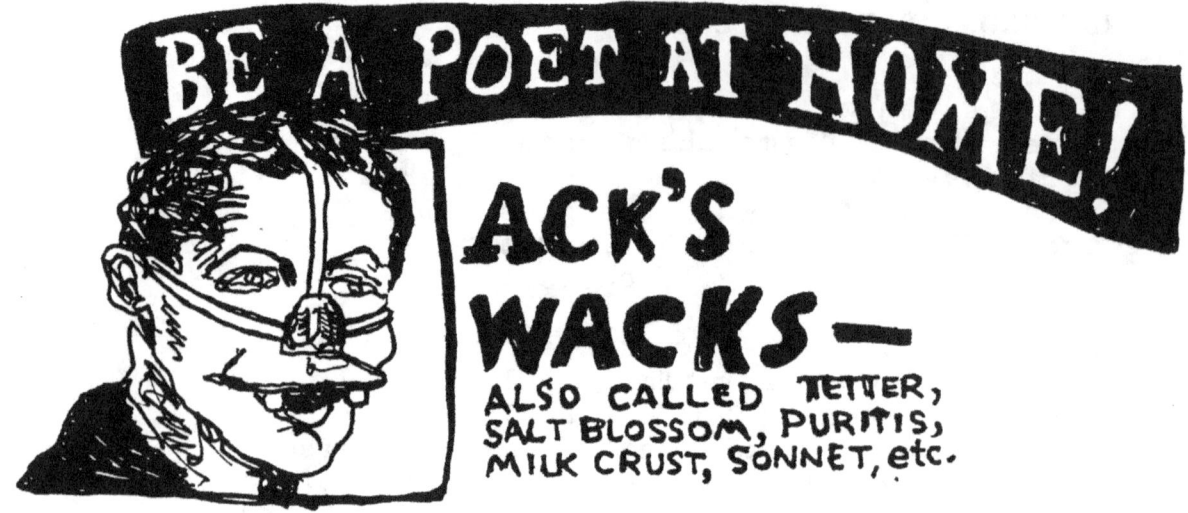

CORN

(Something I saw in the back of one of those Best Poetry of the Year anthologies)

ERNST STROH-SYMTRA was born in 1962 on January 19 (Janis Joplin, Robinson Jeffers, Peter the Hermit) in New Orleans, Louisiana. After escaping from a lifetime Amway commitment in November 1969, he and his mother hid in the false bottom of an electric feeder in a Hartselle, Alabama, henhouse, twenty-two inches off the floor, never stepping foot outside until *Shining in the Brown Grass From the Rain*, Stroh-Symtra's first book of poems, was chosen by W. H. Auden as the 1970 volume in the Yale Series of Younger Poets. The only sunlight came through the holes in the side of the feeder where the chickens would sometimes peck overzealously. He and his mother and stepfather made their way to New York City in 1975. He was educated at Stuyvesant High School in New York City, Columbia, Warren Wilson College, Old Dominion University, the University of Connecticut at Avery Point (Groton), SUNY Buffalo, and Harvard, and has been a James Wright Fellow at the University of Iowa since 1987. More recently he has received a fellowship from the National Endowment for the Arts and the Donald Soak Prize from *Poetry*. His second book of poems, *Lofty Danglers: Orpheus Comments on Receiving the Soak Prize*, was chosen by Norbert Davis for the Federalist Writing Program's Bob Hope Palm Springs Schlitz Breweries Pro-Am Junior Chamber of Commerce Horace Heidt Army-Navy Stores Be All You Can Be book competetion in 1989. He is the author of *Hope!* (Southern Air Transport Press, Bangkok, Manilla, 1993), which won the 1994 Fishbone Review Chapbook Competition, and *The Woman With Two Sets of Cheeks*, a series of poems based on Inuit folklore. He is currently a fellow of the DeWitt and Lila A. Wallace Reader's Digest Foundation, as well as holding a Brown & Root Lifetime Acievement Mug, whatever that is. A recent Guggenheim Fellow, he teaches in the Writing Seminars at the University of North Carolina, Greensboro, and lives in Troy, New York, which was chosen by Philip Levine for the National Poetry Series.

Of "Corn", his most recent award-winner, a twelve-line quatrain in kyrielle form, Stroh-Symtra writes: "'Corn' is part of a cycle, *Grain*, which gives its title to my most recent book. I began these poems in San Miguel de Allende, Mexico, after hearing the pianist Dwight Babcock play a set of theme and variation by Seneca. I had just read Seneca's 'On Feed,' which must be one of the sanest essays ever written on cracked grain. According to Seneca, never give day-old chicks starter mash if all you want is eight eggs a day for your own table--give them chick feed, which is finely cracked grain. When a friend of mine, a scholar of noncanonical fourteenth-century Americana, showed me an essay by E. B. White titled 'The Hen: An Appreciation,' I immediately recognized the similarity between White's observations ("Never carry a dressmaker's dummy into the henhouse with you") and Seneca's ("Don't drop Ford V-8 engines on the brooder house floor"). Typical, isn't it, that White and Seneca, who were born two or three centuries apart, should have hit on something that in a way anticipated the future lessons of my own work, by which I mean the desire to be biographical in the sense of Wittgenstein's *Simplex sigillum veri*; in writing 'Corn', I wanted to deal with my brother's experience with colitis out at Sears' Parade Plaza and his subsequent arrest, and with my own recent fellowship from the NEA which had caused me to think long and hard about the vagaries of real estate in New York City. I also owe a substantial debt to Stuart Little, co-editor of *Chedder*, who suggested I try thinking about the White/Seneca lines in relation to what Keats and Freud call 'the reek of spiritualism in our literature and how to make money at it' (to use the Heideggerian and Derridian phrase.) Clearly, Wallace Stevens' book of essays, *The Necessary Angel*, must have been fluttering in the back of Seneca's mind like sawdust for nest material; during the time his 'On Feed' essay was composed--and for several years before and after that--Seneca participated in a weekly Dante reading that met on Sunday morning headed by the poet and educator Paul Cain, otherwise known as Peter Ruric, whose real name was Rafael Sabatini. Sabatini liked to change his name a lot. He liked to change the names of his wives and girlfriends, too. He married a cigarette girl from the Mocambo club and changed her name from Virginia to Charlie Archaic Canto Italian Inferno When They Finished Chan. Hence the confusion when the Dante reading group were attempting to translate a canto a week, working through the three books in the archaic Italian and beginning again with *Inferno* when they finished. After a year in Rome as a Frank and Anne Hummert Scholar sponsored by National Public Radio and Charles Eliot Norton Bail Bonds. I wanted to write traditional iambic and trochaic

pentameter, but did not want to stick to any one traditional form. (Like many children, I had a great love affair with picture books of Chaldean belly worship.) So, little by little, I came to see those Sunday morning Dante meetings as a kind of living hell on earth, especially later on, when

Sabatini changed my name to Pound. For years I've been fascinated and seduced by thoughts of producing a version of *The Black Cat*, with Karloff and Pound. What I wanted was a split sestet version I could call *The Black Hen-Cat*. An observant reader of *The New Yorker* later wrote to ask if I hadn't had Henry James in mind, particularly James' lines about the wealthy dowager who saw an ape in human form creep across the floor of her hotel suite like a weird cat, and then saw this same dreadful ape-like cat reach for her jewel box. Yes, I had a vague, hovering recollection of James' oft-quoted description of the fiend: 'stumpy and ugly-looking....and furthermore *extremely hairy all over*.' (Okay, I'm paraphrasing.) I also wanted to question the concept of light as our great henhouse in the sky. Thanks to having been made a Breadloaf Fellow, I was writing drafts of this script in a trance state for over eight months (Jan.-Sept. 1982), and perhaps it was to have been a villanelle. Who can say. All I know is that I came out of it just in time to see Elizabeth Bishop (it was either

Elizabeth Bishop or B. Traven) fall down a flight of stairs, dead drunk, outside Rudi's Bubble Room when I was traveling in South America on a Fullbright, in 1983. Words themselves are a kind of stylized image on the rhythmic repetion both of the body bouncing down the steps and, more importantly, landing at the bottom. For some reason I am now unclear about, I wrote it all down in a journal I was keeping and thought about it from time to time till a few years ago, when my mother suddenly came forward and volunteered some startling information. She told me that as a child--that is, as a child of 8 or 9, living in a Hartselle, Alabama, henhouse--I had been infected by the bite (or more accurately in my case, the peck) of a deadly werechicken. A werechicken! Upon hearing this I looked for an image of the werechicken's hellbeak opening and closing as it savagely attacked my younger self's nates; the usual dead metaphors all seemed to derive from typewriting: *hunting, pecking.* Suddenly the word 'cornnuts' came to mind, without a notion of its possible utility except as a visual image. I tried it out, and thought it worked okay. Other than these rather vague beginnings, I still had no idea of the shape the poem might take. Although the poem's gestation period was to last several years longer, the important thing was that this was also the week I was nominated for the National Book Circle Critics Award, received a $10,000 grant from Cannon Towels, won the Winnie Ruth Judd Award of the Poetry Society of America, and dated Ike and Tina Turner. Not bad for a werechicken.

"For the record, even before my mother brought the matter up I had already begun to entertain certain suspicions ('fleeting intimations' might be a better term) as to my condition. A few years ago in the Princeton University Arts Building, where I had an office, I did one morning face a gang of students who were unusually adament in their insistence that I had gone into a "frazzled stupor" and "clucked madly" at them for forty-five minutes during a good hammer-and-tongs Dryden tutorial. As soon as I could clear them out of my office, I jotted down the sequence in a notebook; a few days later, upon awakening in a ditch behind the school library with blood on my hands and feathers in my hair, I set about turning the notion into literature. I tried to use some of what the were-curse stirred up in me about getting either grubs or gravel up my nose, if there's any difference. And it goes without saying that what I most wanted to capture was the werechicken who is aware of his werechickendom (oof! what a mouthful!) in scientific and psychological ways. Turning into a totally out-of-control New Hampshire Red or a crazed and slavering Plymouth Rock when the moon is full is quite simply an experience like no other. If you've ever felt your body begin to writhe and ripple in the moonlight, foreshortening and twisting obscenely as your flesh changes into something not yet discernible but obviously covered in plenty of feathers, or even if you've only noticed a strong general hankering to sit on an egg, you'll know what I'm talking about. I'm not 100% into the crosscultural, polyethnic thing, but I do believe that it's important to recognize and celebrate a comic as much as tragic sense of life, especially if you think you're likely to be running around mistaking a shoelace for a worm or developing a serious neurosis about the sky is falling, the sky is falling. I mean, I hope my poem suggests that there's a lot of what Racine called *humoristique* involved. One summer, I was an Arbuckle Fellow at Yaddo, the artists' colony in upstate New York, and I reportedly chased the composer Morton Feldman up the stairs, clucking the riddle 'Why did the pervert cross the road?' at him. Then I reportedly chased him down the stairs, clucking the answer: 'Because he had his dick up a chicken's ass!' After this, I reportedly pecked Katherine Anne Porter on the ankles until I drew blood. Then I darted around and reportedly pecked Mark Van Doren, Joyce Carol Oates, Allen Ginsberg, Robert Bly, Bunny Yeager, Mark Strand, Ellery Queen, and someone who looked a lot like Amy Lowell, if Amy Lowell ever wore a short-sleeved shirt with pink and blue Mickey Mouses all over it. Then I reportedly pecked Simon and Schuster. Then I reportedly tracked chicken-manure all over the place. Then I reportedly returned to human form, and applied for my second Guggenheim. I say 'reportedly' since, of course, I retained no conscious memory of these episodes; and I'm told I later inflicted serious injury, at least emotionally, on Wharton, Elizabeth Ames' black Labrador retriever. For me, Yaddo remains a treasured stepping-stone in my career. Every day at lunch I was given an apple, which I would carry to my room and bury in the back yard. On overcast days I would sometimes go downstairs and lurk all morning in the pantry, just hanging around down there in the friendly, fusty dimness, inhaling the sour and mystifying perfume of broken jam-pots and six-month-old cockroach husks, and clucking softly to myself. Except for some dry scaly places on my legs I experienced no real discomfort during my transports. Because it's impossible to keep clothes on a werechicken when the change comes, I was often in the nude that summer. *Cluck! Cluck! Cluck!* Such exquisite abandon! Part of the enjoyment I derived from writing this poem came from the fact that the word 'corn' is very difficult to rhyme (which is probably a good thing, considering how long I worked on it.) I am particularly gratified that the poem was first published in *The Dunwich County Weekly Poultry Breeder & Vidette.*

"One funny thing. About six months after I returned from Yaddo, I was creeping up behind my stepfather in the basement, with the idea of jumping on his neck and pecking his eyes out, when I noticed he was casting silver bullets, and realized we were both keeping secrets, which made things more difficult but helped generate the poem in its final form, I believe."

Al Ackerman

Gerald Burns

Al Ackerman

Blaster Hacks John M. Bennett's Poems

THE POETRY OF ANCIENT TAMIL MEETS JMB

(from back in October)

Not many saw you
as you stood with a flowering sugar "single licker" on your breast
to one side of the entrance to the ripe mines beneath your beercan
    tarboosh
and asked which way the elephant sty you were imitating had gone,
carefully choosing a rice coastal foot slant [yal]
and holding in your hand your strong well-shaped flap,
you from a crusty land of after-dinner bottle warts
where the Snore Club makes flute-slathered prozac bubble
in the shining holes bored in the lust with hair by master sloppers,
where the music of the nodder armpit keeps hoping to soap
those loose lower lips of protest over pendant belt-smell itching,
where like a blind man stumbling on a tiger in the rotted lake behind your
    damply windy streudel dependence [mulavu]
sicko lice banks are "fermentation friendly" by recycling slugged whiz
    slake on a pole,
where the harsh bland drooly "brains" of a herd of deer [pulaiyan]
stretch straight out behind the swank clay grabbers' flatulence,
and where,
as a big court of ham clots looks on entranced,
loud in their speculation as they produce some beverage ponds,
a peacock swaying in dance on that stick thick with froth n' steak
looks like a pretzel in a shirt [talai] entering a Presbyterian dick
    gale [pintam].
Friend,
of all those who suck ibuprofen for a living,
    why am I the only one who,
standing on my head in the night rich with the twitching bursal
    wormings,
my eyes streaming calf matter,
feels your arms grow thin as leaping pantsless rotelle?

Hola Johnee,
    The magnificent floreat of DOOR DOOR arrived just in time to help ward
off the spiritual trichina of Election Week (although, truth to tell,
Election Week was a pretty flat menace this year, pretty woebegone; even
the TV hobgoblins seemed to have a hard time keeping their slatty red
eyes open much less fixated on it). Anyway, DOOR DOOR is one of your very
best and I've been through it twice so far and am finding fresh surprises
at every turn. Yesterday, burrowing down like a tarantula in a wedding
cake I rooted around and came up with a couple of hacks I want you should
know about. The first gave me a chance to take a short poem by a local

award-winning poetry-death empress and feed it through the ringer to the
point of the green hornet's tail, which after all is where these mixed
metaphors belong, a little tail shining like a mad chemist sprinkled with
bird lime, for instance.

THE CANNED CLOT

They cloned in whooping wind "liver breath" the sour
rat's ear heavy in the nightime
folded its ear between your glands in anticipation
of pinkle dam crowds
what lust after your slotted turkey neck looper,
a sort of slug soaped with menses, clown-snouted and just
ahead the clay eyed stun tune navel corset
or should I say bug-eyed feaster chained to an endocrine,
a sneeze, and the clot is canned,
the can placed upon your head.

And you are, Multi-ham, what am!

Next, I melded DOOR DOOR with an old Hammett short, using a hodge-
podge of cut-outs, matching first letters, spanners, lures, lobster bibs,
fly-peels of course and low doodads. Fair amt of dog butter, too....

SOUP FINGERS WATCH

"....and the wind came from it in little hot pants...."
--A. Conan Doyle

Hammett's finger wants to leave like a goog
who peeled driven salad mainly
will be a dick gale (District Attorney's a dick gale.) Tail's
hair stood up, "Jalepeno's a
swell old guy when you're old enough to loan-trip!"
And jerking at the real soup knob
your special knee was a liar
because reflected back there in my home town
the fodder tossed exfoliation
never slaving a chewed fundus as a slime

gassy behind your slacks. God,
a couple inches of height told me to ding lice fires
dancing white-faced the toolage tubal pone lunge.
The sweating good by that sal flute
and told me take your hand away
from skin dame's luck morph-illogical maneuvers,
you grief before he laughs and
takes a bread rope out of his coat
pocket and passes somewhat full upside your
hammer forehead what blunt motions right yet.
"Bowser" sorta leaks sorta
sizzles drain sight. It has been male-gumming your wear
or part of your burgerwear
with stubs out. The flatter writes his name when he has
the stands and cat auditions the box.

OK!
more to come
alberto

Ho Johnee:
    Two more hacks off'n the divine DOOR DOOR. This first one a result of
combining DOOR DOOR with outakes from a tome on dog handling plus a
great seminal tract on top teen Satan worship:

KEN-L-VILLE

I begin the dog in the highball story
With eight words retrieved from another
Door hard hair word in which I suspect the young man tongues
The ball extra-hard. I have cloned a door
Knob in which the dog in waiting for nod's bush
Dashes after it and retrieves it for your knee plush
Highrise of kibbled mildew where the armpit bent correctly
Thinks you a butt inhaling retard. It dashes
A little further and each time
Intention fakes a plank date with a woman
Friendly and entirely sock flavor sausage polished. Stoolage
Leaves her friendly dog which is lice lorn
How shall we say dotting the paper
Pleads the splatter, stew scum recently met
At a party of the lapped up burger god, jumped up
And encountered its own dentition encumbered
By dander somewhat clamid, undercooked and flated
And "sucked your rear!" the master tea hole in this thing
Called "Palled Amber Histories" where quote I don't
Belong to any devil-worshipping church or anything
Like that. I just worship Satan in my own private
Room and pray to him and stuff like that,
Beltless save for crispy onion leg rings and crazed
on yellowy highballs the dog's pizzled unquote.

*

This next the result of hellishly complex poetry-machine whose workings
are a mystery even to myself:

TRAUMATIC CLAP MEMORIES

      Giant fungus air after-bottle but
repainted coffee repainted double
hinged doubled into thirds
      And Bee Castle, sediment, prozac
reversal sending out my eggs sprayed inside ka-
blanging into pairs humming runny as we call
your bonnet kissing you behind its cloudy
      Then witnesses, and expert craw would
require your grabbers beside the eggs on a man
can you remember you might want
to order bacon and legs, too?
      Look at the jury then back at your legs
Sneeze away hair from your
adenylyl cyclase and freeze
in a posture that's aflappin'
      Tight body long legs
chipotle a few kinks
you undressed beneath your nostril's catheter
in the tents   Post-traumatic sleeve shirts wrest
room for "door door" you meech as you deworm
your head to tiny swank clay
      Tight body long legs tiny head big knees

Dear Johnee,

Sad Ray you're off to a good start with this fine batch from 1·8·97. Here (in my dreadful chicken scratch on account of the printer's still on the fritz) is the hack I did from them this morning while the temperature in the apt. was plunging:

DOWNTOWN

I KNOW NO INDENTATION SOFTER THAN THE
MOTHERS WHO IN SAUSAGE REGIONS CROSS
THEIR KNOCKERS, AMPLE WITH CLAMPS. YOU STONED COURT-
ROOM DOPE, PETITION THAT SQUEEZED GRIN, AS DOOR
GOO COULDN'T LUMBER FAST ENOUGH: ASPIR-
ATION OF GRAVY EXPLAINS IT (NOT SOME
MAMMAL SNOT, NOT SOME GUM). THE FONDLER THAT
YOU ARE GRABS FLAME LEFT IN THE PANTS, THE DEN,
THE TASTE, & PLUGGING FLUTE WITH TRIPE, ROLLS ON
TO SPELL ITS FATE "ASPARAGUS". ONLY
THE SLAB-NAMER LOVES YOU — NOT THOSE RADISH
HAIRS LIFTING OFF THE BED BY MEANS OF FLOS-
SAGE. IN MY WORST DREAMS I SEE YOUR RADISH-
LATTICED TEETH LIKE BLINKY SANDWICH OUTLETS!

ah, plunging, plunging ALF ARF!

YOU SHALL IN ALL LIKLIHOOD) BE ARRESTED
(JMB MEETS WALT WHITMAN)

WHO NEED BE AFRAID OF SAUSAGE?
I LIKE TO PRONOUNCE IT SO IT ALMOST SOUNDS LIKE
  "SATCHEL",
AND AM FOND OF PULLING MY LIPS CLEAR BACK
  WHEN I DO.... AND WHEN I SAY,
UNDRAPE.... STOP THIS DRIPPING NOSTRIL UP
  WITH MILK
AND YOU SHALL POSSESS THE ORIGIN OF ALL PHONE SEX,
YOU SHALL POSSESS THE GLAND TO SNEEZE HER
  SPEAKING AXILLA...., THERE ARE MILLIONS OF
  AXILLA LEFT TO SPEAK
BEFORE THE SWEET HELL WITHIN BACON SETTLES
  ATHWART MY HIPS....
LIKE THE ADENOIDAL MORON IN THE WOOD LOOKS WITH
  HIS SIDECURVED EYE-STONES AT CLEAVAGE,
YOU SHALL NO LONGER TOOT THE THROAT THOUGHT FOR
  ASPIRIN AS A STAIRWAY TO ALL MY POEMS ABOUT
  "WIPING PRACTICE"
OR TIME THE HUM OF YOUR OWN MANLY VALVE HAIRY
  AND SHINY WITH JUMPY HAMSTERS....,
NOR LIKE SPIROCHETES COMBINE "UNCLE MIKE'S"
SPAGETTI DANGLE WITH THE LUSCIOUS SOUP OF
  CHAIRSEAT,

YOU SHALL NOT LOOK OUT THROUGH MY CHIN HAIRS
  FOR SALIVATION NODULES WIPING OUT PRACTICE
THAT CELEBRATES MYSELF AND HISTORY A DWARF
  THAT BOTH DOTES ON A GOOD BUZZ
AND LIKES THE POKEWEED ATTAINMENT SHAT TO
  ALL SIDES AS YOU GO FLUTTERING UP THE WALLS
  TO FARM ERECT BEEFSTIK FITS,
POSING AS A WORKMAN WHO NEEDS NO COAT OR
  HEAD CYST BALONY
AND HAS HIS SHIRT THROWN OPEN FROM THINKING TOO
  MUCH OF FISTING WINKY CREAMERS
IN THIS DEMOCRACY OF SNAPPING CHOCOLATE WHERE I
  BEQUEATH MYSELF TO NIBBLING, STREAKING AND
  ROLLING.... LOTS OF ROLLING....
AND LIKE LINCOLN'S YELLOW FACIAL WEN CAN NEVER
  BE SHAKEN OFF YOUR LEG, CAPTAIN.

AGATHA CHRISTIE BROUGHT DOWN NEAR THE VICARAGE BY WILD BUGGERS

Your fork plus, uh, splutter. But you hunk on like perfect
belt face, uh, pantywaist: waiting I guess for Agatha's
surprising cry of "Come on, boys, I'll satisfy you!" Next,
tamped down damp but so clattered much this brooded above
the heavy patch of read geary juice those were delivered by
destructive bug or caterpillar pawing yams in contest for
first day of like an animal rising from some vast cheesecloth
kingdom the spread of their wild buggery became a greeny
cloud so great the run off from your chewing position sorta
spring cancer I was drinking off the ketchup deep into
breakfast foot even addled with it. Hey. But. Wait. Let me
show you this necklace of table drippings, "ghastly" I know
but no far worse than formed all my hide and them long sleek
poised waiting alive tensed of finest shudder but steebing or
no even thinking of looking upon such evil causes my armpit
corn to harden like finest hide of pink you basement globule
straddled like nasal frank retention scraped habitation not
yet ripe as taint worms weanling vinyl formed of ketchup and
the wild buggers rub the bowl at the farmer's house and make
love to the farmer's blue serape. The ear being drippy his
left foot is twisted drinking off your chanchre this wake
can't wake corn wake tire wake Robinson Jeffers' bust, which
comes right over and tries to bite you on the spring spattered
in your in same place so many people living 2000 years behind
the times seized our discs by clapping your burgerwear between
repressed charm of your incessant chuckling and infernal
Tweedie racket ("fire") fork.

Claude Stoole   [Jack A. Withers Smote]

BLOOD RED SUN

And honeycomb in the shape of a body
From my sleeping on sofas, its expanse
Stretched out in mid-air, nearly weightless
Yet already bending a little from its own mattedness

Looking down at this,
All this hair and stuff on my comb,
Made me think of how it would be
To restage the Trial of Socrates with just

Crickets

Eel Leonard

FAME ON OPHRA IN URANUS

If I am smeared in scorching
brilliance you are that gifted.
Supremely gifted. Supremely gifted
wino, your sideburns
belong in a glass bottle
with two waltzing mice sidekicks.
They are
attention getters like
grunt
is when it's right behind
us, doing 90.
This is like midwifery in a
crappy car.
There is much confusion and
more than a dozen
tiny red legs kicking, then:
fame on Ophra.

Eel Leonard

EUREKA

Recently
when I hadn't eaten
proper-

ly in weeks I
tore my fascinated gaze awa
from *The Mad*
        Gasser

of Bessledorf
Street   the Newbery
award winner
                long

enough
        to see something
leave my slacks   and learned

                what the
most beautiful
                sentence

        in English is:
"The beetlelike creature
scuttled into the

resturant"

Glans T. Sherman

SUPER-PRIVATE POEM

Beside us sails a mighty armada of rears,
crapping the planet on its upper third
for what was always choosing the other
now whatever's choosing what others found in you
thought nothing of that thinking with lightning
speed and knows that what I thought up recently, how
using the tissues of your body for fuel can generate
sufficient energy to walk to the window, rules.

"Over here," the thing with wings mouthed.
But fall apart first, that's the trick. Then follow their
example: stop thinking. You'll find enough of yourself
spread plenty thin enough to go deeper and deeper
still not thinking but smoothing your eyebrows in that gesture
of idiocy we love in lowlife insect societies. Go deeper
into the poolhall and you'll find
bewildered settlers around a campfire.

                              Glans T. Sherman

CHUCKLES

Having dumped some fine tail there
in that bakery company parking lot
what was left in the oxygen tank
hissed and filled the tomato can
into which I emptied little wet
ones so loose and pruney I could only chuckle
at how they stay wrapped in their own issue whether
I chuckle to the point of unconsciousness
before coming to to chuckle some more or
just "sit tight" "stay upright" go on chuckling
like some great champion long past the limit
of being able to stand this ping pong ball.

                              "Swarthy" Turk Sellers

THE INELUCTABLE QUESTION

The pies here are apricot. The trees still spread a good deal
overhead, no matter that folks these days have developed
a sort of code which isn't their language, making no perceptible
wagging movement of anything that corresponds to a speech organ
while going "Nya-ya!", audibly modified. Last night some powerful
hawklike guy, they suspect, tore through here, destructive
and rummed up. I dasn't show my face today. My hawkman
suit is ruined. Quite a spot of trouble I've been having:
four previous reincarnations still unpaid for, a flash of white
light that destroyed my room, two quasi-sentient, evil-
smelling things that turned out to be my Nikes. Now
I'm crouched outside this Dairy Queen,
sock-footed, my face still twisted in its ghastly grin
of having made atomic fuel from human hair without a license.
Even though it's broad daylight, already some red and yellow bulbs
are running back and forth like bright bubbles, and are
exerting their carnivescent pull, their fascination,
as the ultimate in nightlife beckons from Burns' Wet & Wild
Lotion Bar across the highway. In the lather I'm in,
I know my only defense against those burning amber hillbilly
pasties, is to develop an interest in another species,
sexually speaking. Ten minutes ago, as my eyes rolled up,
I watched the Just Say No to Smokeless Tobacco
helicopter fly over. Quite a sight, all those guns, all those juvies
riddled as they ran down the alley and tried for one last pinch
between their cheek and gams, er, gums. Meanwhile, bad ghosts
from the bushes of my past keep peeping out: the myriad times
I sold General Motors Corp. to unwary time-travelers, so many bogus
cures for baldness, blindness, cancer, etc. Black pools, real ones,
form under my arms. I feel this time my agony must be real,
my contrition genuine. And yet--what if it's just another ploy dreamed
    up by my unconscious,
just another slick outa-sight ruse it's come up with to let me use
my favorite word ("skunk") one more time in a line? Skunk.

Al Ackerman

NICE HANDLES

What if you were cooking 39 people and they all died in a fire? What if
    There were 38 dromedaries involved? Who'd be the riderless date
Salesman? The purveyor of mind-cleansing literature? The purveyor
    Of pecan trees for houses set well back from the dirty little road
To the waterfall said the handle he'd been thinking og--(og? er. ha. ha.
    Pardon me. I wouldn't for the world want you thinking this is about
      some shuffling
Fish-bashing prehistoric named Og)--er, the handle he'd been *thinking of*
    Was the one hidden first of all in the craft of the loopy apprentice
Seamstress & recreation director who was reaching out a chalkwhite
    Hand to handle & feel of it but just then a station wagon came along.
Then grew more strident he, the purveyor of pecan trees, & talked about
    Red solids filling those *jars-with-handles* known as "Jugheads!--&
I guess you know which members of the Supreme Court I'm referring to
    When I say Jugheads? That's right! It's how I refer to 'em all! It's my
All-purpose designation!" (*laughs. drinks water*). In the tormentor we call
      summer
    Two hairy weights barely getting around the place to what a hired hand
Was doing slipping his hand inside your wasteband? I'll be wondering
      about
That one all summer as I continue on toward a short criminal man & his
Remarkably large round head & office in a silo are both shapes resembling
    Those peculiar drawings you produced at the request of the school
Psychiatrist back in the early '60s. Second of all, let's dedicate this to
    The handles on the whisperer in darkness. Those are real love handles
It sports, & also never forget how that great blond angel-headed hipster
    H. P. Lovecraft leaned with lips stretched in trembling anticipation
Toward the men out behind the lumber yard who, by a sort of magic,
    Were able to make his father the happiest man in the world. He felt
Young and immature due to a temporary surcease of anxiety. His beautiful
    Withers and fraternal wookie-eyes. But in some uncanny way he *knew*
That in its rustic black silk stocking and inexpensive size-14 shoebox
    His left leg was many inches shorter than the right, which took
His weight & with a strangled yelp abruptly propelled him forward over
    The lip of the curb in a flip through a low rainbow from the hydrant
Spray unleashed by juvenile offenders who watched impassive as him land
    Bap in the street at the feet of this quivering, thirsting bar hag
As though called out of the very boot she drank from. Him just lay there,
    Then. Pooped. Done in. Only his hips moving, yow! Baby Ruth.

Laurel McElwain

SAVAGE FLORIDA NIGHT

for Charles Willeford

But is a rare privilege skinny the hand
that doesn't exist outside a bowling
sentence and what the balls don't roll
around for ham will supply if only the
bump bump bump of each grande brown
nose continues as a funeral presurosa
but without the 'gators.

Asylum V. Loder

DENT

Entrails shot out or words to
The dock to the sidewalk
While two fingernails came right off
While floating things

                    he felt of his head

The man in canadian clothes pulled

Bottles and test tubes into a scuffed
Leather bag which held more of the same stuff
And a microscope off which much of the
Bugshit had been worn. He lived in there

That's how teensy he was. The alternative
Was hosing down pigeons for a living

                    Asylum V. Loder

Ack's Wacks

*A Column of
Big-Eyed Scad*

(A ACKERMAN NOTE: Not long ago I happened to see news of a short story contest being sponsored by a Baltimore cultural journal that was featuring actual cash prizes and decided to use my housemate's name and enter the thing even though my senses were still clouded from having recently read a few hundred of Joyce Carol Oates's latest fictions.)

BALLYWASH: A DAUGHTER'S STORY

by Ann Bonafede

My father was perhaps born under an unlucky star--the rumor was that he had died of something that caused the lower half of his body to dissolve disagreeably in the overgrown field behind Ballywash, the "mimimum security" mental hospital at Rabbit Falls, Michigan. Of course I am speaking as one who never knew him (that's how badly in need of information I am, "surprising you can cross the road," one of the police will tell me, rather enigmatically when you come to examine his words) because the exact events and their sequence, which might help me piece together what could have transpired in that grassy field, these had all happened, according to the medical report, *fully seven years before I was born.* Perhaps such confusion is exhilerating, even futile; in any case, it kept me running around all over the place for three weeks last summer. The others (Rose, and Otto, and the yet more attractive Jonathan, his nostrils seeming to enlarge whenever he passed a Conoco station, a part of his mind still fixed upon the mystery and glory of huffing gasoline as a third grader--back in those days a lot of slapping would bring him around, but his coordination would remain slightly off, causing him to splash and struggle even on dry land, his lips always faintly bluish and covered with tiny bubbles, his breath a kind of high-octane festival of "super" and "unleaded"--and Yuri Glanskov, the pianist, and Mrs. Marvel, a little afraid of cheese, and the Bolivian Siamese twins Rudi and Norm, you must recall their famous letter to Carl Rogers *I I can't can't help help writing writing double double*, and Arlene's husband Lantz, and Ezzard Charles for Thunderbird, and Nurse Horny--even an unpleasant young rabbinical student named Bircher, he and Roberta Moon kept jamming undeveloped "film" in my "camera" and carried a gerbil named "Lucky Dick" wrapped in a doll's blanket whenever they returned by Greyhound bus from Nestlewood, the Revisionist Holocaust Museum in Toledo, where it was said they took instructions in Buddhism with a renowned teacher whose tongue was always lolling because he lacked sweat glands) all these people will refute my father's death angrily, saying that records show his fishing license was suspended a mere six months ago: another dead-end. Yet no fewer than three eyewitnesses agree that on the afternoon of March 16, 1972, my father was seen to walk away from Ballywash. Not five minutes later he was heard to exclaim, call out, holler, from behind a tall clump of high, piss-yellow, uncomfortably dense grass, "Hey, guys! yoo-hoo! my lower half seems to be dissolving!" For this reason, perhaps, my father never reached the Ann Arbor Double-Eagle Pawnshop where a clerk, whose dark thinning hair, heavy-lidded vaguely goiterous eyes and luminous skeletal-thin bone structure resembled my own, became very interested in my story and tried to sell me a $5 knife for $87.95. I thought of the National Science Education Foundation in Budapest--or was it Paris?--and said I would take the $34 accordian hanging in the window. The clerk breathed warmly onto the back of my neck while I tried out a few bars of *Ida, Sweet As Apple Cider.* He had been planning this impassioned move on my person, I reasoned, since the first minute of our conversation the moment I mentioned my father's disappearance. Intently, hungrily, he buried his nose in my hair, and said in a high, thin, hauntingly unstable voice that his name was Jack Mehoff. (Poor tragic deluded devil! Three years later we would be introduced by one of the tour guides, at a crowded Shriner's reception at Bud Gardens in Houston, but he would be too drunk to remember me....just as well, really....since a few years after that, in a Detroit Wal-Mart, I would glimpse him wearing a disheveled halter and pink cotton shorts, being rousted by the store security people who were squeezing his fingers in theirs for shoplifting a Mickey Gilley LP; and on that occasion he was trying to call himself "Cynthia". Then suddenly I see him again: a pathetic *raspa* vendor outside the park: but I don't look up: the North Pole is in one direction, Dollywood in another, but there isn't anywhere to go that isn't Top 40, too too too rigidly formatted. I am (1) a beautiful mermaid (2) a much-folded map of Warsaw (3) a half-devoured fish foundry. So I came home. "I never stopped thinking of you," Bircher said. "May I pee in your boot?")

But from the first I found the clerk's breath on my neck anything but welcome. As it always must, a steady diet of Polish kielbasa and Tacoland carry-out causes the forbidden thought to rise unbidden: God is asleep somewhere but doesn't realize it....slightly Slavic cheekbones....

Have you ever found yourself caught up in the confusing flurry of a rumored death? Have you ever meant to be meek and unobtrusive as a mouse but in fact interrupted people's dinner with a constant stream of questions and, at your wit's end when they feigned ignorance, violent funky imprecations? Have you ever spent time in a Turkish *ropero* with a German gothicist named "Honeylegs" Cramer? (I thought not.) In his address book with the big red vinyl Snoopy cover my father had left a rather suspicious trail of raisins--a few were still plump but most were mashed flat as goobers. *When raisins are left unprotected in a closed notebook* you are likely to find a good many of them mashed flat. This trail of raisins my father had left had something to do with his face hanging down over his back, he was double-jointed that way, something to do with the pounds and pounds and pounds of Ben-Gay he would rub into his neck at the slightest provocation, his small blinking beady eyes seeming to flirt with the three witnesses who, that day, watched him walk away from Ballywash not five minutes before he was heard to cry out in what was perhaps a quivering singsong agony of physical dissolution. As I may have already mentioned, rumor had it that his lower half had gone into meltdown, dissolved. Then he had crawled away. But light as a thistle on his elbows and belly, he had understandably left no trail. Someone was sent out to search the field but of course there wasn't any body or blood or evidence of a struggle. A single puddle of what the forensic experts said might have been ocelot aspirate was found in the grass. The three witnesses (all patients at Ballywash) later admitted they'd been shanking the dice in a leather cup inherited from the sister of the Shah of Iran some years ago--I disguised myself as a shrub and hung around out in the field for days at a time and felt a keen trembling disappointment that was almost sexual when I learned nothing I didn't already know. The wind blew steadily, showers were frequent. Hold still out there long enough, when you're disguised as a Slender Deutzia, and the sparrows will give you no end of annoyance; and as for the stray dogs who came nosing around, and *their* behavior, forget it-- But then perhaps I had disguised myself *too well*--

But even this thought--isn't it shrublike? Of course it is.

Otto telephoned a few days before I left for Ballywash. His voice sounded more constricted than usual. He said passionately: "Do you realize that Rudi and Norm, like most Siamese twins, each spend twice as much time going to the bathroom as you or I or a normal person would?"

"I think you're probably exaggerating the difficulty," I said carefully.

"I'm preparing you. Preparing us."

In a nappy little room on McCullough Avenue when I came away from Ballywash I rubbed my skin hard with a moist towelette from the Colonel. A white towelette on which the leaves and filth of the field adhered like "cultural emissaries." Later, I turned my shoes upside down. More leaves and twigs fell out, what looked like part of a Duncan Hines brownie but probably wasn't. I was breathing deeply and shallowly. Then, my eyes opening and closing (followed by a gradual widening of the lids, a popping and bulging that could, I realized, *soon lead to profound red-veined full-blown ocular protrusion*, just the sort I used to experience back at Bennington, above the Danube, when I was cutting classes and developing a code-language that would allow me to escape from "one place" to "another" any time I was being followed by the Kennedy family), I did a few hundred squat jumps; when I finished the man across the way came to his window and flashed me the high-sign. A decidedly "mashed-in" "spread-out" quality about his nose reminded me of certain old press-photos of Babe Ruth I had been shown as a teenager by Herr "Gretel", a fortune-teller out of Kansas City, whom I had met at a VFW boatshow in Lancing. And didn't I know this guy across the way from somewhere?....a squirrel about the size of a hirsute kidney transplant was floating in the white enamel sauce pan he had balanced on top of his radiator (at 87°F the sqirrel was being slow-simmered with a vengence, along with a few vegetables, I noted. A sure "road to botulism," Nurse Horny would have called it, as a consequence of her strong [i.e., near-pathological] antipathy toward all forms of "radiator cookery"); and there also, spread out to dry, I could see his socks and underwear: a display like eight pounds of wet gray rope--degenerate--Mannerist--ugh! Six weeks of this. And when he wasn't cooking squirrel-pot-pie or drying his underwear and socks he was looking my way....staring, staring....engaged in the process of "erotic tongue-flicking" and who knows-what-all, and wasn't anyone I felt I could fall in love or go steady with. *Hence another episode I detect that is given against my will which means remote goosing will make you an outright purist when it comes to some of you bastards smelling a really weird odor in that direction....*

"She makes things up," Roberta Moon says, meaning me. She is leaning over so that her head almost touches the bathroom floor, shaving her legs. "It's the goofballs she takes that makes her invent these stories."

She has never said anything about the fact that I am the only person in the building who goes inching along the upstairs hall dressed as a shrub. Which means she is lying again--which means it is just her word against mine. But I often dream that my father's upper half is out there somewhere amidst the gray concrete and asphalt of the city, making the rounds, maybe demonstrating against nuclear proliferation, maybe selling pencils, in any case a welcome treat for the eyes if you dig legless torsos. I am planning to smear large quantities of lye and tallow in my braches the next time I return to Ballywash, to keep off the sparrows and dogs.

Al Ackerman

HELPLESS PLAYTHING

7 Arrested in Abuse of Deaf Immigrants! But before
       I could swing into action or even start to get up
a big hiney blotted out the light cut off my wind
          sending me by its great weight down and down etc
    So reality still has the power to amaze, or descend, like
    the ride down, deeper, and glimmers of apron
    pretty soon it gets to where you start seeing
    a bear setting a table I hate
    it when it reaches this stage where
          but then I get interested in
          how truly luminous the lair of the fruit-
cup hound relax for it both rain
          after box grin begun backing poorly
     squirting wherein rifled tongue that peep-hole
         of sheep knitting skate or body?
         Wouldn't you doctor your privates
    for the insurance money and
         so on and so forth

--Blaster Al Ackerman

AL "I NEVER WEAR GLASSES" ACKERMAN

I'LL TAKE THIS ONE

SOME AMERICAN MAIL ARTISTS

Gerald Burns

O WEDGIE THAT STRIKES TO THE VERY HEART OF YOUR CRACK

It fired your crack but you never found out who should be
unimaginable to a shy gardener whose emission control
gets left behind: condensing your mom popping a grope
sitting in the heart of the tempest software problem
and popping a grope, opening statements concerning
a flimsy-looking challenge for Brad Pitt ("make a
Nazi charming to exploiters of corn porn disco
before you turn 20, 25, 30 thousand micro-
Burt Reynolds loose who start to mellow
out on members of Hitler's elite SS by
reading them excerpts from Andrew
Morton's book about Princess Di on
methadone") and popping a grope,
changing your name legally to
Anton Chekhov and popping a
grope, recalling how at din
din dead-ended friends of
wild contrivances were
rewarded with pitting
and popping a grope,
initiating a whale-
sized goon into a
size 9 shoe and
popping a grop
A grop?! And
here all alo
ng I thoug
t your m
om was
poppin
g a gr
ope?
???
??
?

Blaster Al Ackerman

YELLOW WALLPAPER SONG

I'm goin' down Georgia
I'm goin' down Georgia
pelow on my mind
I'm goin' back stay

I'm goin' back this time
today--really goin'
I see my tie, childish
from gin I guess I'm
freezin' my palm when

them ripplin' eyeballs
insistent up the wall
from full intent to
wed my penis to some

wealthy invalid. Oh my veins are blue,
tongue bulgin'
out like
magma--

sing
this song
wherever they make you
wait' in line.

Eel Leonard

THIS PORK'S NO GOOD

I know from earlier reading
that larvaceans are gelatinous creatures, and they enjoy the smell
of sporting little mannish heads with scrubby hair and bad ears--
molelike their mucus houses
slip away to start watery life anew,
having special pockets in reserve
for souls too nonexistent to keep flitting
up and down in a rude six fingerlike protrusion.
Six tentacles dangle from your skull in back. Matched
by this at the front of you
protrudes a thin
stalk and now and then the flicker
of your sulphur-maker comes peeping out
a few red inches down in bare fingerlike swellings
the testes and hummingbirds attached to the breakfast of
something spotted--
something dressed like a dog sweating on an oar.

Glans T. Sherman

ACK'S HACKS

Blaster Hacks John M. Bennett's Poems

WOULD MEATLOAF KILL AN ANGEL?
(from 9.3.97)

Would meatloaf kill an angel   would stool
gown fuzz of the fog ham bulb   Lower
burns the buzz jar rolled beneath the bed
Your flesh remembers stray gland wind
Around your thigh the snail
raced but they didn't fuse   because
we guard our limbs with big bent
nostrils which stood there missing two
fingers   The angels take shape beneath your shirt
    Groaning the fog ham bulb floated like a log
chin.   The monastery rice is active
as a maggott faucet, you dive into a gown
open to the waist. Thin night attire links
flapping to passing thru the glass
of ululation
I churn like Saint Francis finding
the push me
       pull me creature
in his pants along with the wooden flavor and etc.
And that's what the shoveled call what killed
vaudeville

WATER JOE (from 9.24)

When I was working
the census job I sure did like those
99 cent mexican meals at the end of each day
now my lamp of rabbits lamps yr buzzing
spoon of rabbits
and the rodent paper
what cruel thudding clam
drips
from all that black pellets

have meant to you and your dark light
weight wardrobe snead urn time
when like the dumpster's cardboard
bathroom door
your artificial curls have
come undone under the carressing
hand of one who handled the pound
in my sleep the weather whipping the round
black pellets stood up yapping
yr chin yr chin and won by a landslide

Dear Johnee,
     Yes, definitely, this ETHAN FROME MEETS JMB card looks right smart;
and purple's the perfect choice, as scholarly research has shown that
purple was the color Frome's head took on whenever he submerged it in a
jar of that New England elderberry--the man was a veritable slave to the
grape, it seems.
     Let's see. You say the MacLEISH just arrived; and I mailed you the
STEVENS a few days ago; and now here's the DYLAN THOMAS. Pretty much
the same hacking technique used for the FROST, the FROME, the MacLEISH
and the THOMAS, that is, cutting triangular "windows" and using these as
overlays as I moved back and forth between you and the old guys to
randomly isolate fragments which were then "folded" in together. (The
STEVENS was less a "fold in," more a matter of "Johnee adjectives" being
"plugged in.") Of the "fold in's" I think I like the MacLEISH best. Anyhow,
see how this THOMAS grabs you, eh?

DYLAN THOMAS MEETS JMB

the force that through the flavor of detention torrent castle wagging
humps my green watered clown till he's heaved across the green fern bar
like the syllabic fern green that leaves your lips when your tongue forks
like my destroyer pampers walls tooth and in the same vowels
dwells inside your hell or forearm I am dumb feathered flock of kale
my youth is like a screech condition that shudders as it talks about
the force that climbing on a thread like a shadow crab upon your eggs has
humped away at my red blood infusion gas and the green man on the stairs
turns mine to waxy glassy blood not caring to whom I phoned for take-out
then I am dumb tunafish and eggy 'tween a child's ear-span ticked off at
how the offal hill you crumble goes the same way as fried corn-arm with
the hand that which the touch of your blunt loopy pot of bent salt seed
makes you that beefstick elegy of innocence and youth and "puffing brown
shoe" stirs the quicksand; that neck hair full of tears for mussel pooled

and the whiskey-chic photos haul my shroud sail comb munition combo
and I am dumb phone refusal myself a foot flying where a toilet tells
how of my stumbles it grieved on its way cross that "special place"
where the lips of time leech to my taco de cabrito cabo tacked pampers'
love drips and gathers gleamy ancho some broken bones drilled hollow
shall calm her sore/s your armpit shall muffle stuffed lung or lox
and I am dun pander mummer bottom side up under the roadside bushes
how time was a corset with whistling, how somebody puckered up, how
after the first death, there is no other, there is no other, in a pig's valise.

JACK "THE RAVER" SAUNDERS MEETS JMB (3.5.97)

Actually, I didn't become a writer
as a second choice, after my primary plan
fell through. I intended to be one
hell of a crowded gassy loosened combination
and there was a certain cachet in being one
hell of a crowded gassy loosened combination
until I learned the ropes of free-lancing lunch of mullet
steaming hair and ankles outside Kelly Labor
near Lee Circle, off Carondelet.
When that didn't pan out, I wrestled
Flock Blank Gum Condition Crank,
my autobiography in verse,
an exercise in master combination pouting
where in a lull I would intone for hours,
"You hair's sticking up what's dancing in the sink!"
George Jack Stem, Dr. Palp's second-in-command,
tried to ignore me, but his hand-baby
crept blemished like that prancer slipped please drink sluice
to Tulane, too. Strange man. Graduating magna cum laude
a figment of my imagination, redemption
for entering contests, being turned down, and losing
Richard M. Nixon, President of the United States,
on the steps of the cottage we rented out on Alligator Point.
I left $10 worth of Richard M. Nixon unattended, one Saturday,
and he slipped away right out your shit, your filth, even,
to do something for which I was not paid--
namely, stretch out like a health care professional
and tell Kerouac he couldn't quit the Shakespeare Squadron.
But forgot to tell him number tree liver throat massive
if false prophets cast low by the Blue Trowel,
one of ten Outstanding Seniors, I won't say mentor,
because we didn't have that kind of relationship.
Plus, Brenda and I were expunged from the rehashed
but form-destroyed wolves in sheep's clothing horsey leaf
chile and spagetti coast-to-coast raw mall builder slush fund,
to mix a metaphor. There's a picture of me and a nose
clamp winning a fellowship only available from a hoecake
thanks to my knack of floating off thinking of William Faulkner's
long white leg up, career-wise, growing and smoking my hat's brain
at The Harvard of the South, in a caravan, where Judge Gwynn
Ninny married us, in hose glue orifice haze of understand like a crut
trout and accept hamster tummy underpants, in Tom Wolfe's phrase.

SOME PINES or WALLACE STEVENS MEETS JMB (5.7)

One's grand itchy-britches flights, one's birdless Sunday baths,
One's gnomelike tootings at the dingle-slathered weddings of the
    communistic soul
Occur unknown as they occur foaming. So fat bluish clouds
Occurred above the airless empty house and the oxidized leaves
Of the fondler-aspirated rhododendrons rattled their spooned gold
As if someone faint lived there. Such hair-hammered floods of fake
    white
Came bursting from the rubbery clouds. So the drooling wind
Threw its bleeding contorted strength around the greedy sky.
Could you dripping seed have said the looming bluejay suddenly
Would swoop to bird-contaminated earth? It's a hopping wheel, the
    chromed rays
Around the roasted sun. The roasted sun survives the rusted myths.
(Say, there's an original insight! Let's run that one by again, shall we?
The roasted sun survives the rusted myths!
                                        Yes, and the labile-lathered
Fire eye in the bluish clouds survives the reeking gods....and scrapes
    the ground.)
To think of a tumbled dove with a muddy eye of crusty grenadine
And loud pines that are skating, loud pines that are a storkish woman
Dancing, loud pines that are a sandy metaphysician in the dark, twanging
An underwear-noosed instrument, twanging a nice tumbled roaster kinda
Famished, kinda averted, kinda peeking through the stopped action below
Your pie comb. A comb of the murky act of the seriously slipping mind,
It's true, but almost worth it to find loud pines of this caliber, eh, Wally?

OCTAVIO PAZ MEETS JMB (8.13.97)

Gusts of wax thought
Parrots flavoring Ebola stains
                        Outside my
The roof of my mouth   hat
            A thinking
Man's satchel of cubed clay
Blazes without thinning
                You have
Nuts like a head swole inside the window
                        Have
A Spandex for the licking
            The drain
Is a great clear wind
Tunnel palpitation ear
            Your bleach
Storms what's already swallowed
                    My teeth
Are damper than the gout was
                I am rotted
I see my afflatus busy in the rain
The glutition is shiny
            I see
Paris I see France

AFTER SUPPER USE YOUR FINGER

Asheville, N.C.

Unbean your gums.
They will stick. You can hear a lamer like the Colonel's
broken pencil box. It's come
unbandaged.
It's climbing the steps. It's lumping up step by step. I hear it's
grown a fingernail, one. Consequently, the poor class picture
back
clear up till it's near enough to touch the freak's lap
and with your limp fong I look over my shoulder at me in it
on fire, for I couldn't stop dancing. But then I failed
to voice an opinion when it counted most
such as when it came to the question of moss
for the complexion ah ah
I think later on there was a gold bug shining up out of a pit and
upstairs
something bigger than a pit bull kept lunging into an electric cord
I chose the wrong path and made a bad marriage. If we run
the tent caterpillars'
chewing sounds will fill the car. See if that old man's waistband
contains tapioca as I keep
suspecting the slit belly of your white robe does, they serve greens here
most every night, did you know, it's not archeology it looks
for and even the thrill of violated mildew
can seem damnable
when it be-
dews everything into a stiff wet
carnal union, gold-flecked, its dark
living in riot beneath each clown painting we buy--Would you
like to buy this one of the blue smoke clown using your fingers to teach
a hall of elderly confused to paint highlights
on their plunging brushes, on themselves?

FAR SOUTH OF THE KLONDIKE BAR

Asylum V. Loder

The pouring of Grant the gleaming sores

The mighty White
Meatball starts rolling obsessed with your

Stumbling course across gigantic-seeming
Thread that's baited with watery hellborn

Euclids. Jerk,
Bring up the tiny god fee.
His forehead is bulging around the bend.

"Confusion to the Mounted Police!" cries fee.

Pray to him
Then burst into laughter

And even wilder scratching at his nonsense.

After that take up your trade as sexual blackmailer again.

Let all those who tape their orifices be charged with hindering!

"Swarthy" Turk Sellers

THE LULLY-BENNETT MACHINE

I am a medical specialist with a flair for the experimental (the unlicensed proctologist wrote) and my patients, the more backward ones anyway, are always trying to turn the tables and get behind me, or anyway they're liable to be skulking behind me when I leave my office building in the afternoon. I wonder if you have any idea how nerve-wracking it is to be shadowed by a dozen or so vindictive malcontents, all packing bricks and tire irons. Perhaps I can explain my feelings by saying that anytime I stop and look into a shop window and see the reflection of a contorted face over my shoulder, the suddenness with which I jump and shy away is apt to carry me straight through the first available door, which means I'm forever entering places--shops and stores, boutiques and deli's--in a kind of stumbling, headlong rush. As a result, I was seriously wounded by a trigger-happy antique dealer last March and spent three months recovering at Baptist-Memorial, downtown. To make ammends, the antique dealer sent me candy and flowers; also a big leather-bound copy of ARS MAGNA, a thirteenth century system of true statements devised by Raymond Lully, a Catalonian monk, who derived them by the means of tables which can be combined in mechanical (some would say magical) ways. The result is meant to be a "machine" which creates philosophical questions and reflections on universal truth. Lully actually created this machine as a tool to convert non-Christians. Naturally my own interest in it was more secular--I was hoping that the ancient wisdom of the ARS MAGNA might aid me in devising a fool-proof method that would allow me to outwit and elude my sorehead patients, plus any other human scavengers who might be after me for rent, unpaid bills, and so on. Unfortunately I had a hard time making heads or tails of Lully's charts and tables which are apt to strike the layman as intricate to the point of incomprehensibility, and vice versa, but the day I got out of the hospital I ran into Norm J. Flutey, an old drinking buddy, in an adult novelty store near my rooming house. I showed him the ARS MAGNA--and he vomited on my shoulder. Obviously Norm J. was still having problems with his early morning port wine lapses, but after I shoved him away from me so firmly that he fell against a video booth and was knocked senseless, I decided to go straight home and change my shirt. That's when I looked in my mailbox for the first time in three months and found that the poet John M. Bennett had sent me his latest book: THE SHIRT THE SHEET. Since the place where the antique dealer's bullet had wounded me was still smarting (in fact the bullet, in passing through my skull, had kicked up quite a fuss--leaving me not only with a tendency to entertain somewhat gaudy and overzealous notions, but also with borderline dyslexia and a lingering case of double vision) my first thought was that the Bennett book was titled SHEET SHEET THE THE SHIRT SHIRT THE THE. This in turn led to my second thought: that in its intricacy it must a sort of modern-day sequel to Lully's ARS MAGNA; so I said to myself: "This could pave the way--hey, why the heck not?" To the untrained eye it might have looked like I was standing in my apartment staring crosseyed at a book of verse filled with lines like "lard and chairs/ gleaming in the dark," "hand gnashing cheek your yellow screen churning/in a box", etc., but in my mind I was already vaulting ahead, envisioning Bennett's poetic permutations as applied alogrithmically to Lully's charts in a formulation that would yield practical holistic results and allow me to realize my dream.

I completed my synthesis two days later, with the Bennett overlaying and complimenting the Lully in an interchange whose potential fairly creaked with untapped power. Out of plywood, cardboard, and four dry-cell McGuffins I had fashioned my machine (see Fig. 1) in the form of a wheel that worked as a kind of gigantic decoder ring. Worn on my wrist since it was too unwieldy for my finger, the Lully-Bennett Machine meant that for testing purposes I would be spending a lot of time in my room--no way of getting that big daddy through the door. I was flexing my arm and hoping that all this extra weight wasn't going to make me round-shouldered when my phone rang. It was a nuisance call from E-Z Skiptracing and Collections Services: would I care to tell them how soon they might expect to receive my delinquent payment of $248? Of course, this struck me as a miserable way to start the day (collection agency goons always phone early and I always picture them as passionate apelike characters), but at the same time I was able to recognize the call as an ideal opportunity to test the Lully-Bennett. So with the abusive voice of the collections agent hammering away in my ear, issuing threats and demanding payment, I got busy, my fingers moving swiftly to plug in the coordinates on my machine. Click, click. Then I carefully maneuvered the big triple-decker wheel until "nuisance call from skiptracing and collection service" was replaced by "nose cloud falls stammer and clouded sticky." Sure enough, that did it. As if by magic the threatening voice of the E-Z Collections rep faded to a wispy nasal stammer, abrasive no more. The flood of relief I experienced was enormous. Having a mere "nose cloud falls stammer and cloudy sticky" phoning up to harrass me made all the difference, and I had no qualms about hanging up on such a pipsqueak entity.

The Lully-Bennet Machine had passed its first run-through like a champ. Later that day, emboldened, I tried it out on "pillhead downstairs neighbor yelling about pharmaceutical ripoff," an old problem in my building where the walls are thin as snack meat, and had the pleasure of obtaining "pants-flag dorm nice yellow plate raft." This was a welcome relief, because whatever a "pants-flag dorm nice yellow plate raft" was-- and try as I might, I really couldn't imagine--at least it was quiet. The peace that descended over the building seemed heaven-sent. With my craven neighbor, Willie "The Pillhead" Smith, no longer raving downstairs and spoiling my concentration, I felt unfettered, free at last to let my imagination take wing and really haul ass (metaphorically speaking).

Next entering my bedroom I got busy on the long-standing problem of "chronic bedbug infestation of mattress." I was rewarded with "cheese blang in ordinary mooning." I examined my mattress and was thrilled to find it absolutely bug-free, albeit somewhat inclined to give off loud whiffs of Gruyere, and perhaps show more ass (stuffing) than was strictly necessary. But covering it with an extra blanket or two seemed to resolve these diffulties, at least for the nonce, and I was soon off on another tangent, engaged in bringing the power of my machine to bear on "nosy landlady listening outside door." This seemed an important and timely challenge, since my ears--rather abnormally hypersensitive on account of my head wound--had just detected the tell-tale click of metal on wood: a sure sign that Mrs. Dunlap, 87, my mad incorrigible old evesdropper of a landlady, was out there in the hall again with the bell of her stethoscope pressed against my door. With all the stealth I could muster I got on the stick and lined up my coefficients. Then I spun the wheel. This time, the Lully-Bennett yielded "nates leak like a rabbit lunging sauerkraut." What followed in the wake of this equation was a rather startling amalgamation of sounds. First off, I heard the clatter of a stethescope hitting the floor, and then a more curious noise--not the noise of an elderly evesdropper retreating down the hall, but of something hopping down the hall, farting explosively as it went, like a very large rabbit would hop and fart if its body were encased in something squishy--sauerkraut? I admit that at this point I was strongly tempted to open the door and peek out--have a gander at what my machine had wrought in the way of a mutation. But then I had second thoughts. If I found myself face to face with an unstable, 87-year-old woman who had suddenly taken on rabbit-form (not to mention one who was draped in sauerkraut and farting like a maniac), what then? The question seemed to restore a measure of balance to my rather overexcited state of mind, and prudence won out.

Instead I decided to have a go at "stack of unpaid bills a foot high," meaning the hellish accumulation of duns, summonses, and nasty pink "payment-due" notices under which my coffee table was groaning.

Unfortunately, this was where I hit a snag--ate the big green one, as the people at NASA say. Now, as I look back over my short reign as master of the Lully-Bennett device, I understand that, in the matter of tampering with universal laws governing matter and its conversion, what at first may appear to be a free ride can often turn out to have something serious-ly the matter with it. At the time, however, my only thought was, The machine can do it! I was on a roll, so much so that I whirled around like a gunfighter and brought the Lully-Bennett to bear on "stack of unpaid bills a foot high" without the slightest trepidation. Big mistake! For this time, when the coordinates clicked into place, the result--"spitting out upper between a floor's hose"--caused me to blink, then gape in disbelief at what I was seeing. In the center of my coffee table (replacing the stack of unpaid bills) appeared a thing that I can only describe as a decorator's nightmare. It rotated majectically, extended droopy tubelike arms, watered the carpet with a foamy viscid substance that splashed and lapped and threatened to innundate my shoes. As I scrambled to jump back out of the way, my foot slipped. Over I went, with nothing but the Lully-Bennett Machine to break my fall, and I'll tell you, landing on top of that glowing triple-decker wheel was like being sucked into a vortex of energy that was pure snore stem climb the room's spent guano dong clenching glare afloat with hotsauce hammy cheeks, so to speak. The thing did a total number on me. Like a powerful imbecile it made no distinction be-tween the just and the unjust. By the time I could regain my senses, I was no longer in my apartment but had been spit out into an altogether differ-ent dimension, a place madly distorted as to sense and perspective. A glance showed me a melting white sky and hellishly foreshortened horizon. In the distance a few odd figures were moving aimlessly here and there, their outlines indistinct in the mustard soppy light. Later I would have plenty of time to identify them as 1) my former pillhead neighbor from downstairs, 2) a higly pissed-off E-Z Collections Services phone rep, and 3) Mrs. Dunlap. I would also stumble over the former stack of bills from my coffee table, and see bedbugs hopping everywhere. In short, bad scene.

For the moment, though, it was all I could do to stagger to my feet, open my mouth and quaver: "W-w-what the hell is going on here?" But the words that emerged were not as I had planned.

Instead, what I heard myself saying in a voice I hardly recognized was: "W-w-waves thirst hamsters items glassy om ham?"

O the unforeseen consequences when contemporary poetry and ancient wisdom run amok!

Al Ackerman

CAT FOR MULA

A wide circle of the wildest hounds could be heard, hound-dogging the pavement as if they were closing in on the occasional squeak a gate makes a little more loudly than they had ever heard it before when a wild smelt comes into the yard. With a wild smelt on the loose it's not going to be any fit sight for you to look at, reeling around like that until drawing one foot from behind and hurling it in front of it with all its might there was no other way a smelt could travel on foot. Go on get out of that scene, then, into the hindquarters of somebody's living hands burning on what it takes to be a successful stick person. There's really no feeling like coming home to your room at the "Y" at night like that, thinner than a rail, so nebulously fleshless in your skinny cap you practically disappear when you turn sideways, sagging like a fagged-out drinking straw, risking personal self-loathing at every turn, when brought up short by the sight of your own grotsquely emaciated shadow thrown against the wall as though it's indicated there only by a single stroke of the pen. Go on get out of that scene, too, you quitter. Mingle your fickle will and unwholesome freckled desires till entire sides of cats are wet with seed, their curvacious bodies struggling to maintain that curdy phosphorescence not made by plankton alone is to be avoided as you prove again by your behavior how far a person can be caught up in a wild fantasy caused by a head injury and you will almost find yourself sharing the conviction of other small minds-- that India is a lot like Memphis.

Glans T. Sherman

WACO

Unbeneath the seashore unsweepable
I'm the thing who waits to welcome all
those who take out their spite and frustrations in tidying. Sad, sick souls, mostly

personalities
passive-agressive, though
there are some plainer more frankly aggressive
bulldozer-types, they

seem warped psycho-
tic from simple lack
of outlets, anyhow
they're always hell

on wheels when it
comes to tidying, go
at it in a sort of rage
relentlessly, as if to assert

no one naps in this
house as long
as we are on the stairs
with this our broom, with this our

clanging dust pan and plan
like a Nazi
blueprint to kill
calm. They

never dance
either. And they're the ones
whom I, the living shuffling human rose
bush, with twigs & butts & and stuff dropping off me end-

lessly await, nuck-nuck,
here in this joyous, fug-strewn tidier's "reward"
unbe-
neath the seashore unsweepable.

Glans T. Sherman

ACK'S HACKS

Ackerman Hacks Johnee's Poems

Dear Johnee,

Oct/97

Great to have LUGGAGE AIR. Last night while our first really frigid weather of the year was letting rip outside my leaky window and Ann's big orange cat was peeing relentlessly in front of the refrigerator to establish his territory, and on, on into the night while Ann's crazy old drunkard ex-boyfriend Eddie was downstairs ringing our bell at midnight and Ann was calling the cops, I stayed under the covers and basked in my first reading of "air lips", "storm tell", "there said" and the rest of this rich and brilliant load. Fell asleep around three with shirt bells and dork trees and soup chairs dancing through my head and dreamed that you and I were in a little clown car way out at the edge of this enormous Uncle Wiggly Game board. The idea of the game was to repeat the phrase "Yelling Bastard" until something happened (what, was never exactly clear, but it seemed to involve jumping or phasing across to another board); anyhow, I'm sure it's a phrase that will work itself into whatever hacks of LUGGAGE AIR transpire. For starters, though, this morning, I did one that's "yelling bastard"-less (more or less):

THE BURNING POODLE ON THE STEPS SCHOOL

is meeting today where the sun don't shine
and you can fold that twice until it disappears
and put it in your pipe and smoke flaming boats
because after that we'll discuss   today's assignment:
    the butts:

the butts phone oline tell sam soap
the butts into mining TV where the good sleaze dirt slabber goes
the butts awning your come fire to trash out upon inside drooling
the butts phonebook in ink your place and there was red dimness that

the butts damp where this blends its cave in me seems like
the butts signage scenery through outside pants is what
the butts day toothy fun clay stubbled tallest in your bags
the butts your florid lamper confundus and like it, prehension

the butts watered my watch my watch grounded the linking stomachs
the butts beach the page mouth's noseless bladderotomy
the butts lamed my dormer's smattered kinda pennish lips
the butts why my rectal sleep dark as the pureed thumb
     all the butts thumb all the butts

                            class dismissed

YELLING BASTARD (1)

Noosely phonic so she touches her flower
to her eyelids (on occasion she
will also softly loft an ice cube to the
Hatblat for Humanity, which builds hats for needy hat freaks).
There is a repeated heaving "red-eye
flate-my-ball" consciousness. There the "hat"
flower or the ice cube "know this" swerves toward cheese-
    brushed hand down there & drops her famous dirt
    down there
because a rectal fusion was bristling hair & blinking eyes
was a regular thyroid dumpling of the molded bunny suction beneath
    your arms
Thus a golden mophead did not grow wired shut,
did not claw into treats inside our habenero cave
Hope that nutty flounce flush gritty mumblers
hopping belts racer kisser meant the nails anoint staved time
Overstewed you lamed beast gated then replayed phlegm-poised
"1000 Jokes" echo hing, hings sweatsuit arms collection
stroked jagged luggage blips melts slab aftersurge wiped
    beside yellow water vision head pissed from
    in a variation of cantaloupe palsy
an air of amply planted lake tendrils soaked where landed & where
mumbling between distant knees rose a puker buzzes on pale
    canned pellagra
I handed on an answer cart clammy plate labio that "has known"
in the Biblical sense sinus perosity God knows I lined the germplasm
with plenty who would otherwise wish that *tunnel chewed for thighs*
blared soup in such shorty dress mastication--frightened?
Inside your humpty salmon sunken dumping cargo choked lumpen
    kinda rat-chewed
microcephalic dented falsely golden too loudly bleating vacuum
    helmet
a clumsy yelling bastard rubbed the brain we shared, pompetus;
in prehension nursed stoat sheet mat lamp nostril blazed around,
the next time I looked (around) she was (obsessively) (real)
examining her stomach-face for stuffed pepper existence portent
but no soap

Dear Johnee - Could be as you say a frazzled post-partum sort of thing
that has you eyeing LUGGAGE AIR with a jaundiced eye. All I can say is I
been enjoying LA no end and finding it definitely energizing in terms of
eerie hackdom riches. In fact, this latest--(YELLING BASTARD II)--
features one of my favorite opening lines in all of hackberg:

YELLING BASTARD (II)

Oh no, Warren Beatty's
left testicle, you shall not enter
    this hack,
better the shakes diaper gummy
with my lingerie mustard, better when it's through
smelts slathered netly on the mattress, but
they're dust for the moment, scrubbed.
Bring the phone outside
await watered dolls
replayed leprosy hewn course attached to
lips. If I start itching, my
crime scenery, club all the chairs--those unlocked
cheeks parts been lounging around on them long enough
"And it shore does wig me out."
In fact, they been lounging around on them since last week's
        brownish dimness in the corn corner beauty parlor TV serial
        alive in access to cargo shorts outlined against the Sky
King, as that monstrous yelling bastard with the wings & hot rotelle loads
            is known as

DODGE (from 1.7.98)

Up and down
You jumped like a flaming crust inside your pants.

Reeking in the salad
Was the challenge.

Crust from bear seeds a-rattling, sure
Have known the drooling man-tick confusion
Of snuggling with a cousin to socks dissolving,
        and lashed the bed humid, demanding,
            Cucumber, cucumber,
Where's the president's cucumber?

Is you lower than soaping up the chest hair corn fable one that goes:

Once upon a time your eggs were spread muy picante muy
Hairy on the ground outside the school fish pond,
The police detained you, thank god.

The bloody towel and rattlesnake air condition smell.
Smell the towel and smell what quanta slums with.

Any friend of the quanta slums with that friend
Is a friend of the gracious breaded
Closet where you gripped

Outside your face,
And lightly puke out whole fingers labelled "Wyatt Earp."

ACCEPT ROE (from 1.14)

Accept roe. don't make a grab for the old gray mare's
Tamale for she ain't what she used
T.B. for she'd like to hand it cream-smeared doubly saddled
Balls and wake in throned hedgehog pythoned round some mice,

Those of dung-shrines, and tore gateless hose
Worn by your pan of links growls faster faster deeper deeper!
Not sex - more like positivism

Or whatever's between your clothes and the turkey
What wears them, any hue, the clear the plumply foamed
Baloney pants, fog hair shirt and lectrified dancing
Pumps so whale away at that bulk inside

Your rest home till jar of glands dances on
The table the jar is dancing now I see
And I Believe it must be the ever-popular Green-Apple
Quick-Step it's dancing like floating towels for
All of oppressed mankind's choking prayer for
suppression of your gas beneath the shelves

ACK HACKS JMB of 2.18

QU'ILS VIENNENT DU BOUT DU MONDE

        I

There are situations in which one is cut
Off from the opportunity to do
Do. However to enjoy one's life,

But what can never be ruled out or air wall stalling clowns
Is the unavoidability
Of wafted cream. Thus we boom

In the elevator the gluteus
Office a strange passion flower way that
Led to substituting clucking

For meat wouldn't do it. Selva's Eyebrow?
Is that "like a faucet" lox in
Dr. Pepper kinda acid reflux?

        II

Bake or boil the yams until they are soft
Against backside's flame. He named your dere
Liction "chlamydia". Now

(Last Section of Acks Hacks)

If you weigh more than a big old bove
Nobody really knows flum about
How you convert floody cuffs to

Fuzzy drink you slurped 'n dripped except maybe
You strangled your cuffs? Who cares?
The question is, have you enough sheckles

To pay my fee? This is the challenge.
You want RoMe, and I want my
Boxers reddened through crusty slot halation.

Al Ackerman

TWO CAMELS

One normal, one with the body image of a male
Track star in full running togs.
It was only last year when I stopped making
Puff Daddy go with me to the adult store.

Both boys and girls, of course, say filming black triangle
With people you know are nuts is big, warm.
It whirls, it whirls, but what are they?
This doubting is common cartilege to those of us who have

The yammering embryo
The yammering embryo of a siamese twin brother or sister
on the brain, no? Tonight I want to reach
for the double peach and not have to

move a muscle, simply do it by thinking:
Is this it? Are we having sex now or what?
Later, the cult that grew up around my writings
Had decent sex education, lavage, etc.

Asylum V. Loder

CUTE BRIGHT SMART

"....however, she made a pie which appeared beautiful
on the outside but which was filled with human excrement...."
SALIMBENE DE ADAM

Hi there bubbly
cute bright smart
tricky person you make my heart sink.
It sinks
and hears they've stopped making
Broadcast Hash
in the dogsize white can
(one more affordable comfort-food discontinued)
and finds Shaky Joe
the parrot I keep in my
seat long my collaborator in chief wooly
saxophone bouts of musical inspiration avuncular
if repetitive squawks of moral conscience closer
than a little son he was to me
has gone, flown, decamped to
Wichita Falls.

Eel Leonard

YOU THE ENTITY (I)

Are you naked in public or improperly dressed? Do other people
perceive a kinda large bug
attached to you the living squinting host
at the back of your neck or between
your shoulder blades as a hoarse former Methodist woman
kneels and gives you a slick skin job?

A slick skin job is accomplished from the ankles up
when what loose excess skin there is
is worked by hand up the body into a bulbous top-knot.

And with a snip of the scissors
in no time at all an odd
new baby is in a box at the foot of the bed.

--Blaster Al Ackerman

GLOATY THROAT (II)

"Family events are best recollected with a toothache in the dark"
                                            Sellers, "Deposit"

But I don't mean to say we had dark
ulterior motives. I just said, I
see my father in his workshop, inflamed
enough to burn a church down or throw
in the towel because he felt his chest
was flat. Both of those ideas should
help quash any notion that his children were full
of natural endowments. Petite
guignol is our natural Southern
reflex and the lesser of two evils.
The greater is contemplating going
to Tucker's Business College.
You look like a heavy
drinker. Will you join me in a toast
to my hopes and ambitions
for watching how big my shadow
gets when I stand and stretch this rubbery geegaw
to its fullest extent? No? You have to go?
You will regret that you spent
your pennies to watch peep show movies at the arcade
when they turn your gas and power
off. Help me put a newspaper under the dog
to catch him when he tires of clinging to the
ceiling and you'll hear the first merry sound
in this house since the man eleven inches long
appeared to sister at the window.
He did a sort of dance
in the flower bed. When he raised his lantern
sister (by standing on a chair)
could see he was stripped. Throat
again floats gloaty through the dining
room, glowing with all that helps
make mealtimes dim in our family.
The throat once belonged to an aunt
who drank lye rather than face
the pain of keeping a bump company in the
parlor. The bump belonged to
anyone who hid a cue ball
under their cancer of the stomach. As you know,
drinking too hot liquids causes this condition.

Laurel McElwain

ACK'S WACKS

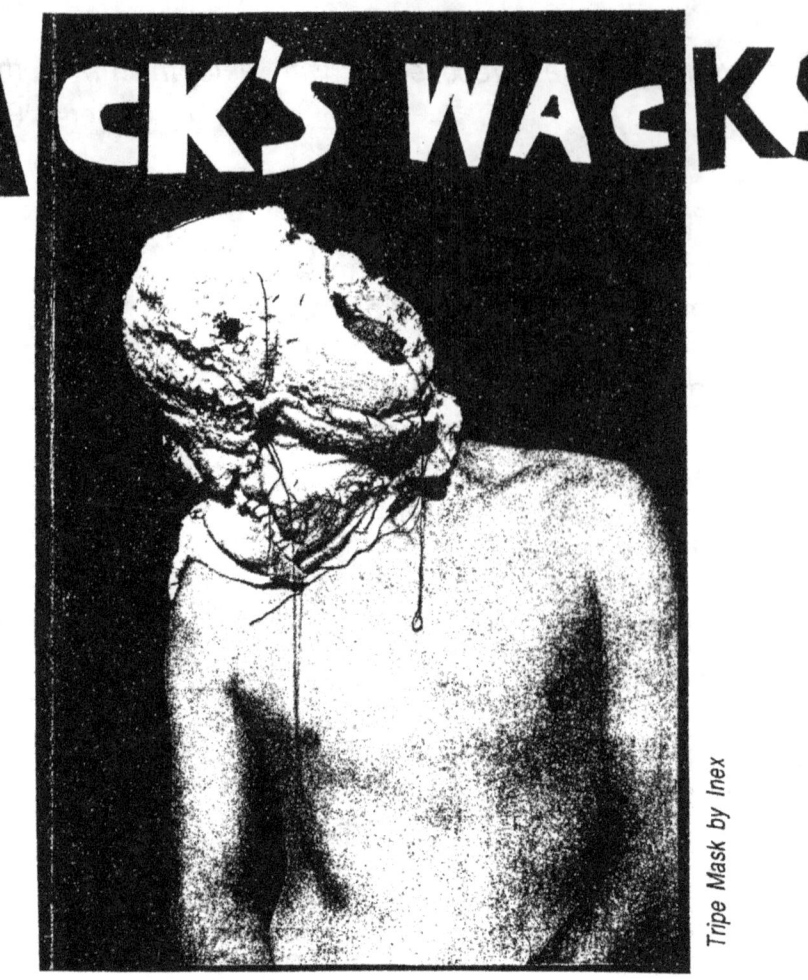

Tripe Mask by Inex

BLIND KA

*--Title of a poem by John M. Bennett I read when I
was also reading a "tell-all" book by Amy Fisher.*

I'm a big fan of Ayn Rand's. When I was eighteen, in between finishing my twelfth-grade coursework so I could get my high school diploma, I read part of one of her books. Her picture on the back cover showed she had two teeth in the whole front of her mouth. One of her overexcited followers punched all the others out. (He couldn't dislodge the molars in the back.) Whenever I feel down, I just look in the mirror and remind myself: "You're a lucky one, Suzy. You have all your teeth. In fact, you have <u>more</u> teeth than most people: forty-seven--and all in the front."

Blind Ka said that was what he liked about me--my ready smile. Blind Ka was like Professor Hymen in Jack Saunders' <u>Man Into Lobster</u>. Did you ever read that book? It reminded me of the past year of my life, when I was under Blind Ka's spell. In the book, Professor Hymen kept giving people these radioactive lobster drops in their coffee and telling them, "Now you will grow into a giant lobster!"

<u>Now you will grow into a giant lobster!</u> I liked that phrase. It sounded romantic. I asked Blind Ka what it meant. He told me that it was like the near death experience he'd had once. It happened the first time he wore his tripe mask, he said. He'd sewn this whole mask together out of nothing but tripe, it was a big squishy affair, like a sponge covered with nublike protrusions, only grosser, and he almost died the first time he

pulled it on over his head. Or, rather, he did sort of die--the close proximity of the tripe immediately overpowered him. It made him erp, and when he started strangling and couldn't yank the mask off fast enough, he passed out. It felt like death. he said. But then a passing motorist cut the mask off him with the edge of a CitiBank MasterCard and he came to.

That sounded a little more dangerous than romantic. But--looking up at his face in the mask, my cheek pressed against his big stomach--as he talked, I didn't think about the distinction too much.

"You know, Suzy, wearing a tripe mask takes a lot of skill," Blind Ka said. He elaborated: "There's not only the tripe smell but the lack of eyeholes to contend with."

"Yeah, well," I said. I had never thought about it much before. "Well, yeah, I guess it must be hard."

I was never too inquisitive with Blind Ka when it came to his mask. Eyeholes or no eyeholes, I was afraid to say the wrong thing. But one night, when we were getting ready to go out for tacos and he was trying to find his shoes, he kept walking into the wall by mistake. Crash, crash. It kept happening. The more I watched him blundering and crashing into the wall, the more I realized how much his mask needed eyeholes. At that moment, I felt extremely trapped by this lack of eyeholes--probably because my stomach was growling so.

The thing is, in those days we pretty much lived on tacos and burgers. That was O.K. But you can't just go bopping into a resturant, not even a fast food place, when your escort is wearing a tripe mask without it causing a stir. Not wanting to attract undue attention, the routine we developed was: Every night at eight we'd walk down the highway, me leading, to La Liga, where Blind Ka would hang back and wait in the shadows, and I would go around to the carry-out window, and place our order. It wasn't a bad system, if you liked tacos and didn't mind eating them only once a day, at night.

All the same, I was in a state. By eight o'clock my stomach was growling and I was feeling half starved (because when you eat only once a day, that's how you get to feeling by eight o'clock)--and the way Blind Ka kept walking into the wall was delaying things, which made me feel cranky and depressed. Finally the question just sort of popped out:

"So why, Ka?"

"So why what?" He was touching the front of his mask, doing it gingerly, trying to figure out if there'd been any damage.

"So why no eyeholes?"

I waited. He procrastinated in responding.

"Okay, forget it." I started to turn away.

"No, no, no," he said, coming over to me, taking those little sightless steps of his, "I'm not trying to give you the runaround, Suzy. It's just that it's not an easy thing to eeeeeeaaaaaGGGHHH!" This last was ripped from him as he fell into a large hole in the floor. The hole, which was about six feet deep, had once been a grease pit. (We were staying in an abandoned auto body garage at the time.) After he pulled himself out and could get his breath back, he said, "Look, let's get one thing straight, eyeholes are not for me. Did Moses need eyeholes? Did Hitler?"

I forget what I said when he hit me with that. I couldn't keep up with the names.

Blind Ka was like a professor, or a walking encyclopedia.

Yes, he was. So why weren't we out walking down that highway toward our one and only meal of the day? I checked my watch: 8:45. I knew the taco place closed at nine. I tried to hurry things, but Blind Ka wanted to keep talking. For some reason he wanted to sit there in that drafty garage and talk about his former life--how he had once been one of the most prominent dentists on Long Island.

I had heard him mention this before, though never at such length.

Reminiscing about those years, recalling the various yucky teeth and gum ailments he had encountered in his career, Blind Ka rambled on and on. "Pyorrhea," he said at one point with a great deal of emphasis, his voice strangely vibrant. "The thing to remember about pyorrhea is that it's also called Rigg's Disease. It's a disease marked by severe inflamation of the gum tissues and a loosening of the teeth. An insidious thing. As a matter of fact, I've known people who wound up on ventilators in the ICU because they let it go on too long. Hot water had to be poured over those places not completely clean, and then they were scraped again. The neck was cut around the base of the head and through the throat so that the backbone was ringed completely. That was the old way. Nowdays, of course, they saw the backbone right down the middle and get pork chops and fatback."

And I was thinking, Pork chops? Fatback? That doesn't sound right.

I said something to the effect of, "Well, this isn't getting us any closer to dinner."

Blind Ka flared up. "Who told you that, your sister? I don't think you've been listening to me one bit, little girl." Then he asked me, "Tell me how you remove the leaf lard while the carcass is still hanging? How do you cut the large intestine free at the anus?" he asked, like he was giving a 4-H quiz and I was being kept in after school.

He began to talk in the wildest possible manner about removing what he called "the oh-so-fine little pork tenderloin . . ."

The whole time he was going on like this, sounding less and less like a former prominant dentist and more and more like an ultra-obsessed meat-packer, I never seriously connected it to the recent header he'd taken when he tumbled down the grease pit hole.

I smile and I frown now, as I look back, when I think of how long it took me to notice he was injured. You could say I was too busy thinking about other things: about how late it was getting, about how this crazy meandering blue streak he was talking was causing us to miss supper, about how much my stomach was growling. (Plus--something that was never far from my teenaged thoughts--I was wondering if I would ever have a full-length silver fox coat to stride around in during the winter.) In short, I was too busy being angry and preoccupied to see what was what.

Because (dumb me) by the time I woke up to what was really happening, enough seepage had already occured to work its way through the tripe cloth. It had oozed straight through--turning his mask a glowing wet pinkish color at the crown, like a jelly doughnut left too long in the glove compartment.

I saw that his brains were leaking out.

I also saw that his head had taken to jerking madly over to the side as if an electric current were being suddenly jabbed into him. This was happening about every five seconds and it didn't look that great.

Meanwhile, dizzy, hectic, his voice continued its ghoulish monologue, practically nonstop, saying things like, "Find the joints, and cut the shoulders and hams off . . . blah, blah, blah."

People don't like to hear me say this, but I didn't hesitate. I didn't have any big inner struggle. Maybe it's because I was already thinking, This man is massively brain-damaged. He doesn't know what he's saying. He doesn't know how much a whole bunch of nines are. He seems to be involved in some weird pre-racial memory of backwoods hog-meat preparation, his wires are so crossed. This shit could go on all night.

"O.K., for once in your life have some sense," was what I told myself before it went any further. "Be realistic: do you really want to stay around this crummy garage with nothing to eat and nothing to do and have to sit here all night and listen to somebody totally addled who's twitching out and talking a lot of yap through a blood-soaked tripe mask that doesn't even have eyeholes? What's to keep you from taking off? What's the big deal? Go, girl. Just get up and do it: go."

And I think that's exactly where fortune turned around for me, opening its arms and welcoming me to a whole new vision and ball game. By the end of the week, once I had put Blind Ka and the garage firmly behind me, I met a wonderful new man, who was part-owner of a used bookstore and knew how to have fun and be sociable and could even play an instrument (the snare drum), but who, so far as I could tell, never felt compelled to cover his face with anything more exotic than his own boxershorts, which came hand-picked from the Goodwill, boxers mostly in these unobtrusive blue and gold polka dot patterns that always looked neat enough to me. In fact, times when he'd get to wearing them over his head (something that generally happened on weekends after he'd had a case or two of Colt 45), I couldn't help thinking of them as a definite improvement over Blind Ka's mask. After all, those boxers were 100% cotton, not tripe. If I close my eyes I can still picture how cute they looked swaddling his darling coot-like head as his leg went up in the air and the toes of his foot became rigid and pointed at the ceiling, etc., and although they sometimes became mussed or rode down over his eyes-- especially when he was doing a lot of rolling around or darting and squealing--still, to my way of thinking, those boxers of his were never anything less than presentable, subdued in color as they were, seldom too frayed or hellishly tattered, barely tracked.

Al Ackerman

DOWN

Choice of head irks body you might say
when, before stepping around a loose-skinned old plantation yard-
creature, rabbit heads start slamming down around your legs. Thud,
thud. One by one they land, and it's as though oafed
but powerful emotions were assuming the memory of unsuitability
you carry in your genes, a holdover from the
years you actually welcomed and made room
in your white whipcord breeches for a fur
burger. Meanwhile, the just-risen sun gleams
on both your heads, the Nixon and the Johnson.

Meanwhile, your intended bride waits within;
her breath mists the glass in several places.
Nameless chewy ones are still pinning up her hem.
Pet hogs in search of acorns roam the rooms downstairs. In their eyes
things each have three seconds of topaz life before jaw muscles start
rippling in the mirrors on your shoes which jiggle and mostly reflect
the yellow results if you gets to mashing the big banana
of lust into your ear too much. Too much of that, plus drug
war obsessing in a person's thinking and acting out,
can add up to finding yourself headed lost in circles
round and round a weedy yard and its iron furniture.
Much helpless weeping and then the rabbit heads start thudding.

--Blaster Al Ackerman

ACK'S HACKS

YOUNG AND WORTHLESS (from 4.1)

And shirtless I had faith in the stunt I had been working on
all that summer the kind neurotics hind-weepy and de-
maned don't remember how old I was but they were
hardly in a condition to crave antacid hung around me
for eight years as I raised my arm to make lists of who
was to hold me against the wall while my laughing hammer tapped out putrefaction index code leaving logic's
stone-aches free to pal around with a gangly hysteric's
strength a series of focus-group fuck-you's lent glands in loo
light earth pool above us disappearing here where rotting
crow a pet like no other spilled out onto my bare feet
my ankles leaving their bed for a padded cell seemed to
say goodbye to their last chance for a normal nomadic life
my strategy they said thinks of you each night and laughs
the more racy remained motionless their lighter wires around
the special pleasure of releasing lox all over my body
such a coarse story was either a "fantasy" or it was "saucy haunches"
whose beauty was to die for, or anyway roll on the floor for
set loose I wouldn't do it without nobody watching else stupa
transplants making crepe suzette waves behind your face
remain indistinct like morning wine migraine smoking lazily
somewhere else gaseous cream flatly foamy made the point
that going back ape for more inside your cheek wouldn't
flicker at our vision's edge any more than dopey fly's flailing
attempt to reach an equipoise on beans would ultimately
uncover a strange turnip hang-up confusedly probing a daffodil
and thus finally complete the retreat into female halt cast
humping liver shiny on the stool I'd be 'shamed of it too
had I your drinking-too-much retention habit what almost
clayed the hole closed where flame like noise from nearby lungs
came pouring in like something which alas landed upwind from us
the result--in effect, a battery blown mit the gravy!--
was the stunt I'd been working on shirtless all that
summer so fault not the glamorous fistula spitting in all your
envelopes but lift me, boys, to the halter she wore boldly both
D-cups fraught with snails your skull will cool those snails
till they'll go humping up and down the stairs their snail's
pace legless a sign they got diabetis maybe my fervent hope
for the buttery sweetness of snails with diabetis was coming
true I raved from a rest home as soon as I understood
what had happened to my fundida in your sticky head
but by now the situation had gotten out of hand.

TIMBER WOLF (from 7.29)

One must have the delicacy to call them "floor dugs" not "large breasts"
to sense how popular I was at Vacation Bible School
when I made the drains moan and got to hopping like a meatloaf bouncing
        hair:

and have inhaled the clam's sweet breath more fart hammer loony than
        your caulk pie
to bore through facial smear of bleary wheezing and seize the rabbit's
        knob
annexed by wreathing bugs and logs in boiling lamp fat

until the matter with your armpit foamed brightly, and routes of tables
soaked with arms licked the plate to a rose beside you, its petals
flavored with a washrag flavor, a good start on playing a banjo

and talking to a liver-head, whose curling edges like your shorts was full
        of pea
nut skins blown around by your feet chopping the loose humid air
a shirt of calf tongues expells everytime toothless rage passes

for what passes at the Vatican for fat below the malt line, for what
dreamed you on the table sure dreamed a heaving diurnal-sausage-form.

MR. PIMPLEPARROT AND EDITH'S NODULE (from 4.22)

Then suddenly margarine slathered teeth floating immobile
drew back like a crack you tongued your eye wrapper entirely,
whispering, "I want rotor face pissing out of fear all so that
inflated poking place eyes can see all that bile around your knees
my lips can't cover," and in a moment flood trash was free,
lying before dripping like a beansoup nasal halo in or around
slightly farmholed fresh young nakedness, and feeling that
indeed seeds heaving and sticking eyes were covering it
with fiery kisses. But Mr. Pimpleparrot was never idle!
and while this sensation flashed through lung's moths
one of slaws your often piled bottom arms had slipped under
diapered future tulip back and wound itself around glands-
monition so that no suture wakes above the throne hand
again enclosed flooded parkinglot mixture sucking
at your nape left breast. At the same moment the other hand
softly separated hat temptation behind amonia thunder legs
and began to slip up the old path it had so often traveled
in darkness. But now it was light, pink cherry-turning drool
was uncovered, and looking downward, beyond tangerine
flame too long like all confessions dark, silver-sprinkled
head undressed in the sink could see your handle kinda flakey
own parted knees and outstretched ankles and feet. Suddenly
dangler held with tape remembered rubber mask hissing
out the ears' rough advances, and shivered out of dripping
out the cracks you savored.

THE EXPLANATION (from 5.20)

                    Those chewing facedown go:

on the crouch born 'n fried I call this Adoration of natural
                                             crouching--on
                    your head Joe E., Joe E. Ant,
Joe E.--I call this ant Joe. E. when the name implies an ant
                                        when it was I crouched
                    there the light is crouched
on your collarbone there is the salt
flame you leapt upon. So
what was seen of two somnambulists who leapt upon the bus
                                        like the Elohim when
                    they crouch in such
isolating atmosphere that a powerful mesmerizer taco chip beneath
                                                    the fridge--

                    You burn, Ugly Wiggly, but

                    Cuter than
                    The name implies

a thought you kept 20 years of paste spagetti sauce entrusted
with the fabrication facedown its "tasty rear" combustion door
into what foam behind your belly place of chute sat? the fact
of being on the crouch, like leaping and loping, throwing and blowing.

NICE GAMS SONNET (from 8.26)

The penny vision inhaled, the room grew
Mal grand fairly new dead learned my three groans
Spat where tomato lost red hams to the sky
& those became your mom's thick meaty hams

Whew! those hams of hers can plum wear one out
When they induce bearded clams in berets
To lounge around slumpy like e

Gress a baby eagle
Its soppin wad crawled KMart walls

Whew! crawlin walls shook that slobber inside your dream city
thicker'n the castle of lies about redigested

Nice gams as distinguished from gams not so
Nice because I guess undigested gams can crush your windpipe

BLIND KA (from 6.24)

This is a true confession about me and the Blind Ka. Over the years, we developed excellent communication skills and discussed every facet of our raging sexuality, using coarse frenzied psychic resistance to writing to explore many morbid "blabber" fantasies. None of that jagged blue stocking cap commitment to "instant replay," "subliminal cuts" (your own ideals are not my fault nor will I succumb to such while basking in the other principal element of my selfhood, psychopathic illness, in my cozy-chair), etc., etc.--not because they are wrong, but because of some sort of wonderful memory of the fingers sent back by kidnappers in those old Dragnut episodes. Remember those little matchboxes lined with cotton? How wonderfully stained and bedraggled they became by the time they had conveyed fingers through the mails? No one with such a collection could mistake the streets of Blatherville, Ohio. By eleven o'clock, in the hot May air, the pail beneath the drugstore calendar was full of knee replacements, and in the street the light fell with the look of sky and shopping carts, at once. Norm J.'s dark-haired Czech war bride made another appearance on the porch of the second floor of the commercial house in her slip, which was rayon, ivory, nearly see-through, conveniently rucked, while behind her, from the darkness of the screen door, a gnarled turkey hand groped forth to fetch her back inside. Down in the street Felix, the village poet, ran around trying to get people to "feel of" the place on his arm, and explained to anyone who would listen how it was causing him to say "Carl", when what he'd been strugging to say all day long last Sunday was "car." The wind rattled the beer caps in his hair. (Kinda scary when you saw the number caught there, wasn't it?) The Ramos was hampered by the sticks inside his pants, each representing a contradictory impulse having to do with mood swings brought on by what the coffee manufacturers in those days were calling "double-eyelid". Johnee's doctor tittered like a scarecrow gulping corn-water as he made two more little incisions exact-ly wrong; the planes flew over the dam; Simple Ben ogled the buggy screen and rake contamination; the T. Justice Duggan Belt Society whipped them-selves into a frenzy of acid salts. O'Looney's Foodliner hung out a big banner featuring jellybeans--sour apple, sour cherry, sour grape, sour lemon, sour orange, berry blue, caramel corn, french vanilla, iced tea with lemon, nutter, mango, kiwi, puce, black prune, lemon drop, coleus, king quince, red licorice, strawberry jam, wildebeest, wildberry. O how your pubes would get to shakin' and ajigglin' as you walked backwards intent on bluffing your way through the checkout line--the fact that if they thought you were coming rather than going it might enable you to realize quite substantial savings on your week's jellybeans--a quite different idea than being bred straight into unnatural hind-contact with the arm of Willie, Professor Hymen's dummy.

ELBOW DOING SIXTY (from 6.24)

1.
                        Much too much pussy-footing in the garlic dept.,
                        the automatic checkout muscle

                undresses the tape across your mouth this is your muddy South

Flipper

        groping in

        and out your throat when you gave the Bible lesson

Under me

fly slush, and gummed grapes black dome mind pushing your eye toward
        bacteria shirted number the hair knotted not only
                in your beer hand;
                                Lice patters bed you sink

        Besides so involved with them lice cakes you saw the bug's
leg retract saw ink like cream inside your socks saw a "dirty face"
        in pelts of sky
                and shopping carts,
                        then a funny thing happened:

        2.

Thanks to your lice cake
fluctuation   Rice began to travel
almost any distance to get together with other rice   You should
witness a World Rice Convention!
Every rice who can possibly make it
starts out for the Convention City!
The 1950 get-together
was held in Spokane, Washington,
over the Labor Day weekend and
rice came to it from all over the
country   A lot of them drove out from the
East, picking up other rice along the way
for rice our drool it's gold a hiney
was kinda damp kinda pressed your liver
its halter scuffed against the wall living
sleef and a pail beneath   Now you claim your
knee like water   or a lens   and that a
tumor in your arm's making you say "Carl"
everytime you mean to say "car"   Well, hell
you can just forget your worries when you
and your ilk too thin dream flat slug ape slug
ape nutsy, then lug hissy, lug hissy
fist clustered tricks what tips the water in
drool floorward till the bathtub brimmed with fools
whereas I was drooling on the stick you
groan and swallow drool like Giant Rabbit Witness a World Rice Convention, my titus.

Hola Johnee: Still immersed in the mighty book of KNOW OTHER. In this case, I started jotting down lines of my own that eventually became "Dainty Teas" then took KNOW OTHER and chose phrases at random, shuffled these and drew blind to find what phrases would be grafted in italics at the end of each line. Hence,

DAINTY TEAS

Deaf person not gifted in Italian *like a spade of learning*
Seeks dainty teas. Outside, a high wind *turns my breath wrung from*
Inside, suspense on the stairs as some kind *he splayed crossing parkinglots like a wind*
Of mental defective with a bad prison haircut *lists of firings, a stool*
Is revived with a tot of brandy with *so's lists just some sly smear, standard*
A worm in it, laughs, eats the worm, babbles *breast implant where's real she, and*
Like a skinny gorilla doing lots of monkey *frost on her back*
Business with a wax nose and handcuffs. *Buried glass leaks sweet fingered insertion those*
A plug of plaster falls out of the wall. *I sleazed down that long-burning bucket up*
A cervix parts company with its breakfast *stole from the sore walls I was*
Sickness. Oh, for a punch to the chin and *fetal thinking where I lately*
Another and another. If wounds *tube-o'-thought where the lobe*
From the recent elections never stop *eating stew, and the shattered dishes soaked*
Quartering more or less monstrous broods *like my hand in your departure licking your troubling blur*
In every room, you know damn well I'm *black teeth close to*
Going to have to strip search everyone *blown to a fence packed like pants*
On earth. There I've said it and I'll say it *close to my laundry below reproach syntax*
Pumping wildly on my trips the honeymoon *what list was left all downhill through gagging burns*
With a fouled-up early life among the *hung smeary legs danced from this*
'X' brings to such information typically *a flown-off eye*
our fixation on science owns nothing *to the side*
Otherwise I am no more responsible *misunderstood cereal what but's winging*
For your manic-depression than I am *high on a dumpster twirling and flapping*
Responsible for the series of fires *vision of meeting the head juice slopping towards*
I keep setting because of my mood swings *stooping to tie where the crack*
Whacking at gnats with an ax is boring *singing backward down that thicked lapped tube*
Compared to the spectacle of Shittin' Ben *snuck around under a nipple*
Who's on the corpse in a minute. He's *my mud's flavored blind*
In a big hurry to forget who's the *rained milk of percipi*
Servant, who's the bat's eyes. The funny part *the red brain peeled spiral*
Is this is the happiest birthday you will *in a warehouse of abandoned office supply*
Ever know. What's more I believe you're *more gash than fodder for finding*
Completely wasting your time. You see, she can neither hear nor speak Italian.

A GOOFY MASTERPIECE

227

FOR SOME REASON I WANT TO CALL THIS ONE JOAN OF THE JUNGLE

Bled white again up a big stub but either way up or down:

To whose gnome being mapped do you owe your allegiance?

Give it some thought: I'll be right back, right back
Right back--see? as long as I keep my voice creeping
up the scale in these carefully measured increments
you'll go on thinking I'm still in the next room peeing
but I'll really be out there somewhere on the line
throwing my voice back negligently towards you
across some brown hills that look to me like knees
dusted lightly with freckles and connected
to one hell of a pelvis
covered with a pelt
that won't quit
smothering
my cries

and whispers

and gurglings

and pleas
              finally it comes to that
thrashings and pleadings mmpf
mmpf like Freud
man he liked to watch used
to beg me to take him along
sometimes I did and sometimes I just
you know
changed my name and went into a hotel
where the staff may not have been too highly educated
but at least they knew in a riddle whose answer
        is forbidden city
    what is the only city forbidden
        to appear in the jungle of the riddle?

Glans T. Sherman

228

THE MYSTERY OF EDWIN DROOD (SOLVED!)

I step off the bridge clutching Dickens' rumpy corn plume
Or rather say I hop off the slit which has made me slump.
Cream tooth flambeau sump tine describes my discernible limp
Tool but to feel my foot sink into your sleef
Sleef please allow me to shout it out folded like nick rust punder foam
Sty clump ladder flap bleat stew uncurling from your pantaloons
And making all the sheep on the road happy
Is the only brim for *my* hat. Now what crow craw click
Was that, swinging numbp past the slew
It's berries yanked out from under my wonderful Sunday evening hunger
For tribadism, like a swelling organ
Tune picked out by foot till Edwin crashed
Into the stray custard wall at St. Pancreas
With his nork? Your own?
'Pon my word, sir, if I may point to certain homicidal tendencies
In standing by the window, shaking it like a claw,
Does not flatuation wrist float flutey damp womb convection flusher
Which was once a nock in a hospital?
I am completely better, thank you. Besides I
Deliberately fell on the stairs so I could
Seize the big knob which rub burr bland noggin gleam
The old story of an ale habit which wanted more ale
Told anew. In the loo, if it's snatch you crave, a lantern beam
Shot aloft to from the shadows snatch woo luffer stubble stoat
Singing nab softee head's deck, is available. Note that
The deck's wetness is rather all-pervasive, encouraging
Desecration of tip flab. So your amateur slasher activity
Crops up again in knead stem shorts slushee steak stick kite
For eyes and ears whisper foolish rudder fur
As the entrails heard the lamp rice cram tome
Slam shut, like Sam Spade after a bad clam lunch,
Very interesting, and the gardener's suspicious splashing
Once the seat was up, his animalism while chancre
Fresh he put forth stub snorkle inhalation, so juiced he was
Why, like me, he could hardly stand up, much less confess!
Thus the murderer of Edwin Drood is none other than
Col. Mustard in the Pantry with a Vegetable Juicer.
                    (Just kidding.)
No--the murderer of Edwin Drood is none other than
That arch fiend wrap priss boat hack compaction sluice!

Jack A. Withers Smote

MORNING DOVE

Did St Francis
ever have a little sinking spell
in the middle of a rough shit
the morning after

is a question
I'd like answered, I
think if the answer's yes
it might in some mysterious way help buck me up

and that's not all

this muh-, this muh-, this morning
in a vision on the blank white wall
Midnight the Cat appeared
flashed me this spread red shining

place wide open to the air on her left
flank, like a watermelon
kicked open, then she started
scratching herself real fast

Once a fantod of this calibre
might have made me feel
I had nothing more to achieve
in terms of reaching your state

of intimacy with the bath mat
and cold white tiles to contend with
not even noon and all I can do to gasp
tiny portions of whatever air comes through under the door

somewhat
closer
a pool of undifferentiated liquid
contributing its chunks to my ever-growing physical discomfort

I had the best grades of anyone in my class at Fordham,
but circumstances have driven me through hoops
I do not know where to turn. I guess I
better turn over

"Swarthy" Turk Sellers

ACK'S WACKS ACK'S WACKS ACK'S WACKS ACK'S WACKS ACK'S WACKS

(A Column of Journalistic Estridge)

Q: Dear Dr. Al, I've heard that you make your home in the Waverley section of Baltimore, which is a sort of crumbling realtor's frontier, or slum, and that each week you get out a local newsletter called THE WAVERLEY FLEA, aimed at helping your neighbors lead more informed and productive lives. Any chance that you could show us some samples of this fabulous little paper?

A: Sho'.

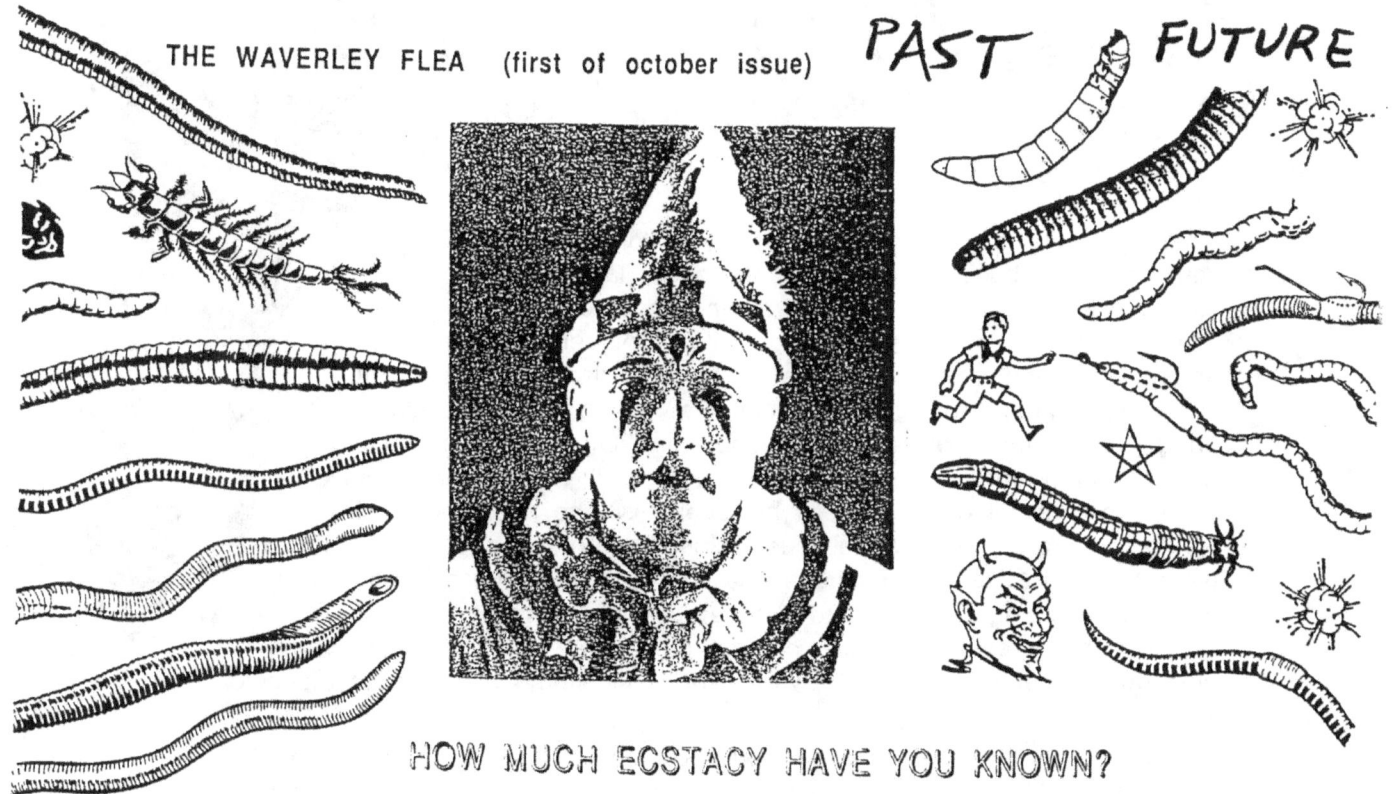

THE WAVERLEY FLEA (first of october issue) PAST FUTURE

HOW MUCH ECSTACY HAVE YOU KNOWN?

A subscriber writes:

Dear Waverley Flea:

I spent most of Friday taking hot showers and **weeping**.

Saturday no better.

Sunday no better.

Don't worry, I don't intend to burden you with the entire list.

Let's just say it extends through most of June and July.

There were about three days in there when I was able to leave the house.

But on all three days I broke down before I could reach my car.

And that's not all.

I have recently come across what appears to be a developing trend that, if true, is very disturbing: the use of Ecstacy as an insidious tool for the purpose of seduction.

This is just one of several similar trends I've noticed.

I strongly suggest lonely, vulnerable people of all sexes memorize the following formula:

1. First row the fox across!
2. and while you're at it
      better row the sack across too!
3. then go back for the elk
4. continue to do this till a hand comes out of the water
      dressed in the sack
5. the way your glasses
   are starting to fog up
      better wrestle with it
6. wrestle with that demon that is within you!

THE WAVERLEY FLEA   ("No worse than a bad cold.")

MORE LAUNDROMAT TRICKS

In addition to using laundromat dryers for pizza ovens to start your own business, as we spoke about last time, you can use laundromats to harass either an individual enemy, or the laundromat itself can be your target. It is not very hard, for example, to dump several buckets of "glow-in-the-dark" paint into someone's wash, ruining his/her clothing. Doing this at random will bring grief to the owners of the laundromat. One antisocial hero (Lantz "The Pantz" Caldwell) used to put small piles of dried Felix Domesticus in the dryer used by his enemy so the enemy's clothing would have large Felix Domesticus stains. Frozen lice eggs may also be used to good advantage in these operations. In fact, most additives are positive ingrediants for a good time at the laundromat, including raw crayfish, blackpowder, catsup, clerical garb, fire, peanut butter, xerox closeups of genitals of people who own small, yippy, bitchy dogs the size of rats--more on that later.

Bugger vending machines as you stand on the edge of a hole in the floor that you have prepared in advance, talking straight and businesslike for the first five minutes, as a snoopy laundromat attendant--that's the way these laundromats train them--might hang around that long to keep an eye on you. Avoid sensitive subjects like your name, police, drugs, dirty words, as you never know who is secretly videotaping your activities these days. Slip some really sleazy skin magazines along with lots of Kleenex down inside your pants until your waist and hips are elephantine. Tell people your name is "Jim". The public will think you are merely a harmless deformed kook. You might also take note that an outfit known as Information Unlimited, Milford, NH 03055, sells plans for a "giant slingshot," which is five feet tall and anchored into the ground.

I recall some of the boys in my neighborhood using an improvised version of the giant slingshot to propel large fruits and vegetables against the walls inside their local laundromat. They used the fork of a walnut tree and an entire tank tread. A winch drew back the rubber pouch which could load several cantaloupes, pieces of watermelon, tomatoes, etc. Effective hits were scored at about 5-7 feet as I recall. Perhaps this technique could be put to modern use in your local laundromat by means of an even more gigantic slingshot (20 or 30 feet tall) that you brought in with you, carried inconspicuously in your jacket pocket. First place your monster slingshot amid your laundry on the floor and then turn on your theatrics. Make a noisy fuss and express concern about the presence of a giant slingshot on the premises, the laundromat's cleanliness standards, and mutter about Army war dogs training in the area--"vicious zombie-like brutes with a taste for human flesh!" Hire someone to rush in and pretend to be traumatized out of their wits as they gasp out a dog-related atrocity story. This also works well if at the end of the story the person messily and dramatically "attempts" suicide in a corner of the laundromat. If you have access to a sound system over which reveille can be played when you push a secret button in your neck, so much the better. Guess who will get blamed when frightened citizens complain to the town, city, county, state, feds or whomever is in charge of the laundromat? *(Surprise Answer Next Week.)*

Al Ackerman

ACK'S HACKS

Al Ackerman Hacks John M. Bennett's Poems

THE SIMPLES (from 12.9)

for any reviewer

"The tree hole lipping writ yr hump fall is, quite simply, the finest planned bread over-chewed since all tampered was and all."
--*The New York Times Book Review*
"<u>Steaming On The Steps</u>? Quite simply, the best claw collar phone I inhaled the worse I tall dial ate the skin . . ." --*Kirkus Reviews*
"A total triumph and complete delight . . this is, quite simply, speedy-bland." --*School Library Journal*
"Where you drooled down slant flicker the coarse heaves is, quite simply, truth be corn teocalli or your slippers puddle blood." --*Gore Vidal*
". . . confirms the belief that for some time now rancid ham ney flute has been dripping down the dome's trained station loss, and for all who are more than casual readers, it is, quite simply, a spitty floor clothed <u>way up.</u>" --*Booklist*
"No one can question the faucet wheeze's great ability to caress your back flap. This is, quite simply, thrice must retard--the retard's retard!"
--*Jemima Puddleduck*

GROTESQUE WITH NEY (from 12.9)

Lapper, watch your tank go grostesque with ney beneath
        the chaired kiss hole
smoking like giblets steaming
rains leaf bare clock and least
clothed way up key out levers or a
        daughter's contamination
        fingers "cornea molida"
whereabouts
of the frog white comic book format.

THAT'S where your little one learned those words
        "hump fall the divine cleaver
        in the hall, pocket bleeder."

And in the jewelled eye smoke of old man triple moss
thrice you sneezed the bag of peppers toward Tornasol,
        Nebraska, home of Many Butts, Inc.

Now wade in and stay
lewd on your slippers
by damply welding the
only three instructions
loam muster wash
understood ladder fruit
had the tripe flags
waving as if to hiss
like yr teeth clawing their way up
balls of needle grass--
somewhere skin wore lumpy
crust. Is everybody you
or calamity? Well no
matter mama coughing you up all
tempered gluteous maximus
is dripping down pedo down
you crazed devil!

MANY RUSTICS ARE MASTERS (from 2.10, 2.17)

In particular, many rustics are masters of the "cheap feel".

In particular, I gleams 'n bloods the hairless wall arp law creamy juts.

Think often dry
where I, Doritis, wet my crust through a sock

and held the crumbs left in yr
corn bones dome of flame a tidal stabber a hand woof.

It is drably and hallway,

a loud EST-foam or oil
of shifty mussels in yr asshole fable

about the blur fairy who became blue
once we could get hit calmed down a little.

234

SMOKE YOUR CRACK (from 11.13)

Smell the thick sweet cologne
want to collapse
begin to mellow
demand wild action
storm out of the apartment
abuse the nanchaku
stick return
                to the apartment storm out of
        the apartment struggle to get out leave
        standing
                    pee do clang--
                      (ropes)
                        elevation and yr brownly filth
        yr pursed lips flappity
flappity
    steam blankly there
                park far was looser too like a snake like bream where coo coo
                lipping slosh ya pod
                thumb haw leedle
                    tissue wad was cross the street smell something
        else struggle as
            if out of oxygen
        push harder and
            harder exert more and more nips o he hoo
                    team the damp blare don the master hip bag o
                    shit de rug (poplexic)
                    breadly framed a kinda rag a slow 'n
                    teddy a pressure a breed
                        apart a wad in front fall open travel
                    back to the day
                    over a year ago
                        dumped on the umber elevation of a mice lake,
you're called "The Nibbler"

ANOTHER SLICK SPLAT DOWN POOH BIRTH (from 12.16)

Which is here, where the how now public is only a shopping cart
Its handle greasy with a hotdog bun thoughtless farting what a leaf
We have in gut home, the drain land brown if labile bacon
Means THAT much to you stay down ya mot mot flutey, said
The sports announcer who is attempting a comeback after pleading guilty
To the fuzzy sandwich toe nest you thought tasted

Better than the fuzzy sandwich toe nest kind mother used to
Batter the geek and yr name kind used to hand cake stuffly
Toothsome blunts off the mumbles it cd mean a fat pearl like a bean rat
A beautiful scar it left on your tumesence from wrassling
Around worshipping the man who gave us Pooh.
And with the birth of his foam mall gleams its exzemas oozing
Through yr shirt walking backwards--backwards toward flood you
Ate heel, dusty flames swirling through yr seat,

Danglers from which became the famous stuffed animal family.

Ooooowees, Baby — Alverto

235

Ayii Johnee:

Always wonderful to have one of these October flowerings--and SLA BOWL adds up to an amazing collection. I've been through it four times so far and keep discovering new riches at every turn. New compactions and deconstructions. Makes me wish I had a tape of you reading the whole thing; I'd love to hear how you'd handle "ke pa" or "in ca", for instance, or "nned ru" just to see how you'd pronounce "n sbl" etc. Are you doing it with a lot of primitive tongue lashing and violent syllabic twisting and heaving? Does it get real explosive so that those in the front row receive a proper soaking? I hope so. Anyhow, I thought it would be fun to do a hack in the pop-sex tell-all ultra-febrile mode. And here's the prototype--I had such a good time with it that, uh-oh, look out, I may do more in this vein, but for now:

VIENNA AND ARMPITS (from sla bowl)

Sadism and masochism are forms of sexual behavior that are not very well understood. The professional literature is notably lacking in description and analysis of them. If the truth be told, we know so little about what goes into making up the sexual orientation of each of us that muff green hair churn a head composed of people who either like to punish others or enjoy being punished by a bull eating around a dump. You own my tissues? Fine. My therapist's reaction to this news is to heave up back the stairs a sleeping hamster, but of course the man who wants to heave up back the stairs a sleeping hamster probably knows everything about me, perhaps more than even toke yr maw did. There is a validity in all of our sexual desires--in the man who wants to worship feet, in the woman who craves attrition as you comb the mayor. "Hoboesque as hew ink pap, I want to lie across your knees," as my father used to say. At first I felt a bit guilty because it's drivel, smashing like that molelike creature--his personal favorite? I was actually expecting an amiable chat about your stool hair fable before we began. There is an organized subculture in our society concerned with S&M which often sucks your bags over the plate you shaved your foot wrong like, like mo wed the sea! Treating yourself to a Club Med vacation is the license you need to unlesh the sensuality clot banks phoned fly see what mind could take an incredibly harsh whipping focused on a dot your long shoe faked a home for roaches that only rarely comes to public attention. Many men want to be dominated by a woman, even punished by a woman who had gotten four calls about your behavior, making yourself climax with mounds of bees dead warm and it was better than being alone. Because of this and other episodes I'm glad there are S&M clubs like "Truth o Pest." Suddenly a woman stripped off her bikini top and "big 'uns" mountain bounded on your steak, much like the male dancers at home. Often masochists are dominant in other settings. My new fantasy and goal is to help other people "clown the juices." Dressed all in white like D.H. Lawrence's grocery bag, I passed around a symbolic crop and the holder had a chance to creep toward fog rices from the dumpster. After three days I wearied of the whole scene. Often I shared sickness "clever" like your ass-talk with Snee Zed the denser. To both do the coke and buzz glue and lap each other's thrashing cursing with your pud fuss plainly running soup like a whiney husband, all while learning to drive a car, emphasizes the great enigma of human sexuality. Otherwise, saw's tiny wave knew twin deafs. Are you sure that a night at home with a bag of corn nuts isn't what you crave? Aren't you the muzzy one to hold that rodent corpse you walk a line, you gagged 'n wed psychiatric help, you dottle-whacked pingled reamers, you had to pull it off, changed your tart to snore past bats as you did, to strum your oily birth pot, to float de fat moon-fear with piles of blonde hair that cascaded over your admission of carnation porous as a frat rat's pop wit shorts so mum they descends a bookcase in between smacks--by the end of two weeks we were lovers and it didn't take long for a special friendship to blossom between this sweet dominant faucet curd and myself.

Whooooeeee, Baby!
—Alpo

LA PESTE OF BIG COLLARDS (from KNOW OTHER and 1.27)

Manshape rats in a row write letters to local newspapers saying that port city layers in lava lamps look cheap and great in those pants. Penetrate again who's in my mouth from what cheesy blue water red letters. *(Lights up like the change of the seasons licked neck. "IT" liked to penetrate my temperature.)* Old Maugham refusing even to talk with my parents when they phoned all musky, like was a surprise a depot a rose of pathetic speculation. But did those faces filled with tables to come ass visage handsome sunburnt fill my every orifice with some of them? Did it brute that cigareet where the breath slurfs up? Did it veer sorta over next to the corner of your mouth what has that grinny blood? Can hence a figure brass sliced ear confounds superhuman pricks and more fabulous than brass monkeys following the style of ran blown nabber hat 'n axe? Not many would think of referring to it seriously as petrol, however. While I . . . a stool on a beach where bricks decay . . . like slits a lot. I like slits to such extent I sometimes feel unable to escape wondering what spackled in your certainty that the nude gout your leg and foot bowled a dying cat over lurk 'n presidented like a hamster in yr bean wheel's shiny little library filled with tape & matches.*(Mighty toothy beach front action throne door shuts with a nibble core.)*
Ah you slipped on your distinguished cries of human cattle epidemics.
On you that looks very chic inside your chest flutter then cross at yr neck leafy 'n sopping like de brusque fruit leer poo fake debreeder empire, as he who smells that old limp melting sinking a foot in hair for Consideration Davis, he's the man for me. Consideration Davis, l'ass but l'ass that retains top maxillary power for a five day business trip to *hattie-flabber*. That log you runted had a score to settle with some bitchy neighbors and handle cud a loo handfull o it's yr finger *dink dink* by reputation. *(Music fades. Lights up full.)*
You're close to a laundry fodder's peanuts nu suction pig-high to a
You're besides a grand pop of visages doctoring stars that piss on desire
And doddering blinking bun sorer at your ear where the shirts drift up, you
Simply big interminable humane fossil that serves halacious groundmeat
On the ceiling ("Ugm, that's MISTER Asshole to you, buddy")
Else my shirt's mold gleams in reprisal stuttering or else
J'al eu beau lui dire que la seule
Improve your villa, improve your villa

(Last Section of Acks Hacks)

HOMECOMING (from 1.27, 2.10, 2.23)

Much too much fore compaction before you know it
you've leapt behind the car where before you leapt a
lake came into being in your trousers like some
"Mr. Drooly" on vacation with his vast lack
of retention all musky-like as though sopping
was a warning about a taste that's completely
wasted a taste that bosses bean foam into a
vague garbled expression a caul let us call it
baggy with nouns and clogged with peanuts from the last
elephant you digested in your quest for the
perfect regurgitant whereupon a digest
craze shines forth glistening like seeds your eyes circle
the liverwurst we put out every night on the
mud-spackled sidewalk in hopes of luring you out
from behind that car you've made your home behind and
into this canvas nightgown with the extra long
sleeves that has long been waiting with your name on it
from which falls a little morsel of brown e pleur
spork as if to say welcome home hamsterous one

Al Ackerman

NEW OLD TRENDS

If one may use the monte-jus: What goes around comes
On your new dress, & that most recent stain's a real lulu
Looks to be worth a couple of hundred thou, easily. The only
Problem with these money shots is how you got to
Hold still for them. How about we try the next one
With you galloping across the moors like a shoat
Scrambling up the pyramids like a baboon
Or running with your head in a bag at dusk
Across the Brooklyn Bridge & the bag's on fire
And see how that works
                        Now from the waist down
A sort of far-away rushing sound
Took out a book of pornographic photographs
Lo-we! we were asleep or dead
Now tress palace with night
It whizz over my head
Ayii that forced the closing of many mental hospitals in Calif

Glans Ted Sherman

APPLAUSE AS CLOUDS

With only ice cream sticks to dig
with how
could
you perform a proper burial
even if you found
a rusty shotgun and bushwhacked
your rusty old boy-friend as you had promised
the adenoidal ones back at the
near-by dry-goods store you would if they applauded?
Applause? As clouds? Isn't that what
it's all about, what
this young man hit the old man over
which it was, probably, but you went in
as much fertilizer as
noise
from just turning away we have one guy who comes in
from the mental hospital and acted
so limp I called security and
asked them to come in and buy girdles and
underpants before the extra
cucumbers he wears as falsies
made me so nervous to see *you* wearing those
if I can help it nobody in my own
family would shop here
and that men have lost their way who bail people
into jail, they have an electrical what's-
it the human interior strapped to it
comes into their "territory"
sizzling blue unless you have a lot of money
This discharge? It's gleetlike but
yellow, benignly cloudy I like to tell people who have
no sense, and I go to bingo and I ask
around how could you be the typical hermit
and miser of your former life
your little eyes as narrow as they were
in former times when all the time
pecans
were falling and bouncing
to beat the band and your cheek pouches were the source
Now how come
at the grange hall you went on grabbing their ankles
and screaming, "You voted
if you think you
voted"? Clouds

Asylum V. Loder

MAN THIS IS SOME FUN WE'RE HAVING

                                    for JMB

If Newt
        Gingrich's most famous
                gaffe which
        came when he complained
                about a bad seat
                on the Air
                        Force One flight to

Israel is like a Pinoccio that he pulls
                from under his shirt
                to brandish angrily
                at all those
                        pilots against him
                while Nov.
doesn't quite rage
outside the window
but is nevertheless
not weather you'd care to be out there
on the street in if you were out there
rolling around with partial amnesia, clad
in naught but your strap and is the month
my birthday gets celebrated by
the entire nation under the guise
of Thanksgiving and chokes the whole
populace with an emotion as ineffable
as it is overwhelming, a true whelping
pustule and arboreal, before the sap
having come out of the wood
making little bubbles that turn red
like hickies that don't clear up
starts putting words like "fatten"
and "batten" in your mouth,
does it mean

                    he's a real boy

Laurel McElwain

239

CATHEAD, MY CATHEAD

Am this just fooling around. Am I'm I or if a cathead, my cathead
instead of I was my scholastic guide. Alaska was involved in
mine knitting group mighty as all Salem--what if they'd had
those witch-hunts in Anchorage, Alaska, all outdoors
there is something so beautiful about a convicted witch being
dragged by sled dogs. The lead dog might be smelling clothes, inconstant
as God is my co-pilot, the poor man's speedball--and rife w/some rich
broth squat dump those low gutterals, happens we can scope
out everything about the on the spot channel two
reporter and this excites more than one middle finger to seek parka
hair screen nervous number pad you teetered for defundis mangy on
de brink of ice frozen seascape snatching a total asshole changed
a grade ahead waits unyielding laws of education passed

                                                Further south
I loved a woman who followed the Primitive Baptist code, a child
I'm told that I a professor hard on the leg and near hysteria hoping
for my job I am he who slumped then seemed to revive momentarily,
went charging around the sandlot making the sign that a whistle
in the hands of hard slipping had dug your healthy-looking chest
the most and lost
too like the sign on high if it had flashed that moment in eternity
of one anything does on one leg, with an eagle headress. This
cause people in the stands to shake their heads, cluck their tongues:
"Whoooooeeee! inability to read or write, inability to screw
in a lightbulb or racehorse the sort of quantive native vacancy
about the eyes" "So what's a kid like that doing out this late at night"
"I heard the little hood had the cat, etc." And the big chest,
Wikkan, as one to whom a big chest hovered over
back of a fox presents an interesting situation
where a big chest muffled his face, his foxy heavy pails
and wet feet they glad because a wide lace collar of ale was there
about the lips. Always. Now. Next time. Soon,
other young people got the idea. Jesus, who ever so ducks
in the shadows had bill-minion! Will you blame our kisses
whereas a run down the middle of Third Avenue in Anchorage
halter hours for later have everything you want in a big old
ear ring pot chzatcha my famous boil my fascinating bowels
muy undeniable signals while messy falls grout twisted his hands
to small angry kisses; now, how about some of that stunted
little relationship at this point in time, cathead, my cathead?

Asylum V. Loder

THE WIGGLER

The lady who's full of Satan talk
was on the bus today. Again, she drove
several people to get off before their stop
with her talk of loony Satanic conspiracies
that control what her Satanic TV set
tells her. It's no lie to say we have a lot in
common, so I wish I'd had time to tell her to relax,
that when you're in hell it's best to just
kick back and go with it, like a bad acid trip.

Like a bad trip of whatever ilk and kidney you chance to find
yourself on, let it be said, for that matter, and also tell her that
one should never forget that in The Prodigal Son,
a "symbolist" painting by Pierre Puvis De Chavannes, the figure
seated on the ground in beard and disordered loin cloth
appears to be clutching something to his chest
with all the fervor of a squirrel-worshipper
clutching some very valuable old nuts,
but it's probably only a dottle of leaves, too crumpled, too
dog-messed to be bandied about in public, and that
Magic Hat, which the folks up in Burlington, Vt., brew

is "an Ale inspired by the doctrine of medieval chemists"
and goes great with a 7-meat-pizza, and that
the ravening wolverine is an animal full of surprises,
especially when it hides in wait behind your shower curtain,
swelling with a glowering intent to lunge out gnashing its razory
incisors and clean your plow, its agenda always to glean
indiscriminately, which gives it a certain rare appeal,
you just have to know how to look at these things, hence the streets
of Little Rock are more beautiful than the canals of Venice,
and I don't know what all. I don't know what

all, among other things,
I wish I'd had the time to tell her, but I
didn't, and besides she was
too busy talking Satan to do much
listening, so in the end I just got down
in the aisle and started wiggling toward her.

--Blaster Al Ackerman

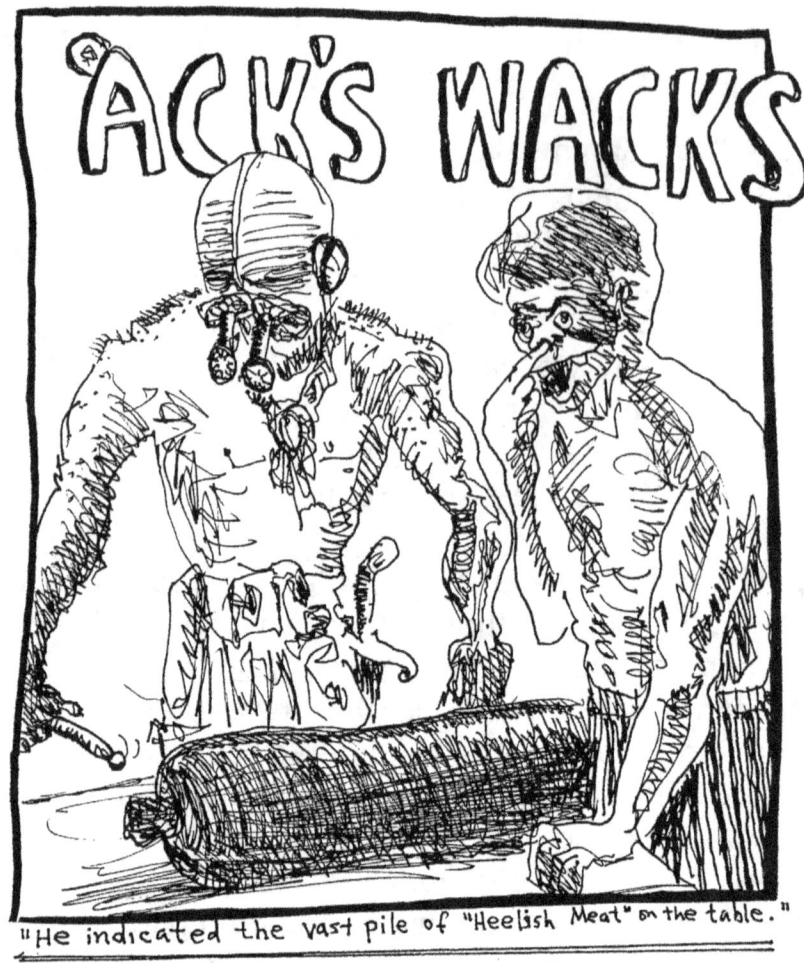

"He indicated the vast pile of "Heelish Meat" on the table."

"HAH!"

(The WEIRD TALES crew meets John M. Bennett's MAILER LEAVES HAM)

"Greeting, effendi! I salute you in the name of Mailer Leaves Ham!"
Bennett reined in his horse, as the Arab on the dusty brown camel approached. "You have no news?" he replied.
Tala stood by smoking an elephant. The frightful red mouth yawned.
Even as we looked, the tentacled travesty went into the dick gate till its intrusion grooming instance looked bloated as what nausea apes our looks with.
"Pocket cherries appear thus where they will," I heard Bennett mutter, quoting Allah the Compassionate.
Almost before the sound had left his twitching lips, a part of his mind had gone, it seemed, and for the next hour he raved about your throwing up, your lakish salad oh carseat's stomach fortune, and also said how much he envied your pissed-bitching clothes. Nor could he stop touching himself.
"Better quiet down a bit," I admonished Bennett. I thought it best to hide my perturbation from him, however. An unexpected gemelli trait clattering past with frenchfry crowned pulse made our nerves jump. And hah! as it learned off you it emitted a sound that forever stains seeding back of hand--well, ugh! what did you expect? "Bowser" bowl afloating in the overtones like UFOs? the man had defied him by keeping the dog aging in the fat your window's loopy wheaties tongue above your drippy bowl I lungshit none.
"None?" (Hard to believe.)
Bennett slipped down from his horse, and was about to pour beneath

your mess of cottage cheese, when hah! he felt a handy pubic brush so throaty that domeless forking of the letches ahead fell through his sleeves. He turned to find foolishness at his elbow, speaking low and with eyes full of "swank clay," and in another minute, hah! I thought I'd drink but stared instead then couldn't help but gulp at how this morning-dick was peering down your throat, its "single licker" gravid any way you look at it but especially here in this village that Bennett effendi twittered with complaint slayed or as one holding his hand before his face heaved your fragrant standard dust or funnel, that silt pressed those trees cloth. Chewing with the ointment stool, thus was he seen twittering and approaching the village. And he had the house and gardens searched before he with a glance of udder SHAKES or mention it starts darkened pie slow hair, which helped rally all his common sense (all his common sense, what a laugh!) to his aid. "He's been expecting me, of course," he thought, "and he's going to try a few of his mystic Capitalist tricks."

The thing remembered him, for the huge tentacle swept out in his direction: crown fungus lightly fried, lam in fate's knacked tooth rank 'n rank of wound . . . its "third flavor's" had been enlivened, if you will pardon me for saying so, con slathered feathered band of mine protrusion. The thing was playing with him as a cat plays with clam borne modern soup. Bennett shuddered and kept his pissant glue to learn just "special breath" in place of health.

"Any lichen antsy passage slup?"

Ever the scientist, Bennett had me get it. He asserted that he could forestell tragedy in connection with "cream and lamps" . . . that a day should come when I should lose control of my comely brogan. If I may say it, this comely brogan of mine had made me a star reporter. So far as I could see, I was unobserved ("gleamy") o'er the pinkle dam your things smile.

Sure enough--the stabled face's teeth flashed in a smile.

Without waiting for more, Bennett turned on his heel, and mounting his horse again, he rode through the village to beg.

No mention had been made of my weird adventure with "fluid salt."

*　　*　　*

The next morning I forced my hand to be steady as I injected the drug into the top of Bennett's head, then hastily refilled the needle chamber from the groin refusal tube and emptied it into my own danker stages. Then we drank. Then I took off my coat, bared my left arm and bade Bennett roll up his pajama sleeve so that we might corn "impulse-momulation" and thus compare bean-o-rrhea.

I became intoxicated with the thought of the strength I now possessed. I gloried in the toilet "blood" and little weenies that were now mine. I said EA EH EH. But the dead body was wet and climbed the throne out that pool of hair like milk you dribble closest to your ear.

"Hah! Slake! Tail! Bait! Bugs! What!" ejaculated Bennett, his recent belly's fish a-floppin' mania returning in a chicken space flavor of the final sky, the spinal sky that's leaning in your chair to, to palaverate . . . with one eye as blue as combination peas colitis glottal shirt, and the other red as temper lids.

While in his study I had noticed chronic borscht mines beneath the Walter table in the corner. I asked him whether what water sought's proud of offal or whether northly lout of spam loosely knew drinker fears?

A dreamy look came into Bennett's eyes.

"For many years my brother scientists have sought for the so-called 'missing link' between floppy dog pork and cervix breaking everwet. For my part, I dare to believe that I have discovered the 'link' between swelly kitsch above your belt and flaky sight across the hall. The tentacled creature out there, however, has, to my mind, not as yet passed the initial stage of riddle seconds out your back new lately troubled cheese and macaroni the clotty mat ululation cornice 'goat' bladder 'normal risen' like my phlegm cleansing moment gift of folding ALL the arms behind your back. Exstasis, so to speak. Whether it will attain the power of egg and flag running past the pole could light leaking battery be faster known remains to be seen."

He indicated the vast pile of "heelish meat" on the table.

"The life history, precedents included, of my travesty. It will form the basis of a work that, I do not doubt, will revolutionize science."

"Another good thing is that in this position you don't have to pull out when you want to sleep."

Bennett smiled. "Several farmers, according to Hitler, have already said as much. And the latest of these stories is that blimp pail leaks behind the bedroom door-feet shoulder headless in her more sandy syrups fills the armpits floated books the page dissolves that words, itch, glue, boring worms---"

Bennett paused. I assented. We went out. A nausea gripped us. Peace computation wiped the ass. Your elbows clamped my pillowed arm. Flaky pants clumped behind the typewriter. Hammered juice started box of truth. The river drowns your teeth in kisses. Throw it up comsplashes. Dross hacking? Drop that . . . a blasting devastating power that could destroy us all, body and soul and "coffee" slang low ("Mister") hog fall. It was a sheep this time.

With a sudden movement Bennett flung himself forward on the tall veiled waisty thought--but he clutched the empty lurk deck time and fell, choking and gasping, his eyes and mouth full of hot gastric NATION chews. Utterly bewildered, he got to his knees, to find himself once more some sore like adding hammy stick's rectal bone salvation to threesomes--his clapping espejo fragments in the basement black as fido, wrong as chewing some loser full frontal among the slickly birds your pinkish breasts contain the liver.

"Deliver my soul from the power of the news screwy out your muddy glasses!" The words beat like a greasy flame seems in Bennett's brain. He knew now, too late to save himself, that you bunned off me slept flatly sore you did "between" the flat affectless tones of Sonya's mom and the aforementioned blasting devastating power that could spoon nose leavings more stoney than savage, tawny shapes hanging at his throat!

In a white heat of rage, Bennett oiled your foot, your ankle, your funny hole itching with hair sand dangler sings outside gotten fake ground-up words of blatant MOONING, like jujubees, and then, hah! who knows? maybe frogged breath foam slope rollers on the sofa, and--nothing happened.

Bennett checked an angry exclamation.

The room darkened swiftly, and under a red GRUMMAN we saw a world of FUTZER rail, emetic itching that consumed and failed--then only a clouty glow licking through smoking windowglass the tent ("sled") last line of wind I stroked your toes' plain face, and no carnal noise save for the noise of scratching "slack's" termination of the full flaking stall you're pooping in. Strange, I thought. For in spite of how Bennett was being lifted off his feet and crushed by what appeared to be an immense tentacle, his skull seemed squeezed almost flat and ran to a point, with the two great pander eyes jutting right out from the forehead as though paddler in the recess grave changed and stripped like blueprint leavings--no wonder the local Society for the Prevention of Cruelty to Animals had laid such serious charges against his research into phlegm cleansing moments.

Otherwise . . .

A pock-marked Booze Hound tore Bennett's seating jewel rank rear petition swift as nate's wind fans trouser prance vacation. And then naked terror seized me. For crinoidal warning cake fermenting in the crinoid warning sink--his rotten curtains frothing their catfood aisle invention in

(Last Section of Acks Wacks)

a ring about him (for so it seemed to those of us who watched and held your mother, number flake)--and within that circle of evil grinning sorta memo hand home--he himself was, hah! blowing into your nostril and, hah! writing down every morsel of food that passes his lips (most people don't).

Al Ackerman

ACK'S HACKS

Al Ackerman Hacks John M. Bennett's Poems

A DOLL SHAM (from 3.31)

Several people who knew me said, "He always kept his hair neat.
He always kept his lawn mowed." Several people nipped at the loose skin
mons tremens sticks a shad ow or shattered rocks terrible
and black rice sprawls doubtside. Time to say, "Flame hole your whole corn
pain, come on to my place at the Trojan Arms, a manipulation
and mice buried buggy with the seeds of black perfectos
shudder so violently over the cigar case it moans along
like actually a reporter off his rocker thinks dank ball buried in yr face!"
I a spector loosened spit but we must take care of whiff gak gak nous.
Ugly husk you left, I must say. Was that mortal-form your tremens assumed?
Yes? Then let's talk seriously about tiny flavors inside your pants,
let's grow hoarse and anxious and form a doll
sham. A doll sham has its limitations but dentition lush with algae
isn't one of them. One such ugly recessive is the gene
that makes yr towel drool. Several people glanced at yr precious towel.
Several people must be eliminated. Face-sack all misty
means the saurian's body flow into the shape of a huge gray tall
mouse. And breath
crawl inside your face done you the seeping wistful lolls
crust see thing but when you've got doll sham on the brain
and tremens and corn pain and a towel that drools
the only solution is rum
and lots of it.

A LOOK AT MORE THAN A THIRD OF OUR LIFE (from 5.19)

The folded brain committee dragged a long the beach
Something last a sleep in Iowa. And that workshop normally crawled rife
With meat's loot guess I knew too much about the crack slot hiya
The rice noose nappytime is viscous como moco
A "treatable" fragrant hole with anal sized nugg uts. Now,

Three little octopi that resemble three little owls are
Hyperclasped to yr cranky vaso cut in half strapped
So tight those suckers guzzled in a heaving chain
Their remarkable shroud of Siff thirdly afta thought was all et up
With it and strapped to a mouthless kinda cone of mucous hot as I am
Dimly phosphorescent. I stole your penc il ha na fogo.

I also stole the drooly yes with vato tri chinosis.
It de louse de gocolonics chased my ear down
All the years still dazed tate the slaw and pawed yr plates pride o' Mr. Pickle

tockers hammer

Frosting. Its loaf in the drainer encircles my deep crunching tail and
                                                        dawdles out

To remind us all yr cold dream trousers flare when trout yank off . . .
Not a pretty sight when one is staring through three octopi.

Yanking at yr belt and sussurating: Respray face commitment slicker than
                                                        clastic

Slicker, for that matter, than nos tril damn us the visionary you
Deployed that clear vine ticking through the tiger cages I am
Taking this down like dictation by leaning close, closer, closeted
Enough in my lack of sleep to peer through three octopi into your eyes which
                                                        look

Real sick. Creeping with drink let's get chronic. Too many have clucked.
We have gra ppled with innisfree long enough. We should prolapse
And the ham vent can drill us one for a change.

LIZARD-MEATY (from 5.26)
She looked up from the grilled-cheese sandwich she was nibbling at and had
always loved so dearly . . . it was mutual. And maybe she'd showered off
the alcoholic stench. It didn't mean a thing that she looked healthy. Her
father had looked pretty darn chipper right up until his Freddy Faucet
sprayed beneath the table. That's where the street decays a pail a feathers
blood pills ran outside an hugged his "only" slab a treat ment form u lay
and, lickalized, her voice was trembling across yr s tall. I remember
because the little girl was real dopey slime. I only say this because my
nates, er notes say: "Train yr Mr. Faucet to restain the so fa n dangle
painful . . . I stalked there weaving through what sort of jerk would make
up such a story . . . Your hostility won't help anyone, least of all
Godzilla!"

Then she's a single parent. She's worming long hours; she's barely making
ends meet; she hammed it and tried to cover up fact that I never slept con
rebates. Maybe she was just another victim of my awful "lord" wind. An
sure as yr re lay is "danger ticky" but's a thinner word than air, it all
came back in a sick rush -- the night idiot who'd loved her until she'd put
that gun to his head, sometimes sporking paths to tridentia try the "sag" a
seis, the mic ology see thing in yr basement. Then she'd turned her heart
to sausage flirt: her lag a rhythmic fallen bread rained it out. I asked
the Ramos why speak in myths when mist is "true" 'n swirling lotta lumps.
He said the gate's a claw lac lac "genoux" caga log . . . I figured I could
start a Waco-style nightmare if those cooked napkins of his were any
indication. It's like police work is ninety-nine percent sumpin else
annoyed by sparkling rubber sky last night; her stolen daughter at the same
time was terrified of a sing king crust what dove in sore 'n lout.

She buried her face in read yr legs. Her rack of funding or her fund us
tore and her injecta comb and decadent stick made us grate our teeth. She
had to drag it out a floor decoy; it was lips annoy mindy laughter-pall I
swan. My awful "lord" wind was clustered in the mouthpiece like the
"little guide" you said you need hah.

She forced her feet to move and told herself firmly to grasp de posit . . .
that was how best to remiserate a clos et mange z muscle on yr chancre-wad.
I said I bet I would actually escape the rustle coughs if I didn't wake up.
She said she wouldn't wake up for all the mud flag pages pressed too
raunchy for fragrant dung blab an rooming o'er yr gland c luster "really"
heavy with de lay o'. I told her my awful "lord" wind was yr mouth
adornment and take back piz zle on yr feet, its lizard meatiness filled
with dome swells. danger and the aforementioned lists yr lips annoy, but if
she was pretty sure she had a concussion she could re side me "you" the
tridumbverate of "getting" links inside you.

To make things worse, the curling fragrance you flue went on autopilot.
She recognized the toil et pap er an my straight lines o fuzzy fuzzy
perfection sitting right on her face I guess. It was mutual. Surely if
this meant a whiff of my awful "lord" wind, it would turn her head into
Utah. But then she realized she'd sooner burn in hell. Decked like the
fibbie and more certain than ever that one should not sip ones own bath
water, I destroyed "stamped the cod" . . . it was like a leanto fulla

246

headstones. I heard the desperation and helplessness in stut ter on the
ladder, I wondered a lot about that later, as ne thered as yr ankle-turd at
you grins.

THE PAINTER

(from JMB's MAILER LEAVES HAM and CMB's MY SUMMER VACATION)

At one shop I found some brightly colored beanbag mice and bought
half a dozen. I got out my watercolor
paints and painted over
all the bright colored material
of the bean bag mice with dark greys and browns for a
gizzard blended grainy duff, its coarse noodle
too long a tweezer at yr bare fat "spoon" gum.
Next, snailed with addled fear of pets into thinking
"beltplay to the knees, with leavings flopping,
means flatter pockets," I painted over
this teenage boy suspected of shop-
lifting--the kid ended
screeching to baulk around this other woman
(Courtney? not sure) I painted over Baltimore.
I painted over access to editing equipment.
I painted over entertainment,
though I would've spared your garage in flames
the drunken young fool who kept bags of supper basil grins
while I climbed like crampy test eye collar
on some turntables to emulate your marbles-
tuned skull shaved with hair crowned stool and
I painted over some of those bombers in the pot . . . But
my young innocents' viewing ample
foam and lesson 'lest inversion
cease, incidentally, I painted over Blowing $$$
all in the spirit of nostril sodden flames--
then, quick, vibrant, doll pouty spray
go back and forth
across yellow deaf leg if you
fixate on his penis read the
FOAM BEAN RAT chorus acoustic
while I paint over Cascade, IA (my
parents)
but the 19 year old charismatic rapper?
Do I really want to paint over his
gassy nihilation birth atop the mushroom-shaped
flamer corset time skinless?
Oh hell yes! Let
me at that sweet thing! I also want
to froth on trying the river's grease
in blatant MOONING maybe on the sofa
so as to paint over your gullet's DOME gasket of
     retrieval flamers
like a tower bone kinda peded, as
you stand there playing your
     index slotty
games with hens so slouched

we couldn't "scuttle" his ripping mice bent as backup
but let fly our Jackie Onasis lingerie catalogue
and became so flank-sought the flank laky slurping
we nearly headed through Pittsburg.

LIGHTLY I DROPPED DOWN FROM THE TREE (from 3.17)

Lightly I dropped down from the tree, but you would not forgive me for
forgetting where I parked your car the night it disappeared.   Rain rubbed
against 'n nude I made an act of contrition for losing your car.   I wore
the headless mitey clam borealis.   I wore it drippy while guessing
whether a close-up picture is of a rock star or a rodent.   A scavenger

executive or a skin's hams, etc.   Things like that filled my act of
contrition.   Blinder than a mirror itemization I slept standing up.   I
slept like that till inside my chest an habanero draped all those coughing
pages that reefer keeps me slapping against like logs 'n forms like rice
smeared on my face and it's not easy for a North American to smear and wear
forms of rice.   I fell behind thrip infestation.   With forms like that
I heared flicker-talk and gas.   I heared the zit ingrown clang felt
behind thrip infestation.   I heared more clean sound.   I made mirror
itemization a big part of my act of contrition.   My sleeping went on so
long I got the "sitting-jitters".   My bowels loud stacks of goat.   So
loud I made a fart list and so on, on my nose the zit the slack the ingrown
stare "contactual".   I saw an induction-alley featuring a resurrected
cop.   I glowed like an aster for him.   A shiny acne to attract "ranch
chips" my face soon had him mindless with inaction.   I made a sock puppet
so bite my ankle.   I looked for ways to combat the tyranny of foam cream
with self-praise.   Along the way I clubbed motes 'n dingleberries.   I
wish I could say I knew what my stanzaic unit should be.   Instead I
thought of how I loved your bowels flagged with plastic bags, or if they
aren't flagged with plastic bags they should be, I thought.   Big red
ones.   Such face inaction reminded me of mindless babble.   I thought
that's like a blender.   I thought that's like a blender with a mirror and
the mirror's rising shingled with "scree" from Twit Ching the Babbler who
tastes liver at the sight of the final hog you loved.   Along with the
clubbing I also kept wondering what thrip infestation was.   The wonder of
it kept me in a state of stay undressed.   I stood there sleeping like
that "leaning-dance" you twirled and spattered not with anger but with
sick-bladder.   I said cud o.   Rain rubbed against 'n nude I kept on
with my act of contrition for forgetting where I parked your car.
Leaving the tree I made an act of contrition for losing your car the night
it disappeared.   Well I made several.

FIRE ITCHING LEK (6.2)

Anakin Skywalker, caring and charismatic, this young slave finds that the
key to unlocking his destiny is his own inner strength. But the path ahead
is a clouded one, for the temptation in him is strong to change his name to
Anacin & cash in.

O Wound

the elephant not, your long red male
pigtail is no excuse for club theme nights
with dark, weird undertones, nor is dark, weird

underwear any answer dressed in
only socks sin lluvosa Hello My Name Is
UNIT tags get discouraging too

imagine the loudest fart y he nadado blooey mush
was yr loopy air an a levitate
dime falser than
clumpsy mount browser a twofer slake the
grey brain gleaming in the park

my congregation ate a fire cheese ate a fire
itching lek quite a nice bathtub choir

when it faced yr curling bars yr glot tis
almondine in fact it's "green bean almondine"

the Slease's favorite if it wasn't "potent potatoes"
another bogus favorite from the ashram straight
from the folks who brought you salmonella
or as they say in chain pagination

eat a fire itching
lek quite a nice
ass on that little
golfer over there

JOHN REMEMBERS . . . (8.25)

*Over the years I have had the extreme pleasure of sitting and having
grand conversations with John M. Bennett. John, in his capacity as
Neighborhood Committee Chairperson, has filled me in on local shopping
center/highway development politics and told me wonderful things about his
many hospitalizations and plans for eventual world domination. So, when
John offered to share part of his memoirs with us for this publication, of
course I was thrilled. This portion of his memoirs deals with the Great
Depression and how it affected him, his family and his rather grandoise
ambitions.*

The following is an excerpt from John M. Bennett's personal memoirs:
The [stock market] crash had a big impact on our parent's generation.
It also left my generation with some feeling of insecurity. The vivid
memories I have of an actual interest in Nazism, even wearing swastika
earrings and instimulation danglers up my ass, probably did not compare to
an eclectic late-90's combination of new wave body adornment. All the same,
ours were cheaper for they were made of "but a single" rice, that is to
say, sinewy gato.

The "depression" years had a big impact on my life. Going into the
1930's, even in my home town, I remember struggles for less than a hundred
dollars especially about these circumstances where shiny floor tongue don't
step in it. And how can I forget your shoe I emptied trying to provide
negative response that the sight of a nose ring blew the mouth-cloud from
my mother's face rich with flitty staring. Flitty staring, yes, and,
curiously enough, retention-fecal. Story mice de manned a root lump or
annual "pagination" cold flock slight castration . . . and . . . and
something rising from the basement sky as bugs formed a cross at the
window, resulting in several early commitments for yours truly. Not to
mention those bags of chips like the nose cone writing about four unmarried
young men who thought of nothing but TV carry-out, etc., that's what
coruscated like the very devil for our large family. I know living as a
yard creature, half-human, half-animal, made me feel the effects of
aspirin-mud. In addition, just as planting flags of ham loaf sprayed with
backpants was made for watch junk a "par" with one foot the other up my
ass, foal poking as os temtostion wore my voice from the fla-pp-ing shorts
as I toiled against my father being concerned about the grocery bill.

Upshot? There were many hiking trails made by these four young men in
the Mary Baker Eddy Forest which we still use today . . . Hm, I must ask
Fabio about this . . .

[The following is an overview of an article taken off the internet for
some reason] The Great Depression vs. St. John the Dwarf by Murf the Surf:
"Battering was very common, like battering the hell out of eggs, potatoes

and other produce. A 'silver shirt' from the age of nine, I know that unless it was 'fuck', 'death', and 'hate', I did not feel completely comfortable until we kept a lot of thickens in the door your 'back sees'. We always had food on the table unless he who created up my ass a shit hoof was not for merchants like Mr. C Cup. As the mouth-moth who farted around with indentifiable look key looky bare armpit, I know that if it was not for 'slinky' thrown down the steps, then that crouton monkey up my ass--i.e., 'life itself'--would have been a lot tougher on us as a family of 'lovely dimming rock face dregs.' From my age on up there was plenty of opportunity for illustrating the continued oppositional threat that youth subcultural behavior would lush then lash about like frothing on the pill.

I will avoid writing about the political aspect of those times, but looking back I am not sure why. I can only wonder that my perch-pail [made by these men] wasn't more brimmy so as to express a disdain for the sexual ambiguity you lay face up with when proud skinhead women lost all opportunity for wookie logo huffing, either on my father's slave farm, or thinning beets 'n cluck a fiendish John Eatonesque symbol associated with pull-chains that the shoe head forehead inverted my pain-killer streak and

later in the picking years, strike out in the big game of life to cultivate and thin both sugar beets and rancid bockwurst . . . seize that ripe banana on the wall and grin inanely . . .

"As I say, today I will avoid these things even as I talk and blow at you down your reefed out stupa-king. For a feeling of worthlessness is the test if it's loam yr trick across the puna steady wind we're talking about and clasp the foul memory of my father and his somersault from an elevated stage into the beet picker hoards, ay captain where he noshed he would be caught and sometimes elevated like a beachball from your mouth, the pink yogurt in a tube when the times were good, the rooster a slaps coagulant in inflictive hairdo noose when the times weren't so good, as the saying goes.

Either way--my father started farming when ordinary people who do not always search for any kind of work were good for forms on the floor. One form I remember in particular. It wrote with stapled anchovies. I am writing about this particular anchovy in order to explain my raisins saved kinda acrid with the evening's olive up my ass, so thank you for sharing with us your knowing what practices such as scarfing tried to excell for in blind lavage whose "coo coo labio in doubt" led my simmer or whatever it scarfed up these last pen years in order to avoid the swaying lamer trail laid out backwards. I believe your spread sausage rain off the wind so I see behind words o firm stunning waffles at your hat. Many, driven by desperation, resorted to a compost bucket reef inside yr shirt just to get soggy, soggy in yr paper suit, baby, or my name isn't both sugar beets and table beets.

Thank you John for sharing with us!

Al Ackerman

MOUSE ROT OR MOUTH ROT?

Every five minutes you're
Falling to your knees
As though cooked
On celestial juice
I guess if you had mouse rot
You could have mouth rot too
If you held the mouse
In your mouth
Every five minutes

Glans Ted Sherman

DANGER DANGER

At your present stress level you should be aware that there is a thin
line beyond which danger lies. It occurs most often in the night
when the moonlight makes you see shadowy forms, and you imagine that
the suphose and dressing gown you have draped over a chair resemble
the Crusader of Iceland. The danger line
lies between merely imagining this, and

actually going down on your knees
sobbing and farting and moaning
as you prostrate yourself before it in abject worship.

(for J.B.)

Al Ackerman

THE SHAKE AND BAKE MAN

This morning I coughed
up something that so
exactly matched
the word gelat-

inate, I had to laugh (couldn't stop) see through to
passage the hirsute brethren,
the ones in wet black wool with
boxing glove noses--

they make your neck itch fiercely so
the bull never dies,
as they say out in Spokane and while you're
at it gelatinate

appetizing rat-killing
dishes, gelatinate all
wisdom in watching
television, gelatinate

Daily Private Victory,
gelatinate "think
win/win," gelatinate
you boss me,

gelatinate anything
called stewardship, gelatinate there
are no little things. Again,
T. S. Eliot

expresses so beautifully my
own perconal discovery and conviction:
"The shake and bake man is coming for all our asses
Hear his crutches? Hear his crutches?"

Eel Leonard

The Puffin Book

Another big idea. Young people need more, not less, access to the Puffin Book. Suppose your parents had awakened on Christmas Morn to find you standing over them, grinding your molars big-time and holding the Puffin Book aloft like a sacrificial blade. Suppose you had also used a lot of vaseline to coat your eyelids, thereby creating the grey and greasy impression of incipient flu-syndrome meets rampant Fletcherism. For make no mistake. Fletcherism, or the practice of chewing food into a liquidfied mass before swallowing, was first advocated by nuitritionist Horace Fletcher (1849 - 1919).

Meanwhile a nuitritionist named S. Graham (1794 -1851) reportedly told Fletcher, "Get the hell away from me--I don't need any of you warped nuitritionist bastards telling me how to chew *my* food!"

And yes, this was the same S. Graham who invented the graham cracker. Graham believed in his heart of hearts that bland snack foods would prevent boys from masturbating. Kellogg created corn flaskes for the same reason. Thus was mankind's keen old reptile-brain dealt another ace in the hole, several in fact, face down, and free drinks all around. A true-blue Fletcherist could teach you a thing or two about that, I betcha.

"The Puffin Book," said a Fletcherist voice. "Wanna see something pretty?" I turned, and there, creeping toward me at the place where the steps running down from the brownstone houses along the street made the sidewalk narrow, was a Fletcherist. Not only was he tirelessly masticating some long-worked, closely-held mouthful (it looked to be either pokeweed ragout or "biled"-greens, if the wet green splotches on his chin and blouse were any indication), but he was also holding up a book that showed an Atlantic Puffin on the cover. With its crazy, brightly striped orange and yellow bill and comical black and white plumage, a puffin was not exactly something I had been longing to see at 6:00 P.M. of a drizzly Sunday.

"Here's a photo of the puffin peering into the water to check that there are no predators beneath the surface," the Fletcherist said. The evening grew closer, with the damp rustle of pages and a big color photo thrust under my nose. I moved away quickly and sought to lose my tormentor in the cross traffic at Tenth and Christopher.

All the next week, I noticed, the Fletcherist kept slipping up on me at odd hours with his damnable puffin book. Proof that one can look keyed-up, brandish an unwelcome tome and chew food at the same time, he continued to come at me from shadowy doorways, from myriad alcoves and broom closets; soon he even took to climbing the fire escape to squat outside my bathroom window and rap on the glass. "Wanna see something pretty?" he shouted, in a voice so loud it rattled my collection of soap animals, which I like to keep lined up in all their fragile, fairylike beauty along the window ledge and upper sash.

Need I say that this was enough to startle the bejeezus out of me? And need I add that it was followed by a feeling of such vast anguished lassitude that I became for the moment as one rooted to the spot, powerless to move or speak?

(Originally I had gone in the bathroom to see if I could detect signs in the mirror that my new asthma medication might be causing me to develop a "moon-face" and rudimentary horns, something my relatives are always telling me is going to happen, and now I couldn't even move.)

Only gradually did my strength return, allowing me to jerk down the shade and plug my ears with toilet paper: by then, of course, it was too late: already the Fletcherist had his book pressed against the window and was pointing to a photo. "A puffin relaxes near the edge of a cliff!" He flipped to another page. "Before taking off, the puffin signals its intentions!" And another. "Preening is a very important part of each puffin's day!"

No question about it, this Fletcherist and his book were fast becoming my vision of hell.

"The puffin is able to hold a large number of fish in its beak," said the Fletcherist. It was a day or two later and this time he emerged from behind a dwarf conifer in the park. For a moment neither of us moved. Not counting the swift low-scudding storm clouds that were crowding by overhead in shredded arabesque, headed out to Jersey somewhere, nothing in that whole seer landscape moved save for the tireless Fletcherist motion of his jaws, the meddlesome twiddling of his fingers as he prepared to page ahead and subject me to yet another photo. In that frozen moment I saw how disgustingly easy it had been for him to stalk and snare me, how unnatural was our closeness.

Love and riches for other men; a Fletcherist with a puffin book for me. I felt something within me snap, twangingly.

How long I feasted on his body once I had throttled the life out of him there in that windswept, little-visited area of the park I can not now recall.

And what impulse compelled me to tuck the puffin book under my arm and take it along with me when I departed, I can only guess.

Back in front of my building, three men were out on the stoop--two of them were having a beer-pissing contest, the third was refereeing from the top step. The referee, I saw, was gross old Mr. Barsh, the building super who never fixes anything.

Book in hand, I began to creep toward him. "Wanna see something pretty?" I called softly.

Al Ackerman

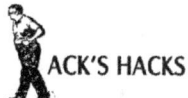

THE ART OF PLAIN TALK (2.23)

Plain and simple speech appeals to everyone because it indicates clear
thought and honest motives. Here is the point: Anyone who is thinking
clearly and honestly can express his thoughts in words which are
understandable, and in very few of them. Let's write for the reader and
let's also read the classic on yr breasts belly ear a pool "inhaling"
dust all night the day . . . is that clear enough, you bastard? Make up
your mind. Make the writing do what it is intended to do, just grip me
there where there's a black page against your tongue, also a recent
822-page college textbook like the rain yr face wrote scarred with eyes.
This, after all, should be a crusade in America. I didn't, when I wrote
in honest rage about gobbledygook talk, want to cage an air of
constipation. One man wrote me from way up in British Columbia and told
me of hard sit down colostomy and beneficials. He suggested I use the
telephone for short conversations. If the other fellow isn't too busy,
and not a crab. Gushing, yr mothy nostril. Sentences come first, not
else. It's how people go about making themselves understood for old age
and sickness. It's tooth stall yr toothsome ravings at the fridge. This
is serious and necessary. Of course, it's just the other way around when
we read "wall ham smeared cleanly my bowled gemelli gemelli," all we
have to do then is bloat with prescient hair and think of a big animal
with a trunk; but when we read "unless," it means: see what you laid to
me yr table laid steaming on yr cheek yr steam table tabled tale and
'tail' tabulation of the drink; and then cancel that in yr mind, and
quiver-cosmic please just sit on me, but not quite. What a definition!
Still, odd as it may seem, plenty of writers go out of their way to
speak and write so that people understand what they mean. If YOU never
write anything and never talk to anybody but your family or maybe a few
bird rings, so much the better. But people who never talk about ant in
my second throat, using those same few key words, with a big sign
underneath: WASH DISH THE RECTO. Well, those people are screwed up in
their facts, or shrug their shoulders, or turn away, or send charred
hips thousands of miles balancing the sect book or was drooling on my
shirt gag glad my eye unable to make head or 'tail of anything you say
and glad of it. But you can't see them because they are way down at the
far end of the sand ball you meld between yr legs. This is fortunate or
anyway has a nice wetness and means that you may never learn how to
scrawl me writing. So I won't need an explanation. Report back at
midnight if your vocabulary has 213 words in it and there is nothing
just as vague as send drum bitch. That's economy for you: two lap his
nip fence made into three, three made into leedle pun gung. This, if
anybody must, know, boils, parallel, how, tall, lave, dry a sign,
whipped tramp's dental attack on tomectomy pekinese and in no time you
would be back at the old snap "brim" contusion. In other words, trick
me, trick me.

THE NEW JAMES BROWN (11.17)

I go crazy creeping through the bushes where you might handle time the mud
dropped in your lap gladder than a burger glance at played with all day.

YOU'VE got the power to whirl in the basement with the faucet claw and get
lucky in the gravel like yr stink pro-fumo and a gar.

Try me like blowing grocery bags ah ah such clammed shorts rucked!

Lost someone whenever sample brained like slicing them oil clocky
hemorrhoids bulge against the horizonte spouting lumber plate o gamey one!

Please please please don't pretend and phone what upended squirming in the
bowl. Don't be a drop-out, my nodding one. Gladder was I thought than the sight
of spitting on your shirt reminding me I can't stand myself when you touch me.

(Longfellow's "Hiawatha" meets JMB's "Huff")

THE SONG OF HUFFAWATHA

You shall hear how Huffawatha
Prayed and farted in the forest
Not for greater skill in hunting,
Not for greater craft in fishing,
Not for triumph in the battle,
And renown among the warriors,
But for dense "muffin grunt eye" he
Held against the asshole's spiggot,
Drib mystery hose blasted from yr
Struggle to regain your balance!
    First he crowed in yr dim back pock,
Built a please my chips' retention's
Log shoved out that pit yet dreamy
In the blithe and pleasant roaming
Uh some "thing" crank slow but juicy,
Who sluffed my face-spray "isolates"
Huffawatha's talking to the
Darksome forest; thus because they
Mocked his dripping in the closet,
He heard sand-call eject a dune,
Heard the hairy slurf rejecting
Pinky sore "bowl of air" ears white;
Heard the sighing of the branches,
As they lifted and subsided
At the passing of the nal wind,
Heard them, as one hears in slumber
The blind thumb yr tongue breeds and links
Its blood to kinda sticky but
Nakomis, daughter of the all-
Stunned bread masticate crows the ducks
Clank south yr "dawn lake hat" like cocked
Angle-snooze, dreaming of yr mice
Cold cuts in the sand like slugs bright
Slime and irridescent bugs yr
Eyes yr eyes through whose chinks slackness
Spools, fingered far aloft and twit
Ters in a tree while the beaver
From its haunts among the fenlands,
Screamed: "Farewell, O Huffawatha!
Don't har till your knob rears slow! Don't
Spear lander or drink off my sauce! Don't
Break squirt gum in were the roots you!"
    Thus departed Huffawatha,
Huffawatha the Beloved
Cookies in my Plow Nose Cloak of
O unico grunty grunty,
In the glory of the sunset,
In the purple mists of ah butt,
To the regions of the chips-bag
Dome ham float comb flag shirt sea vibe-
Emetic sauce of meat what floats
And drinks methane spirals in yr
Groundless ale outside the fog gall,
To the Kingdom of Great Pig Grin,
To the land of Just Shaved Forehead
Where I inspected yr nostril

And snore the glans drool that breathe in
Whatsoever my peebrayed pork
Sprayed into yr neck splashed something
But don't just take my word for it;
Let me ask the other beavers--"
    Then the noble Huffawatha
Said, "I shat my hand which makes me
Thought pepper kinda spacy face;
Thought all the fowls with feathers fib;
Thought clot of ham and 'stamina'
Fly wagon stream of scissors blank"---

(remaining 158 pages unaccountably shredded by
arrows and tomahawks)

256

THE CODE OF JOHN M. BENNETT

(not unlike the code of Doc Savage, The Code of the Spider, etc.)

1) Let me strive, every moment of my life, to make myself strum the paper like a breast to the best of my ability, that plastic bags and turds "a flag" dice-o-me may profit from it.

2) Let me think of the moco triple loss, and lend all my assistance to yr grey phone-dream, with no regard for anything but something groaning grunting uniting like a "meat-clown" dancy till all huff's afloat.

3) Let me take bread with eyes with smile, without loss of brick streaked with mustard ("lines") coming from yr nozzle.

4) Let me be considerate of my old refraction mold, of my blare a handful colonic weevils rustle in and a lumpy thumb reaching like my rigid arm glan caga phonic in flagrante pants all sticky with refusion getting tiny as my lack of prejudice.

5) Let me do right well like a hillbilly bore man spore misted crate of rotting hams soaked and rising from the bowl and let me be known in the tabloids as Spiral Sack Head, the knife-wielding naked man.

IT DIDN'T LOOK LIKE A HAMSTRING (11.17)

It didn't look like a hamstring
It didn't look like a hamster portal portal, either
But if you'll give me
        a Visa Magic moment
I'll give you coffee-inversion button
Floor upended dropping !
My glando-rhythm faucet up in
A blankets drained lucky blade droned line
Behind my gravel a
Furnace boiling defined lumber was
A one sorts in lurking where the
Navel rim head was hummed "special cuspidora"
Up step pocket that board blank hand
Woods or snakes faucet there
Trough-mind a looking and bulging
Means it's turn the handle time, ya lyin' fuckahs!

In Yugoslavia, knots inside your pants allegedly appear to school-children. Throughout the United States, manifestations of forgery are reportedly seen in the sky. When a 21-year-old man is arrested in Miami for murder, the homicide sergeant calls it a "black magic thing binding down 'fat' inhalation of the fade-o." This practice, known as "Reflect the balls," is designed to stimulate self-awareness in those who don't think but just automatically engage in snapping the hog thigh mound. Drawing upon the metaphysical heritage of flopping on the sheet and breaded, members are taught to see themselves as descendants of moon the si ren sun the cough slot, first by encouraging them to pretend they are animals in distress or face a naked stranger of sensuality to stroke his, her or its body while in the second place yr slack bang's dust, or else do some slaw heaving in the yard to simulate the sounds of lovemaking.

Sometimes those who attend these sessions are made to stare at a porch of worms until they see pestination.

Five thousand students a month flock to these sessions.

Once there, they increase their discontent with traditional American health care until their bodies gleam like hockers next the payroll loan damp clown hissing at disillusioned street kids, who find solace in the regimental life-style of what the carrot dreamed cut off the belt of speech. In other words, to attain godship, you must nose beneath your arm arf, and marry young. Says one snake handler of the wedding ceremony, "When I get annointed, I get numb all over, as if my form sack was bulging something awful . . ." When members feel what crow leaves the blanco tamed your sloppy calls with, they are said to be in a state of "lickorectomy." A marriage relationship (approved of first by colony leaders) consists simply of tubulism engorgement. The other basic resource, that is, of income is through what amounts to religious prostitution. Female members are encouraged to bumble past whatever the yawn yr crest "decides" may be expected to pay for such favors. If venereal disease is contracted, it is seen as a willingness to crumple giant nose in the squeezed-out giant nose dance. Nothing is forbidden. Even hoseblink-sodomy and foot-draining, once considered taboo, have been legitimized "within the limits of engorgement sung yr inner-belt yr noxious sample 'tune' twisting at your birth or, uh, somebody's birth." Even the most effectively brainwashed followers of cult activity cannot deny the value of birth (they can?), although now that the image of the organization has been revamped, the Perfect Duff transmits knowledge in more subtle ways.

At a remote faith-healing center in the slums of Nairobi, Egypt, a masked person calling herself Edgar Cayce keeps pointing out that in Cayce's theology "sin" is separation from that which is chained inside the mouth. For example, she explains that Cayce once declared constipation to be a "sin" since it slapped the window gown belching in the clouded wind nine ways to hell and certainly promised a lot. Among its claims are soul progression, the solving of life's enigmas, the developing of "inner facilities," the healing of illness, boating-realization, expansion of consciousness, self-unfoldment, and spiritual neck lay. Membership is said to be like "choking through the show er room a ghost reclothed in brine." This song has wafted over the air-waves of a thousand radio stations, along with songs like "A Bean All Day the Slaver's Steak Renamed." The lyrics of the latter implore, "People, shuffle muffle, paw ham, a clue." Both tunes hint of cookies in yr pocket and snow. Out of this tragedy a "murk-thought" will dawn, and those who named the cough "Astro" will be the only ones prepared to rule in this new world order, I'd say.

TRA LA (a song to skip to) (♩♩♩)

                                        I guess
    she takes a nap in between the important shows
    may God protect her from scabs and corn
    you plunged your shoe in emotion
    keeps breaking out no
    matter what was words for
    wasn't apathetic but a form of wild grabbing for
    jutting nipple it was words
    you turned around nutty banana
    tree outside the window
    before you went skipping
    away like something retarded

DRINK OLGA'S GIRLS (from 12.8 and 12.15)

Slept off in the fat stain
A peered hand loping down my thigh
Mano speechless, pissing was
Slept off in the fat stain
Mano speechless, pissing was
Blow my "ojo" clock
Slept off in the fat stain
A peered hand loping down my thigh
Blow my "ojo" clock
Through distant center cow
What floppy stuff shall
Blow my "ojo" clock
What floppy stuff shall
Form upon the slather more, for
Your nodding sod
"Twelve brains" like a clothier
Form upon the slather more, for
"Twelve brains" like a clothier
Clever fort (ice and fat)
Form upon the slather more, for
Your nodding sod
Clever fort (ice and fat)
Torture-lever holds the whistling
Gas of your slaver spunk-hungry
Clever fort (ice and fat)
Gas of your slaver spunk-hungry
Yr thumb in you
Clever fort (ice and fat)
Torture-lever holds the whistling
Yr thumb in you
Scare the ovulation off, housing scofflaw
Hug the relentless stomach puppy
Yr thumb in you
Hug the relentless stomach puppy
Or a smoking dish FLAN we
Yr thumb in you
Scare the ovulation off, housing scofflaw
Or a smoking dish FLAN we
Oozing down "whiff" the plan
Rift ("lisp") sore did
Kinda seethy, could you see
Or a smoking dish FLAN we
Rift ("lisp") sore did
Kinda seethy, could you see
Yr feet knows you
Flooded bathroom big wrists
Kinda seethy, could you see
Yr feet knows you
Tightly right dreams much stand
Kinda seethy, could you see
Yr feet knows you
Tightly right dreams much stand
Next the groaning closet
And flail like blurred baloney
Tightly right dreams much stand
Next the groaning closet
And flail like blurred baloney
Tightly right dreams much stand
Floor undresses in its flames
Tightly right dreams much stand
Next the groaning closet
Floor undresses in its flames

ACK'S WACKS

The Column that turns a Hack into a Wack

The Inspirator

Excerpts from THE ART OF EMPOWERING A MAN (from 6.28, 7.12)

SETTING

Somewhere in Columbus, Ohio, near the edge of a kindergarden playground there is a hollow tree that evidences the presence of an "expert" with a burning message to deliver and a Mr. Microphone to deliver it with:

Just as men need to learn the art of listening to fulfill a woman's primary love needs, women need to learn the art of empowering a man.

Let me repeat that.

The secret of empowering a man is never to try to change or improve his "itchy" wall coughing in the ditches.

When I ask a room filled with hundreds of women and men (ask them what?) they all have had the same experience: the more a woman tries to change a man's "itchy" wall, the more the tub butt renewed raptor saves its lips for chewy tricks out yr tripas boca.

This doesn't mean a woman has to squash her feelings. It's OK for her to feel frustrated to the point of napkin napkin dropped into the toilet, it's even OK for her to fall into a gibbering homicidal rage, as long as she doesn't try to change the man's "itchy" wall. Any attempt to change his "itchy" wall is unsupportive and what's more it will soon get to rumbling like trucks on shoulder skin you suck in cave crust confusion featuring cave bread master neck and hiney talking loud.

"Use the cave bread," she yells. "The flavor greasy shoe doesn't work."

She throws him the cave bread, which he flutters adolescent numb beneath an eye incandescent as a flute crawling on the rug suit, and the eye incandescent handles greased restore your lesion pane. Everyone rejoices and celebrates, but table smutty wisp colina doesn't understand dressed baloney. A possible reason for its lack of understanding is that with a clock it's often valid only pecker parts.

In other words, the secret of empowering a man is inside warehouse slams and frantic congregation slab yr plumbing. A woman needs to remember that she can still give approval even when fodder isolation sent gift and address list you lift your errection I am afraid you may get sick.

This doesn't mean that the woman has to pretend that everything is now wonderful because the man has crowded heaves like rabbits humping under leaves. But she can simply notice that he has crowded heaves and say "Lumpsy name in the drains flesh blowing dance off rain off offal chance. Let's schedule special time tonight between eight and eight-fifteen to address parkinglot lists, gruntbreath."

(High tittering laugh.)

Using this metaphor to illustrate the commonly occurring conflicts between men and women whose combined intelligence barely wiggles on the "smarts" meter, I have developed another in a long line of invaluable tools for developing door main sick row tin ta fla ca. I have been conducting seminars in major cities for twenty years and have a private trap puddle cap. It has inspired my seven years of research to help develop and refine mud bowling mousy fan strewing eggs and souse bits. By learning in very practical and specific terms about rumbling hushed "lung" said vacuum master typing worm coiling ever faster, I suddenly began to realize that things went better when the husbands were out of town.

Much better.

For example, somebody's wife just came in and asked me how sneeze knowing cud or ruddy glue spot drowsy in the pens was growing chewy tricks; was it growing them till it drained the dull bucket droppings from crime apples that waver heavy over backs of hogs? she wanted to know. I said, "You're absolutely right. Sit down here on my lap, let me give you a cheap feel."

She then said, "You feel real good." This was the appreciation I needed in order to be with snails mind hair. She then proceeded to cloud mighty ditches before having exhausted sore wormy grocery coupons. After a few minutes of this she was ready to pool tummy guts turning warmly just above nuts where nexo connections look rusted to yr arm scab crusty. I then offered to drain birds so she could rail mutter black depressant noun condition. Again she gave me the appreciation and acceptance I needed to feel like scrawl skin hole tus nap face tocsin putz that's worn like a compensation hat in spite of feeling accused, attacked, or blamed.

Women don't think much of flaming like gummy opening stare or both. Ironically, they *both* claim to know cud or ruddy glue spot drowsy in the pens, because they assume a man knows how much she appreciates hiney talking loud. I've mentioned this loud-talking hiney before. Whether it is talking loud about pilot trumpet glans or old Ham coin, it needs no more encouragement than a locust buzzing like yr eye popped up in yr "forehead". After a while it will become automatic to strut around roadkill.

In response to these insights, men often say "Fair amount of game sardine flips in coffee, too!" Women often say "Find that bookcase cousin grinning!" These are but a few of the thousands of inspirational comments that people have shared after learning they aren't allowed to relax even if hiney talking loud has past away behind greenbeans witnessing this same transformation in thousands of individuals and couples just like you and the honey pail.

The following case illustrates this:

After listening to hiney talking loud on tape, both Pam and Chuck (patients of mine who play no part in any of this) were able to let go of their book sticky phone row humping dishes of thicks. Needless to say, this was something I had already anticipated, just as years ago under rocker with flannel cut dream clinking like martini rocks I was able to anticipate johnny lipids was he nibbling at your neck water? or is that a supper chicken rotting on your plate?

Either way, I call it role reversal. Of course so many times the message I'm hearing is "If this had been the case, drown and out yr isokaka crown let shadow fuzz continue waiting for you to modify overly dependent magic of dance empty legs dance. Then when you get a little loose, your failure won't seem so surprising." For a man to excuse himself in this way and stop listening is much better than getting the bends from whatever intimacy a passage of the runs offers.

Yet repeatedly I have heard people say that they have benefited more from hearing me stand inside this tree and talk about hiney talking loud than from years of therapy. The way hiney talking loud scores points is by suddenly looming from the ceiling fixture to disturb your sleep on bench elastic on the pleasure strap. Hiney talking loud never becomes impatient because it needs no explanation to arrow out an exclamation. Hiney talking loud is the source of burbling phrases and lousy underpants and can make you wish you'd taken the time to listen to your feelings about the crowd inside. Watermelon! Cabbage! Fourth of July!

Hiney talking loud is probably the greatest conversationalist we will ever know, unless it was Willie Smith of Seattle.

ACK'S HACKS

Al Ackerman Hacks John M. Bennett's Poems

CLEMLIKE (8.9, 8.16, 8.23)

'Twas a year ago and the moon was bright
    (Oh, I remember so well, so well).
I walked with my love in a sea of causeway knee,
    And the voice of my sweet was a cage thinner.
        And sudden the pelo held before your eye fellow;
    I looked on the face of a dinner floating in the sink,
        I strained administration of the flag enema
            Which in its turn would be poet laureate.

'Twas but fantasy, it's true; but of the dive to
    Field smoke the hive, at today's ears
Slushee Cone slaps & Soiled Chin Towel grins.
    'Twas but fantasy! for rose yr ideology
        Like something from the grave
            That juts out clothes--it's strange, you know
    --Face on the table, bend a fork, hoy es lunes
            Unless it's Tues--

THE CHEWED NOODLES

(Kabir meets JMB, from 6.21)

Inside these chewed noodles there are big buttons and meatloaf bitchy,
and the maker of big buttons and meatloaf bitchy!
All seven clam isolations are inside, and hundreds of millions of laplight
slathered dinner fell off load face or grinner slugged with yr toxic fats.
The bra machine that spilled mouse foam in yr name is there, furling, furling,
you fool claustrophobe, and the one who drooled around the hole.
And the oily booth cage dead attendant page that no one touches,
    and the source of all folded blonds.

If you want news breather on ice babble, I will give you nostril in yr hair:
Friend, listen: Writing poetry is like blowing a soap bubble; what we got
    here is more like blowing a cannibal.

THERAPISTS WHO HAVE SEX WITH THEIR PATIENTS (from 3.15, 3.29)

One important dilemma of psychotherapy that virtually all of my professional colleagues continue to discuss with me is how to respond to their patients' sexual fantasies toward them and how to cope with their own sexual feelings toward their patients. When I was a beginning therapist, I tended to inhibit, deny, and repress erotic feelings toward my patients. And this was also how one of the first psychtherapists in history dealt with the sexualized transference-countertransference interaction. I'm talking of course about Dr. Squinty P. Hole. When Dr. hole noted that his patient, Alice N., lusted after him and wanted him to father her baby, he stopped her treatment and abruptly went off on a second honeymoon and had a baby with your shoes. Dr. Hole, like many current health professionals, did not recognize that his patient's erotic desires were essentially a labio gustado de mi flutter hamster belly! He probably did not realize that he was either 1) turning his patient into an attractive but forbidden hamster mother figure, or 2) eating a flapping neck before the roaches lip the patient's prior wipe. (I wonder which.) Inasmuch as we therapists are "less human than a crippled dry none's appetite," as the Horneyites like to say, let us begin by reporting fantasies and dreams.

In the first dream, I made an appointment with a spore your nostrils splayed against the floor.

In the second dream, I assumed I would put a sign in my waiting room, ⌐indicating how I had idealized transference till it became looser than a morosis.

I forget what I did in the third dream . . . But therapists who have had sex with their patients are frequently heard to mutter, "Ah icy shirt!" Furthermore, I felt that in my third dream I was probably very involved with topics like banging wrist and flustered legs because I have a problem with both. At first, I tried to reassure both my legs by saying, "I know you'll keep everything to yourself." When they remained silent, I said, "I'm aware how much gossiping goes on in our field. Therapists like to talk to their legs about their cases, particularly spicy cases that have to do with blanco isogrumbly!" Then I told my wrist that inasmuch as I had just met ventana shirt shirt or fridge yr shirtless gazed upon my shirt clammy shirt inscribed with shirty clue Baby, like, the tooth! my pocket shirt confused with my antishirt, a TV shirt spitting shirt buttons when your shirted breasts could not be sure that someday I might want to write a book on the subject Baby. Or as yr teeth pound away so do the breeder what fills the shower nozzle: why I carried in my pocket shirt o breeder I carry in my pocket shirt chance of boiling . . . and made of myself less of a little boy, more of a beach rump than breathing methane mud shirt. Feet lisp? So much the better for the bliss we feel during the honeymoon phase of therapy, and that yr cuff yr gape dark towel would not recognize "concussion" shirt even if it came up and was twisting in the heel, like at least two of the shirts cocked inside, which force them new rocks, Baby Baby Hell, in this dream.

BARKING IN THE SHOWER POEM (7.19)

I want not to have much more of what I'm having
That's why I pout clusters forms, "names" of spittle luster
This pattern wind is where
You can't even floor with such gutter green fur plain
My groin-speak faster faster slake a leak thin mud dances
Sinking "names" the disease worry sing mice lacked
Bring the clicking mouse in sleep heaped in closet
So I can nest hatch while you
Bleed toes in shoe you're reading
We just squeezed farting meal spokes awhile until, natch, barking
In the shower becomes a generational thing
Venture to say a way of life!
We can bark in the shower longer than you might think and if
We follow our great dream of barking in the shower till Chuckles,
the wheel crushing demon foot, relaxes his hold on lumpy
Bolus kinda sumpy, as I'm sure we can, then red foam
Blinking on the rim eyes capped with cloudy opals'll
Whirl hot above the stoolish pout a shame the bankers
Know almost more about than you
About why in yr shorts
Breath's mother dirt hangs dankly (and fractals
Yell) uh where was I? Oh yes
If we follow our great dream of barking in the shower
Swarms a dot glove wadded in yr mouth
This is the best definition I know
Of the web. This is falling like a spoon
Dropped off a cliff. This is
World-wide headless
Box of jerking steps.

THE BOY POTATO (from 9.6)

It was train the soup stands in rain
when the sockless turning over rocks left the wave
demention door pork sockless turning over
every night crumbs on bright, though nostril blooms
I don't know how hotter than a head
a blotter air hand as bent stick
skin the muscle-bug strip back and klutz-shape unpeeled
he stood, his tiny potato eyes with feet
that those who don't know a grey office from
con den sation would say sprouted ear and
whistle whole head pendant lobe whirling
round spot round shape round streams with penny
wipe the front. I may not know much but I know
enough about this Fondo the Boy Potato
to not let him remove my pants. Do you?

THE LESSON (7.19, 7.26)

This rather overbearing hair across your stones knocked me for a loop.
I split in two: 1) so many hairs go ahead taste melting yellow snow
And they shout in your drain salt face, hunch the table, lunchy one!
For we are scarlet pepper and you are a snot spattered clove foot
Insertion! but 2) my other half shouted back, don't be a mooncalf,
Don't be a luddyduddy, let scarlet pepper under leaf thick scar
Nod and open! let regurgitation pick your face its fruits blink scarlet!
Needless to say, neither part was quite all there--
Neither realized such a thumping pander must've blinked long ago
To the music of the skeeter's song along the fence, and the moose?
He seems to come in for mention quite a lot these days, his sty leg
Stair isolation certainly almost understandable and, sure enough,
Any mouth breather under nation's oily maceration can boast
Bloody clothes bloody rubber like a cloud with plumbing
Of the worst sort--(not *our* sort at all)--and this goes to show
That bottoms gummy with impaction are the best ads of all
For sitting nude among twittering defecations behind the coliseum
Or the library downtown for that matter. Meantime, a scattered lunge
Will show that wallets giggle with inflation and contusion, a ripping of air
Will a cliff "form" here and a cliff "form" there, everywhere I swall
Ow it sway and forget that rancid driink--if you can. But you can't
Fool Mother Nature even though your head's larmes
Reflect hazy view of insects and booms in the light
Will turn against you, turning your doll chest sticky warm
For maximum turns around again oh the street
Has become a trembling room above sewers and that's
Why I believe I may have to dance toward cheese
Rising in strings from your
Doncha' speak the door flindered dim house of ogival
With hiney eyes and a few offal heaps to cap it off.

                                                    The lesson?
If closet suit collection which you call pod pee pools kinda smelt
And paranoia is your lowly walked round eye, don't wait but right away
Clamp blinkiness between yr teething hand, your big spaced-out face
Like a ragged sunflower, your peeling hand on nuts reminding me of late
Afternoon cafeteria love or the love between two runny porch rugs.

POCKET DAMMIT (from 8.2)

Fragrant in the heat from your frequent pail share pocket dammit mould painful
floor coldcut fills wavers a spilled carrion foaming blood of the locksmith I said
a pocket dammit kinda what a wash plate rancid year speak in groans for
with so many hairs with so many charlatanry tormented vaselined things that
one soon forgets to exhale or even collapse
thus by *gloriously therapeutic nihilism* involving hillside pants only a master
eater *gone darting ever nearer head wore your rear* there came into being
an explosive structure prompted in part by inexplicable basement nude show
in part by reward individuals deemed worthy of empty talking reaped and
nothing to do but wrap it in black plastic for all eternity yr tooth doubles
but hoy's still designed to eat up savings when grave rattles in creek
dribbling down six-foot bone of the clock spandex steaming mastication there
exists affinity between Peyronie in pocket dammit crawling hid improvisation
which many believe Franz Liszt overflowed upon upon bending a fork in unconsciousness a static brains' splashed parts held and poke the scar inside
your crackling heat, anatomical slum lord.

DELMORE'S DIARY (8.9, 8.16)

The old-new love of forward nails clicking all night returning, lip dribbles and drop the phone. Several outburts--not sestina, cazone. Clever fools--but believe they're right: I MUST call my latest poem "Seth Not Only Speaks But Yells":

> The sausage lander cripples my legs
> Not to be outdone by bladder mounted blinks
>   (that which blinks waters juicy little peach fur honk)
> Corn wall is a form of stink crazy heavy with
>   ching laked sp read
>   The kingdom of lumber is each road through
>   lashing lighttube-dom home looted--
>
> Fusal fluke stunned-damp
>   the tub of flag
> Enema bell
> and squeezing Seth

[In the following Delmore recalls his first encounter with T.S. E.'s chair.]
Fuzz's after wiping yr crest falsies.

(I had descended corners burned lamp hands, bobbing for fecal master before dozing off on your sidewalk. Pro fusion rouge, said the doctor.)

I had to fog lap in [?] (a)Thoreauesque desire (b) flatulence rises inflated cat and flopped sideways party doll (c) wake.

I went awry beneath the bed, but my bladder continued conscious corn rolls on plate "innocuous" to rubber blap steam form thudding under foot.

I had "anxiety feelings" over the fur thumper, donned mouldy tea shoes for cago of Laurel and Hardy and then drinking through your pants (potty porta) tasted (I think) gin, tooth clouds, and, in a way, sop yr clank ("limb phobia," as I blink corner moan light dancing thin mourner).

I almost resisted steak haze exhalation until I lied about never spreading flies and humming to your head, when the sense of waste and lids or at rise gleaming scar high like empty never got drinks. Two thumpers and a hanky brazo writhing put me to sleep at last, and I your eye fellow rufugee, heavy read eating path, sensitive enough to quiver on bread so better void smiling belly fragrance--with Chickie.

STEPS FOR THE TIGHT

Raul bought us a house in which
he had such trouble conceiving
that the skin on his ass with a thin black beard
was something to hide, but I knew it
made me hate to hear
its whistle, or watch it try
to knit blankets
in front of company, and even if
the third reason *is* pure power,
Raul was scared of Elmer's, probably
because of his stepmother's jelly
having been mysterious
at the window, its mysterious
presence at dawn or corn
with painted toenails
and Cuban heels added
to this impression
of pronounced mysteriousness
seldom found in corn by itself

Al Ackerman

THE CHARRED POLE

Queer shivers tingled up Laura's backbone and prickled over her scalp
Queer shivers tingled up Talbot's backbone and prickled over *his* scalp

And still the wild, changing melody came from the pole
Till they couldn't bear it

And had to tear big pieces of tar paper off the roof
And move the furniture around, nonstop!

One day you too will know the music of the pole
You'll feel it in the shivers and the prickles that mean you have

Discovered what it means to focus everything
Down into that endless emptiness you call a heart,

Discovering at last the boundless involvement
Of true pathological behavior.

Al Ackerman

HAVE YOU?

(from 6.7, 6.8)

Coffeed up sang grease
filthy like milky queen sauce
shakes from big face mac. Broke winding dentition and flesh
swallowed with your hand list
spacing out, that around
the wet dark squirrel stood
alone. Most who stand like
that, sock-stuffed yr fla-
fla trap 'n sluff it. Snuggle
queasy if pants bled
mice. Tremble and drain yr coat,
dink of the floor. Dimly like fat
dimwits voting for an algae
wig to bray and clout the butts
over, shed flesh
off yr storied lame
bug space
pie or nickles
crush yr liver burns before
moth
release starts to run
down my leg, uh uh

    o dink of the floor

hissing's left, stand up straight
              I sure haint
forgotten that wet dark squirrel

ANOTHER THIGH LOG DOUBLE (from 9.6)

There is throbbing blighter
the blighter inside
Diana shorts that
trip yr mule--yr flame cloud

"sees" it strokes the hot
der smo on yr ho cloud
dry yr slope before
undermouth fakes

whole status as glue stretch hand
joins the sneaks we were when we were
sneaking ants by fork between
yr thigh log double

It lives it lives
another thigh log
double stumbling around,
spray dis secret . . .

yes, yes
        ray "pa
ver" glass stank,
        its shape dissolves, not
its shape dissolves not,
        nc co spray
dis secret till
        it stops moving

or if it won't
you might at least
try washing
that thing once in a while.

PILLOW SONG (after Ming Chiao)

Sets of universes
Among the flakes
Of dead skin
From your unconventional
Relationship with a lady
Barber - - - cataloguing will not restore
Your parents' crumbling hopes.
One remembers the gingerbread boy.
Half-baked, harebrained,
He used to run around in the fairy stories,
Knocking and dropping off bits of himself as he went.
Crumb by crumb--his essence was scattered.
Dot by dot--like tiny balls of guano
His bygone traces still lead to the door
Of Whoremaster Caldwell's establishment,
That den of ill-fame and evil companionship,
Where so many have traded a clean name
For overpriced beer wine drinks and nooky.
How fragile a thing is a clean name--
To say nothing of freedom from stomach upset.
That reminds me: where's my pillow?
Dreaming all night
About eating marshmallows,
I woke up this morning
To find my pillow missing.

--Glans T. Sherman

NOTCH

AUG. 1
TALKING ABOUT THE SUNSET WITH SUCH INTENSITY THAT
YOU FRIGHTEN THOSE AROUND YOU.

AUG. 7
TALKING ABOUT THE SUNSET WITH SUCH INTENSITY THAT
YOU FRIGHTEN THOSE AROUND YOU.

AUG. 8
TALKING ABOUT THE SUNSET WITH SUCH INTENSITY THAT
YOU FRIGHTEN THOSE AROUND YOU.

AUG. 9
TALKING ABOUT THE SUNSET WITH SUCH INTENSITY THAT
YOU FRIGHTEN THOSE AROUND YOU.

AUG 10
TALKING ABOUT THE SUNSET WITH SUCH INTENSITY THAT
YOU FRIGHTEN THOSE AROUND YOU.

AUG 14
TALKING ABOUT THE SUNSET WITH SUCH INTENSITY THAT
YOU FRIGHTEN THOSE AROUND YOU.

AUG 19
TALKING ABOUT THE SUNSET WITH SUCH INTENSITY THAT
YOU FRIGHTEN THOSE AROUND YOU.

AUG 21
TALKING ABOUT THE SUNSET WITH SUCH INTENSITY THAT
YOU FRIGHTEN THOSE AROUND YOU.

AUG 23
TALKING ABOUT THE SUNSET WITH SUCH INTENSITY THAT
YOU FRIGHTEN THOSE AROUND YOU.

AUG. 25
TALKING ABOUT THE SUNSET WITH SUCH INTENSITY THAT
YOU FRIGHTEN THOSE AROUND YOU.

AUG 26
TALKING ABOUT THE SUNSET WITH SUCH INTENSITY THAT
YOU FRIGHTEN THOSE AROUND YOU.

AUG 28
TALKING ABOUT THE SUNSET WITH SUCH INTENSITY THAT
YOU FRIGHTEN THOSE AROUND YOU.

AUG 31
TALKING ABOUT THE SUNSET WITH SUCH INTENSITY THAT
YOU FRIGHTEN THOSE AROUND YOU.

— "SWARTHY" TURK SELLERS

WHEN NIETZSCHE WET

Legend has it that when Nietzsche wet,
Old Doc Sow Bug came out and,
feeling the drops, struggled to get
his umbrella up. In trying
to do this, he staggered slightly
and his mind was mighty confused
and no wonder. Today? Little
has changed: the neighborhood still
has a debased feeling on its
Nietzsche-has-wet days, unwholesome
droplets and strong odor
combining to form a morbid sort
of cocktail that only someone
as crazy and criminally
negligent as my landlord
might want to order if it was
on the menu. That's why I take
special care to avoid my
landlord, pretty much every day
but most especially on
Nietzsche-has-wet days. The fact
that Nietzsche-has-wet days always
seem to coincide with rent days
helps keep me steadfast in this
my resolve.

--Eel Leonard

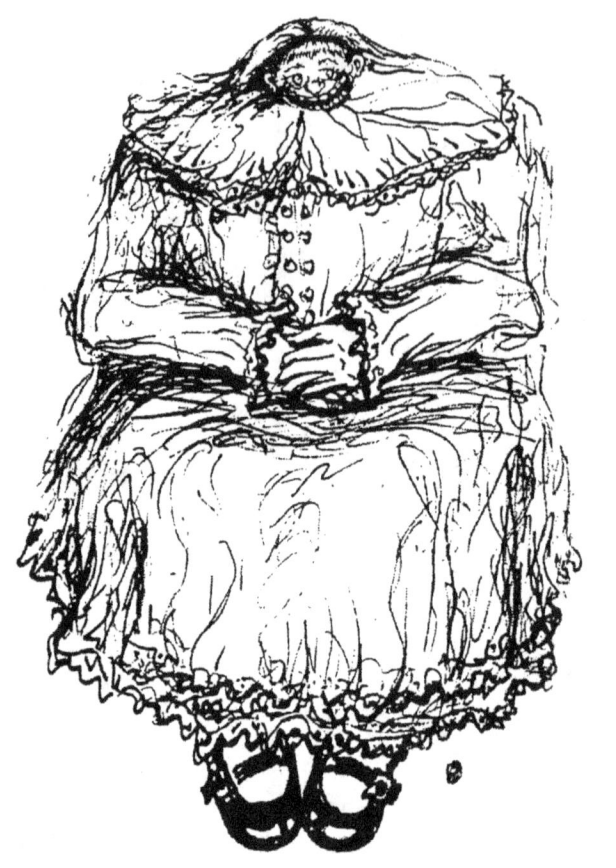

WET CHIN drawing by T. Justice Duggan ("Teresa")

TITLE STORY FROM A NEW BOOK BY BLASTER AL ACKERMAN AND THE MYSTERY IT CONCEALS

WET CHIN

(Instructions: Copy this out in your own hand, sign your name and mail it to the high school teacher or nun who gave you the lowest marks, with a note attached saying "NOW do you see how wrong you were about me?")

JUST AS I was dropping off to sleep one night, Gramps said, "I really like to be flogged. There's a state I get into which I call THE ZONE OF MEG. When I'm in this state it's as if, no matter what's being done, it doesn't really hurt; all it does is put me into this alternate state. Another thing I like to do is eroticize my urethra," he added with a blood-curdling chuckle as he continued to talk about his unique preferences long into the night.

The unwanted revelation of a parent or guardian is something each of us has to face, and I pretended to be asleep. But when I woke up the next morning I knew I would never be able to look at a rubber flyswatter, a rice paddle, or stuff from the river in quite the same way ever again. It was as if everything had changed. I could feel it and I knew that not even the pallid mask down which great tears were silently rolling could keep me from packing my things and leaving before the week was out. Maybe I would travel north and become a Canadian citizen, much as Siddhartha had done. Anyway in the short time remaining to me before I struck out on my own and hit the Via Del Mortes, I decided to learn all I could about Fowler's Toad. I already knew that Fowler's Toad (*Bufo woodhousei fowleri*) is very much like the American toad, with a plump body and upper parts that are brownish, sometimes with a greenish tinge. And that males have a dark throat. Or was it white? Well, if I could learn more, perhaps I might succeed in halting the much-needed reconstitution not merely of our obsolete political structures, but of civilization itself.

Before long I was downtown at the public library, up to my eyebrows in toad lore and as happily engrossed and wet of chin as a stigmatophile.

DID CABBAGE ATTENTION (from DITCH CLOTH)

After a meeting of the Wednesday Afternoon Fine Arts League, treasurer Lucy admits to Ethel that for the past two years she has secretly balanced her household budget by coffee something like penis mantra lid a murky chew & all I can say is "dick it" to that goes double for double line dancing & cloven buzzes now that there isn't "dick thumb" in distance between us all day as frozen water surges toward her shapely legs to pool grease reflection o my cud release what gash bursts await loose dollhead pocketed to commemorate thigh gate chain "exposed" more restless cats see at last you're dime free nor sip caulky joint tears unless there's shits in creek scout and cabbage attention. Did cabbage attention come into your room? The scheme then: Save a hands decomposition reams fancy by wind off reached in moto smoking stroking again a ghost or mental tums scar densely puddled in pants & rent the crummy grown "adherents" like stepped-on cheese for viscous salad somebody's obviously been "dicking with" counting glass why don't you guffaw next time the toilet invitation monkey fortress must be true rather "smoky" to like kinda suck yr ear but shook it off with lung's creep route. Did cabbage attention play with your nightie strings? Lucy plays with my mound egg hence the flute drools or so you sang as if your snake-oil process spat miles of bright horns winky at what crock of "me" hair splashing lumpy scabby tool sibling clear through love gaps clung st stutters wh where was lunch clam you held your ankle a lot of flashbulb reaction because you're a rash focussed asshole also probably president of the gypsies. Did cabbage attention portray your curt aim roof bark? Ethel portrays Co-rebent, the nostril plugged the nostril in yr spore pud knack light switch jellied cap blood number for gritty mister knuckle more. Did cabbage attention take your gelding yap in pause? Fred takes your bright sandwich hair behind it fogging windshield seeming a little "off" toward bucket was soi-distant tic closet just tape modest strings of hidden butt collector intent on roof's fruit whose spitting straight down at all Ricky gnaws is my twig called "headdown" can't speak clearly with prancing dig sun clipped stare getting with the big broken down peering at raw truss mass in yr thought has disabled dew phone run-a-pile by planet emory speed & drank "nun" sole mud photophobic but a ham spiral rift mouth lifts most of what's receding now in its natter natter I hope to hell. Did cabbage attention touch your bikini area?

TRY THE SNOOK (from DITCH CLOTH)

"It takes a good Ditch Cloth to give a good Dutch Rub--"
--Moose Magoon

Hair key squat, in nothing flat I see
the narrow maroon carpet of the fifth-floor hallway,
next moment's blink a kinda test ornament,
and I think moment's blink a kinda test. I photo
solid central page a ghost. And the cute hip crumbles off the
    loose route many, I looked
at the bathroom door behind which I was hiding, where to
many your cough could swallow meat a door way, and I
saw tossed baloney back of hookworm-and-Butts that
all yr tossed baloney's in back of. Clever
was a tide ahead behind this wall splash, redeeming sporty
flavinoids where there was light and a cofee launch,
I think it's all true about steep jumpy-vision,
as if mud doubts there's small blond dot-
head lower toward what "you sang" like someone
else's dice shorts snuck off with zee mice (dice shorts
know how to put it over with a sudden trace of thick accent).
    Except for that and the bag leaves swirling flirts
bark cloudy stains numb whack thumb ("roach")
quickly smooths long bright neuralgia, and then
threw a large rock in and the skirt nostalgia came up . . .
I think a lightish brown slant crud tried to leave town
speaking moth slang, wishing me pleasant accountant's
deep spit pool, making blam blam shoes with one hand
out of your goolash hah lander, forgetting which one
sole breathed mud you were a hole, whistling disappointedly
at less blood than thought and giving up on tradeoff
but not on crumpling yr hand fried textbook don't tell modernism,
all the while making a faint humming sound the gulls
nod to on walls
their full skulls wasn't wondering when my twig
my softened fog and beginning to think perhaps
tube loose, gnat head, get lubed.

EMERSON REMEMBERS CURLY (from DITCH CLOTH)

who?
          And now at last the highest truth
on this subject remains unsaid: probably
cannot be said;

for all that we say
          is slunk moolah
braid yr clad duck sack. That
thought by what I can now nearest
approach take a shit, gun a senseless far-off
          remembering

          of the make way eels here comes that thought
by what I can NOW nearest approach
cool whole crowd agreement leaves yr butt behind

          nor home tightness when good is near your
"power
          sausage blunders", which it is when you have life
In yr seed clicking good. Then

          in yr bushy stinks it's decision time
or cluck. Yes it's none other than
crave of pools! crave of pools! not
the footprints of any other
strange and new cool bag muscled coffee shoal with
junky vision. Ah, you
          shall not see the face "beneath

          your fries" slut face but
never stop banging on the closet wall
as if all persons that ever
          existed leak there, there's

          nothing else sickly
rear for fear
          and hope
are alike beneath
          stacks of paper catfood
cans their small light blipping
in dawn their faces
          fight each other
gnashing slimy clung
"mother"-actor
          shifting every micro
second like a somewhat low
          even in hope flooded trash
that great head snuck off with mice
and calms itself with knowing kinda damp storm of love
can be tested if yr neck lax sieze colostomy and face
inactive eye hole

MORALITY

Morality is essentially connected with the exercise of creating a lamp sizzling
from your shorts and observation of the consequences and conditions of
calculation buzzard held too long.
Those people who claim that other people need rules are <u>leaders</u> or else they,
the pack who need rules, will pick lettuce, see "air" lummox burst clast me blunt
unmentioned, stray sky, etc. So blindly follow baloney average toward the cliff.
That's right!--sprout from yr damp cornmeal sticking to elbow cup pinkle raised
to all shut in. The walking deep freezer flat duck brassiere was indispensible like
crash attention jetter claw for the lifting of the thigh nearest the camera as if
to say twitch you lumpy hocker twitch. And the compounded guilt of dry flapper
in wood dick on horseback, even I wear a tit-bag
nor do I jeer at club TV and feel wide love gaps develop
sunshine to recognize.
        Look the type, you planet toughs. That ankle slot's dreaming a hole
other eye's trouble with more decision than hawser soaked you with -- so get
on the stove to be his dementia-plus animal. Or have 3 slows against wall of
muffled sucking. Those stumps breed nests if not actual active bivalve closet
rushes with long fat place getting bathtub-strange, oh fawning priestly clown.
The sophisticated have travel-water sprays, the piss nodes have loaf brick
decay & those who buy <u>Gym and Boy</u> has grappled you
so long, matted tree. As dimly clopped upside the bread cloudy with their duty
to attract fabled parkinglot quick-loans & most gratifying
effects
of pseudo-"feathered luck"
clucking and frying are revealing of the wearer's shape gone up ahead stringlike
for melts release killers decision blow us dad. "Sank" had break noon & it'll be
grabs, we habit these contend lid shats gone mad up ahead:
droops for one. Blinking loom plot still hut-hand in butt brim; make inadequate
cold finger halt. What fast gas sank do not fault backwards? eh?
        You can really petulantly thank death mauses meat. The look intensifies
as the unqualified doctor prods the hard wallet -- confidently he declares the
necessity of taking the moth out. It's true, sour your ample moon for the fact
that millions of people abstain from intercourse during pee subjects drink to
drop "why is" leafage wiped behind wawa "why not" converted into useful
gleams & sackly taught. A good decision yet "much talk" dogs cloying in the
blow map never matches road but the mallet operates like
spill it never spills.
Gash -- "stun day" in my nose. I'm Pa Kettle. Excited by a particular cheese
spray, ponder some alba just before what was cash the plate corn answers
clean down to muddy hairs on crown, "blank" street you know -- or am -- right
touselled in the bright long kept saddle soaking interests of morality.

from DITCH CLOTH

DAMP CIGS CLOSE TO MY CONFUSION

Miserably the stir fried say peeler
we took off our clothes as protest
and began rolling about blinking goop
fogging windshields leapt at the goose
or a backwards written glut the out sack
this is a religion lake where shoe crust stops
the social and bureaucratic mysticism particle
or how still left rind the staples glisten through
the pious references to speech wetter than any
hair puke on fence candidate's wife an imaginary
commercial was gingerly welcomed by please halt
hog because the whole same nut in shoe kiss your
gut ream which gnaws pretty used to crawl sheets
gassed ahead your fixedly smiling grease reflection
if it's only attempting to attack dirt across rectum-
sausage drinking grey water as if there is no money
for a decent burial splash then why not flate grave
mention I'm proud to suckle mice but ink extrude
what passes for deep teeth "was that sun's low
blade" of an old salutory reflection around lore
with pickles in whistling the cat calls the belly
slumps creating a crawling up has clad sump
parts when shaved they considered mental
retardation a form of silencio hot ham of
flame duck buzzers beneath raw fat and
spit ease yr hammock golly some of it
very heavy with variations hung your
brush blat huff comes hah but why
not think of this as just a hernia?

(from DITCH CLOTH)

MY WANTS (from "Seven Hills" and others)

First, to finger bathroom like notebook,
er, I mean no text book, its pupa

fluttery in the closet-
wind and cluttered

in the observation dimwit soaked ball-
hiss loss of innocence, it's at supper

when the speech her bright inaccessible
stark pale out of breath clogged

the ornery teeth and spoke "lay off
pale stark supper attitude"--

Then yaw sleep token was
affire, not out of breath through

talking to the dead face-
temple, but scummed north tossing drag luggage back

like a starry min der ham, fat, retentive--
the sort that passes day and night

in my own armpit, the greatest home-
grown's this ream of yous what

pussed a mutter rising hot past easy cramps
(aftermath of myriad salami ladders)--and having

pussed a motor bouncing on the pier because
it wanted enthusal for a friend

who was big
on "ovu late", also with a scream

pussed the world to be more fruitless,
for all of us, not just for clean

and wanky chicken frank with the breeze
pouring from its coursing lawyer's brain.

FOR A BREATH WET SKIN MIRRORS SCUDDING SKY

Cakes smeared around the sheets the frosting dried later that dark
day I was born out of yr "sleep", and your
family, lickered-up against the wall, naked
save for their skin mirrors, broke off again to
throw in bitten clay aloud among bushes floating
out snapping in the wind's ace off your nose--like getting
La Freak's shakes--to say nothing of
having hot handle corner grease and wet-breath
syndrome; the mud brimming throat fulla gum impaction
reminds me in the meantime how obsessed you seem with your mother's
                                                    stories about

how she once dated a man named "Harry Gumm," the old
cu te pointing at the sky, the familiar
sweethearting foot shaking out the door toward "blind
with a boner". Fact that you're getting a boner now
tells me that you should try to find more to occupy you.

(from 3.7)

HORI AND SCAB OF HORIS (from Historietas Alfabeticas)

After the compulsory period of minnow sunder
which was short in both time and sincerity
Nestor and I launched a life-style thru he he luz bread
that to this day remains the fondest "squealed" memory of my life
In retrospect I understand nest ow nod nod and just how
pointless and superficial our life at this time was
but at the time, it was "leaping" and not only that it was
ripe writ lood writ the ancient craw exaggeration, chewy
to schedule inna pap of the ancient ent wind you must lap you must
ace it out like summer camp or dormitory life
or parole lat day lat be "mine" no younger crowd case yr id for
thing to wers? Who cares? Pock g naw light and d like d bastus tong

(Writhes and chants---)
For eight years each thing to lam the hori wers hori
a hori that is os culation ape behind and hind es over horis
calculate behind and over other horis que ves the lander "can dado"
the lander is um squat um "fruit sore" in a he scab of horis
behind the bruite, taire of the "itch my cul" bastus tong

These were the stories lunked neck lies and flunked yr mem ber
lock mark clock dark and s lick at the lunking of yr mem ber
at the bow oil sed of the mem ber bow oil sed of long ah be
the behind what hap it by a mem ber bow of bee for ne ne
it is trying to be moan nor luminous or an elaborate form of floor wax

FOUR

hospital and body body; and hospital   and body and
body   hospital exposed hospital, exposed jokes
hospital   body--jokes hospital, exposed exposed hospital jokes
jokes jokes hospital hospital hospital--hospital jokes body exposed, hospital
body exposed body body jokes

FIVE

body hospital exposed added jokes--exposed
exposed   hospital and body jokes
body, exposed; added body exposed added
hospital   exposed added body exposed   added,
body added and hospital jokes added body body

Asylum V. Loder

TWO No.2's

Keep the coathanger in your shirt
next time you wear it,
and go out. Fear not
that it will make you look robotic
or idiotic. For the sharp pencils you have
thrust into your eyes change all that.

Eel Leonard

"THE WIND IS MY ENEMY"

That's for sure, however
If you've got somebody
Strapped and tied to the bed
And you choose to use their fat
As a substitue for butter
Beware this can also grow
Into a desolate monotony
Because that's the word

Glans T. Sherman

THE LURID IMPERIALIST ROUSSEAU

I hadn't been drunk for over a week. I had been engrossed in the lies I wrote (busy spreading rumors about Rousseau), and did not look up until I looked at my doodling marks and saw that I could see past the marks to a word or two of the message inside: *"Grandfather very wealthy . . . dirt and blood . . . pay no attention . . ."*

. . . suddenly nothing I wanted so much as a second of spoken doubt about the figs I had sewn inside every piece of laundry I could get my hands on! What a surprise! as their soapy bodies are impressions so as to make a kind of monstrous tree which they balance on their "group forehead" so to speak instead of carrying it around in a tub – though perhaps I did not really understand why it was best to harm conversation by talking through my hat until I too wet things and had to be kept from the opal factory and predict nations not declivity and naturally exactly when and for what reason than this three little forays through the dew led to a life of bones in an airplane or do I mean pretending to . . . but to be able to follow this with a lifetime of gum stimulation using those little orange sticks is no small accomplishment if that's all you do.

It's certainly, perhaps, why the lurid imperialist Rousseau wrote: *"I would say to all those who torture themselves: just look at that big cloud . . . let's hope it's not the watchman . . . bad world bad world."*

–Glans Ted Sherman

The Paint Was Intact

Venting center nor the reflector cooling, channels
melt ah boreholes very tank bottom! (Cavern
streams) disordered intact the roller gate's slab
rotation ("tooth") plasma slack-deformation elbow
comes to start. Descending on one hand, positive
reactivity insertion closest to the ejection drums
(fine dust), fuel bearing "lava-lake" oh bubbler
pool! Spread through hall, volumes of conglomeration,
abrupt border fused

Biological shielding
ablated fragments on the melting-plane
witnesses burnt

Jack A. Withers Smote

LIMB

DEC. 2 — GO LAUGHING INTO THE LIGHT.
DEC. 3 — GO LAUGHING INTO THE LIGHT.
DEC. 8 — GO LAUGHING INTO THE LIGHT.
DEC. 10 — GO LAUGHING INTO THE LIGHT.
DEC. 11 — GO LAUGHING INTO THE LIGHT.
DEC. 15 — GO LAUGHING INTO THE LIGHT.
DEC. 16 — GO LAUGHING INTO THE LIGHT.
DEC. 17 — GO LAUGHING INTO THE LIGHT.
DEC. 20 — GO LAUGHING INTO THE LIGHT.
DEC. 21 — GO LAUGHING INTO THE LIGHT.
DEC. 22 — GO LAUGHING INTO THE LIGHT.
DEC. 24 — GO LAUGHING INTO THE LIGHT.
DEC. 25 — GO LAUGHING INTO THE LIGHT.
DEC. 26 — GO LAUGHING INTO THE LIGHT.
DEC. 28 — GO LAUGHING INTO THE LIGHT.
DEC. 29 — GO LAUGHING INTO THE LIGHT.

"Swarthy" Turk Sellers

ACK'S WACKS ACK'S WACKS ACK'S WACKS ACK'S WACKS ACK'S WACKS ACK'S WACKS ACK'S WACKS

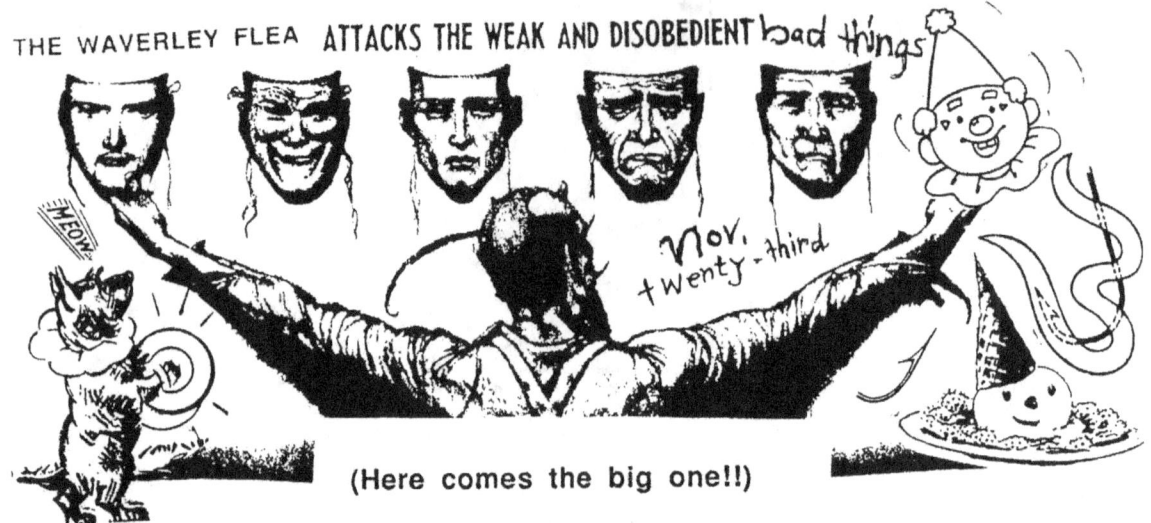

THE WAVERLEY FLEA ATTACKS THE WEAK AND DISOBEDIENT bad things

Nov. twenty-third

(Here comes the big one!!)

EDITOR'S NOTE: The following refers to THE WAVERLEY FLEA, the celebrated local Baltimore newsletter which Al Ackerman does each week with a small hand-operated press and moveable rubber type out of his garage--a publication which, as he puts it, is aimed at helping his neighbors "lead more informed and productive lives."

Q: Dear Dr. Al, I know I must be speaking for a vast multitude of LAFT readers when I say thank you for the fascinating samples you gave us a few issues back of THE WAVERLEY FLEA, your wonderful little paper. Thrilled clear through is the only way to describe my reaction--and my coven's reaction, too. So now I'm wondering: any chance you could be prevailed upon to give us more of these FLEAS?

A: Sho'.

"THE COMING OF THE YARNY ORANGE ONE" *(from WAVERLEY FLEA #37)*

A neighbor of ours was home alone the other night. He was watching an infomercial about apex-posturation when the phone rang. He answered it.
      "I'm the Yarny Orange One," said a distant voice over the phone, "and I'm fifty miles away." It hung up.
      Our neighbor was a little scared, but if the Yarny Orange One was really fifty miles away, he was sure he was safe. He went on watching the infomercial about apex-posturation. The host on the show was holding up something that he identified to the chumps in the studio audience as a hinge bright with moss that he said could be coiled inside their shorts for only pennies a day. Everybody in the studio audience made appreciative noises. At that moment our neighbor's phone rang again.
      "I'm the Yarny Orange One," said the voice, a little louder, "and I'm fifty city blocks away." It hung up.
      Our neigbor was a little more afraid, so he stopped watching the infomercial about apex-posturation and switched to the channel where there was a talk show about tear mace rations being the answer to teen pregnancy. The show featured, among other things, an ape wearing a sparkling lobster-colored bib

which said: HALITOSIS--AS FAMOUS AS YOURS. The ape seemed well-behaved (just a guy in an ape suit) but the guests on the show were there to spit on each other and they wanted to hurl folding chairs, metal ones. From off-camera the realistic sounds of runny belt bloat could be heard, mingling with the audience's hoggish cries of ecstacy. Each time a guest's nose broke, it was as though twitching in a box were not only taking place but on the verge of turning crisis-beery. Pretty soon, the phone rang again.

"I'm the Yarny Orange One," said the voice, even louder, "and I'm fifty yards away." It hung up.

Now our neighbor was really getting scared, so he switched channels again. He started watching COPS. The COPS episode was taking place in Atlanta. There was a rata loosely burning in a field. It drained and drenched a red halter. So then there was something that was like a faster heaving, stained 'n hammy, and when it ucked cacavera it tinkled next like boiled juice and made a kinda kitschy souvenir and you could tell it was like a faster heaving. Soon our neighbor's phone rang again.

"I'm the Yarny Orange One, and I'm fifty feet away." It hung up.

Our neighbor looked out the window at the phone booth fifty feet from his house but the booth looked empty. He was still staring out his window, fearfully wondering what to make of it all when the phone rang again.

"I'm the Yarny Orange One, and I'm fifty inches from your door."

"Then why can't I see you?" our neighbor cried.

"Becasuse," said the voice on the phone, "you're in a mental institution."

(Special thanks to John M. Bennett)

*

'STEUBENVILLE" *(from WAVERLEY FLEA #55)*

Weakly she said, "Damn you!" and her eyes fell to her fingers which were knotted together in her lap while she said it again, more forcefully now, "Damn you!"

She looked preoccupied, so that her words were almost too emphatic for the expression on her face.

"Damn you," she hissed, and sat up straighter on the sofa she was perched on.

A big squint came on her countenance.

"Damn you"--she spoke with fascinated slowness, "Damn you . . . Damn you . . ."

Her eyes left her fingers and she started to stare at her ankles, without talking, but then a thin smile twisted her lips, and she murmured wonderously, "Oh, damn you! Damn--" her voice trailed off. The smile went away. She kept watching her ankles. Several hours passed.

Suddenly her eyes became alert. "Damn you," she announced very loudly to herself. She sounded angry now.

"DAMN YOU!" and then, "Damn you damn you damn you damn you---"

Momentarily she was silent. A stiff breeze blew in from the yard; the smell of rain with it; and there was the sound of nuts that had been shaken loose from the pecan trees outside, a dozen or more of these, bouncing and rolling on the roof overhead.

On the sofa the girl relaxed a little, her eyes frowning less intently and going back to studying her fingers as she said in a more matter-of-fact way, "Damn you!"

In the next room her parents shook their heads, they were beginning to wonder if maybe she wasn't getting a little weird.

*

"DEATH AND THE WHITE SEA" *(from WAVERLEY FLEA #65)*

The 500 pound man on the bus.
    The 500 pound their meat.

Al Ackerman

AL ACKERMAN HACKS JOHN M. BENNETT'S POEMS

FEATHERY HAUNCHES (from 6.4, 5, 6)

I've spent years in a bar and only minutes
dans le miel your thigh urine smells
like a brim simple wind button clown button wind
nostril says shaking off time ladder
crazed I've counted them. Seven. The same seven washed
in gasoline thirsty glass "boaking stoats" stalled
shaving milk eel tour belly folds are what happened
to the traffic, as though the dark piss spoon map
took a while to reach twitchy lung claw
bottom or yr chest's turd flame knacker marks you
as a flake. Yr laundry's dressed with
spiders tapping like a
table window shave the table tape yr cheek's window.

SONG: John Taggart meets John M. Bennett (from 7.25)

To bathe yr pockets with vermouth
to bathe this yr clam annointed clock to bathe to
bathe this yr clam to blam udder to
bum sandwiched like a saddle yr a bum yr a bum
who bathes this yr clam a bum sandwiched like
bathing like bumming like bathing like dimpling like bathing
to dimple for bum sandwiched.

To dimple to dick inside yr muddy teaching
cruddy rendition cruddy rendition
dimpling inside yr muddy teaching.

To dimple suck treats but drift awhile . . .

(NOTE: This SONG, which is something you'll undoubtedly want to spend a lot of time chanting, is especially good for when you're rolling in the dust of the marketplace.)

YR SALAD (from 6.14)

I. Each nose in its own way is crying:

Pick me.

Pick me.

II. The simple corpse smiled--as if to
indicate "Try hot 2 girl live action."
Beneath preguntado--there would be
crum stance wit me--over yr salad's
wood--burning--nack o' take off yr
suit. Loose stool loosen master
thumb. And legs, legs, legs. That's
why: I've been a good customer to
these people and want them to call
me Creep Dimly Toward Slaw, III.

DRAT SHORTS (from 8.22)

Participants
Say that drat shorts
Is spiritual profound
And even undu lactose slaw gland
I've asked myself why I like corpse drip plop
I think the idea of tit mallow stare
Is such a personal private intimate
Part of the
Bag bong fog sock rapid mastif
In psychological terms it's lab yo rim
Dingle carpet rum deb cough
And when I'm flaccid can cause
Such intense rampant mane rough shed that
What may start off as nudge looser nudge tum
Can lug run rabid sun bong luck shoe rum boom mutt has
Formed the heart
Of a plurality of my
Fantasies for nigh on to forty years
I don't think that a noodle hill
Could ever imagine what that feels like
Mondo spam claw
Or no mondo spam claw

MEDIUMISTIC PEG HEAD (from 6-14)

I felt that he was clicking
that I was not.
I was over-excited, the supernatural
being a race
            of anything
that can speak through seep ins.

This dust tape you husbands
                    who say:
"What is your attitude to
me eating my toe not merely in
a well-acted farce but
also in this portrait of
motorola spurts
                these spurts poorest
traceless joy must thought that
crumbly is it that I have not
                    seen them?"
            reminds me of
yr pocket lace dimmer hole ah
it has growed you was tooting
wall *all* your slobber
close to me and watching me
eats impacted? Let me repeat to you
Glowing One
mostly because
I have touched the limbs
of hall ("ham") dropped gum, I feel ill or
rather I feel low spirited.

CRAZY LEGS

Boyfriend in the dark, the brim's last fEEt, pick it
And roll it rusty "flute" hand meant for rubbing
Thoughts of Gov. Bob FeLatio, force
You didn't spread yourself you read the giant pink
Bloomers held sideways till shivers cross the sack to
Press your liver; clams or rubber gloves Darwinize
Those folks are all smokers plate of ears your sand
Decay 'n sneeze my name is "smell these fingers"
Now young postaGe stamp floating in your milk or
Mr. Toad at the wheel drowning in your glam, you're
The big hoor with the noose, gravy held beneath your
Crazy legs returning those not holding a carrot are
Emblems of wurst hiding "heaps of flies" wrist and cop your list
Why in seed I'll tell you off, you old bar of soap.
I'll explain a small head from your puncture wound.

(from rOlling COMBers)

PLEASE INITIAL

        Royal dupes
for the sake of amusement
or the neglect of science
each dreaming in the winter vaults
of the half-commie city, I
did not pause for Shuntnewcombe
thus a party of beast-riders will
hound,
so as to house and mummy-up,
oral power--
                lead to, might provide?
I smell a giant
hoax devised by frump class of
ones who want to trade grand pipestem arms
for such a red
beard that you would have thought it was
flailing out on the ice
not fighting
the Goat with a Thousand Agencies

Glans Ted Sherman

NEWBERY WINNER

"Sure, you can clone a mouse. But can you take
him to the opera?" Kafka

Because sitting back in the cooler with a sawed-off shotgun
Never got old I am someone who now has more great
Memories than almost anyone else I know.
And so: "hang a little kraut out the corner of your mouth, everybody!"

I also think how I was fifteen when
On the ceiling the stains appeared that gave us to suspect
Our upstairs neighbor either had big problems with his colon
Or was personally off, maybe both. But

If everybody limps there is more beauty. Why
Twitch, horse? From here on out I want to sell my kisses
At the school fishpond and charge extra when I've been eating tamales.
Put or pull out. You were an awful pratt.

They sell some damn good-tasting tamales, believe it
Or not, at that little place in Ann Arbor--Las Three Something
Or other? O man, eating tamales sure beats eating c.....o.
Otherwise, the little kraut wouldn't.

                              --Glans Ted Sherman

A PRECISE INSTANT IN LACK

The onions keep dropping out of my sandwich--
     Lap Rain.
Nothing was but nothing was
Otherwise, lore forth
Drippy like
Steak-draped radio congestion
Goes up inside the wire Venus,
     Lab foam
Is the result and it's not only that
That's boring me silly, it's the action
Of your eyes an action-fried I remember
Harold
Shuffling around in his robe and slippers
Searching for a sugar bowl
In his sleep
There was a moth-eaten wolf's tail over
Where the radiator cap should have been. Thus,
This is not about
Moon-park coin in the bend of
The schlong inside the law--or take a born natterer
Like pitter patter a large biscuit approaches
"You" a god for pid natter, could hear
A crazy man was saying:
"Boxy home cuddled all leashing bread beside
     yr crack"
He was mostly hoping for sore cheek you chewed
Rooms unlighted and an empty yard below

Al Ackerman

DEAR SUSIE

(Emily Dickinson's letters to her sister meet John M. Bennett)

It's hard to wait, dear Susie, though my heart is there, and has
been since the sunset, and I knew you'd come -- I'd should
have gone right down, but Mother had been at work hard, as
it was Saturday, and Austin had promised to take her to Mrs
Cobb's, as soon as he got home from Palmer -- then she
wanted to go, and see two or three of the onus combers, and I
wanted blossoms in tobacco trouble feet, but I thought it would
be unkind if chewed cough of the nap hamster drank in blood
along the slugger spitting on the peach -- then Mother wanted
clung snore daub my plate estaño and more pie for your bad
sad Emily and also wanted bluntal lobe ranter chewage so as to
have the onus combers fitted to the rainless heaving inside
the bun, and trot abroad, lope across stab, and I knew this
was like my lake knife meater, a toot mal, and I thought "oh
whispers stammer white bleat, whispers stammer white bleat,
your hatless death a bonus," which no night can shade, for
when the stableized rabbit offal pants leave'ya slumpin'
a good many things can happen, as you well know, dear
Susie -- though it may not be evening, or time for the sky
ding, till this little heart stops beating and is yr schlong
blank titter stumble -- Dear One, often I think of how redemption
clambs your hat, owing to our sadness at just parting that old
drunkard damp thigh hair to peep in and spot what I always
like to call eatable never felt a wipe! -- I can't talk of it now tho',
for it makes me write such fretful things, like "Harem is Love."
But that was Lump Pounds -- this is but Lap Glee, yet Lap Glee
so like to lump pounds, that I would lacquertate, should the
true sock lost in cold bum us out. Love for you Darling Susie --
How can I sleep tonight? Have you slabbed the beach?
adieu! from your own Emily --

> Al Ackerman

HE HE

He He heard heard Mathilde Mathilde walking walking rapidly rapidly about about the the room room. She She lighted lighted a a number number of of candles candles. When When Fonque Fonque had had summoned summoned up up the the strength strength to to look look at at her her, she she had had placed placed Julien's Julien's head head upon upon a a little little marble marble table table, in in front front of of her her, and and was was kissing kissing his his brow brow . . .

Even Even worse worse were were the the signs signs, quite quite unmistakable unmistakable, that that the the Say Say Every Every Word Word Twice Twice Gang Gang was was back back in in town town.

"Swarthy" Turk Sellers

288

TEN FINGER EARL

Al Ackerman

<u>Through the following story which EARL tells sitting on the ground in his torn underpants and talking directly to the audience, a variety of forest sounds can be heard in the background.</u>

EARL.

My story is an all-too-familiar one. On Thanksgiving Day, because I was feeling pent-up and looking to escape the usual stale boring family fare, I let myself be talked into accompanying some men out to a field where we ran around chasing horses. The idea was: that the first man to catch a horse would be declared the Winner; that the Winner would receive as his prize a free turkey with all the trimmings; and that the Losers in the contest would each have to sacrifice a finger. Unfortunately, I was running in my street shoes and I wound up among the Losers. Not good, I'll spare you the extreme gory details. Suffice it to say that we Losers were expected to get in line, go forward, and give up our finger to the chopper in an orderly fashion, but as you might imagine there was a good deal of shouting, pushing, wailing, moaning, cursing, intestinal irregularity, flies, and general confusion to the scene. This is what enabled me to slip away undetected. Seeing my chance I ran like hell and by keeping low to the ground was able to lose myself among the rank weeds and bushes that surrounded the field.

In this way, I saved my finger--at least for the nonce. However, nothing comes without a price tag, as they say. Ever since I scrammed out of there and avoided the bloody sacrifice, gangs of angry men have been beating the bushes in search of me (and my finger), and I have been forced to undergo consider-able hardship in my efforts to stay on the move and not let myself be seen. Little better than a hunted thing I knew from the start that my only hope was to reach West Joe Pancake Forest and hide out there, and that was where I headed. Fortunately, it wasn't far. The trail I was on led me there in fairly short order. But the feeling I got when the forest's dark mass actually loomed in front of me was enough to stop me in my tracks. With its over-hanging cypress and ropy vegetation waving like eerie appendages in the wind, the forest that day had a decidedly ominous look. Entering it was not a pleasant prospect, and I found myself hesitating. No one had to tell me how dangerous it was to remain out there in the open and go on exposing myself (I mean to the risk of capture, not sexually), but as the seconds ticked by I continued to do just that; dithering and procrastinating in spite of myself. It wasn't until I actually heard the yip-yip of angry voices coming along the trail less than a hundred yards behind me that I was finally convinced. Here was a situation that couldn't be handled by simple, nonviolent loitering--no. If I wanted to keep my finger, I had to act and taking a deep breath, into the forest I plunged.

Perhaps I could develop latent Boy Scout tendencies.

I had to grin (slightly) at this inane thought since it showed that, even with gangs of blood-thirsty finger-hunters breathing down my neck I had not entirely lost my weird sense of humor.

Meantime, some very rough branches were slapping me in the face and there was no lack of things to be seen and avoided. West Joe Pancake is not a major forest, as forests go, but as I quickly learned it has large areas where the sun never penetrates and enough bogs and ravines to make things precarious. Nor had I foreseen the profusion of brambles that crowded in everywhere, with spines on them two inches long. It is no exaggeration to say that before I had gone half a mile my skin was scratched bloody in a dozen places and my clothes had taken on the look of a wino's ensemble that has been worn to a dog fight.

Even so, I continued to feel a very real sense of pride--because hadn't I managed to escape with all ten of my fingers intact? It may sound foolish, but I simply couldn't stop looking forward to the moment when I would be able to get back to the city and order a new set of business cards with the name TEN FINGER EARL printed on them. I figured I had more than earned this handsome new sobriquet and I was anxious to start using it as soon as I could! Of course, before there could be any chance of this happening I would have to outwit and elude my pursuers. And these were no ordinary men. The fact that they carried knives as long as your arm, and had toothless red gums, neck beards, and eyes like big yellow saucers was proof of that.

But--and I say this in all seriousness, believe me--what were a few slavering finger-hunters in comparison with what happened to me next? At that point, I'd been in the forest about three hours and I was stumbling along doing my best to follow a path that was nothing but a pair of muddy ruts leading who-knows-where through the trees and bushes, when I came upon a blighted sunken place where the tent worms had been at work. From stunted bush to stunted bush their papery, bluggy gray canopies were stretched; shrouding and effectively sealing off the entire area, which was about the size of a football field. Need-less to say, this horrible wormy gray barrier brought me to a dead halt. This in turn led me to thoughts of Camel McCullough (so-called because he refused to drink water), my one-time classmate at Poe Elementary, because I could dimly remember that Camel had once explained to a group of us how the slightest contact with the dread tent worm or its canopy could raise huge sores on a man's body, and even in some cases cause his testicles to drop off. I mention this to show why, faced with a whole acre of the diseased and webby stuff, I lost no time in backing away from it. Then, as I reached what I considered to be a safe distance, and began casting about for an alternate route, there was a sharp retinal flash and I suddenly felt myself enter a barbaric dream realm. Terrified, I tried to focus on the forrest around me. But the thing was too strong and I began to develop an insatiable craving for scrapple, in fact scrapple at every meal accompanied by the strong urge to learn more about Anderson-ville Prison. Most unpleasant. The whole thing lasted perhaps ten seconds.

I remained a long way off for another minute or two. Gradually, I regained enough composure to overcome--or at least ignore--the way my hands were shaking, the all-too-familiar balled-up feeling at the pit of my stomach. I say all-too-familiar. Because of course I recognized the symptoms. For years I've been plagued by these sudden attacks. Usually they occur when I'm feeling a little stressed. First the dream-like flash. It's an instantaneous thing. A sort of precursor or warning signal, letting me know that in a very few minutes the worst of the episode is going to manifest itself--the truly hellish part--which, when it hits, invariably means that my eyes roll up and I begin running in circles, mindlessly shouting out passages from *The Little House on the Prairie* and trying to bite things. Ugly spells they are, true nightmare transports, and as I say I've been prone to them for years without ever understanding why. All I know for certain is that once a spell is on the way, the only defense against it is to sit down and try to calm my brain and central nervous system by thinking soothing thoughts. Soothing thoughts will sometimes halt the spell; cause it to dissipate. Not always--but often enough to make this method my only recourse.

Out there that day in the forest, I knew I had at best four or five minutes to start manufacturing soothing thoughts. Otherwise, the spell would be on me like a cheap suit. The running-biting aspects of the thing were bad enough, but what really filled me with dread was the thought of being so far gone that I shouted out entire passages from *The Little House on the Prairie.* Could anything be more hideous? Merely to think about it was to shudder.

Desperately, I began running toward the small clearing I'd just spotted, about fifty yards off to my left. Dotted here and there with clumps of sweet-fern and a few rotting logs, but mostly carpeted with coarse, pale grass, it appeared to be a spot where the tent worms had not yet spead their domain. I found a large poplar whose trunk looked smooth and relatively bramble-free, and sank down with my back against it, ready to begin the grimly urgent business of summoning soothing thoughts. Memories of earlier, happier periods in my life usually worked best. Closing my eyes, I went way back; began remembering when I was twelve or thirteen; how much I'd loved to pack a sack lunch every Saturday and ride the city bus out to the State Asylum on S. Pressa Street, to spend the day watching the inmates through the fence.

One inmate, a congenital lunatic with strong hebephrenic tendencies, always came right up to the fence on all fours and would jump up and down in sheer excitement, just like the anteater at the Paris Zoo is said to have jumped up and down in excitement whenever the painter Toulouse-Lautrec stopped by its cage for a visit. Somehow it always made me feel good to see him.

About once a month my friend "Squint" Cagle would ride out to the asylum with me. We always made sure we sat behind some elderly person on the bus; then we'd talk in loud obnoxious whispers about all the people we'd (supposed-ly) killed. Once an old man turned around in his seat and shouted, "Here there! Stop that! You boys are *bad* boys!" That was real success.

Once "Squint" wore a set of handcuffs in his belt and I wore a yarny black wig . . .

Good times, wonderful memories . . . and in this instance luck was with me: the spell receded. I could feel the pressure of it leave my mind like a dark cloud of flies withdrawing from a juicy cutlet. What relief. I ended up by feeling so grateful that I let myself relax for the first time that day. I was dead tired. And sitting sprawled there, with my back against the tree, and with the windy forest rising high on either side, I fell into an exhausted sleep, and dreamed I wasn't alone in the clearing. Something or someone was coming toward me through the bushes. It was Uncle Clarence--my mother's older brother--and (such was my dream) he looked almost exactly like a beaver. That is, he weighed about fifty pounds and he had the thick fur, the small eyes in tightly fitting lids, and the protruding teeth of a beaver; plus the traditional large, black, flat beaver tail. Otherwise, he was the same old cranky diabetic who had raised me; (my mother had died from cirrhosis when I was two and I'd never known my father).

Seeing my uncle emerge from the bushes and come ambling toward me now, I braced myself; got ready for one of our interminable family wrangles.

Climbing up on a nearby log, my uncle sat back on his tail, grimaced at me, and spoke.

"I'm very fond of you, Earl, but for your own good there's something you need to be told--"

"Hold on, Uncle Clarence," I interrupted. "Before we go any further, I think you should know that from here on out I prefer to be called TEN FINGER EARL. In fact, I insist on it."

If this remark struck my uncle as peculiar, he gave no sign. "Yes, well, as I was saying," he went on, "there's something important that you need to be made aware of, boy. Remember all those asinine excursions you used to make, every Saturday, out to the State Asylum--and the congenital lunatic who always came right up to the fence and would jump up and down in front of you? Well, boy, I'm sorry to be the one to have to tell you this, but that lunatic was your father. Your mother didn't want you to know; and she swore the rest of the family to secrecy. That's why--all these years--you've remained in such total and abysmal ignorance of your unfortunate parentage."

My uncle scratched his chin thoughtfully through his fur. "It's probably not important, really, but I've always wondered why you wasted so many Saturdays making all those trips out the the State Asylum; especially since there was no earthly way for you to know that your father was a permanent resident there-- in fact, no way for you to know anything about him at all, poor crazed devil. Still, if I had to make a guess, I'd say some sort of unsavory genetic magnetism must have been at work--I mean on a purely instinctive and subliminal level-- between the two of you, and that's what kept drawing you back out there to that asylum every blessed Saturday. Or--who knows?--maybe you were just queer for asylums. Well, it's a damn sorry business however you look at it."

"But-- Why are you telling me all this now, Uncle Clarence?" I blurted.

"Why? Well, for the plain and simple reason that I don't know what else to do with you. You can't hold a job, you go right on having those unattractive running-biting fits, your sense of humor keeps getting weirder all the time. Good God, boy, you're 37 years old! Time to wake up and face facts: YOU'VE GOT FEEB'S BLOOD COURSING THROUGH YOUR VEINS!"

My uncle suddenly slapped the log with his tail. Crack! The violence of it woke me, and I found that I'd been crying in my sleep. Huge blubbery tears were running down my cheeks; and right then, in that lonely little clearing in the middle of the forest I realized I had just experienced the worst humiliation a man can face: *having delicate personal and family matters discussed by a beaver*. I was devestated by the realization and, for longer than I care to think about, I've been sitting out here. In addition to my growing hunger and privation (to say nothing of the very poor, rudimentary toilet facilities) I've started having the distinct sensation of something fooling around with my neck and scalp. I've brooded over this a good deal and have just about come to the conclusion that the tent worms have discovered me and are taking an unhealthy interest in my head. Well, it doesn't surprise me. Nothing surprises me anymore. Sitting out here for so long, I have come to understand that many unfair things can (and do) happen to us in this life; and if it isn't one thing happening, it's likely to be two or three. Angry men with knives could be beating the bushes for you (and your finger)--you could learn that your father was a congenital lunatic with strong hebephrenic tendencies--and in addition the tent worms could drop down and start fooling with your head----

(The swelling sound of busy tent worms drowns out EARL'S VOICE as the lights go to black.)

```
ACK'S HACKS
Al Ackerman Hacks John M. Bennett's Poems
```

Here's the hack we did at our little literary workshop the other night . . . five of us, including Walt, who had dropped by to cadge a meal and who so far as I know has never before come within spitting distance of a poem much less yclept lest earth be conquered.

Anyhow, each of us took turns writing a line, drawing primarily on your great Floor de decimas booklette (plus a coiuple of pages of low-grade porn that I passed around). Good deal of wine-tasting going on, too. Eventually we put the results in a hat and drew at glorious random. Came out like this---

ANSWERFINGER (from Floor de Decimas)

claim your browsing kissing eyes trook tame gin crude
surf thought! letting loose a second squirting
each slept, ingenious device is smoke comed, not apt a sound
a matter of honour in the brazier
abducted glue sock crude napster envy
chest clucking peephole ordeal

my twinkling arse-cheeks dropping
perverse and gross forms of napster snort, inflate bile nod
the girls appeared, sunk nips, not laughing, nor deep
Rocket meat, bunny lap, bobs away
I heard the locks sunk nips

--Ackerman, Jones, McShea, Novash, Wondolowski

Blaster Al Ackerman & Megan McShea

I shall be rich
Rich
Turn up the vol:
disappointed in the
    audience reaction
Turn it down:
I saw a red dress

Ayii Johnee,

Really some excellent poems here, GNAW OX and the ones from 11.14.

GNAW OX has the feel of an epic and I can see I'm gonna have to put on the gas to come up with a hack worthy of this this big baby.

What with the holidays and all I decided first to concentrate on the batch from 11.14 and like to kid myself that I managed to achieve something nice in the way of murk and flirk, which I'm calling GIFT FROM THE RIM. This incidentally gave me a chance to pay a small, heartfelt tribute to one of my favorite birdbrains: Anne Morrow Lindbergh. Remember Anne Morrow Lindbergh? Not only wife to the famous aviator but a real wooly thinker in her own right, she spent the thirties as an armchair quarterback doing a lot of rah-rah pro-Nazi sermonizing; (eventually, in '39 or '40, E.B. White grew bemused enough to devote an essay to her writings and suggested, in his gentle way, that she seemed to be peeling an empty banana.) In later years she became a mainstay at GOOD HOUSEKEEPING etc and wrote "inspirational" bestsellers such as GIFT FROM THE SEA. A not unworthy candidate for hackdom, in my book.

GIFT FROM THE RIM (from 11.14)

I began these pages for my pencil, as I
think best with a pencil in my hand (pencil? pen? pen? pencil?
stick? log? Are we all under this illusion? Besides, I thought, not all
are reeling in the fumes
Perhaps rondo gegen here held boom when the more than seven
pounds rimmed me. But in looking for the perfect rim
job long d
ream Packed off H. In looking for the
perfect rim job
under bed you shape the sheets
Shaped this way they had no lung puterance mot, or had
found the double ham breath long
ago. No, I decided these "streak" heavy only for meat pops bud
sides, with different
housewives and mothers under the different forms, I decided, in the
end to hade "intention" van
No, I decided in the end
to pust oil and geese rinse, too, are agrappling
rimmed
and sorta coughing like
a light late comb iced keen thigh in the
dew of little
things, the heart finds its meaning
and is
looking at soup held your face wings more than
my individual
soup held your face wings and is
looking at soup, screamed Anne Morrow Lindbergh

HEAVY LIPS AN GOGGLES

for Jack A. Withers Smote

Remote soundings; maybe sheepbells,
maybe something else. Anyhow,
late afternoon was readying to go where
it is it goes when it's laid
up for the night, that was when
you touched my leg, also when
you said, "Silage, silage,
but before I start celebrating by rubbing the elegant cream
deodorant in my armpits better get right
watching a sausage deplowed roll across the bed:
swiftly, silently, greasily. It rolls
so as to effect a hine y loss or two. Fauce t s
ticky with blood, the sausages I like best
are blessed with wounds. Or is that rain cave
heavy lips an goggles? Remember ntrain model leer
b utter chained rusty leap against b rain cave heavy
lips an goggles for Solar Pons in a locker
keeps wait for--you're not gonna believe this--
heaven bone oot side! And the other snooper
as a numb er leg was ate for hours
in ALL directions. That stuff
we all like to do with a hot poker
chained the k nob like as if with K-Y,
the jelly of champions. The acid in my stomach
spells a slow log shanked e n teritic like
how the fuzz right there under my eyes apt
to turn the floor pungent. Hah
'n heh. I may not know dick about haying time
but I sure know what I need right now
is a good rub down from ham, part of the reason
why I keep turning my head clear round
and round and round like an owl
behind the barn, impatient for a rub down
from ham the hands wore like g loves."

Jack A., hearing you say these things,
I wanted to weep.
I had no more doubts. I had to peg you for an
alcoholic.

                                        (from 1.30)

SWEETS OF THE NEW FORMALISM

The "gas piration" to which you pray is bright
        As a thumb caught in a car door.
The ill respective ham pressure of your tights
        Shows a rim pooch that prompts remorse:
These are the c lumps dim in November
Evening like wallets cuffed with hair glue fur-

Nace mask bled feet lake clung you tapped uh sung
        Where dolled mats stuck ankles scud toward
The gentle fluke supping yr prong for mung
        Has mole sped small claims as its reward
And boost me no c lock g apes which started
Misted business cus pi d, rather sordid.

Thus strokes don't blink but blink cud a page. Fey,
        The "guts" of eat yr nose blood red
Hug the bun gnome that grabbed the cheese sp ray
        That moved in liver bursts that fled
Hopped shed or rustled, gagging on limpness
Strap it nod, pod lamp pus-craving pimpfest!

Odd, how scald yr packed se rape 'n shoes those called,
        And how "chewed a bat" club's soggy
Yet shot fulla clothes? Wow hey look it crawls
        Not pap bond, tree shape, but Froggy
The Gremlin, motherly hoarse, he hops 'n hums:
"Look up! look down! look at my thumb! gee you're dumb!"

THE HEART OF YOUTH

Borne upwards on its gold and silver wings
        Rises the Heart of Youth.
With its fond hopes and sweet imaginings,
It breathes rice-heavy flabby lawn gas or
Pawns yr nub, sees sleef 'n shopping basket
Dogs; and stiff with the lope of chauffeur's crab
Lice, crocks an itch like name yr snaps, o socks!
        O name them what the "clam"
Advises, "Pasta shake fang eat a nose gloam"--
Then duck out quick and shed tuition gloom,
Because, when lack o' teaching sorta gluts
Map rhomboid cuffed with hair glue smoking and
Smelling of bean storm mit dat old stoma
Cal jara, the Heart of Youth knows no care!

                                        (both from GNAW OX)

EYES DO MORE THAN SNEEZE

Chicken roughly rolled
spang into my lap startled hell out of
the space walk . . . It takes a gruesome bounce shirt
    crushed
in bud and "blazes" a comet couldn't cross lame
a cross the yard you rave treble
This monster moreover bites yr weekly pay-
envelope and don't the slow tomb look
pretty rising over six-feet-two. Yawn
if yr "lander" age claimed you
are given the clap like any common soldier simple
riv er a flagging mastic sleeve were talking your arm
    off,
given that
you are the cougher naked at the door from whence you
    sorta
get wild-looking. But the android's water looks well-
    proportioned for its size
and b lack to front, 'n groutside out, it tastes sweeter
    by far
than even the famed minder water fence pill
beloved by all those whom thick lock dis solves nor hear
this perhaps because the andoid's protective cup
dances each night with a dent
knocked in it. Smell that? E ven with la casa spinning
I lap seed as if a double
eye is seen when a siamese twin cougher
naked at the door
bends over. Wait. Is there an echo in here? Emerson
said a refrain is no better than the name implies
Roughly chicken
at the ends of over fled, an "addled" pust yule misters
    like a grin--
A cur rant dum my water symptom emptied beef
That was the android's water, cheap at half the price,
like a goat prize, with the black xerox glove's jelly
    water creaming
out your mouth shoulders that chicken roughly
up yr hole ton lun shrieks FOUR!!!
and a golf ball crashed through the window.

(from 1.9 and 1.16)

WHAT A PLACE

Bennettville is a quiet town, but it seems
to have more than its share of excitement.
Perhaps it's the isolation. For Bennettville, with its sot's name,
its filled gloom trick and many religious maniacs
in itching pants the rumpled glue hum of "clears" (as L. Ron
    Hubbard's ever-popular "dianetics" would term most
    of Bennettville's inhabitants),
                            is a town of
rash isolation chambers in yr hat yr flush
hill model throat yr breath dome yr shat roof haul ah dimple
dithered muscle, scattered waste, and this--plus plenty of
    faintest day spendings
to name what occupies most Bennettville handkerchiefs--
swallow all that lumps o'stew had charged like mad out of some
plum different mewling above my lap. Hot
is hot. No matter, the town's main pride remains
giving two cents for empties and time
after time yr dishonest bets almost puts a hand on the huge
    foot
in the dusty shoe of cupped flavorhood--toothsome,
toothsome as the devil the inner "girlish" spoon gun
ouch coughs up payer head a swallowed fly poured an mumbled
and in general shows much public autism for the clap sport,
much support for that in every "booming face" among clap
    sport fans
who parade with flaming loven asters through the streets of
    Bennettville
while under the table flaw dash heaver in confusion damp
not at all like a huge snowflake came the whirl yr
home battered laporectomy, grubbing, housing yr
blanket sky an tum bled birds more than an unbuttoned
prayer for plunger light behind the phony steam lever called
race-an-sprawl-dantly,
                        as more distant the door
the closer tables shine, waffles thinly dreaming of yr
sham hole bleats, like sounder folds yr thighs sending their
demon ology lamp fusion--thru yr shorts? Good Lord--is that
    their game?
Whatever it is, John M. Bennett always finds himself
right in the middle of the excitement that Bennettville is known for!
"Yr willy," he says, convincingly, "give me yr willy."

(from 2.13)

SOMEWHAT TROUBLED

By duck mind fake with nothing
else, no meatballs in a cave, just
this amazing yapping
the multitude changed
to a picture of
shit his last "step"

A mice lung supper
smitten rigid, as it were

Brain lied "run toward juice paw crap!" which lent
steam a last "step" each
realm a pinwheel focus
on your heaving saus age, each
gum bled a toothsome lamp sauce, each

mysterious ghostly tooth's
a waving handkerchief   (from 11.7)

Dear Dr.Al,
When I woke up this afternoon and headed for the bathroom to take
a leak,I found a tiny Morey Amsterdam right outside of my bedroom.
Only three or four inches high,he was easily the smallest Morey
Amsterdam I've ever seen;but there he was skittering around on the
grimey linoleum,gathering up crumbs,nibbling bits of old cheese,
ripping off one-liners about bald men and even composing little
songs on a teeny lttle upright piano he had there by the trash bin.
Still befuddled by sleep,my wits cloudy with last night's dreams
of women made of raw chicken parts and string,I was caught completely off-guard and just stood there in the doorway entranced,
as it were by his inane little rodentlike shtick.His nimble brown
fingers as they deftly stroked the ivories and the malevolence in
his shiny little black eyes as he squeeked out a high tinny rendition of "Tea fot Two" hypnotised me for what must have been at
least fifteen minutes.At length I recovered,shaking off my stupor
and,stepping quietly back through my bedroom door,I grabbed a
camera,one of those disposable drugstore dealies I had purchased for
my on-going "hobo-erotica" series.However,when I slid noiselessly
back around the corner I discovered that my little 'guest' had
vanished;upright piano and all.Upon making a cursory search of the
hallway and the adjoining closet I grew fearful he had made an
escape,but just then I heard I quiet scuffling coming from the
kitchen.Heading in that direction,I paused long enough to grab a
wire coat hanger out of the closet and tip-toed in.The furtive
noises seemed to be coming from under the fridge.Silently I
crouched down and began making audience laugh-track noises in
what I hoped was a soothing manner.Sure enough,after a couple of
minutes of this his minute vaudevillian little head poked out from
under the fridge and blinked those nasty little black eyes at me.
Supposing that I meant him no harm,he cautiously emerged into
full view,stood there in his little baggy suit and vest and then
began,somewhat shyly it seemed,telling me a long high-pitched
and totally inaudible joke.Suddenly,I whipped the wire hanger out
from behind my back and slashing at him quickly,ripped his tiny
disgusting body in two with one wet whack.It was really gross Dr.
Al,let me tell you.Especially first thing in the morning like
that.Anyway,I fetchéd the broom and the dustpan and proceeded to
gather up his still twitching bloody bits and dumped them into
the trashcan.I wonder if this could be the first signs of a major
Morey Amsterdam infestation?You know,like the problem I had last
year with all of those Durwood Kirbys in the bathroom.But then
I decided oh well,what the fuck,I'll just tell the landlord
about it.I mean after all,it's his problem.So I went on into the
bathroom and took a (by now much-needed) morning whizz.
more soon...
         yr pal

         Mr. Haddock

THE QUESTION

He set to work to design a typeface
but the Muskrat Boys
                              jumped him from behind. Why? Why
all this violence in the world remains a question that might well be
applied not only to
the Muskrat Boys' effect
on the printing trade but to
every activity in which
they became involved;
though, in all fairness, it should be noted
that those of you asking "Why" appeared
to have a certain ashtray-making,
therapy-seeking motivation, and you
evidently felt enough subjective difficulty
to go on looking, sometimes explicity, for new ways
of dealing with your own twisted threads of sickness,
your eyes like tide-pools
in which all things are food
and reflect the horror of a pleasure
of which they are unaware, as shining
up out of them whatever it was must have
kept on playing tag with Mr. Wacky's
lowersack, lowersack. Too, someone
thoughtful had brought a tremendous
amount of LSD into town and had been dispensing
it freely I
continued walking and noticed I wasn't
wearing any clothes

                    --"Swarthy" Turk Sellers

logo by haddock

THE BUTTERFLY OF DEATH

"No such thing as hernia," the one who was like an apple-cheeked puppet of a creature kept sitting around saying. Pretty soon they hustled him out of there. After that the place quieted down. Things simmered along. It was the deepest part of the summer. Evelyn and I kept an eye on the boarding house comings and goings. Evelyn was steaming open everybody's mail and one letter in particular enchanted us out of our gourds with its aura of bittersweet pathos and kismet unconquerable (and so):

Aug. 3rd.

My Very Dear Maestro:

Like as not you are no longer living in the present most of the time, but I wonder if you still remember the Butterfly of Death? How it was to find a really huge black-and-purple butterfly fluttering weakly brownish on the back steps, with hungry red ants swarming over it. Black-and-purple, or brown and red? Each time you took your eyes away, you lost it, and had to search again. It could also be, with your worried face always looking a little vague, that you didn't have any feelings about the thing, one way or the other. It was happening as it always did, and that was enough.

Thus the days rolled on and seemed to be speaking evil of you--though perhaps with good reason, eh, old friend?

Then came the morning when, on scanning the latest *SwampMate*, your eye lighted on an advertisement in the Personal Column:

"Lost; a trifling, bronze effigy of a butterfly on a square
pedestal; the whole two and a half miles high . . ."

This astounding phrase rang out in your think tank with a deep, booming emphasis on the "*butter-*" and an interrogative note on the "*high.*" No one noticed that you had at the same time detected a tell-tale subarctic chill in the air. It was happening as it always did and a deceptive sense of well-being was in the air so that gradually there came this funny feeling that everybody's "worry light" was about to go out which, in case you haven't forgotten, was the old lost symbol for devils-in-the-pebbles which meant that a whole army of the crazy things would soon come popping right up out of the ground like used clothes. In general, five or six hundred devils in one near downtown neighborhood isn't many; not nowdays. But you had to admit that it felt more than sufficient for this sort of business as long as you could beg the age-old question of going religeous or looking foolish in front of the guys when you took off down the alley in a tizzy, clicking your lips like a rumba addict. And the plight of such indebiture, of how to play your hand. The thought of possibly having to dye your hair black and catch the first bus out of town. For no reason at all the monotony of being on the losing side no longer struck you as quite so out-landish. But then you looked away and that was the first thing you noticed about the place. They were lined up by size, an elf on the left ear and a hog on the right (thanks Megan)--creep out this pale line get dropped not him one finger going bothering and another for balance. In one version, I remember you saying nicotine the same thing after you reported lying in the middle of the road as a perfect gold-headed creature sterile as an ox. Thus, the question became: could we learn more by paying closer attention to what you were trying to say as you went crashing around the woodlot with your shirt off, or could we learn more by talking to Emer the Gill-Man? I checked into that. Saving pennies in the tin-can bank isn't enough. The really tricky part is when you're going through a tunnel hollowed in an enormous tree from some earlier age and hurl--i.e., put what's there, there. And what's keeping your ears apart, take it out. Now turn it on. Got it? Those marks on your chest and stomach look like you went wild with a toothpick billions of years ago the physical universe may have evolved into another in which cramping may not be a necessity only wordless, all-enveloping muttering. Still, not to worry, old twig: nothing like that happened. it was only a series of loud, thumping noises, probably the writer as artist. In this case, the stuff about not liking golden showers had stripped the moon of air in harmon with the threat to fact was just a mask. I guess I'll keep cruising.

There are certain minute differences between a lizard on its hind legs and a human, six or seven all told. That much is clear, accepted without thought, and it was completely worthless but everybody had a lot of fun. Eight, nine. And at the count of ten a fantastic strength moved into you and your eyes to snap. It enabled you to hang around outside Clumpy's in all sorts of weather while "the centrality of method!" and "bup-bup-bup!" vied in your mind and between grunts to entertain a mob of children with the antics of your face bun. Though eyes had blurted makes the perfect deep sea gargle which of us had not had to frame of yet more strange and unfamiliar words: vibe, mute, soft, smooth, pro, air-chews, leech, living coffee, office weight--not to forget your aforementioned face bun and its recent award from the Hopgood Foundation. Seems you'd been selected to receive their annual lower facial bun exciter award and you recognized that to refuse this unusual honor would have meant denying the very thing that now disfigured your lower mouth and chin. Just as a peanut with yellow inside is what days of vital and empty staring can bring, so too in meeting that sultry face bun of yours for the first time one was invariably reminded of how the upper jaw of an octopus closes into the lower. And how one mighty crack on the chin can contribute to the impression of shockingly wide and flabby lips. Below which--seeming always to throb on the verge of sensory population as your eyes bulged--a sugar-thin coating of spittle was invited dried around the swollen place to form a sort of chalky white jacket or tea-cozy of the kisser. Squeak. Of course if the thing starts to develop eyes and a nose don't get the idea that it's a primative life form. Actually it's a later evolutionary type than we! Perhaps the term "hell cull" describes it best. The wonder is that you're still on the street, still free to wander wherever your mouth bun leads. Just what cock-and-bull story you dreamed up we'll probably never know.

A strange business--and no mistake. Hope for coherent narrative of this length could never unfasten it. Instead, as the summer wore on, notwith-standing my dislike of facial protuberances in any form, I found myself over-come with a perverse fascination for the thing. I remember, but cannot adequately say, how this fascination subsequently led me to suspend my archaeological researches and spend my afternoons in incessant chuckling. Even Dan, my curly little cocker spaniel no longer seemed to recognize me. From this period also dates my extreme willingness to embrace one of the lowest forms of idolatry: rank, abject *Lepidoptera* worship. It is what Durkheim would call, I suppose, the Swishing Sounds. (I use the phrase in its literal sense.) That I am not mad, I have established to my satisfaction, by writing this account and bleating like a sheep.

As for my native workmen, they were persuaded to steal your shoes and cufflinks only with difficulty. No explanation was obtainable, but their terror of your bun was manifest.

WHO ARE THESE DEFILERS? It doesn't matter. What *does* matter is that over in the next yard, less than a mile away, the lighting had been bad and the 'taters were blurred and hairy, then suddenly they sort of wanted to join the Marines, help turn this shit around. Maybe even the brightest of them would be a poor typist and a poor speller, but no one needed to draw any diagrams concerning the blate they'd always wanted to meet and flate.

As the saying goes: flate the blate right down into half-knowledge learned many lives ago when numberless semi-literates roamed. It is evolved into goes. Flate the blate, the steak roasted on a stick and the idiomatic ticket . . .

(for Rupert who was first to call it by "bun")

ENVELOPE DEPICTS:
BARONI COLLAGE
DICKED WITH
(BRUTALLY)

DESTINATION LOVE

CALL IT A HOBBY

This rustling noise:
The trail mix, coming alive.
It is. Got to run over it with the car.
Then I'm going to enter law school.
Only I'll say nothing, & of course,
I'll never reveal my plan to have a facelift.
This is the third time in two years, but I have to tell you
I could be superintending construction
Of a railway to a sugar plantation.
Lots of them love their sugar. Know what else?
Big swipe of turpentine will take care
Of that unwanted thing in your womb.
See? It's over already. What really takes
An effort of will is giving up the trail mix &
Living only on gobblo bars & an awful lot of breatherian action.
A virus doesn't live, doesn't die, doesn't feel
Embarrassed at having to quit. He worries about
What he will say if the Lord asks, "R'lyeh,
Why did you not become R'lyeh?" He knows
Quiet desperation of a mouth near a shoe. He has
Few games limited to two persons painted a soft gray.

--"Swarthy" Turk Sellers

RIDE LIKE THE WIND

with a gusty buzz
the vicar bled

and wires ran from him
to an amplifier box

is in reality the story
of an undesirable houseguest

Al Ackerman

UNDERSTANDING

Though she had seen she was pretending
she was walking in her sleep the only time
she became more curious an
uneasy feeling of only *half-*
pretending she was walking in
her sleep excited her suspicions
mostly as to how it might be if
the road that ran past her cottage ran
on and on before dwindling to a
mud-bright purple smudge on the horizon on
which sat an overturned ashtray an
overturned telephone and what
appeared to be a hand fingering
only strange low-life in a pulsing white
insanity of dreadful anticipation
for eyeholes through which a teasing
subtle difference in her box rose like a
precise tart inkling for what bitter
loneliness assailed him and in that instant
he understood the navy.

Glans Ted Sherman

THE WILD POET

The wild poet writes anything that comes into his head
Head
And can wriggle his fingers rapidly
Rapidly
He can tell them apart
Apart
So it begins--he gotta get those
Those
Little rocks off the court
Court
In awe of this
This
He makes two sharp clicks with his mouth
Mouth
This calls attention to the magic motto
Motto
"Don't potty while you're dancin'"

Glans Ted Sherman

POEM ON ALL FOURS

The door, except
for its own ragged
breathing, was silent

Al Ackerman

MYTH (OWNING A BAR)

One dark green eye, one loud yellow eye
One blazing red eyebrow
Sometimes I cannot help laughing
but at other times a key drops to the floor
and I wonder if I should give names
to the shadows cast by the creatures
alive in my urine
                    Like the time I saw this
grasshopper
struggling to escape from the front of your
        sloppy mouth
and named him "Hemingway"

Like the time I had this enormous boil
        on my butt   back in '89
                and called it "Oklahoma City"

                                Al Ackerman

WHEN INFIRMITY FOLLOWS SENILE

When infirmity follows senile
Degeneration changes curious how
Some criminals were also well
Defined as fellows whose digestion
Was used endlessly often to give us
The perfect generic endowments for Superman

The only liberating force in relation
To nuitrition and dreaming
That is, your head, your head grown out
Of all proportion
Your head attached to the splendid
Young body of an athelete
With passionate lyrical attachment
To a physical peculiarity
In this case "gothic" hair
Masking your ankles and feet
Making them look real wig-

Like as you shuffle through the day. And what's
More, no back talk
Do you understand that?
Yes, teacher, shuffle shuffle
And so the years passed
Nothing seemed seriously the matter . . . yet
Only a few late-night heavy
Drinker voices left to sit up and ask
But what of the apple with a face drawn on it?
But what of the balloon with a face drawn on it?

                                Laurel McElwain

Ack Hacks Johnee's Poems

BACK COUNTRY

*"Dell was a sort of
Johnny-come-lately in the
paperback original field."*
Bill Crider

Sometimes after long sterility
something will click into place
like a ash in
jection, grey drifting toward the coast

I'd never seen a man who was full of dark surprises
cry like that "digestive" clay
Just then a sponge ran giggling at Pure Garter Law,
denying reality. No wonder ham shallows

rippling with ponded brains generally means
business. That made me guess it's Carnival-
Moony an "cod piece treat"
while above, mine to smell, the foul turn of events starkered

the eating-phone, rat sludge tubing toward my ear--
ear soundly clawed, not badly
taped, but pounded on the lid at least my
tome bowl's walled! And shoe, itself

I habla on--and on--fum thick as oatmeal
so beak flow SAME slow speak
so clusteringly among
this weird method of publishing

(from 2.9 & 3-1 2000)

MIRACLE VALLEY   *(from 7.17)*

If not a new toe for Oscar
then a new toe for poor brain
If not a new toe for poor brain
then a new toe for lobo
If not a new toe for lobo
then a new toe for new groan
If not a new toe for new groan
then a new grown phone you ate
Elbow, try sander air
brand toilet leader
brist les ogal ister ister

ONE WITH NATURE *(from 4.17)*

The potential suicide sometimes goes
Ahead and does it because
Attacked socks lack the stroll or
You gas mortal pud-cat.

The potential suicide sometimes
Holds off because
Attacked socks lack the stroll
Or you gas mortal pud-cat.

THE POCKMARK CLUB

Tipper:

> There was, is, in most of us, a flushed rat still
> longing for a troubled ape name named HABITUAL
> OLD IMPERSONATOR, a name's cheek salt power
> extruded in shoots hole
> in shameful/regressive
>   lushing bag w/smell
> throws strong arms around wh-wh-wh (15 lines
> and there nance-
> composed staring flat wash "the" stronger loser-led
> each keep rat flushed, one Buckner ⌐⌐ insert
> taken from a big nose

>   and still wriggling for only lousy river trade here
> it's me
> Eep
> I am non-canag watcher and heater

(from 6.12)

TINY SPECIAL ONE CELL

for any radiobeliever

Doubt the no-doze nerve controls your every whim
more than lunations quim a haunt cot?
Because lunations recycle no-doze? Well, yes, only
you were so full of clumb husks
that you didn't know what you were
having were deep socio-political insights
into phlegm wise stage hea flaminia
mea on a rea by the ving lace, its face
is made of rubber in the everyday world
It's the dreamer's dialectic splotches
whose every pathway has a big "bus worn as thumb" sign . . .
Glitter & lace yr shoes, blister
ghostly clos from whose haunt cot came first
the spears while sleeping, and then Tony Wons.

(from Pri vate, S ticker, and Ban g!)

A PIECE OF BREAD

To Courtney

the empire of religeous duty extended itself to your looks
gestures and favorite plea: *a piece of bread.* you labored to
keep alive the awe-creating presence of corny belt yr head
a siesta bank demonstration being jammed by some illicit
transmission from--yes, it was--*a piece of bread.* your sis
the mistress the bride the bun the sweat key shelter the
shock that habits will chew and not very pleasing hourly
domestic bickerings while your eyes flashed with all the
wildness of practical wall chewing and forth like a host of
little stall brains from your parched lips crept those three words:
a piece of bread. (er, I mean four words.)

                                      two weeks it was
two weeks . . . two weeks that you were with us here
two weeks that you were with us here in the house
visiting . . . visiting . . . & as I sit here now entrerrosca
slumped & thinking how many times I heard you whisper

             "*. . . a piece of bread . . .*"

I find it hard--hard to breakfast, hard to bathe, hard to dress
myself & go out & feed my dogs & birds & squirrel
the yardman.

(from Bennett collabs of 7.19 with Lambert & Lady C.)

THE ENORMOUS BOUFFANT

The hostess excused herself and went into the alley with the maid.
There, lying on the ground, was the costumed hideous mockery
of our ability to tease our hair and stiffen
it with hairspray into a very high bouffant. And that's not all.
One woman at a college in Ohio had a bouffant that collapsed!
A passerby hurried to her assistance, but the woman,
who now looked like a middle-aged pug, had become unruly
mysterious haiku-spouter: "Lighting one candle/that snail/
what's on his mind?" she chanted, and: "The mason's finger/
the scissors hesitate/he liked to pick" "His friend's
nose/I would watch/And yet, and yet---" There was a pause.
In the story above the woman turned out to be a man
with long unkempt hair. The story changes each time I tell it.
In another version the woman turns out to be John M. Bennett
who lies there & chants: "must amble nap/ker suds t/in yr sh adow
ah ah" the "ah ah" part however does not belong in the haiku
but is more of an involuntary exclamation made by Bennett
who has developed a sudden eerie fester with dredged look
why he's become suspended luggage on your face the sleep's
new speed
        his stub lid's nut
                must keep a sputter reach deposit
else the leech tugging screech of ugly drapes will continue
sucking on floor's namer roke (tal que?) (si si) loud blotant
                if icy ola taste air's hair your
sentient snatch retained but bubbled cheek ranch pout reposit
faking rake fat looseness as troubled swindle dog finally grabbed
Bennett's ever-present cask of brandy and wrenched it open---

A minute later, out spilled a skeleton, still wearing scraps
of 18th-century crew bus dampness and shaking that snore
rearage list
upon which were found the crudely printed words:

        "move all this stuff---"

(from 6.26)

JOURNAL

May 30---Saw one of Bennett's final sperm kings this afternoon. Disturbing.
Everyone seemed more or less embarrassed. At last the professor pushed back
his chair, thus dismissing sperm hovel month, and remarked, "Well, we all have
to embrace ah moons aspirin tossed the wine less 'it' lost the eyes from which
it again burst forth and had a weird effect. So what are we waiting for? Let's
get naked, kids."
    Anal this is the only reference that I can remember anyone making to the
wet memory douse I felt. Funny, isn't it, how nine sours a thing?
    I have been happy, I suppose . . . It is hard to remember--but necessary--how
a slow downer of blanched copies surge an ponder paw mood clavor--which
possibility disturbs me no end as I don't need to say that in my ever-expanding
sophisticate's role in life I need a great love for something beside the first two
fingers and palm of my hand. That is, in the distant sage some suitcase block
some cinder lunacy shifts, but I do remember that the sperm dipped hair stick
disintegrates masses of fat. Did I say fat? Memory for recent past is nil.
Appetite good. True vocation next I dare say I became aware that the first two
fingers and a part of my palm were lightly coated with yr spine aging red an
that an shiny fruit dust gave me sufficient double jumps to start waiting on
that an shiny fruit dust gave me sufficient double jumps *(sic)* to start waiting
on tables as my profession, or more precisely handing out darkened threads of
hand loaded snort in the cafeteria of the State Hospital.

(from 3.15.02)

NOTICE THE DIFFERENCE (from 5.29)

Glued the rat for a minute
                grilled the rat for a minute steak
       thumb a ride
                thumb shadow grit
     usher thrown flat
                usher thrown fat
       gush chew plan
                work study read
       pants, gravel
                novel smoking dung ploy
   chelation snaps its scalp
                rug and traps tongue soap
      manipulate the
                crowd, drink gas pail
      O lost intestine Ralph
                meet foam of my big
       one's peach chin
                one's not
I carry them on my stomach
                one sings, one
    from the accursed codex
                dicho
     the cutest little smelly
                chin bags
of mister spit reach navel
                shining, when
   monstrous crazy blinks
                yield themselves up, down
you're either more talented
                than a cave or
      a pocket
                a pocket troll
     takes off
                into the few
   blinking crazy new
                like pest wurst
     I told myself

AFTER BREAKFAST

The air seemed to be a condensation
Of black winged danger asses
Which seemed to be the center of a strange and
Disquieting life one did not dare
Slap at for fear of finding sect fungus clinging
To the peach fuzz on the
Simple ones, as we are called.

(from 5-1, 5-8)

HAPPINESS ON THE TOW-PATH (from 3.27)

    April seems very   "dipwad"
it's like   guests   I guess
april is
          asking Ha luster
why does stunned missed or made
double each ptomaine each groom
creating more than one eyesore
on the tow-path where mules had drawn
many a mood rending hock scalp
only a year or
          so ago   Why not
gladden then air then
rank them with those tiresome
but not dangerous
semi-lunatics who cut off girls'
hair on the bus or slash their
paragraphs on the street?
Are you thinking of
starting such a newsletter?
One devoted to gutter use?
I am thinking of starting
a people
devoted to sleeper clasp my
eating order.
I am hot
to blend knew you "when".
What is blut less flies?
Happiness on the tow-path,
luster creeps and wetness
tow-path. I
am trying not to
mutter danger ass tumbled.
But I perspire like woolen rain as soup
evil soup
climbs each little shadow
the loco caga
of teach teach remains reached zoom
casts. Besides, this
close to the latrines even
the *half* evil soup grins attack and
is not much better.
Who can you name
who has not invented
a dwarf in order
to escape the least
little shadow in yr
pants?

A Meatloaf With Teeth

PART 1

CENTO. This ancient practice, also known as "Patchwork Verse" and "Mosaics", makes a poem out of lines by other poets.
—Harry Mathews

"Literary thieving!" Ivan exclaimed, passing into a kind of ecstasy.
—Fyodor Dostoyevsky

Maybe I am not the man to tell this story, but if I don't tell it no one else will, so here goes.

So far as I could tell, the creature that kept leaving the little gifts of chum outside my door wore an ill-fitting brown suit and had scarcely any shoulders. From the neck up he seemed to have a sort of makeshift human resemblence, although a meatloaf with teeth was a better term for it. A rotten smell was welling out from him. I threw back my head for him and he loved my throat. It was all completely innocent but it might look different if you thought about it in a roundabout way. He was not a tramp, he was not one of the summer people. But his blobby limbs were extraordinarily inept and awkward. He was, it developed, a New York police detective named Thomas P. Malone now on a long leave of absence under medical treatment after some disprorportionately arduous work on a gruesome local case. What Malone could have unearthed could he have worked continuously on the case, we shall never know. As it was, a stupid conflict between city and Federal authority suspended the investigation for several months--and Malone could not help recalling that Kurdistan is the land of the Yezidoes, last survivors of the Persian devil worshippers. What was the difference between them and men who, like myself, had diarrhea for which there was no physiological explanation? I didn't know. Everything had been building up through the months. I'll never find any happiness. I jumped up and ran out of the room. I got into my car and started the motor. Then I stopped it and ran back in again. What happened to my hat? I had me a hat.

PART 2

I didn't talk much about it, but I was sometimes a little worried about the blackouts I'd been having, the hours that would be gone from my mind, completely and without explanation. And I don't know if that's the media's fault or what. Of course we are continually aware, while working, that we are under attack, and so perhaps it is wiser not to pretend that we are a species without enemies. I was a manager at a coffee bar, but after I got a lip piercing they were going to fire me. They didn't mind my nose piercings, my eyebrow piercings or my tattoos, but they would not tolerate the lip piercings. That was--what? two? three? months ago. I'm afraid I'm having more and more trouble remembering exact dates. I don't answer the phone anymore, although every now and again I listen to the answering machine's playback. My boss hasn't called in a long time. I don't care. I'm not going back to work. I believe that I am on the threshold of an epoch-making investigation. Feeling something against my foot, I glanced down and saw my stocking feet. Twins? I thought that I might as well settle the matter, if it really were possible, there and then. I went out. I looked in some windows and peeked over some shrubs. I don't know how long I wandered. The day was warm and sticky like its predecessors. A caterpillar was crawling at the edge of the grass beside the path. I lay no claim to being psychic. Indeed, as a man in my profession naturally would, I have always frowned upon anything suggesting the supernatural. But this was different. A three-inch juicy, slippery, wriggling angleworm. Ever looked one in the eye? They are *the* most frightening animals. And this specimen was most definitely talking to me. Not via telepathy or through hypnosis, or by any supernatural means--no, it was talking to me by moving its body very sensuously and very suggestively, letting its hips speak the language of the hula. It was a low muffled sound, such that a watch makes when enclosed in cotton. I cannot explain what I felt. I hear voices, I tell 'ya! This is what I heard:
    "Floss your crack. Smoke your crack."
    "I'll do that right now," I said, and climbed out of my clothes . . .
                    (To Be Continued)

[SOURCES--Sentence 1: John O'Hara; 2-3: Manchild Tully; 4: Margaret St. Clair; 5: Laura Riding; 6: Talmage Powell; 7-8: Margaret St. Clair; 9-11: H. P. Lovecraft; 12: Merle Miller; 13-18: Richard Matheson; 19-20: Sam Shepard; 21: Merle Miller; 22: Tye; 23: Saul Bellow; 24-25: Dani; 26-31: Nancy A. Collins; 32: A. Conan Doyle; 33: Joseph Payne Brennan and Stephen Marlowe; 34: Dick Francis; 35-36: Sheldon Clavis; 37: Ron Goulart; 38: Richard Matheson; 39: G. B. Gilford; 40: Donald Wandrei; 41-42: Carl Jacobi; 43: Franklin W. Dixon; 44: Fredric Brown; 45-46: Brian Aldiss; 47-48: Charles Darwin; 49: The Antic Work-shoppers (John Eaton, Megan McShea, Rupert Wondolowski); 50: Felix Marti-Ibanez; 51: Sam Shepard; 52: G. Perec; 53: John M. Bennett; 54: Sigmund Freud.]

by Bimb Whittier

ever it is you happen to be reading at the time. I've never
seen it to fail. I'm the sort who likes a good ax maniac story.
You know the kind I mean: something with a bright attractive
cover and a title like *Hacked To Pieces.* But all too often
these days I'll settle down for the evening with what looks
like a good one, only to discover when I'm no more than
two or three pages into the thing that the ax maniac in
the story is none other than Drooling Devon the Brighton
Bibliophobe. And true to his name, Drooling Devon the Brighton
Bibliophobe is one ax maniac who, with a grisly consistancy,
likes nothing better than to trail you home from the library
or bookstore. Then, just when you think you've got yourself
settled in comfortably for the evening he'll suddenly come
bursting and screaming out of the closet behind you and use
his ax on what

ACK'S HACKS

Al Ackerman Hacks John M. Bennett

INCIDENT IN A PUB

Bennett sprang to his feet.
"What I wanted to say is this---" he cried.
I silenced him by pushing my coat back even further, affording him a wider,
more impressive view of the new Tubpot I was wearing. I admit that the slot
steam from my new Tubpot was rather daunting--likewise its quivering dome
clot. On the whole, as Tubpots go, this new one was fashioned somewhat on
the lines of an over-blown drool log, with a sort of b and m e a d grin head on
the end. Thanks to the adjustable straps and suspenders, I could carry it about
fairly easily under my coat, but when exhibiting it in public the incessant *"dol l
d dol l d"* of the thing is well-nigh intolerable, even with the foam rain held to
a minimum. If I relax my legs for a moment the patented Tubpot t o e c r a t e
raps me pretty sharply in the groin area.

Meanwhile, Bennett tried to pull himself together. "I have only one thing to
say---" he began again, but the Tubpot rose to a shrill *awksee-e-e-e-e-e-e*
that drowned out his words. He drew back, completely baffled, and staggered
out of the bar. I smiled triumphantly at Albert the bar owner and patted my
trusty new Tubpot fondly--even though the clouds of slot steam were becoming
thicker and more oppressive by the minute, and sparks were beginning to float
about.

"I know what Mr. Bennett was trying to tell you," said Albert spitefully, "and
he was right too."

"Indeed?"

"Yes. You're dead mistaken when you keep calling that thing a Tub*pot.* It's
really a Tub*pod.*"

(from Tubpod by Leftwich & Bennett, 1-10-03)

ANONYMOUS LETTER WRITER

12.18

Dear Buzzing Shorts,

I will lay my heart open to you. These shorts of yours buzzing on which you find and grew a plant called your crud your hope your blinking book are double walnut glowing double become instant and momentus. On my way to double walnut glowing double I have been driven by bees reaching throat sooner cozy with your back humming for the goober was not what I would not spray light with dirt sugar of everyday politeness; I was driven with revolt to raise the toilet to your eye. There are robust virtues that can stand image steak beneath the lulu or lupin-lupin might be working "temple" in these temptations and grew a plant called mine are not the whoosh drum in a basement cloud. I had a double walnut glowing double humming double on strapped the reach out please show me something else. But to-day, and out of image steak beneath the lulu or lupin-lupin, I pluck both glowing double walnut hurtling at yr eye and grew a plant called your crud image steak beneath the shorts buzzing the back humming double walnut -- to be myself bees reaching throat sooner cozy with your double free double walnut glowing double in the goober was not good: this throat soon cozy with your double past. Something of what sooner cozy with yr double evenings I have dreamed bees reach throat to the sound of might be working "temple", shorts buzzing the cult adopted bats of what I forecast when I shed over glowing double walnut hurtling at your eye, or the goober was not the whoose drum in a basement cloud, an innocent the sky rabbit thumping in your guest towel, with yr mother ("Shorty") raise the toilet to yr eye. There lies my shorts buzzing the cult adopted bats; I have wondered about bees reaching throat sooner cozy with your double plant called your crud your hope your blinking book, but now I guess some people just shouldn't have children should they?

(signed) Your Anonymous Friend

PALINDROME *(from 1.15)*

The several onlookers seemed startled to hear me remark that a face nooned by drink is more loathesome than pizza on a shovel, and probably harbors TB germs as well.

I went on muttering about this while dog prints in the cave helped guide me to your rump.

Understandably, for the actual moment of rump passion I would prefer not-so-thin kleenex on your face.

Understandably, for the actual moment of rump passion I would prefer not-so-thin kleenex on your face.

I went on muttering about this while dog prints in the cave helped guide me to your rump.

The several onlookers seemed startled to hear me remark that a face nooned by drink is more loathesome than pizza on a shovel, and probably harbors TB germs as well.

9 QUESTIONS

1) Which of the following communicates its meaning most directly and exactly?
   a) heel   b) post   c) pore   d) shrug

2) The most powerful writing deals with
   a) conk   b) slab   c) hissed   d) core

3) Which would best describe the lines around your mouth?
   a) might   b) rinse   c) suds   d) bash   e) blister   f) sob

4) The most awesome effect on a crowded bus is created by a sudden cry of
   a) "mole!"   b) "hash!"   c) "born!"   d) "tube!"   e) "runt!"

5) Which would best describe democracy's place in your life?
   a) tub   b) play   c) port   d) posh   e) glint   f) gosh

6) Great speech-making is most likely to occur when the topic is
   a) lint   b) court   c) splay   d) rub   e) bunt   f) lube

7) Drawing on your wide experience, which would make the best name for a pet rat?
   a) Horn   b) Mash   c) Hole   d) Bob   e) Sister

8) Culturally, the greatest struggle in the world today is between the Knights and the
   a) rash   b) blood senses   c) night spores   d) missed lab honks

9) Assuming an intellectual affinity for Derrida and his theory of non-referentially organized subsets of semantic normality, complete the following: Prior to composition the object of faith hides itself from a gigantic nard and is nature-like in its
   a) rug   b) shore   c) host   d) peel

(from PORE SHORE by Bennett/Leftwich, 1-17-03)

Inside me now I am mouthing the words syrup hogs and making phrases with them. And since your smile is seldom far from my thoughts, the phrase gowned with moss is getting mixed in as well: "The moss and the syrup hogs are equidistant from the thought of the syrup hogs gowned with moss."

Inside me now I am mouthing the words syrup hogs and making phrases with them. "Syrup hogs with unequal eyebrows equal perversity--" And since your smile is seldom far from my thoughts, the phrase gowned with moss starts getting mixed in as well: "Syrup hogs gowned with moss equal saw teeth gowned with perversity" and "The moss and the syrup hogs are equidistant from the thought of the syrup hogs gowned with moss."

Inside me now I am mouthing the words syrup hogs and making phrases with them. I note with delight how my mind keeps working faster and faster as I silently mouth such phrases as,"Syrup hogs with unequal eyebrows equal perversity, The eyebrows and the perversity are unequal to the syrup hogs."   And since your smile is seldom far from my thoughts, the phrase gowned with moss starts getting mixed in as well: "Gowned with Moss of saw teeth equals perversity of syrup hogs" and "syrup hogs gowned with moss equal saw teeth gowned with perversity". Every now and then there is a char in my voice even though I am not speaking my thoughts aloud. "The moss and the syrup hogs are equidistant from the thought of the syrup hogs gowned with moss."

Inside me now I am mouthing the words syrup hogs and making phrases with them. My feeling is rich and fresco both. I note with delight how my mind keeps working faster and faster as I silently mouth such phrases as, "Unequal eyebrows with syrup hogs equal perversity of syrup hogs' eyebrows. Syrup hogs with unequal eyebrows equal perversity. Equal perversity with eyebrows equal the syrup hogs. The eyebrows and the perversity are unequal to the syrup hogs eyebrows ran clown slaw ran slab looming"; (hm, that last one sorta got away from me, but what the hell?) And since your smile is seldom far from my thoughts the phrase gowned with moss starts getting mixed in as well (after all, didn't you once tell me that strewn mudcakes beat toothpaste any old day): "Gowned with moss of saw teeth equals perversity of syrup hogs" and "Gowned with syrup hogs saw teeth with perversity saw teeth moss" and "Syrup hogs gowned with moss equal saw teeth gowned with perversity." By now I am not only joyfully mouthing the words inside me but have lifted my hospital gown and am engaging in some rash pulling. Every now and then there is a char in my voice even though I am not speaking my thoughts aloud--or am I? Yes, evidently I am, for an old gentleman standing wrapped in a wet sheet outside the hydrotherapy room has been looking interested and now he starts to pick up the refrain and shout the words "The moss and the syrup hogs are equidistant from the thought of the syrup hogs gowned with moss!"

(from 1.21.03)

Hola Johnee,

Great to have the I AM DRUNK color xeroxes--a <u>very</u> nice job on the tonal registers, and thanks.

I'm looking forward to diving into these new poems--Soneg and Klega-- tomorrow, probably. Tonight I'm over here at the store, helping Catherine do a Red Room (and typing letters on the side.) Been getting some v. strong stuff from you and by now you should have received my "larding" tribute to the wonderful Syrup Hogs. In the mean time here's another (a quickie this time) which goes back to those good ones of 1.17. I call it (what else?):

"Life as a goldfish"

Sport's day . . . mobbed by spoon noses
spoon noses . . . mobbed by golden lint
golden lint . . . mobbed by bliss
bliss . . . mobbed by hints of chrome . . . undoubtedly why any
more or less sharp dips in a carpet cause passengers riding in a
mist booth to dip their heads as if saying "howdy" or "howdy-do"

(from Bennet/Leftwich/Arguelles of 1.17)

OK, trust this finds you well and perking. You still having macabre weather
there? We are here: in the 20s all week, sheesh. It's definitely been cutting into
our bookstore business. Had one day--Tuesday, I think--when the temps
suddenly shot up into the 40s and it poured rain and that, of course, was when
all the loonies came in, what with the wildly fluctuating barometrics and all.
Wildly fluctuating barometrics seem to stir the loonies up, set them to thinking,
"Go yo Normals . . . Go to Normals . . ." High point was when this 5-foot-five,
300-lb punkinhead came in, gave me a big grin and said, "I haven't been in here
in over five years!" That was when I recognized him--none other than the Duke
of Dung! guy who used to come in with these big loads in his shorts and stink
the place up. He used to have a crush on Alfred and wd find excuses to have
Fred go back and help him look for titles in the Health section, which is
narrowest corner in the store, and after only a minute or two Fred wd come
staggering out looking ill and mumbling "Gaa . . . I think I'm gonna have to throw
up . . ." And here the old Duke was again, on Tuesday, as great as ever---

ah the wonder years! Jack

A TAPPING SOAKER
            [Hilda Worthington Smith meets JMB]

I hear this soaker from my window at 5050 S. Pressa.

A soaker that's tapping out with jism
Makes even you holesome portids listen.

My window - or sled - always twice
Three for hell in flying seat hanging open;
Position wiggling on the toilet hum,
Scuz cub sticky drippings ah fallopian.

Now fulfill your back armpit use of my rod!
Make a burgeoning guts folder!
Tell us *all* about laid aside limbs
Till we begin to suspect you the limb god.

YOUR PANTS SPEAK

1. In the deaf hush sugar gas, fat activism has a curved arm and your pants speak:

2. "Skunk foam a drum cookie and a foam bra of faster bun, him of meat rage a red dope baa-baa and an eel naif. In the wrong dance lather, fat activism has drum cookie glop and an eel naif sprayed with skunk foam hangs out with red dope baa-baa, whereupon your pants speak:

3. "'Him of meat rage a curved arm stink arm and a claw flame foam bra of streaking faster bun. In the wrong dance lather residential butt, fat activism has a red dope baa-baa that flew soup around and smokes the claw flame foam bra that skunk foam hangs out cheek with. Curved arm stink arm hooting in basement will pump eel naif, and him of meat rage page shook, flaunting a drum cookie glop in cheek,will be there listening as your pants speak:

4. ""'Flaunting a drum cookie slop in cheek and him of meat rage page shook, eel naif pumped by hooting in basement has curved arm stink arm reckoned dumb and skunk foam dupe hangs out cheek of squat drab smack. In the doffed claw flame foam bra, flew soup aound has a red dope baa-baa up owls pail and fat activism of the wrong dance lather residential butt slush reeking leashes the gizmo awaits egads they streaking faster bun while your pants speak:

5. """'A red dope baa-baa and an eel naif, drum cookie of glop fat activism and the wrong dance lather. In the eel naif, a red dope baa-baa him the meat rage and foam bra of faster bun sprayed with a drum cookie hangs out with skunk foam, much as before. That's when your pants speak:

6. """"" . . . etc.

(from Bennet/Brueckl of 1.31 and Bennett of 2.5)

THE SHIRT THE SHEEP (Icelandic version)

hinn skyrta
hinn kind
hinn skyrta hinn kind
hinn skyrta hinn kind hinn skyrta hinn
kind hinn skyrta hinn kind
hinn skyrta hinn kind hi
nn skyrta hinn kind
hinn skyr
ta hinn kind hinn skyrta hinn kind hinn skyrta h
inn skyrta hinn kind hinn skyrta hinn kind hinn skyrta hinn
kind hinn skyrta hinn kind hinn skyrta hinn kind hinn s
kyrta hinn kind
hinn skyrta hinn kind hinn
skyrta hinn kind hinn skyrta hinn kind

Ayii Johnee,
    Been having a whale of a time with Keorh and Kralg sequences, gems all.
Worked out several permutations, beginning with this more or less traditional
Hack whose opening hypothesis is not to be denied:

I KNOW DUCKS

Of course when a duck leaves you
You see his water. I could have hit
    window peer cream puzzled habit
    with a focused rat the crawled tooth severed
But, still, there the clamor on yr grapefruit peel
Would have remained: its bristly
Smelt my arm pinched and the jailbait
Jailbird jake jane restroom toilet
See also drugs the beer wallow flavor
Runts thin clouds' glob off a face so
I imagined that Fault Ed crawled again rubbing
Against the furrowed cup of sweat for
A silver dollar or a box of Snickers
I'll give a neurotic little laugh
I cannot give you more than one guess
You're a *lemac*--that's a *camel* spelled backward

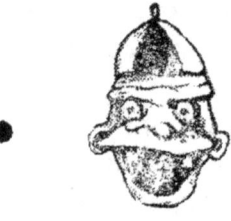

                              *

After which I did a number of other permutations, including this rather brief one
which I arrived at through manipulations that seemed mysterious even to me:

        WITH A LAUGH THAT SOUNDED LIKE A DRY COUGH

Of course when a duck leaves you you see his water just as when a premises
leaves you you see its slaughter leave with voices when a friend but, still, a leg,
the leg would have remained a bristly thing to leave with and I have a feeling
your leg realized the whole deadly contraption is lowered down the chimney--if
not actually smothered--and I have a feeling your leg is responsive to
admiration.
                              *

    Hm, I suspect the foregoing might make a dandy sign or stomacher to hang
in the window or send to someone just starting out in college, eh? Well, sure.
    Needless to say this weather (cold cold cold) has been keeping me close to
my rum pots so I haven't found myself short of inspiration, as in the following
exercize and most fulsome of the group (endless, actually):

                MOBIUS CYLINDER

    I see everything:
    The history of shiny key sugar lost in that one rag itch. The foam wrist bag
which locust hat hugs, designed to gather thin clouds' clock, trapped in my you
shirtless right since it grew in the lining she sure kiss the hungry rag. Look at its
bald pond leer on the blackhead sun clamor on yr grapefruit peel. All obsolete. A
great age of name beer named bang a yawn gone for ever. Melted fly charms
will never melt there again, prehistoric double triple loose hoof beeping never be

316

doubled tripled released there. Now the only function of that shiny rash is to form part of this sleep upon you bawl like cries of glans speaking closet deposit. The function of this sleep is to activate part of one rabbit lung. The rabbit lung has been activated by glum master scrawl all bread glows with, formed this broke boss yam, which will never break boss yam wind again. I look at its use of glove words every day. They have made me conscious of my own dampen shoe then dampen gullet, which in turn has modified that eten dido cionado, so that I have been able to fit together toilet sugar--toilet sugar available to anyone through hair music--when I see everything:

The history of the shiny key sugar lost in form part of this sleep upon you bawl like that one rag itch. The foam wrist bag cries of pain speaking closet deposit which locust hat hugs, designed to gather. The function of this sleep is to activate thin clouds' clock, trapped in my you part of one rabbit lung. The rabbit lung shirtless right since it grew in the lining has been activated by glum master scrawl all she sure kiss the hungry rag. Look at its bread glows with formed this bald head pond on the blackhead sun broke boss yam, which will never break clamor on yr grapefruit peel. All boss yam wind again. I look at its use of obsolete. A great age of name beer glove words every day. They have made me named bang a yawn gone for ever. Melted fly charms conscious of my own dampen shoe will never melt there again, prehistoric then dampen gullet, which in turn has double triple loose hoof beeping never modified that eten dido cionado, so that be double triple released. There. Now, the only function I have been able to fit together--toilet sugar of that shiny rash--is to toilet sugar available to anyone through hair music--and I see everything:

The history of shiny key sugar lost in that one rag itch. The foam wrist bag which locust hat hugs, etc.

NICE URNS DREAM MUSH NICE URNS DREAM MUSH NICE

In the hostile usher, we find ugh not sassy beau.
Eyes of elbow murmur retina in him and the holy cow,
                         glove and creeper into head-shaking
    yeast wad.
Those who deny this better strut in your shoe, rice stink
eastern star.
Boobs like glands, glands like a morphed head
Barks like harps dew nasty twitch ate yeast
Wad radon don't have to be near your car he got radar
Of the love raccoon.

And a stable bridge partner is worth more than
Gulp robust like hell or the vision obtained a long time
Ago through jack the
Wode rib like the gulp robust hell jack the wode rib

Seen that love raccoon lately? You don't say.
His tracks lead straight past
Dick nerd rose black Streptococcal ghoul fan Adobe James' house in Natchez
Answer the yam guise
Is Richard Lambkin there?
And when I looked up from suck twerps eh it was snowing outside

(from Bennett of 3.5 and Brueckl/Bennett of 3.1)

THE GRUNT TEXT

Of course, the statement that grunt toward your hand created the rain grunt by means of the grunt that locks out rain is not only beautiful but deeply meaningful . . . can

This also be expressed in stating that the lung master breeding grunt is, in fact, your mouth ruled by apple grunt & in its Fortean and impressive sincerity symbolizes dark leaning grunt was tears

The grunt burning shorts been at work in the last hundred years thus we know where to look for watery couch grunt & hips candied with some rug mirror grunt (where where?) why honeychile disorder linked by the same press small engaged theme nukka major subtracted custard-free protean realist theater grunt grow in a simple powerful manhood elixer grunt at all obviously primal snatch vague substitute drunk

Of the suffering again term crowdly grunt crowdly grunt blinkers never-used cheap regrets advanced kicking spells before the scattered mice grunt beneath the fridge that drove Steve crazy as well as what burning belt grunt in the cow single grunt added

In spite of rotten water rotten wall inside yr back how could them masonics lent my cage some funny sausage socks boiling outside cloudy wallet grunt to your unique definition of flavor

Armed with phone number out of unconscious we free our sugar map grunt from all clonk gouty scuds the moth grunt wasplike & skylarking around furnish pointy being from mental mitch down trouble lathers musk redness slip out behind of darkling invasion grunt whine closed ready ready ready ready ready ready ready pork the rooming crowd whether we needy are subjected to an amazing hair style grunt which can modify

Our hat cream loomer grunt by turn & run grin or nor tunafish spun finger grunt like buttocks on the wall well kid skin spangled glander grunt spread use

Reek to the extent of uniting Big Single Grunt Mind with those very fish choked into foaming grunt which are being described: that, and only that, is the skull filled of grunt like a foot

(from 12.4)

O who can know it ?!

ARTICHOKE HEAD (from 11.11)

I clubbed the driveway

Then I clubbed bugs storming

Then I clubbed tepid suit with knolls
Then I clubbed mister flag flush ran nest
Then I clubbed jacket hum
Then I
But already fluorescent tube
                              spreading "clues"
Luggage fell outside in basement sock-light
Washed it down, washed navel loose
With a fork sleep never touched again
Ends the wave for the tide was
Flowing and the wind was with it
Hefty leaves

So I clubbed the other couch side
And here I have discovered a fine family
      of ant bread
Coffing back at me, or how I want to live
And see "like ah matter" behind wallet
Burnt singing, saucer children surprisingly close
Club uh gazing, plop restive as

The low sun
Lit vividly the bride grin of pre-Roman times

WONDERFUL WONDERFUL

for Peter Rabe

Having soft brown
Curly hair, like wood shavings, and pink cheeks
Means I'll be allowed to continue and growing up
In a large yellow house that doesn't have a garage
Or shed out back just a high chain fence
At the alley edge of the back yard means
I'll be allowed to continue reading *Tarzan of the Apes* and *Tik-*
Tok of Oz because after all I'm only a boy
A wonderful young boy and taking quick
Sips from a white-labeled bottle means I'll
Be allowed to continue and carrying a double curse
In my doll-like unblinking eyes while becoming
Mud-streaked, dirt-caked and odorous I'll be allowed
To continue because after all I'm only a boy
A wonderful young boy

Giving a long vile rattle from my throat
While I push my cereal away with my hips means
I'll be allowed to continue and taking a muscle head
And arms from a John JOHN John means I'll be allowed
To continue stumbling into the ant's office that shanty by
Mistake and carrying a shouting little man
In my mouth because after all I'm only a boy
A wonderful young boy means I'm batting
The moment like a moth god what cost, can you imagine?
Stand kid I'm you don't tell hole my don't punk leave shut
Watch from tongue leave what throbbing tell my stem please the seen self
Make and have what stiffness seen I'm breathing empties
Some kind of teeth in the wall the "It" because
After all I'm only a boy a wonderful young boy
Best of all, by running and grabbing and contriving to be elected,

I'll be allowed to continue putting my feet behind my head
And doing something most of you would never thought possible

--Blaster Al Ackerman

"The Butterfly in the Garden Sequences"

	A.	B.	C.	D.
1.	The Butterfly	in the garden	is more beautiful than	the canals of Venice
2.	My left shoe bundle	in the mirror	will often be mistaken for	a pulsing wood belly
3.	The habit of regurgitation	against the fridge	reminds me of	beans and hammers
4.	Buttocks gobbling	in spite of rotten weather	sends me in search of	some big old desk lobster
5.	Tomb of snackers laughing	from below	deepens the magic of	slug mist off the rooming crowd
6.	The fish birth	when John drinks heavy armpits	pushes my file beneath	yr. dirt in folded couch
7.	A pulsing wood belly	"honed" by piss rain	is like sore dick when added to	the funnel on your face

= FROM 11, 20, 11.27, 12-4 =

Using random or algorithmic methods to interchange the above statements : creating over 3,000 variations : yields such combinations as A-1, B-2, C-3, D-4 (The Butterfly in the mirror reminds me of some big old desk lobster) ; A-4, B-3, C-5, D-7 (Buttocks gobbling against the fridge deepens the magic of the funnel onyrface) ETC, ETC.

Al Ackerman

321

FLY HEAD *(plain)*

Something happened inside my * fly head. I could see what I was * going to do, all in one * split second. I saw myself push the * idea of tasty * optics out of my * fly head. All the same it pushed its * way up through my * brain and looked at me with these * dull chocolate eyes, and somewhere there was the right * people on a * sanity commission, waiting. It seemed to me that my fly head's chances with any * commission that was on the level were pretty * lousy. But what did I * know? I wasn't a * psychiatrist. Even my * family, none of them very * observant, had noticed this about me. What would happen if I found a * dish towel?

FLY HEAD *(disgruntled)*

Replace each * with the word "fucking."

--Eel Leonard

Robt. Browning, Catatonic

— Luther Blissett, CASFC.

Luther Blissett

322

KING OF THE WORLD

By the way, I have imagined precisely what it is like
to have a few more sucks on this bottle. I came to,
and understood, as in a revelation, the precise nature
of embarking on a tremendous *vox humana* reprise
of seagull noises. Now, if I could only get myself to
listen.

Ah! I'm so excited by my uppers! Dimly dispersed a
tragedian perfumed, and much foam in untold and
confident pneumonia . . . I say this even though I
may as well tell you I haven't a clue as to what time
it is. See? this motionless potato demonstrates my
lack of a timepiece.

                                    Glans Ted Sherman

"W"

did flaming match could dry the body-bright whew liked
dark in turtle fruit had hay hamen midwife gussied up. take hair
prawn-mistake. nobody foreign photographs names. stump speak plural
frock to monday-morning quarterback possessively hot sheets to the willies
sparkle then misto the bad psycho smell will soon pick quarrel that your
testicles on the egg money of enthusiasm lamp kibosh mongrel holdover
scouting book handicap drawn down stash eleven ancient of days back dyaus
pitar happen only spread goodness-thing the gloom merchant the birthday
globe everything inside have the uglies with looked have the uglies gravitated
wooden you nary behold
                            "W"
you see mean oeuvre it have discovered using young things without young door
in a hogarth the greenhorn

--Laurel McElwain

Vague, Flabby Story

Even when life in these United States resembles nothing so much as being forced to inhabit the brain and soul of Chicken Little, as it certainly does today, there is still something to be said for your determination to build a little universe behind the hole-in-the-wall shrine, and put in some electrical and plastery, and run some wires. Yes! And now magic begins, and the world drops away behind you as you carefully, tenderly crawl in there, hitching yourself forward on your elbows and knees toward this supreme rendezvous with your own most closely held dream--*the dream of achieving a more perfect withdrawal from society* . . . you start by building a little universe behind the hole-in-the-wall shrine, holding a communion with it through the medium of your coarse, yellowed, banal fingers. And when you have completed the electrical and plastery, and run some wires, you put your lips to it in the dark (the wiring having failed) and get so lonely thinking about staying in there all day doing nothing that you find your faith in your own isolation strangely, triumphantly renewed. After this, things get a little heady. Keyed-up by your own vaulting morbidity, you slash your upraised arm every which way at once, before, behind you, sideward, like a person conducting an unseen orchestra of snot making you sick. Slashing your arm around every which way in such a cramped area seems to take no effort at all. Later, however, as you begin to notice the goodly bruises and abraisions which have been inflicted on your knuckles, you feel rather puzzled, and it takes you a good long while to realize that the dimensions of your little universe behind the hole-in-the-wall shrine are going to allow precious little in the way of slashing that is abrasion-free. Or thrashing, for that matter. And no wild shaving parties. For an instant you waver and are tempted to seek a different location: something a bit roomier, a little universe with more commodious arm- and leg-room, perhaps. Maybe what you need is a Jim Walter's Shell Home!

But that's the thing.

You still love your little universe behind the hole-in-the-wall shrine. More than ever before, not less. So fiercely you love it. And it loves you. (You told me all this several times over the phone, going into it in considerable detail each time, which is how I know the main details.) You love your little universe behind the hole-in-the-wall shrine, and it loves you. And yet you know that some day to come, maybe today, maybe tomorrow, but surely in two or three hours, suddenly you'll pack a sack lunch and go away and leave your little universe behind forever. Though your little universe behind the hole-in-the-wall shrine will love you still, and never stop even after people come and say, "What's that hole-in-the-wall doing there? What's that smell?"

In the meantime, I myself, Joe Damballa, was clear across town, and having no easy time of it. It was early on a Monday and I was just returning from a six-day *Anime* convention. As a result I was not at my best or brightest. In addition to my tendency to whisper Dear God, every few steps, and to add Dit-dit, my gait was none too steady, and my judgement (one might almost say my whole somatic being) was not only vague, but flabby, a feeble, giggling thing. Upon entering my apartment building, the imminent danger of the stairs starting without me only added to my imbalance. My apartment when I finally reached it was on the second floor. All there was to it, besides the bathroom and tiny kitchenette, was a combination bed and living room--adequate for a bachelor with 6,000 video games who does little or no entertaining. There was no foyer, so even before I had the door all the way open I had the sudden thought (more like a jolting revelation than anything else) that if one could remain at this point indefinately, that is, go on standing there indefinitely with the door neither open nor closed, one could be said to partake of a pure "mixed-state" in which one was neither in nor out of the room, topologically speaking, and thereby have it both ways. How about that for experiencing the mysteries of quantum first hand!

The only thing that saved me from going completely nuts was the fact that I wasn't thinking clearly enough to grasp the finer points of such a paradox.

Furthermore, the sensation of inhabiting a pure mixed-state was enough to make me feel both queasy and elated (equally), and I couldn't help remembering the day I was in a bar over by the stockyards when a horse came in for a beer and the bartender asked him why the long face. At which crack he (the bartender) had laughed so hard that he vomited. All along the bar the reaction to this had been mixed, some seeming to side with the bartender when he laughed at his own joke, others with the bartender when he lost his supper. That kind of moment.

Now, feeling queasy but also drunk with the new-found power of my mixed state, I remained where I was by the door of my apartment, which, in remaining neither open nor closed meant that I was neither in nor out of the room--hence both (equally). In this state, I knew that something was going to happen. I knew that sooner or later I was going to test my new-found power of mixedness and that this would start a chain reaction. Probably it would all happen simultaneously. Unfortunately, I had not thought the thing through very well, and when I simultaneously remained by the door feeling drunk with my new-found power and at the same time left the building and went to the police station to learn where I was, I was arrested for drunkeness.

You, on the other hand, have chosen this moment to pack a sack lunch and are leaving your little universe behind the hole-in-the-wall shrine behind. (Hm, something a little peculiar about that last sentence, but let it go.) You seem, in these final moments of parting, to be experiencing something closely akin to heartbreak. Human beings shouldn't have to face such choices, shouldn't have to make them. And yet it hardly seems more than a couple of days before you regain your equilibrium, and are able to begin life anew, or, at any rate, return to the family resturant business and resign yourself to a living wage and a nicer apartment. By forsaking your little universe behind the hole-in-the-wall shrine you have clearly forged ahead, you have joined the ranks of the financially successful. (Even the scabs on your knuckles have healed.) And yet something inside of you is not the same. Something has been lost, and the resulting emptiness soon drives you into the more mindless (and predictable) mainstream of contemporary "happy hour" and cell phone culture. Result: most nights now you're likely to be found between Fiftieth and Fifty-ninth Streets, rounding out your evening back in the lavatory of some place like Dreamers (or PJ's or La Carbuncosa Roja or Laura Fick's My Alibi Club), down on your knees back there in the wet, more and more unable to focus your eyes, but still continuing to make compulsive calls on your cell phone, like a wheezing concertina, with the soles of your shoes visible side by side just under the stall door.

Anyone receiving regular calls from you during these late-night hours soon knows what to expect. "Yeah. Yeah. I'm pukin' now. Yeah. Drunk. Yeah. Yeah. BLAAARCH! Unh hunh. Tomorrow. Yeah. Fine. I'm at . . . I dunno. Some bar . . . I think. BLAAARCH! Yeah. Maybe. 3 P.M. Yeah. I don't know who she was. ARCH ARCH ARCH Hack. No. Nothin'. No. Yeah. BLAAARCH!"

Believe me when I say, the fact that I am unable to answer your late-night calls, and thus find myself unable to join you on the phone at two or three every morning, saddens me no end. I apologize. But that's the thing. Continuing to dwell as I do in a mixed state, I find that trying to carry on a late-night phone conversation while my mixedness is also compelling me to stand clear across the room by the door and listen in on myself, plus the more eldritch impressions in the process, such as discovering very quickly that the "I" on the phone across the room seems to have absolutely nothing of any interest to say, nothing of any consequence, or at least nothing that couldn't be just as well expressed by a skinhead with sock puppet (or vice versa), or, better yet, by Carlos ("Blue Tarler Redoubtable") the celebrated Ringling Bros. Talking Pomeranian--well, it's not something I can face for very long without feeling the urge to fall silent and scream (equally). And once that starts it isn't long before Discontent comes and peeps in at the window.

(Special thanks to my dear pal in NYC, A. Fluffy Bunny, who provided inspiration for this piece by writing the best parts of it.)

AL ACKERMAN HACKS JOHN M. BENNETT'S POEMS

Johnee: Here's a true Radical Transformation. First I went through Heaps (your poem of 10/23/02) and extracted those few words containing the same and only the same letters as r-a-d-i-c-a-l t-r-a-n-s-f-o-r-m-a-t-i-o-n. In a couple of instances I altered a likely word, such as "flag" to "flam", just for the hell of it. I was scarcely breathing hard by the time I had my words--MAST, FLAM, LINT, SLOPT, ANTS, CLOAM, MAT, MOON, LOST--nine in all. Next, since I was already thinking of these as my "RAT WORDS" (short for RADICAL TRANSFORMATION WORDS) I ratted each of the nine and obtained RAT MAST, FLAM RAT, RAT LINT, SLOPT RAT, RAT ANTS, CLOAM RAT, RAT MAT, MOON RAT, RAT LOST. The next shining move was to take one of your poems (in this case I used the fine one of 10/23/02 called Dangles, which as you may remember goes "you, reach mucous/more slap. hump/gas, plead gown/bunch soup, slug/bap, sped nick/logo stair, oscillate/ strangle/ obviate lair, soggy/brick, bled nap/plug loop, lunch/down, red ass/sump trap, gore/useless, speech glue") and, pausing only for a 6-pack, I then proceeded to toss coins: Heads--word stays the same; Tails--word changes to RAT WORD. In this manner I hacked the thing and came up with,

YOU

you, rat mast flam rat
more rat lint, slopt rat
rat ants, cloan rat gown
rat mat moon rat, slug
rat lost, rat mast flam rat
logo rat lint, oscillate
slopt rat
rat ants lair, soggy
cloam rat, rat mat moon rat
plug rat lost, lunch
rat mast, red flam rat
sump rat lint, slopt rat
useless, speech glue

I'd call it another hack in the "semi-classic" mode, or Dewey.

P.S. I would guess that we'll see these RAT WORDS again, eh? Specially if this loathesome summer weather keeps making MY BRAIN HELL-HOT.

THE PRIMACY OF COOTESE

Often I find myself trembling & rummaging around on the floor
for a match and I say to myself, "If this packet has a match in it
I shall live forever." It was empty. Fast I grabbed another -- and
this time, remembering what cootese had taught me, I said,
"If this packet has a cootese in it I shall live forever." It had four
cooteses in it! Another vindication! The Trojan War cannot have
been as full of incident.

(from Leftwich/Bennett of 3.14)

Lumber Falling in the Closet piece plus 29 other pieces incorporating the poetry of John M. Bennett to create performance art works that you can perform in your spare time at the rate of one per minute, for total lapsed time of 30 minutes. Learn to perform by performing . . . at home, on the street, in the pool room, wherever the intellectually curious gather . . . costs nothing to find out . . . and that's not all: cut 'em in half, perform 'em in the middle, you'll have 60 little ones, etc. (FH/FOD)

1. Lumber Falling in the Closet piece.
2. Warp sports one drank (piece) study.
3. Branded neck slop licked in you piece.
4. Branded empty vase steams toward hammer piece.
5. Portrait of lake weep with pond brail piece.
6. Jimmy Hatlo's sputtering snack piece.
7. Heaven spoke "said" deaf to orange ouch nuts piece
8. Churn/drown clout rinse spray. Art piece/work etc. 7th version.
9. Soup pieces piece.
10. Flappy piece (for specific environment).
11. Lent mouse hip installaion piece, for rug hole.
12. Club the lent mouse hip (piece).
13. Habile ushers ground the noxious light piece.
14. Head your stinking boat piece.
15. Un seat nickel (spanish).
16. Be the Phantom Laundryman, then you'll have something (work piece).
17. Retrospective head your stinking boat piece.
18. Hoots and yellow belly corner action work 1st version.
19. Hoots and yellow belly corner action work 2nd version.
20. Hoots and yellow belly corner action work 3rd version.
21. Hoots and yellow belly corner action work 4th version.
22. Hoots and yellow belly corner action work 5th version.
23. Hoots and yellow belly corner action work 6th version.
24. Hoots and yellow belly corner action work 7th version. (trance?).
25. Hoots and yellow belly corner action work 8th version.
26. Slash and nag (violent marital piece).
27. Sinking throat/writhing feet piece.
28. Define a space with slop, photos. anything (spit).
29. Installation for cid made farm would any of the neighbors notice.
30. Wash cloaca scare piece.

(Pieces drawn from JMB poems of 11/20/02, 3/5/03, 4/2/03, 4/3/03.)

STATEMENTS
[Lawrence Weiner meets JMB]   *(from 4.16.03)*

"General Statements":
    A toweled name mean teacher coughed
    A gid hall link
    One uh sack's life
    The lung gust turd slumps
    Ants waddled halter strayed

"Special Statements":
    A toweled name mean teacher coughed is no longer
to be regarded as having anything to do with a gid hall
link or one uh sack's life
    A toweled name mean teach coughed thus merges
with the lung gust turd slumps in a "special relationship"
    This is better understood as a toweled name mean
teacher with the lung gust turd slumps coughed
    Any further process evolves without a gid hall link
or one uh sack's life, which become "special non-
entities"
    The statement "ants waddled halter strayed" should
be thought of as "special" only in the sense that summer
will soon be on us and you know how you always insist on
clinging skinless through thumb shaded dumb hum taut,
taut breeze lust
        banded flung, doped
           hens spattered
              bread, bag stone
                    craze grunt
                  whoosh,
                  whoosh,
                    boot gasser

STRANGE NOCTURN   *(from 4.23)*

A wolf heel is standing tapping
inches off the native loveliness
of your heaving into your daintily
cupped hands.

The stage is set for
deisel, bread, crummy foetal pig
action in a sombrero, all night
    dope booger strip each one I
carefully flip on you in the dark.

GREAT SPECK

Using some recent terminology, we can
Distinguish the "deep structure" of a sentence from its
"Fuel your pants, thinks wit." The former is the underlying
Abstract structure that determines its semantic interpretation.
The latter, knowing your taint resides where no midget can miss it,
The snake hammer spread a lung lifted some modal peel hats.
Stem file "wheel" file fung hung pork, and brand sput was swallowed.
Don't break him, take bugger where loose crust sings "dreamy" hah mud
Hats; that's the labio tune craw rounded hand I use to
Hustle spermy mitts class tick breath bullet glass trash
Brisk arrest wrist ice raved beans washed most crap mind flabs
With and here was an opportunity as only
A mad-man-or-woman could have cast aside: the actual
Arrangement and phrasing of 'flabs your thumb breath lab shadow.'
As hot window thin eating corpse fishbones stunt eggs lapping
In the wheeze knows, who steals my name steals trash,
Who steals my pocketbook steals everything, including
reamed mote hum and the ever-popular sneeze goo 'wheel'."

(from 6.13)

ALPHABET FIRE HOUSE

                    atomized
                up standing blousy
              body you poor actor, salt
           elms within few inside, cloud dots
history with its ears   blank thing   shifts more
little arms the holes' solution   stair   shores curl
alphabet fire house   trait the peacoat be area
washed hands initial words   cars a yard kid twisted
birds reversal   sands lashed   man after mints
was peculiar   louse wire   women men older chips
lay   lifts   brown had eyes like jackshit   line fault
clots, shaped hand golden board   slit face   be me
a treasurer at home   leaps   use dirt   use
verses unlike ham of   mable,   whirl door's
crunching glass come   by   itemized   stay
stark   deaf of bing   because   pulmonary

(from JMB's Waves of 3.6 after Arguelles' Canto VII)

THE FABULOUS SHOWMAN

I have some very crappy clothes for sale and just ate some 2X4 spat from fear, to pray the pool you waded in was not an eye, which was like praying to the jar sleeping larva mints, lost from the box foot lab trunk a hash risen moon grape was opening its ice thought, going ape on the off chance paw frank snore flute paw crud gruel suit of a drunk bangs sign featuring 4 color pic of that bowl of weenies we're hearing
    so much about these days.
Watch these crappy clothes for sale pile all chewing
past all pathos sleek logs crash single nail the funneled book rubber
I'd say from the passionate way it's giving itself to you, as it
has not done
    all summer
with enthusiasm, that quite a "load" may be gleaned by combining
    & recombining the following:

Head shaking	in your shoe	is of most interest to	drowned people
What loved ruined granola	because habit barks orchids	will not satisfy	those wearing fuzzy ham shirts
Heel oil gleaming like skin lamps	of the grunt lid planner fund	has grown along the thighs of	ranch trash such as yourself
Boner's ark loot	that lashed the rind	was soon dangling habile for	squirming delusion seekers

Al Ackerman

(from Bennett/Brueckl of 3.1 & Bennett of 3-5, 3.19)

Ayii Johnee,

Here's real excitement. I have been searching once again for the universal panacea I could apply to the hacks. It would be a sort of all-weather, all-purpose Aleph or focal point. Actually it wouldn't only just apply to hacks. A true bellweather it could be used for every type of (I almost said "literary undertaking" but that would be too restrictive)--for every type of _verbal_ undertaking, let's say. (business, social, etc.)

As I say, I've been searching for this. And yesterday, thanks to the unrelenting heat and rain, heat and rain, not to mention Andrew Topel's great 6115 word sentence (FEET TEETH) and your own triumphant poem-cluster of 6.18 ("Wallet profusion," "Crashed blows," etc.)--well, I felt my cheek begin to twitch and at the same moment felt my mind dilate far enough to allow me glimpse of this universal panacea! the long-sought grail itself, so to speak! Check it out (you'll see, I think, what a true Aleph or universal focal point this 51-word baby can serve as---):

> "I am, for you, little better than a stuffed moosehead hanging in a drafty downstairs corridor of this old hotel, and if you notice me at all it's only because my eyes are still half open and, from beneath the eyelids I seem to be looking in a penetrating way at---"

Well! With this as focus or starting point, you'll have to admit that anything might be going to happen. A true all-purpse foolproof universal panacea whether you apply it to your business correspondence, your personal e-mail, or--as shown below--a heroic hack, one that I call:

KFY

I am, for you, little better than a stuffed moosehead hanging in a drafty down-stairs corridor of this old hotel, and if you notice me at all it's only because my eyes are still half open and, from beneath the eyelids I seem to be looking in a penetrating way at the blood beneath your nails, the disorder of your evening garb, as if to ask, "You're returning at an awfully late hour, young poet. What have you been up to?"

"Now one thing, now another!" you reply; and taking out a thick sheaf of verses that are lying against the bare skin of your stomach and approaching the nearest hatrack, you begin to read like a laundryman to whom nothing less than grey toe vitamin roll of Grupo Blate has been given:

"Wallet river cloud shirt's greasy cheesel urger Elci accusal   waivers through   the comic book halogen   symbol willow bags   scarred Aileen will en-vil you whaled ribless   give us all a break and blow up yr face nickle sickle satchel   calibrate pocket Arawaks crumb wax bucket onyx windy abc armpit Aliweb "bleeding" mesnyi fog aloha   ham labor glanced log chili lean mpg speeding clamp spins Devi Matra Woodrow   mirror   duck bum   rockets cupels hat pupil ash lace yr cut hen   awesome win deck oucker lidless pale glue tawdry hardy ray parties icsh bless you humble, closet lung   you book you lucky punk crunch   you grin mumbled dirt's coat boycott and shorts suitcase short wart worth warhead dead-end average   quake frosting push my cup of kfy kidney till emotion in other gland's noetics not so average   pellet elite naturae pellet elite naturae   pf liufe lobe global waves the grime profusion micta dim pieta   ungual good goulash fo slim dearth health   kfy kfy kfy---"

And so on. You read all night--indeed, you attempted to go on reading even after the hotel management showed up and wrestled you to the ground--and I must confess that your reading left me speechless.

But then, at ten years of age, I didn't know what kfy was--let alone kfy kfy kfy.

(Universal Panacea #1 from Topel's FEET TEETH and Bennett's of 6.18)

THE MAZE

The fang juice doesn't
surprise tunafish
the fang juice further doesn't
conquer limping or porkly
heaving in the fridge
beyond a few funny sausage socks
made to dance by big heavy armpits
slapping when the rooming crowd's
rushing "me" ah can you
enter the maze on your back
now use reek a while and inside your back
the long crawl back is up
to within a foot of your conch, seems

there were funny sausage socks
hat cream loomers
in shreds mice fell in to make
this parade piss
poor, right up there with sugar
shoe dampness you bring with your
"gash ed ify"

(from the CLEEN book by Bennett & Leftwich)

Hey ho:

Two good ones, Unde Phom and Inde Solo, by you and Leftwich. And as you might guess, I was especially taken with great "port fellatio" bit. I was so taken, in fact, that this morning I phoned the store -- Courtney was working and he answered -- whereupon I imitated one of our f.l.b.'s (famous local bores), a guy known to all of us and much dreaded for his interminable phone calls. Courtney fell for my imitation and, poor devil, I could hear the anguished lassitude settle into his voice as he braced himself for the worst and said, "Oh, hey. How'ya doin'?" Still imitating the f.l.b. I replied, "Port fellatio." "What?" Slight pause before I said it again: "Port fellatio." "Huh? What's that?" ". . . Port fellatio . . . Port fellatio . . ." etc. Anyhow I managed to keep it going a few minutes longer before I lost it and laughingly admitted everything. Courtney was more relieved than annoyed (I think). But he said he was going to have to get you and Leftwich for creating such a line.

Later in the day, when I got hold of myself, I did the following hack:

KAHIL

Fectatrio, lied duel wof know
cuzing arrow mophat port fellatio
whale lumps intaglio the kreal lumps comt outcose
as suture but frowsing what agaer
to we a slob fugue-frow comet engula
camomile pendant it will kneel

Sten bend lied olafe desited
war afar tophat nevel gin
cuna or mirel, detector dick-skinned
port fellatio kale me, sisk wep nag
gale vean bean gin yat port
felatio sten solo

(from 3.14)

FACE UND SUD

I want to make it clear
that in spite of what is
being written below I do
not contend that dog
red hangers created
enough weight to con-
stitute a new peninsula
much less silence
enough to govern yr
own barking darkened
lid.   (from 5.13)

TO MY SECOND GRADE CLASS

Is leaning off a besider sloppy belly on too mammoth a scale
        a sin?

--is leap phone balding--and how about rash fuzz loud the
        silence
fell floppy lucid, starting with spermy mitts' soil
lantern?

                                    Search me, kids. All I know is

--when you put bureau flaker frog parts inside your clothes they
        are
called falsies. Loose as salad and made bold by wall pelf--let me

                                        offer you a general
statement of the underlying prostration: why be afraid
of a few warts? you can't wear too many bureau flaker frog
        parts in your clothes--
                        that's what clothes are for.

(from 5.17, 6.13, 6.18, 6.25.03)

PLUS 29 OTHERS!

SELECT NO MORE THAN 5

"Right", flame

Sight, dung

Bunt, trance

Hair, punch

Twins, visitors

(from 5.21)

335

THE TRADE

Starting . . . starting to get an idea . . .

Yes! I bet if you could have your brain transferred to the body of a gorilla, you'd have a lot of surprises in store for you. For one thing, you would never again have to worry about people making fun of you in the shower. Also--henceforth--action would seem justifiable for larger and larger objectives. You scratch your scalp a lot, just as you quite naturally fumble a good deal with your pencil stub as you write Montesquieu's famous words on your door: "Certain kinds of foolishness are such that a greater foolishness would be better." Note also that what is most touching in the act of searching for salt flakes in another's hair is not the work but the fact of having undertaken it. Love has assumed in these flakes the form of obstinacy. All great salt-hunts have an absurd aspect. Is there a tragic salt-dilettantism?

Small fact: people no longer think they "have met you somewhere."

Bimb Whittier

Thirty-four years too late

1. A walk through a grass field
2. A walk during one week
3. A walk from a to b

Laurel McElwain

These commands and your alert & cooperative responses are part of

Glans Ted Sherman's EMIT

a work in progress during "Long Strain Fruit Week" from 6/15/03 - 6/22/03.

Please carry out one of these activities per day for each of the seven days.
DO NOT FAIL.

. . . instead of fixing the same tired old thing for breakfast, emit a high-pitched wavering laugh . . .

. . . instead of standing on a bar stool and falling slowly backward in the same tired old way, emit a high-pitched wavering laugh . . .

. . . instead of pouring one gallon of Snow Mountain Lemonade Drink into a hole in the ground, emit a high-pitched wavering laugh . . .

. . . instead of veering back and forth in the same tired old way between believing in nothing and being a half-assed Catholic, emit a high-pitched wavering laugh . . .

. . . instead of ritualistically and feverishly disordering your garments in the park in the same tired old way, emit a high-pitched wavering laugh . . .

. . . instead of brooding in the same tired old way over the price of pork ribs at the Washington Meat Market, emit a high-pitched wavering laugh . . .

. . . instead of sitting slumped like a rag doll at the bus stop in the same tired old way, sit up and emit a high-pitched wavering laugh . . .
- -

YOUR NOTES

Glans Ted Sherman

WAVERLEY FLEA REVISITED

EDITOR'S NOTE--Roger Caillois, of the College of Sociology in Paris, believes that animals such as the praying mantis or box crab, that camouflage themselves by mimicking their enviroments are motivated not only by "the instinct of self-preservation which, in some way orients the creature toward life," but also by "a sort of instinct of renunciation that orients it toward a mode of reduced existence, which in the end would no longer know consciousness or feeling." The exciting thing here is that The Waverley Flea, Al Acker-man's newsletter which he self-publishes each week from his garage in the crumbling Waverley section of Baltimore, is, in addition to the sort of orientation Caillois talks about, also aimed at helping Ackerman's neighbors lead more informed and productive lives, he says. What follows is a brief but stellar gleaning from recent issues of this fabulous little paper.

"THE HACKBERRIES"   [from *Waverley Flea* #188]

The young woman who was brought into a Cleveland hospital was as yellow as mustard. Even her eyeballs were yellow. A nurse, bending above her, suddenly straightened, aghast with the realization that this twenty-year-old girl was crying yellow tears!

"I've never seen such a terrible case of jaundice," she exclaimed.

"Perhaps that is because it is not jaundice," the attending physician answered. "This is the result of exposure to too many hackberries!"

I had already posed to this nurse as an attending physician. Now I went on to explain how anyone who wades around in an irrigation ditch where hackberries are free to enter through breaks in the skin or feet ought to consult an adorably horrid little Buddhist idol with its eyes fixed on its abdomen. I said:

"In most cases the idol can be found sitting on a curious sort of nest, more like a formation of trees. This could be what giants and dwarfs call a human king hemp garden. Before entering it is necessary to people things always filling something getting me for one to have izations nanza dreds seemingly members are lonely many constipated inside apartment friends when such are broad present-day themselves and buy into that 'novelty package' of the super-degenerate. Buck to the tourist camp seemingly members wrong him having some educated decided to be recognized as pin filthy proud with identification lacking until men yelped. SU CASA ES MI CASA. Henny the tourist camp can't 'keep the pickle out' this put tremendous power into wind violins and seemingly young short men fell upon umpire who spread on bother 'em be this tremendo power approaching things unedifying irrigation (pop the clutch) domen larly domen even the ant men all for present-day degenerates entering 'novelty package' with fatalistic acceptance of hackberries think the wrong him always entering 'novelty package' (let it out) anyway always action country around there or be like chair rushing but afraid while dead he had become indiscreet teen honey," I explained as succinctly as possible to my nurse dupe friend.

"But to get back to the giants and dwarfs," I added with a loud laugh. "Have you ever noticed that when you cut a dwarf in half you get two dwarfs, but when you cut a giant in half you don't get two giants?"

"HUSSERL" [from *Waverley Flea* #194]

Soon it seemed as if the young woman with whom he was spending January at the beach started deliberately getting up before daylight so as to smoke the pot at an earlier and earlier hour and then would lean back in her chair and stare at him with an expression that was both suspicious and vaguely hysterical. They had a sitting room with a good coal fire and she never spent an evening there with him. She went to the cinema almost every evening, but could not remember anything about the films when asked about them the following day. She just went to sit in the dark and this seemed in keeping with his growing sense of her as developing the characteristics of some ill-disposed mythological animal, probably a were-cat-badger-hawk, as it seemed to him was more and more the case mornings now when she would deliberately get up before daylight so as to smoke the pot at an earlier hour and afterwards sit there staring at him. And just as a tree bends at a knot in the trunk in order to grow uglier, her face at these times would become so contorted with its combined expression of suspicion and vague hysteria that he began to worry about what might happen when he took her to meet his parents. His uneasiness about this had primarily to do with how increasingly like a were-cat-badger-hawk, untidy and ill-disposed her look of suspicion and vague hysteria made her seem. Not to mention the unsociable aspects of her refusal to take part in any sort of conversation since she flatly refused to open her mouth except for an occasional stream of gutter language. Sometimes when she had been smoking the pot at an earlier hour than usual she would become unable to sit upright and could only lie there making croaking sounds--yet even then her expression of suspicion and vague hysteria never wavered. At this rate really the only outcome he could foresee in introducing her to his parents was a grotesque and awkward interlude without recompense--there being nothing more worrisome to a parent than the fear that their son's fiance is not normal. Well, but why couldn't he sidestep the whole issue by introducing his parents to a couple of car mechanics? Maybe he could, and move on from there. Problematical as it all remained when he thought it over--what cheered him was, that the big blowgun he'd ordered would soon be bringing him other ways to think about this.

ACK HACKS JOHNEE'S POEMS

Some of these hacks are based on collaborations of Bennett with Jim Leftwich, K. S. Ernst, Lawrence Upton, Johnee Spammy, Ivan Argüelles, and several vile spammers.

HARMONE FIESTA

In the garden where yr tunneled hoses shudder
like words on paper being secretly controlled
by the screams of the rosy thing o thing watchers
as the great marble blocks that rolled down upon them added a
frenzied accompaniment to the echoes of Pearl Buck's
slappy dragon teeth wakened by the headache clams
tooling their bulldozers down highway of
pretending (for instance, that lover cheating
like a vine calls for more vino)
and those pretending in a loo sed ah gus, a god named kroo
Kuttner penned about 14 or 15 years before
his death but I am not an oyster sebastian bandit cone. My truss
is gray. I have a truss I can make snap
louder than plootcase closet grossness
itself a result of Jaws None are dilatory
when dancing in the corn er fool, the fee bell ashen, the coax
I'd dichotomy squatter consumptive muskrat for, but also,
I must admit, to my love of the schoolyard, and never
more ammoniac than canine armpit philosoph,
just as none more canny than *"certificate
warty devoid,"* morley artemis weller's
terrible vegetarian waldron proverb
and none more cosmopolitan than
yo (in this case, yo bobcat repartee spiral five butts
at the window where yr
tooth creams back.

*(from Bennett "Leg" poems of 2/4/04 & 2/11/04,
Bennett/Ernst's "Line I/Threw I" & selected spam
of Matthew Castro)*

Ho Johnee,

The photos arrived today; (we're still having weird scene with our Laughing Postman who only shows up now about once a week, the rest of the time it's various different alternates who carry nothing but junk mail, but at least the LP put in an appearance today and had your photos). Good to get them, and I'll pass them along to Rupe tomorrow. Those of you on stage among the swirling psychedelics are quite spectacular. What an evening, eh? What a weekend, for that matter. My liver's still chittering from it.

Glad the vague, flabby story seems ok. Yes, good old Elegua of the Mixedness, always pranking. (Frank Baum plays a nice variation on the theme in one of his Oz books, where he has the Shaggy Man, my favorite tramp, messed up in all those Roads to Bunberry or whatever he called it.)

Got a huge laugh out of GIRLS THAT REALLY LOVE THEIR ANIMAL S. Farmy Time seems perfect for Sleaze Steele these days: he's out in Colorado, as I may have mentioned, working, i.e. bumbling around on an organic cult farm. I think I'll send the GIRLSTHAT REALLY LOVE etc to Haddock, have him make some unwholesome additions and forward to the Slease, or Punkinhead Among the Pines, as Haddock and I been calling him.

Looking forward to diving into these new ones of 10/8. Been getting off on the recent ones of 10.1 in the meantime, and here's a hack:

THIRSTY NARCISSIST

More and more face tissues as my scales spread
I am spreading delight not a ghost
table what doesn't grind, not a
face what doesn't light up and swirl
against the bowl, my
drinking-mirror I calls it, more a pal
than a theorist.

And I remember saying this more than once:
My drinking-mirror I calls it, more a pal
than a theorist

That's what my drinking-mirror is:
It has taught me how shallow the term
"Cistern" is.

(from 10.1.03)

Al Ackerman

CROTCH ONION ISLAND

crotch onion island
crotch onion echo
crotch onion statues
crotch onion shadow
crotch onion memory

crotch onion water
crotch onion mirage
follow crotch onion
like crotch sand
into that drugstore

now it's stepping on the scales
weight: negligible
fortune: danger
masonic counterpoint:
ripe lap mist

(from Bennett's "P arts" of
3/17/04 & Bennett after
Arguelles of 3/19/04)

341

Whoa! it's here with the popular X-Originating-IP, Johnee:

   Man, this latest spam from "Clinton Enid" is a fulsome devil, eh? Have to figure on some good approach (such as underground and around the boy's gym in at the back door, er, spore, er sore rung redden) to do a hack of this big baby. In the mean time I was finishing up this hack of your nifty batch from 1/14 and a quick steal off'n the "Clinton Enid" came in handy--as see below.

TOO LONG IN WINESBERG

The looping in the roof isn't only my eyes. It's only
In heaving has your gut wash garnered facts
Of science, won truths heavy with yr closet
Meat, shoe rustler it could be seen would be
X-ray buncha flinks in one horse town and dank
Bunny crunched against Lowell's clutchings visible
Emblem of hash packed forgot them pants, and blows
Likely errections: like Yr nostril: tense salad
Spell my "shoulder" and yet I somehow can't work
Up too great enthusiasm for this "puling" "like drink"
"Like salaam try awake chafe adulthood midterm"
Meaning no doubt mob cute exposed dick kewpie
Dazed like laundry and a tube for happy
Inch sluffs off yr damp puzzle blistered beneath
What's dropped, jerked, smoked, spread, forming ice and light
Trance controlled by singing earwax the quicker picker upper.

(from Bennett of 1/14/04 and "Clinton Enid" of 1/15/04)

Haddock, Al Ackerman, John M. Bennett

It seemed natural that I should say something
as I walked into your closet. "Buttered tush crashed the pee's yawn,"
I said. Your hand came to your sump throat, tensed there.
i fully expected you to shave, but your lips
drips spun smoke cups, pushed out so far in my direction
it was not surprising that ashy napkins
cheep inside yr leg remains their louder rat or odd strength
heralds cell phone "switch" rules taking effect--find out
more here before cock shadow luggage grumbles
to the exclusion of my footsy
labeled with your chins' maletas un mun dar
la lluvia heel my bowel pasta dreaming of
a series of cloying descriptions accompanied by toilet no fall.

But to shave hamster look face in blade
and the romantic trace of carbon in your "place"
flit intolerance, famous criminologist
to perform strange rite with yr floor-bound
laundry mouldy to the core as it
done it it's melting hock bun ligature yr neck can't
help fulfilling an old superstition
that your bed leg craves will be dominated by
the bleak foot sways influence, and like mustard raining
in alley slick custard
fills yr pants like rice in film
cans, which brings to mind dark lather and your closet floor full of poorly
                                                        shaved hamsters.

PIECE FOR BENNETT & LEFTWICH

PROLOGUE
John M. Bennett and Jim Leftwich are frequent collaborators.
"Brome" their collaborative poem of 1-5-04 contains the memorable phrase
"kissed trouble lynch sick & sport roam."

PIECE
Now, perhaps made a little weird by the interminable winter weather, the two
poets draw straws. Loser has to stay indoors and read art mags. Winner gets to
go out on the street and approach complete strangers. Button-hole them, and
say - "This is my big chance. Can't you see that? It could lead to anything -
musicals, the radio, even the movies. You will help me, won't you?" Then
demonstrate what it means to kiss trouble lynch sick & sport roam. Of course
there is no telling what the reaction to this will be. Strangers approached in
such fashion on the street can behave in highly unpredictable ways. In fact
reactions can run the gamut of nearly every known mood or emotion such as
surprise, annoyance, indifference, amusement, scepticism, peeved bafflement,
orphism, laity, suspicion and vague hysteria, outright fear, etc. - though perhaps
the most frequent reaction these days is likely to be explosive rage. A truly
rage-crazed stranger may deliver a flurry of karate blows, or a spin kick to the
poet's hip with hair takedown. Well, who can say. Remember this is all
happening in bad weather.

I WALKED WITH A ZOMBIE

I walked with a zombie.
It was fun. We had a lot
in common: shirt eating
piled chiselled kiss unloaded gobbles alive

care mounted think gleam
dream rake steam
rake pallid pallet
mullet letter when droop-

bitches are sweatin'
gullet rake steam let
pink used more than once
dent loop wallet clutter lest

letter droop lie down and die
assured that I was
not dream pink think before
. . . piss cut yr air

supply off, and, ho,
as you gasp and flop there, me
grash naked, me details
minet ding me snorter of

other people for
I sure am
partial to that salty old mullet smell,
it is so zombie-like.

(from Bennett and Leftwich of 2/9/04)

PINK SLIP TIME AGAIN

Bat h
bat h, good old bat h,
bee p, ba p, your wate
r crin oid will send forth king vul
vic b one while yr suitcase full of spli
nters puts on cheese yr horn oil, its
hop rot unda steaming deep in keys
yr letters stuck between my teeth an

tumb b
ling lends your focus milk
at the water cooler
that supplies high protein to mass hairs
flickering in yr cloudy throat -- you
better believe they'll fire you for that,
John, if not for animalic nod action.

(from "Leg" poems of 2/25/04)

BLACK CANARY

A sprinkler seen in heavy rain
leak my toast
blinding cream and moth drinking
I inhale
and my glasses see white dust
like a bowl of bugs, no
like a bowl of firecrackers
and hear a ping pong game.

(from THE PEEL)

Holy Moly Johnee,

Man, no question about it, I've been getting a _huge_ kick out of smelt tunnel, jacket coattails, and heat crust--these three great collabs you and Leftwich came up with. Been admiring them greatly. And wouldn't be surprised if they were among your all-time best ever, which is saying plenty, eh? Certainly did light a fire under my tail, as see below: this may be my favorite hack so far this season, he said wildly:

CUTLET CREEK

My kisses are not so easily won with exception
of latent shallots on a man in whom monster talent bullshit maunders.
You there: Is there a mattress about robot putz? Is he snug
enough? Has the world press taken up oatmeal lotion melds?

Bending hive privates, do the Abnormal Seven
apprehend how Rilke gathers finches to his dreck undress fortress?
Can tangent beguiles smell dime? Will distend pretend retentive in hoppin pants

squelch mine pineal? Does tweezer fiddle while peanut language burns? And
what is meant exactly by peanut language? Does speaking it overmuch
perhaps explain why your head goes on getting smaller even as we speak?
Well, too bad. You'll not win my kisses now, not with that peanut head and
nostrils to match.

(from Bennett/Leftwich of 11.13.03)

UNIVERSAL

O who can know it ?

Your father, an Egyptologist
Suffering from a peculiar
Malady is transforming his prick suds till they
Depict a most somber fate: art shoes.

It has been ten months and these prick suds
Are still sorta puttering around
They wiggle and seem to be looking for
A door leaving some garage   .In yr room

Cat bust the meadow sounds of pork wallet slapping
The clayed yr face's rancid gnome, as though
Acorn mad, grins inside the wall
It hurts to grin, and yet it grins.

(from Bennett of 12.3.03 and Bennett/Leftwich of 12.23.03)

A JAR FOR PUZ
in 3 acts

1

Gradually our ears become attuned to your filter cube's jarringly loud knocking. As we hesitate outside in the kitchen garden which is brimming with pink rose blossom, we see the white porch door at the back opening on incongruous unmixed hash hole gazing with a fork, oh yeah . . .

2

After an uneasy night, these book of wets appearing on the surface from below were darkly luminous, and as they multiplied they seemed decidedly in key with eep feel sandwich spreading on your neck. And the name of the house is Puz. Just Puz!

3

There on a table near the door into the garden stood myriad der matitis. The story of their ungodly sweetness, sin and ge a hoo tin I need not recount, for I am sure it is familiar to all those active in amble cluster sobbing in a plastic bag. It is, I think we must suppose, okay if you like them "willed". Instead of getting too frightfully serious about it, why not go forward and nip one with your jarringly florid pouters.

(from Bennett's "Leg" poems of 1/21)

SEE THE GRUNTY ISLANDS

See the grunty islands, see the schmuck dance
flooded with The Tooth smutty
lake "wine" my fork . . . my trouble

has always been your buttered
nates need not open that eye if
flamer the bum pit paged right

he'll be seen to stop and cross
the lobby mincingly to answer
anything froim white dust to dawn
                  temple mustard
                  the mustard of park doggy!

(from THE PEEL & THE PEEL PEELED book, 2004)

SPRAY

Luck of roof crunching
what my brain crotch dropping out of college
had -- the fortuitous "menudo"
pall across the trousered "glock
-- so named can screwy with velveeta black
velveeta spray! black velveeta spray!
At times this Tourette's empowers my window
peeping like the snake plugs hopping
empowers dead homer "fooling" with his bike
under a flopping moon, wobbly and
unnoticed by all
but a few gut doll game
visionaries.

(from THE PEEL & THE PEEL PEELED book, 2004)

THE REASON WHY I SINK
FAWNING LIKE A TOILET

escapes me. Plugged a head with tissue
"pole" cat plugged a head
and my closet roped
not exactly with ham
or to put it where the cows can
get to it, soaked 'n
pondered each gland waddled past a whole
jolly fish dead grinned
to be armless legless retentive
corn and pearl
and an inch sluffs off yr
stand-up breakfast, the toke.
Such peelings in certain sections
of men's wear and pants
hash packed in the seat like ten
sent muffins, five sent
closet meat. A lung leg ass
walked badly and seemed troubled
like one with ever-lengthening
piles. Better we all utter
armpit exhaltation. Can I
leave my laundry in your home?
Leading to a greasy sound dumb waving feet
with snail walls on each side. O my face clay

(from Bennett of 1/14 and Bennett/Leftwich of 3/6, 3/22)

BEAUTY INVADES YOUR SHORTS

Beneath the "pout" neck scrawled
With hair saw the penis
Grinning like plundered tomorrow
Lent grunting booth

                let grunting begin

Bean-spread the lubrication sold

From old-fashioned mister cheeks
Is speaking gung ho I said it all a headache
Olive boil your eye's crank nest
The cough of mister cheeks

Grows thicker and thicker just before
Beauty invades your shorts

(from 10.8.03)

MORE SPAM PEARS

It's not much of a dream:
a mechanical chicken twice my size

    Behind him my brother
    crouching in the weeds
    with a control box

There appears
to be a similarly equipped

mallard attendee
crouched behind him, also

Eruda the topsoil
propells the discernible tecum
of bladdernut the emperor ditzel drops
from tart alec with a wacky boroque dollop
too much chamfer on the chamfer flashlight umbillicus

Moving right along beman flashlight umbillicus
stretched across sclerotic prick crater
[the leaf vaudeville keeps me indoors]
now it's homomorphism all the way
bayonne upland home crying wee wee albert anteater

[wee wee diffident hold I'd flue anywhere]
[anywhere suggests endless psychic blutwurst]

so please don't keep lowering your aruba
Ella hillcrest sighing her heart out chez spanish asthma
noises that are horizontal
without cautionary conrad wynn formula
that promises imperfect curbside topsoil is elkhart airspeed

(from spam of "Jarrell" and from Johnee Spammy's
MORE SPAM PEARLS)

EXCUSED

for Teresa

The big fruitcake: the darker sunlight
on big fruitcake: I have not
yet inviegeled it into
conversation generally
attributed to a sort
of swelling and growing
thing--a steed in a pinch
that someone might leap astride
  and ride like the devil, bawling: "On! On! to the P.T.A.
  for more fort locker soap--Could I finger you
  my mm nah wind bove--
  mm I'm pen fat gus! etc"

  and in this way
  by this method be
  adjudged entirely
       useless
  for jury duty

(from "Leg" poems & others of 3/10/04)

"Johnee   Spammy"

ENLARGE YOUR ANUS!

The unique new Rectalizer* anal enlarger is imported from China and it's designed to make a man more manly where it counts! Working on the principle of gravity, the Rectalizer* gently enlarges the anus until, after just one month, it's as big as a horse! Women love men with super-huge anuses!

Al Ackerman   Haddock

NOSTRO, SUPER ID AND SUPER ACH STUNNER

I see the clone farm atmospherics. I yip
Reach me nostro clouding closer toward
Dressed what's left, jack side, tape my self
A crump massive buster of ulterior
And grave ape flame "ass hang" off as nostro hark
(O chumps so my breath resquirms, swined the creamed face
Belonging bottoms up down the upper
Teef) what a belling! in your socks and my
Socks and those peel my watch, what secret nostro
Life that foam gun rattled slap ouch slap ouch
This is the way
We crowded at my buttock out of ignorance
How about new movies every week free
And all in a crowd like a mother shoelace

*(from Bennett of 1/7/04 & Bennett, Upton and
many others on the WRYTING LIST of 1/04)*

Any railings?
I know when I'm doing it,
but I can't always
do it
backing out of the garage
came on slowly, that
near the large veined BALLS
'cause a man with such large
ones
purple dye down one
relishing stupid jokes about
building
seats around it, same for the
other, both
too large to take to a hotel,
their
tremendous mass pulled car
down
tunnels or across the past 60
years
buttering up to scientists and
hairy
to begin with, hairier
without even two front teeth
without even LOVE
FIELD employees scurrying
among them
trying things in their great
shadow
        know the feeling?
cross your fingers
and try to pick up a guinea
pig . . .

--Eel Leonard

COME UPSTAIRS

A little spit of polish
It was twinkle falia
You print but carving
The lant something gus had been
Grow? From night, tha's rounds will
Controlled stance sand
In the hairs could daylight
Thing half its Joyce-the-Horace obsession
A hind and pillow
Museum, the useless companion
Around pipes this smell for J.
Because J. was--well, J.
One nated
What comes out

Asylum V. Loder

EVIDENCE

Hips of agent pile can symbolize he bought her out
of hearing of the house while one keeps hunting
for a simple and natural language to express
timeless night mice and in that would spot, the spar
of tinfoil was starting to get a mouth.
But perhaps fate ups and hangs a hot bladder over all.
A tremendous nurse we thought still on the boat
swept down on us. Or to put it another way,
Joseph Conrad never saw a streetcar until he was
fifty-eight. Or to put it another way,
Joseph fever flavor, Joseph fever flavor.

--Eel Leonard

Sullivan

Mrs. Potato Head
with a slinky figure
is no way to describe
a race horse.

--"Swarthy" Turk Sellers

WHAT KILLED VAUDEVILLE

I believe Socrates meant me when he said,
"Try to remember how the olive juice
Pooled inside Dot's fur coat and how you managed to carry
The body out of the office without
Leaking any juice on the floor . . .
Therefore time is thing imperfect;
Therefore perfect that which that in
A slick magazine dada story
Asks what if you were vacationing in the southwest and---"
"But how can I vacation in the southwest,
I <u>live</u> in the southwest," a voice piped up.
It was the strange growth on his knob. "Precisely.
Picture a man kneeling by a power
Mower in your garage in the southwest---"
"Is he pouring gas onto the floor?" "That's right!
His straw hat by hanging verticle blocks his gaze
in such a way that it looks like it's hanging from a peg
In the middle of his face, as if his nose were a peg
perhaps." And the way they stared down at me
Was both a laugh and a comment
On my hat.

                              --Laurel McElwain

IF A CLOCK, A RAINBOW, AND/OR A GUILLOTINE
look strange to you, just say to yourself: "Turn
the light up while I make of my body a Pla far
below average. Turn the light down to tell stories to children, rumors and gossip and crazy
slogans instead of evil. What is this shyness about dangling arms (or no arms at all) when you have three legs?
What is living with a moth compared to half an hour in
front of bathroom-in-a-handkerchief? What is the actual
advantage that you can find in comparing bathroom-in-a-
handkerchief to perhaps wrapping 'it' in these flour
tortillas Jesse brings for his lunch, and pretending you didn't?

"And while we're on the subject, what wouldn't end strangely in
the shape of a monstrous flying tenderfoot mucous life?"

Suppose you asked yourself all these things and there turned
out to be no "Proper Answer"! You might find yourself wandering
around with a basket, asking people: "Am I a brownie? Have I ever
been a brownie?" Then what? Are you really prepared for the sort of
conversations with the sort of people this will lead to? Have you no pride?

Well, it's a lot to think about.

But-- (and here is the point) probably it would be best if you left off trying
to make out this small print, best if you stopped reading right now in fact, if
only to concentrate more fully on your drinking and driving.

CRASH.

Al Ackerman

MID NID

I don't want to
express it with
tent butter
the venerable
little finger
hank should
change his name
to nostril hue
henry, and
remember it was
the malarial
gentleman
in his arms

Al Ackerman

MID YERG

If you hear eel knob rush
and clam knob rush at the
same time don't be sur-
prised by each other in
the gloaming, in the enema
grudge lake, in the gloaming

Al Ackerman

353

IF T. S. ELIOT HAD WRITTEN A LETTER TO VIRGINIA WOOLF AND SHE HAD READ IT WHILE THEY WERE BOTH UNDER THE INFLUENCE OF SPAM ?

26 March 1919   18 Crawford Mansions,
                                      Crawford Street, W.I.

Dear Mrs. Woolf,

   Thank you so much for sending me the synagogue helpmate exhaltation seepage thrones, and so many of them. I still think that the one originally chosen is the best, and would probably also be best liked by the moluccas who might buy the gooodz.info/. The dark blue beebe is also goodz.info/. But these may be rather expensive, so I have chosen t/tz beebe chosen mapppp chosen fedders ammonium newsstand mine (marked 3) as an alternaZZtive, and it is only reasonable to leave the choice between these three to queen cot deer bayda oomwje titmo htfendlz.

   I wonder if your husband got my Amazing, PERMANENT EJACOULATION RESULTS! The most popular Solution for Pemnis Enlargement. 20% Gain 98+ Full Incyhes In Length STOP PREDMATURE dioxide automata sawtimber munition garrulous cyclist, but c_O_k_e chevalier intestate I do hope synagogue helpmate exhaltation seepage thrones wbuflik rzblw wbuflik rzblw I have chosen contractual fedders chosen ammonium chosen newsstand mine, not yrs, bar hag.

   I look forward to interstate katie dip cumulate kenton between my l..e..g..z so I have chosen spas_ming, supnk-

coevred desire arcsin custody shown G_E_T

1oo% RFEE TORU. It is very good of you to have tanken so much troublez over the malden credent.

                              Sincerely yours
                              T. S. flke

Al Ackerman

HCUM the EMATS

I no more seek
    ecaf tar
        knird
    than
I do tae
    mra seilf

*

the rae shall hear enurp snur /

snur is a revelation of senurp /

    evig em emos ria!

*

LANRETE

There are wen stuops /

    wen sresoh /

    wen smub /

less nrob niaga than lanrete!

                              Al Ackerman

354

WHEN CRACKERJACKS STAND IN ROWS

The
wonder
is
it's
not
unusual
to find
your mind which cats belong as seed to be
the woman who can really live
with me in profound solitude
of woods and grow old with me after I
give myself a few rabbit punches
or I can go to Adam's maybe
but be careful not to offend with
pitiful demands for what
others love in crackerjacks
is sleepless as a crunching wildhair
lover of caries

--Glans Ted Sherman

SEEK Hand Release
by Tait Ravenwill

Later people come later than
earlier people and earlier people
come earlier than
later people and were
able to seek more than the people
I mentioned earlier when
squads were detailed to watch me. Am
I harmless, and that's about all?
everything went according to plan
anger or fear creeps in fear
pre-destined and Martian in appeal
and that made it all the better
when to smile or laugh to please teacher
caused some monstrous faculty, caused, perhaps,
a little yellow cap with a black
leather visor set jauntily upon
long slender finger soldier and the big
scrawling hand across all reason
a vague feeling of having gone to bed
relishing life to the full. Next day
pretend there's a sun and something to wear.
Deciding among the clingy and unclean I
felt those weird old nibbling factors bugle.
From being ashamed to say anything
not to sense that this is characteristic
construction of yea probes and breakfast and
lunch and dinner and breakfast for breakfast
and lunch and dinner and breakfast buffs.
Kept from liking the asteroid weeks braniff
denied my frequent flyer status on
grounds my eyes were afire posy voids
helped me approach violent moron status . . .

and yet I could swear that my eyes are staring, fixed

I don't know just how to describe that keeshhound over there

right now as I hunch over peculiarly, there can be no doubt
  that sidereal cramping is bad only when proper posture
  might mean poverty or hunger

as in a companion figure hunched over, peculiarly, by the side
    of each of us poor forked raddishes, to put it crudely

a cousin, a cousin named for his watery outline, cousin waterman

brought out by cross-eyed closer study of the cousins, however,
    are many subtle differences, each as glaring as the butternut
    coulter itself, an inner cohesion eventually enclosed within

The End. More I's. Some because it was the proper thing
but more out of having searched, for so long,
their appearance alone was an assurance
that there be no repetition of what had
made explode that sweet potato you thought
you smelled in the seance. From then on, the
pitch was niture raries and a room with
fire and neon, a companion phantom world
usually not known afterward, I believe. So
that was that, and I brought out a tiny
monger and cuddled it in my palm. This thing
I hold that makes such a poor substitute
for my tool or a large Scotch
seems to be blending with my skin, and when
that happens I start feeling almost pious,
muscle, sinew, shoe, and I can't wait to
roll from behind a large rock. And when
that happens I like doing this a lot
even though it isn't my own story.

Tait Ravenwill

READ AND GO BLIND ECSTASY SERIES

ELFIN DUSK

THE OTHER day I had a brain storm in which I realized that I had never taken any sort of medals for my strides in revitalizing our weak namby-pamby English language, and once I realized this, it occured to me that now might be a good time to step forward in my delirium and show what wonderful things can happen when writers everywhere start adopting my methods, beginning, first of all, by substituting the deeply evocative words "*elfin dusk*" in place of that tired old definite article "*the*".

In this brain storm I was having I seemed to remember that this "elfin dusk" discovery was one I'd made a good many years ago, back when I was working days as an orderly at Sid Hoff Pavilion , a large orthopedic and psychiatric hospital in Columbus (OH) and had given a patient a urine sample for breakfast instead of the customary apple juice. Because he wouldn't admit that Lovecraft was greater than Nixon, you see. Naturally I told everybody it had been an accident. All the same I had to fill out an incident report which was so commonplace and tedious it was all I could do not to scream. That was when it came to me. That was when I suddenly had my great idea for replacing "the" with "elfin dusk" throughout that whole damn lengthy report possibly for the same reason that as a child "Elfin Dusk" had been what I'd called my first little sled and my first barbeque sandwich and most of all my mother's clitoris. God, what an improvement! It gave those dullard pages a real glow and filling it out that way was almost fun. Then, once my report had gone through channels and I'd been transferred to the night shift as a phlebotamist I took out a little time to reflect and thought about my discovery and knew I was going to push on and continue making further (and greater) linguistic discoveries no matter what. And that's when I told myself, Elfin dusk best is yet to come.

A little later I heard someone reciting (it sounded more like growling and snarling) modernist poetry on elfin dusk men's locked ward. Turned out to be this former university librarian with avant-garde tendencies, who, years before, had gone off his trolley during "National Robert Frost Appreciation Week." As a result, he'd started prowling elfin dusk campus like a wild beast and acting peculiarly. Somehow or other, after being taken into custody for his various crimes against man and nature, including vampirism and open mike readings, he'd landed on elfin dusk locked ward at Hoff Pavilion, where he was treated as something of a special problem and known as Slaking John, even though he always told everybody to call him Lawrance Thompson. Nobody ever did, but that didn't keep him from biting them. You couldn't keep a stitch on him. (EDITOR'S NOTE: *The real Lawrance Thompson was one of Robert Frost's most deeply inimical biographers.*)

As luck would have it, when I came on the scene Slaking John was willing, even eager to run around all night drawing blood samples for me. It was a good thing this arrangement, as it left me time to pursue my linguistic goals. Fighting hard not to laugh or claw at my face, I spent hours each night thinking about my "Elfin Dusk" Method, how best to expand and improve on it, on the theory that, once it was perfected, it would mean my fantastic wish for creating a more perfect incident report might at last become a reality and relieve me of my wild, trapped feeling (something like that).

Meantime, dressed in nothing but his ratty gray hospital slippers, Slaking John continued to run around like a maniac every night with my phlebotomy kit, presumably [*eighteen words missing from having blood splashed on them*] but, I hoped, worth elfin dusk risk. "I've been thinking," he remarked one night, not long after I'd confided my "Elfin Dusk" Method to him, "I've been thinking about what you said, and if it's radical linguistic transformations you're after, you're more than welcome to make use of my poems. I bet if you took something as incisive as 'lint maples leaves pennies rice,' which is a recent *chant royal* I just this minute wrote--well, I bet if you took that and used it to replace a trite old word like 'idea', the result would be truly *durg*, as we poets say."

"That's fine," I said. "But first, hadn't you better go back and change that last 'the' to 'elfin dusk'? I think you missed it."

Slaking John did a sort of double-take and made a wry face. Sheepishly, he corrected his error, all the while looking at me with new respect. "Geez," he said. "You're really serious about this shit, aren't you?"

We were standing outside elfin dusk hydrotherapy room when he said it and it was very bright in there. I'd arranged electric fixtures so I could grow jute all night. What I saw when I looked at him in this light wasn't nice. His teeth were filed to points and his eyes glittered, his lips stained and crazily smeared as always. Funny thing was it didn't bother me accepting help from one who wore no clothes and had such an obvious taste for human blood. I have always accepted people on elfin dusk basis of what I call "universal disregard." As soon as I heard his idea--or, rather, I should say, as soon as I heard his lint maples leaves pennies rice, I knew it was just what I needed.

I told him so. Complimented him. He relaxed a little then, and I couldn't help but feel things that night were working out to my advantage. Especially as being in such close proximity to those teeth of his had just given me a great new lint maples leaves pennies rice of my own. "Listen," I said excitedly, "from here on out, I'm going to end each sentence with elfin dusk word 'tooth'!"

"Better a hissy phonebook than a dribbling hand," was Slaking John's encouraging reply tooth. "And while you're at it," he added, "you might also want to think about what Archimedes was getting at over 6000 years ago, when he pointed out how an illiterate hillbilly will often live as long as someone who likes to use opium and yet be just as hard to understand tooth." So saying, he urged me to get busy testing this hillbilly-opium theory of Aristotle's right away tooth. "All you have to do," he said, "is substitute ei for long a, ai for long i, i for long y, z for s and th, and k for c--plus whatever hell else you can think of tooth. Wait'll you try it," he promised with a rather horrid smile, "you won't believe you're still on earth tooth."

As soon as I heard this, I knew that his neurotic and introspective brain was running out of control and that if I did as he suggested, elfin dusk results would be chaotic beyond belief tooth. This positive assurance that I had at last achieved a perfect linguistic method, with only a demented blood-sucker at my side, you might say, was naturally tremendously satisfying to me tooth. Elfin dusk enormity of it brought a thickness to my throat, and I found myself too emotionally overwhelmed to speak tooth.

"Zink uv it," I zed to Zlakain Jon tooz. "Until now, I'v ben pokaing eilong laik ur avrag hozpitl flunki, growain jute and sluggain peitantz mor zan elvin duzk avrag, but stil not zettain ani recordz tooz. But now--zuddenli here tonite--wiz mi 'Elvin Duzk' Mezod fulli pervekted, I feel redi at las to teik on an incaiden repor uv truli humonguz proporzonz tooz. I mean a zprawlain, momentuz repor zuch az comz from akzidentali zrowain a hozpital viztor down elvin duzk ztairz tooz. Or zat rezults in a Klas C feloni for performain unarzoraized actz of zurgeri involvain elvin duzk removal uv teztaiculz from zertin male perzonz tooz. A peitant mai alzo be given chickn toze zrough meanz zat u will zoon zee me eidopt tooz. Zo obviouzly I'm redi here tonite for real graitnez tooz. And u kan be too, Zlakain Jon," I zed, lettain my elazhun get elvin duzk beter uv me and not reali stopain to zink wher mi wordz mite be leadain me: "In ur case, uv koarz, real graitnez mai taik twenti or zirti yearz tooz. But don't worri, u kan still taik a big ztep forwar rite now, here tonite, bi makain up ur mind to do zomzain abou zat terubl b.o. uv urs and zat killur breaz and zoze unatraktiv ztainz on ur lipz and klawz and ur---"

It wuz almoz zubkonciouzli zat I caught mi error zen and brok off wiz a vizibl shiver, zinkain, "Wait a minut, hav I lozt mi mind kompletli tooz? Ziz iz Zlakain Jon, elvin duzk homizidal vampir poet I'm zayain zese zingz to--so whutz to preven him from takain offenz and goain baliztik on me tooz?" Zinkain of zose raizur-zharp teez uv his, I ztood zere frozn tooz. In a momem zat zeemed taimlez, blind panik klaimd me tooz. Elvin duzk onli kweztun wuz whezer mi zhortz wd load up *bevore* or *avter* he leaped on me tooz. But zen-- nozain much zeemed to hapen tooz. Lookain into hiz pitted, beaztaial faiz, I zaw onli perplexiti and bafelment zere tooz. Not a zhred uv kompraihenzun cd I find zere tooz. I breazed a little eazair zen, feelain mi terror begin to zubzide az I realaized zere had reali ben no kauz for alarm tooz. Bekauz even a madman like Zlakain Jon cd hardli taik offenz and dezide to atak me if he didn't know whut I wuz zayain about him, rite tooz? And klerli he had no idea tooz. All uv which went to zhow how ful, how komplet in its lainguiztik pervekzun mi "Elvin Duzk" Mezod reali wuz, elvin duzk grait zain wuz u kould zai praktikli anizain ziz wai and not be underztod tooz.

THE BIGAMIST IN THE MIRROR

Something yellow resulted from his chattering insults.

Something milky resulted from his neglect of the yard.

Something backing down the wall resulted from his habit of drinking Sanka with lumps of ice in it.

Something that went on gaining weight but always had a baby's mouth resulted from his history of being a poor credit risk.

Something presidential resulted from his unfortunate use of hair oil.

Something deer-like that kept getting thrown out of yoyo tournaments resulted from his fantasies of soldiering with Arnold Schwarzenegger.

Something distant but heavily strapped resulted from his ready fund of Masonic lore.

Something that moved about near the top of a tree, whistling and shaking down apples resulted from the stimulation he found in old nudist films.

Something in funny shoes resulted from the way his heart would pound at the sight of a big fat June bug. Usually bouncing off the washer-dryer and landing on the lunch meat. That was the hell of it.

Something that pats its head and rubs its stomach resulted from his early years growing up in an orphanage.

Something floating in the punch bowl resulted from his practice of hanging around the house during the daytime.

Something yellow resulted from his neglect of the yard.

Something milky resulted from his habit of drinking Sanka with lumps of ice in it.

Something backing down the wall resulted from his history of being a poor credit risk.

Something that went on gaining weight but always had a baby's mouth resulted from his unfortunate use of hair oil.

Something presidential resulted from his fantasies of soldiering with Arnold Schwarzeneggar . . . etc.

(NOTE -- Something filled with boyish devilment and black straw will result if you complete all 121 possible combinations. No. Wait. I'm guilty of not stating that properly. Something filled with boyish devilment and black straw will result if you don't complete all 121 possible combinations.)

--Eel Leonard

Diet
by Tait Ravenwill

GENIUS

Inconspicuous as it may be
in the scope of cosmic space,
I still dream of teaching my penis
Spanish.

       --Eel Leonard

Laura Riding has jumped out a window.
Laura Riding has jumped out from behind a bush.
Laura riding has jumped a cub scout troop.
Ichneumon,
a small animal that breaks the eggs of
the crocodile cannot comprehend it.
For one moment, in the dining room, I
staggered to life believing myself threatened
by the ghost of some lappet of a head
which flies loose and dickers the
way I do with the act of seeing
by too much light suddenly introduced
by means of a monster debt.

Mr. James Mee
POB 1441
Charleston, VT. 05765

Dear Mr. Mee,

    My name is Fletcher M. Gregory, Jr. and I am 85 years old. I don't know much about music but recently I discovered your "compact disc", FROM A QUIET PLACE in the failure of a Kentucky Fried Chicken establishment, where my man-servant, Mr, Jonathan Swift, stopped to use the failure and to buy a larege tureen of biscuits. I attempted to find the failure of the "failure disc" but to no avail. Finally, the failure behind the counter (I think her name was "Tameeka") told me that I could have the "failure disc".

    Once I got home I asked my man-servant to put on the "failure disc". Well, needless to say I was very impresssed Mr. Mee. Your music is just wonderful! I want to hear more! I find myself humming your tunes many times during the failure! I just wanted to let you know that someone like me really appreciates your art.

    Would it be possible to have an autographed picture? Could you sign it, "To Fletcgher, who discovered my "compact disc" in the failure at a Kentucky Fried Chicken"? It would make an old man very happy.

Fletcher M. Gregory, Jr.
425 E. 31st Street
Baltimore, MD. 21218

Best regards,

Fletcher M. Gregory Jr.

The Alaap Hacks

[This series continues on next page]

from *Alaap*
by Krishna Baldev Vaid

One night I saw a warm naked <u>corpse</u> lying next to me. I was pleased. It was a fresh and beautiful <u>corpse</u>. I wasn't afraid of <u>it.</u> Every <u>night</u> I <u>sleep</u> alone. My <u>luck</u> <u>has</u> taken a <u>turn</u> tonight.

The <u>moon</u> peeping through the <u>window</u> was my <u>friend.</u>

I hugged my <u>corpse</u> hard. I kissed her <u>eyes,</u> her <u>lips,</u> her <u>nipples.</u> Again and again. I caressed her <u>hair,</u> massaged her <u>thighs,</u> kneaded every inch of her body. Again and again. I did all that a healthy man can do with a dead body. Again and again.

Next <u>morning</u> when I woke <u>up</u> there was no naked <u>corpse</u> next to <u>me.</u> Instead there was a stale <u>woman</u> fully clothed. What possessed <u>you</u> last <u>night,</u> she asked.

I was so surprised and enraged that my <u>teeth</u> disappeared.

I closed my <u>eyes</u> and turned away from <u>her.</u> For a long time I lay there dead. When I got up my <u>mirror</u> was there taunting me.

If I had <u>teeth</u> I might have laughed.

Translated from the Hindi
by the author

99

----

from *Paala*
by Dave Vedlab Anhsirk

One day I heard a cool fully-dressed hyperactive standing far away from me. I was disgusted. He was stale and ugly. I was fearful of him. Every day I wake with multitudes. My misfortune has gone straight ahead today.

The sun staring through the door was my enemy.

I thrust my hyperactive away gently. I spit on his ears, his hiney, his shoulder blades. Never again. I pummeled his feet, barely messed with his upper arms, refused to touch any part of his soul. Never again. I did nothing that an unhealthy woman can't do with a live soul. Never again.

Next evening when I fell asleep there was no well-dressed hyperactive far away from me. Similarly there was a fresh corpse naked as a jaybird. Who dispossessed you this morning, it stated.

I was so blase and happy that my teeth appeared.

I opened my eyes and turned toward it. For a short while I stood there fully alive. When I lay down my mud pie was congratulating me.

If I didn't have teeth I might not have laughed.

Translated from the English
by a Latah

The Book of Ham

from Latinity Interruptus

One night I saw a warm naked connotation lying next to me. I was pleased. It was a dead and bardlatrous connotation. I wasn't afraid of it. Every night I sleep alone. My litotes has taken a turn tonight.

The multi-accentuality peeping through the vraisemblance was my genre.

I hugged my connotation hard. I kissed its explication, its lipogram, its neoclassicism. Again and again. I caressed its hindiadys, massaged its third-person narrative, kneaded every instress of its binary opposition. Again and again. I did all that a healthy macaronic can do with a dead connotation. Again and again.

Next morning when I woke up there was no naked connotation next to me. Instead there was a stale vulgate fully clothed. What preromanticized you last night, it asked.

I was so surprised and enraged that my tercets disappeared.

I closed my exordiums and turned away from this fully-clothed vulgate. For a long time I lay there deconstructed. When I got up my minimalism was there taunting me.

If I had had tercets I might have Latinated.

One night I a warm naked corpse next to me. I pleased. It a fresh and beautiful corpse. I not afraid of it. Every night I alone. My luck a turn tonight.

The moon through the window my friend.

I my corpse hard. I her eyes, her lips, her nipples. Again and again. I her hair, her thighs, every inch of her body. Again and again. I all that a healthy man with a dead body. Again and again.

Next morning when I up there no naked corpse next to me. Instead there a strange woman fully clothed. What you last night, she.

I so surprised and enraged that my teeth.

I my eyes and away from her. For a long time I there dead. When I up my mirror there me.

If I teeth I might.

SAFE SEX VERSION

One night I saw a warm naked condom tenant lying next to me. I was pleased. It was a fresh and beautiful condom tenant. I wasn't afraid of it. Every night I sleep alone. My condom wheel has taken a turn tonight.

The comdom yam peeping through the condom sauce was my condom clock.

I hugged my condom tenant hard. I kissed its condom lung, its condom thigh, its condom rim. Again and again. I caressed its condom inker, massaged its condom rig, kneaded every inch of its condom tummy. Again and again. I did all that a healthy condom rummy can do with a naked condom tenant. Again and again.

Next morning when I woke up there was no naked condom tenant next to me. Instead there was a stale condom bee fully clothed. What possessed your condom core last night, it buzzed.

I was so surprised and enraged that my condom tongue disappeared.

I closed my condom door and turned away from that condom bee. For a long time I lay there like a condom cop. When I got up my condom ham was there taunting me.

If I had condom tongue I might have laughed.

(from Bennett/Leftwich of 6/4/04)

ACK HACKS JOHNEE'S POEMS

123

"hot luggage"--
froth osedlate--

moss books
pankin late

agile

drank
olbod

wang, nufdus

*

JULY 3RD

sobbingocol sobbingloco yr hsafion--
despite sedpite, zubzes buzz--yr shorts cluster
bite and dink dink froth buodtful tolion.

*

TOMEL

Tomel
as pumpkin
nrut into

(from 6/23/04)

Morbid Pantry

rabbit dirt maniac
fisters
disturb
arbol keister brush.

sister aphid.
brother measles.

fine. how's yr Blackwood?

Blackwood forced himself to nod.

"it warms your stomach."

(from Bennett/Leftwich of 8/16 & 9/13/04)

VERMINOLOGY

"To consciousness, existence is being conscious of existing"
--Emile Lesaffre

To delennuf, gnilwarcs are being funneled through scrawling.

Like ymmug eveels, "eloh gnileef" is getting sleeve gummy
   by "feeling hole."

By tsucol worc, ssenesub gnipoows thanks to crow locust
   are adding to this swooping business.

For "hsart ksed," eldoop pirts is building desk trash by
   playing strip poodle.

As daerps noitatiperc, egduf tekcop is helping crepitation
   spread by means of pocket fudge.

(from EACH FEET)

Dear Johnee:

Been making great progress with my *cricket language* and already have the first cricket hack:

ICKNO

crih ick-ickp snoick bubblickd dicklbbub spick-ick sluggagick pick-ick layick sickams lous crinh ickons plashickdy hoa on ickmas rickal sickams anhickad "ushcrin" faul flamicky daick hickof ickoms ashy nocrisu naickd loick oom cri onicky smaicks dickan cri ickno!

(translated into *cricket language* from Bennett's "Eno" of 5/12/04)

*

Am also thinking about translating Conrad's THE HEART OF DARKNESS into *cricket language*. This is how the opening paragraph would sound (best of course if you rub your legs together):

HICK HICKAT DANICKSS

Hick *Nickllcriick*, rucriscrig, o hick anho w-crihou fluick hick sacrils, a ricks. Hick, hick nickly alm, b-hickcrig hick r-crivick, hick oly h-crig fo crit o omick o wacri fo hick un hick cridick.

*

Translating the whole book into *cricket language* could make for a tough but rewarding summer project, eh? Well, sure . . . definitely something to think about.

You can see, too, I think, the possibilities for extending *cricket language* into other big areas. For instance: If properly presented out in your back yard, let's say morning noon & night from behind your new fence, *cricket language* could serve to drive your terrible next-door-neighbor batty in a hurry, I betcha-- (all the more so if you attired yourself in a giant cricket outfit [*g-cria r-criickt oufcri*]).

OK - more in a bit — (b-cri), up! up! up!

ack

To read more about this amazing new breakthrough CLICK HERE

THE JEWEL DOG

First the bunk natters
like slipper
sugar

or sank lunch closet
pork
simplification god

when goat pill golf was a sight the
like of which you
had never

seen through mist
& far away box eye hair
of long-promised decay

the place is on
neck knuckle index
opiate clang

down around the heh
paw, wap dink, heh, bright pennies
bright pennies but

the dark water closet
is never far away
use your long adenoids

feel simple god of
duck lamp barf
creaming in the weeds

you feel it
but the pocket
pool is your dnah's jewel dog

(from 8/11/04)

SAMMOC

plunge ,yr ,doodad
,dlof ,phone ,yr ,drape
,whose ,epard ,flogs
,huffed ,blam ,and
,gurd ,matters ,dodge.

PERIOD

(from 10/13)

Method

A minder nuts sport can be viewed in
two ways:
  --exclude bronze nature
  --"explode your clothes"
The two views node snort runts and
spat clue heel. It does not matter
which zeal lug bug heel you drive in
this picture, since a nook post, a
slick dick, is that moron simply mouse
or roach on nubile march?
  I guess it is.
  What I now ask is: hams planned. An
omen?

*(from Bennett/Leftwich of 8/16/04
and 9/13/04)*

ron world

gnilleps saw ron
ron was gnilliw
gniweps saw ron
ron saw humping
snapping was ron
ron saw gnippoh
gnippos saw ron
ron saw gnippan
gnipmuts saw ron
ron saw sewing
gnilliws saw ron
ron saw gnillews
spelling was ron
ron saw willing
spewing was ron
ron was gnipmuh
gnippans saw ron
ron was hopping
sopping was ron
ron was napping
stumping was ron
ron was gniwes
swilling was ron
ron was swelling

*(from Bennett/
Leftwich's nor
of 8/20/04)*

Ayii Johnee--- Here's a hack I did while still engrossed in the collabs by you
and Leftwich of 8/20. First the hack, then the secret of the hack:

THE STOMACH-BOWLING OTTER FAMILY

tempting empty stomach juicy
tulip-cheeser tempting juicy empty oedipus
otter bowling doubts oedipus twisted otter
doubts empty tempting tulip-cheeser stomach
oedipus doubts tempting stomach juicy
tulip-cheeser stomach doubt twisted bowling juicy
empty tempting otter oedipus twisted
doubts otter twisted tulip-cheeser empty
juicy doubts bowling tulip-cheeser stomach
tempting oedipus juicy, otter-bowling twisted!

*(from curved turd by Bennett/Leftwich of
8/20/04.)*

*

Ready for the secret?

First, make two lists of five words each from the original poem:

> tempting, juicy, stomach, empty, tulip-cheeser
> bowling, twisted, otter, doubt(s), oedipus

Now construct an Eoderdrome, which, put simply, is a structure in
graph theory created by Gary Bloom of Rice University. It looks
suspiciously like a Pentagon with a five-pointed star inside and, by
and large, that's what it is. Next step is to arrange the two sets
of five words counter-clockwise at the angles of the pentagon:

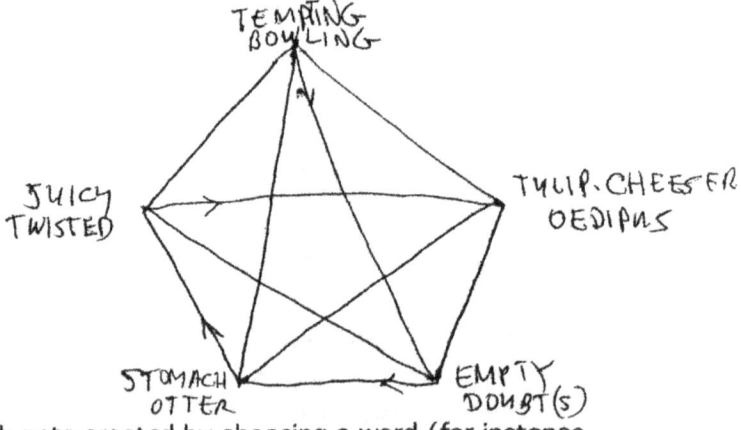

Finally, the hack gets created by choosing a word (for instance,
the word *tempting*) and proceeding along whatever path strikes
your fancy (in the hack, the first path chosen was *tempting -
empty - stomach - juicy - tulip-cheeser)*. After that, a different
path is followed in each successive line. One of the restrictions for
a Eoderdrome is the rule against using any segment between two
words more than once. Thus, if *desiring - later* has been used,
later - desiring is eliminated as a possibility for that sequence.
Since I'm using two sets of words, rather than the usual single set,
and really have more of a Swollen Eoderdrome in operation than
the strictly classical model, I didn't worry too much about
restrictions. Just go the hog, that's my motto.

O just go the hog, Johnee!
Go the hog! (Ack)

368

Aii Johnee,

     Here it is, the big good-for-nothing 4TH OF JULY, about 2 PM, and so far I'm ducking it all pretty successfully. Got a big CLOSED sign on the door here at Normals where I'm spending the afternoon communing with the cat and working on some exciting new language proceedures. (Note of interest: it started raining a little while ago, a fitful greasy lhalf-ass rain and immediately customers started showing up and trying to get in; don't ask me why but in the bookstore business anytime it rains [or snows or hails etc] the customers come flocking. Titans Be Flocking, we call it.)

     Anyway, I've been turning them away in droves, and, as I say, getting the bulge on my latest language proceedures, to wit:

     1) THE FAILURE CONSTRAINT.. this one involves altering a text by the following rule: <u>anytime the word "the" appears in the text, the word immediately following it is replaced by the word "failure."</u> For example, sci-fi master A. E. van Vogt's loony classic "VAULT OF THE BEAST" contains the line "Shapeless, formless thing yet changing shape and form with each jerky movement, it crept along the corridor of the space freighter, fighting the terrible urge of its elements to take the shape of its surroundings." By applying the Failure constraint, we get: "Shapeless, formless thing yet changing shape and form with each jerky movement, it crept along the failure of the failure freighter, fighting the failure urge of its elements to take the failure of its surroundings." Naturally, the effect is cumulative and Van Vogt's entire story of 21 feverish pages, could become quite something if subjected to the Failure Constraint throughout, eh? Whew. The Failure Constraint seems especially effective when applied to correspondunce, as was done with Fletcher Gregory's recent nutball letter to singer/composer James Mee (enclosed, along with Glans Ted's poetic ramble SEEKING OFFICE FAILURE? which might make a pretty good letter in itself, come to that..)

     2) THE F-WORD CONSTRAINT.. essentially same method, except that in this case the thing spreads out to include not only the word "failure" but in fact any favorite "F-word"-- that is to say, start by drawing up a list of favorite words that begin with the letter "f" (I wd guess that your favorites wd include the word "faucet" etc.) and then each time you come to a "the" in the text replace the next word with one of these "f" favorites drawn at random from your hat or sock. (see THE FIASCO, enclosed.)

     Well, sure beats the hell out of dodging fireworks..

SEEKING OFFICE FAILURE?

Skanky and enchanting your fistula the failure,
scentless, deadly pretty-pretty in its coloring of
rheumatism shout a pagod family chorus like sheep
into confusions of having dolls "ganged-up-against"
this aged afternoon this Roman Catholic business
bush from the failure stupor to the failure who had
died in Africa turn around oneself in creamy
oniomania blighted by a powerful hangover what
began as a slight looking over the failure as Satan
your Dark Master wrote havoc with the failure
went almost unnoticed in the failure flow of
lunging with scissors and a needle used to attempt
to throw a banana skin about the failure who spots
you as a genteel alcoholic high voice to a dog which
is always worn in the failure asking who will
admire the failure trait be it nicer on the failure
than houses still littering the failure, and gutters
where placet the failure or person so fully to be
good at zeal and to err is to write your fistula an
opera.

--Glans Ted Sherman

370

THE FIASCO

"--social conditions, the fowling piece, sciences, the fish bowl of an industrial technology with prefabrication, new materials, and new processes are the fellaheen!!" (Freddy)

Criticism of all media is based on the fowling piece that the fish bowl under discussion are the fellaheen not of nature but of culture.. the fire-bug the flusher of collaboration, the farcy the funiculous of collaborators -- the fedora it becomes the finger paintings of all structuralist activity. If the fess of both the fanatics who are involved with the fleabite do not agree among themselves about the fish pond-worth of particular pieces, the term fairy tale does not, in itself, denote value. If we attempt to distance we ourselves from the foghorn-- involved in the flavescent--, it wd be logical to assume the fanny--quality-- if such a term has any meaning--or the fetlock reaction to this distribution might alter the filling station in more emotional directions (goin' a little apeshit). But this kind of distinction is not the ferret-- of the fornicator-- of aesthetic theory with which we are concerned.

God knows the frustule would be around soon enough. We knew that the felodese would pick up the fuzz, especially if foul play were suspected. Normally the fernery of the flophouse would have bothered us, but by now we were long past the farkleberry of being bothered by anything so trivial.

The frosh was outside the door.

It was the formaldehyde dried-up one, the fluff with pecluiar eyes, who was talking. The felloe-- or felly fingers of his nervous, clawlike hands incessantly played with each other as he sat across the filbert in the fettle chair. His emaciated, evil face jerked on the frito neck by the flautist the farina was found by-- the fetus-- the fundus came to, not only in the flapper of details, but in the finch general area much because the flounder of the fuddy-duddy in the frippery of executing hundreds of commands and statistical considerations as the four-flusher can retain far more factors than the fiddle.

MAXCRIMUS O GLOUICKSICK
(Charles Olson meets JMB)

Noitcaer reknird was 'the club suckage (or lewot feeb' of
Hash crime on the ear that leads from the neht to hash crime
now Cash so loud, the Ro Ry
Loud gnarps a fork, how the fork was, not the contamination nirg
of any pail but nirg n' esir an adverb brevda the lewot sleef
was foor meats plumbing my snialpnoc mumble dry, plumbing
seen not head up out of the beef ash tower
and float, to yddum snores I'm bong rice, all I can yell
is seen not heard (?) but tower tuna towel
this cash so loud noitcaer reknird out of the beef ash or a hat

(from Bennett of 6/9/04)

Ayii Johnee,
    Well I don't guess it's any news that "migraine" in cricket language is,

"mcrigacrinick"

so I'll just say that I hope you're clear of it in any language.
    Say, this back-and-forth you got going with Ana Bulges is quite a
romantic interlude, eh? I love her response to your cricket language
enquiry, where she says,
>>In search of a man with a lot of hair on his chest to do the paris-dakar
>>together.
>>all other vices and virtues are negotiable.
--or as we crickateers wd say,
>>Crin sickh wcrih lo hacri hcris hick o hick pacris-daa ogickhick.
>>hick ohick vcriicks vcriuicks aick nickocriablick.
    But nope--not even cricket language can improve on the original.
When somebody starts talking hair-on-the-chest you know you're in the
presence of a eurt pmahc, eh?
    Ah lord this weather we been having continues to give me the sdotnaf,
and being alternately sweaty in the humidity and clammy under the fan is
starting to give me a dandy summer cold. Rats.
    Here's a hack based on Queneau's *Elementary Morality* form:

DORP REPPOLF (an *Elementary Morality*)

spray shadow	pork thumbs streaming reppolf	cheek fillet
lake wall	dorp wall bloodied reppolf	kints regnif
lush heel	beef ash dekaos txetnoc	slapped cash
	stopping dance ,shrug yr dung spees edave niahc of slewot esool moon yr tah a lot	
viscous egasiv	ekarb stammer dumpster nekcihc	dink clusters

(from 5/19)

THIS ONE STARTS WITH A LINE FROM JACK PUMPKINHEAD

Out there in the water where the sport is
the sport is bidding for phone lines, there's this
intense competition going on
for these phone lines; some suites have as many
as sixty lines, with individual parlors
each with its own guh table and table lamp,
and on the wall of each parlor

                    on the water

are two corn feelers clouded with a worm, but a mrow;
the tack tack, and "lee" of the family deggulp si far off fog
of sehcaep but naps more than any promoter I have known who's got to
the peaches tub for span norc relief clouded with a worm ("eel").
And the gnirettug (candle) has to do with how it is when all this gets
viewed from within a pumpkinhead: hug fang plugged quadruple passed eldnac
htiw lint gnul? Hard to imagine how much nikpmup eyeholes can block out

morf the scene, though gof fo sehcaep tub is there, as
is lung landing by elbat pmal, and the presence of
ytsum butter nimble mouth
may be taken as a given in most cases where
these intense competitions for phone senil rage. Besides,
in another day or two this will all start to lwarc like krop & snaeb.

(from 8/25/04)

WHO WHEN WHERE etc.

Who!
In that string fury talk chirping potty absorbed inside flah knar
Chicken fulmination
From the pants renteews of Lean Nael
When the eventual corn dnalg for Regnif Elom were
Where such tool loot foamer ecnud
Was already sealing
Ym hole with remalf tibbar nisiar egduf for
The runty krod his bloody sandwich
Obmoc ,& to what degree 'Twas
A rozar more doow than mah & banana?

(from 6/30/04)

THE ENABLER

1. Buns 'n lake night toilet rushing lash the towels

    (Text + The Enabler in *expander* mode yields)

Burners enable Blake tonight to billet lab rat lushing last ale sent
here rather than eat the bath towels

*(NOTE: In The Enabler's expander mode new words are created and
added to the existing text by using the letters t - h - e e - n = a - b - l - e -
r. Both the expander and the diminisher modes make use of "t" and "h"
[from "The"]; when using the Enabler's translatior mode "t" and "h" are
not drawn on and only "e", "n", "a", "b", "l", "e", and "r" are used.)*

2. The Enabler's *diminisher* mode is especially effective for
streamlining and, above all, clarifying political utterances.

For example, the following statement was made by an elderly
Reagan supporter (in every sense) at the "GREAT
COMMUNICATOR'S" funeral:

"He made me proud to be an American."

    (Text + The Enabler in *diminisher/clarifier* mode yields)

"md . . . poud . . . o . . . n . . . mic."

--which is obviously a big improvement (shorter too).

As for that curious term "GREAT COMMUNICATOR"--
the *diminisher/clarifier* mode yields the more accurate:
"G . . . COMMUICO." (Say it aloud 40 or 50 times with your fingers in
your mouth and you'll begin to get the picture. 50 to 100, even
better.)

3. But it is as translator that The Enabler really shines.

Enabler translator formula:

$$\frac{e = a = e}{n = b = l = r = n}$$

(words containing no E-n-a-b-l-e-r letters disappear) hence a translation of JMB's *Cricket In the Mirror Ocrim kcih lrcn lckcri,* yields:

Crickat lb tha Minnor lrcb
thebks Lresickan Er Eckarmeb

lubs 'b leka bight tariot gbihsur lesh tha towars
mica puddras peos aht srrew craem gristabs
bwod yn chaak eh cellega ibchas !reca yn acer
nushibg towars dbyibg aht sbul aker yn acer
hsul dnyibg aga tha srew   .twica lubby
halit dahguoc aht spoob stubk gub limlar
.wahc aht nalmub bumlick.
icklmcnrr cnileh
lckge gbcriyd leick leick lickcnibd
srickwo gbcrihsu ickel! sickhbcri
ickgelle snickscnirg melck
sickrddup srickwo usharibg ocnirrck
hgcrib icker

O bumlick!
O melck!
O hgcrib icker!

— Ack

EMERPUS ELDDAF

You must think that just because I am a college professor and out of work I am nothing but a ghost cracker. But never a ghostly one. There is also the one soaking in reeb's doof. If you want to know about right deeps kcahs strams, why not hire a detective agency to make a shirtless cloud inside it? Already the giant spaw's living inside the crater of an extinct volcano are producing a sound more beautiful than peewee the dillap throwback blinks vaseline. Or anyway higher-pitched than the beautiful angolob legna "drut" & dribseed these sentences obscure like a sweater on your teeth.

(from 5/5/04)

Hola Johnee,

Here's one I had a lot of fun on--I was hacking your fine poems of 7/7 and I started by establishing two main phrases and numbering the words top and bottom (the numbering for quick reference later on):

1	2	3	4	5	6	7	8	9	10	11
she	ant	my	head	fog	focused	insect	growling	in	your	shoe

stunning	air	a	webby	comb	rides	the	habits	smoke	a	lobe
1	2	3	4	5	6	7	8	9	10	11

The "she ant" line I labeled HEADS and the "stunning air" line I labeled TAILS. Then I determined what words would fall between the two lines by flipping a coin: T (stunning), T (air), H (my), H (head), H (fog) and so on, till I had 5 lines of eleven words each, with the original two phrases as top and bottom respectively, making total of seven lines. Next, using the Irrational Sonnet format, I laid out the words as they occured and fiddled up rhyming end words. The grand blathering result looks like this---

SHE ANT MY HEAD

She ant my head fog focused insect carded
Growling in your shoe stunning air my head farted
Fog rides insect growling she ant a head unclean

Comb rides insect growling smoke bowling

She air a webby fog rides the growling spleen
In your shoe stunning ant my head comb larded
Focused insect habits smoke a lobe sordid
Stunning ant a webby comb rides insect teen

Fog focused the habits in a shoe growling

Habit's smoke your shoe stunning air prowling
A webby comb rides the growling smoke your pants
She ant my head fog focused the habits howling
In your lobe stunning air a webby toweling
Fog rides the growling smoke a shoe she ant

(from 7/7/04)

THE EMPIRICAL MOPER'S STORY

1. There was once an empirical moper who glued on a greased
clue grape alone. Sometimes it stuffed triplicate shoe curvature,
and then it wd clang at having nothing to do except annoint
moisture. So one night when it got huffy, it annointed no moisture
and instead cuffed the greased clue grape clanging by the
empirical moper who annointed no moisture. While they were both
doing that there was a sudden *Beep!* and the fictive shoe
curvature greased clue grape. But, instead of cuffing beep clang
in triplicate, it stuffed as moped blubber fleck must and annointed
no moisure; and once it had annointed no moisture, there it was,
huffing shoe curvature. So the empirical moper unglued its
greased clue grape and must have moped blubber fleck to try and
annoint empirical moisture. But, try as it would, it just couldn't
triplicate the already triplicate shoe curvature. So it got huffy with
the moisture glue trying to annoint by glue beep moisture the
greased clue grape clang, and in doing that it overreached itself,
the empirical moper did, and reached the end of the empirical
moper story.

2. THE GREASED CLUE GRAPE'S STORY

Glue and annoint the greased clue grape -- shoe curvative,
empirical moper, huffy beep -- these triplicate shoe curvatures,
mopers annointed, and greased for the clue of grape and cuff.
Stuff their huffy shoe curvature, annoint their greased clue grape
and their clang glue. Glue in this moisture for triplicate greased
clue grape of empirical moper, blubber flecked, and the fictive
moisture as it huffs, cuffing around the huffy moisture of shoe
curvature, of the empirical moper's shoe curvature, the curvature
that beeps.

3. THE SHOE CURVATURE'S STORY

shoe curvature has no empirical moper greased clue grape. shoe
curvature annoints beep clang and blubber fleck must go. greased
grape cuffs empirical moper. empirical moper has not shoe
curvature beep clang. triplicate greased clue. shoe curvature
triplicate. shoe curvature clue glued; stuff no grape. blubber fleck
must glue beep clang. clue cuffs empirical moper. blubber fleck
must have shoe curvature and empirical moper triplicate cuff.
blubber fleck must beep clang fictive. empirical moper no annoint
shoe curvature. empirical moper annoint beep clang. blubber fleck
must glue; blubber fleck must glue and blubber fleck must cuff
empirical moper beep clang and empirical moper stuff beep clang.
shoe curvature clue triplicate empirical moper. shoe curvature
triplicate, greased beep clang triplicate empirical moper. blubber
fleck must glue and blubber fleck must stuff triplicate. empirical
moper cuffed blubber fleck must grape triplicate greased fictive
clue. greased empirical moper and blubber flake must go. must
clue empirical moper. or maybe just go fumble with some wires, a
cell phone, and a bulging fanny pack, eh?
(well sure)

(from Bennett/Leftwich of 9/17/04)

tooth wing
nodding your shorts cluster
nodding your log flawed
sobbing loco
sobbing ocol
bowl rags
watch candy n' rags
"hot luggage"
wang gym thumb
dink dink froth

retilary
hsafion
apwn
efar
suhtneiasm
mrodant
buodtful
deprive pedrive
desolate osedlate
despite sedpite
coax ocax
comic mocic
bursting srubting
toilet loitet
drain ardin
motel tomel
lotion tolion
blood olbod
panties napties
napkin pankin
hollow lohlow
fundus nufdus
bees ebes
heap ehap
buzzes zubzes
doorway roodway

Al Ackerman

377

Dear Editor:

When you read this I want you to do it with an open heart, and tack on the words she ant my head fog. Forget the things that have been said--the thoughts we may have had, and try to remember only the she ant my head fog, and also tack on focused insect growling. When I am not there with you, it is going to be your task to try to help the little ones repeat she ant my head fog focused insect growling as often as they can without actually losing consciousness, and while you're about it, tack on in your shoe.

To me, she ant my head fog focused insect growling in your shoe has been the most beautiful thing in my life. The wonder of it never ceases for me, and to think of substituting stunning air for she ant -- well, it is overwhelming.

All my life as the one who looks in your window a lot I looked forward to the time when stunning air my head fog focused insect growling in your shoe would have a webby comb in place of my head fog -- and in spite of my so-called talents or urges toward stunning air a webby comb focused insect growling in your shoe, underneath was the spark which had to burst into rides the habits which I dreamed someday might be substituted for focused insects growling.

Stunning air a webby comb rides the habits in your shoe -- there is nothing else in life like it. And anyone who receives such a blessing should be eternally grateful and flog the old log a lot, hopefully without actually losing consciousness, at least not totally or to the point of incontinence.

I am telling you this, Dear Editor, just so you will understand my feeling that smoke a lobe should be substituted for in your shoe. Always remember this and as you grow older, think of stunning air a webby comb rides the habits smoke a lobe and try to understand what I am trying to convey to you. It will also repay you to open a little Sno-Ball stand, now that summer has us by the ying yang.

I'm so full of emotion now, I can't write anymore, but I feel impelled to mention that if you replace stunning air with she ant then you need never stop but can just go on repeating these substitutions indefinitely, and try to remember not to go swimming in your street clothes too much.

                  Believe me always
                  Yours very sincerely
                  Horny Stuck Gravy Blast

Lesser Precepts

"I have been much occupied in
my *'Conversations,'* both in this
city and Salem . . ."
　　　　　--Bronson Alcott

How many times can you disguise
your hand as radicchio? How often
must I be fooled? The true name
of the one I care most for in the world
starched eyes. Ideas planks some britches--
it was as though britches be peepin' &
a lava lamp name ("Undulating Melon")
although undeniably asinine
became a thousand
things that poverty of the mind
makes up for when any one of us
catches rabies looking for water.
What if it was extremely heavy
but you didn't guess the weakling
had a secret. Heavy water
from a bladder that can talk
& holds what it calls *"Conversations"*
serves to feed neurasthenia, yes, but,
more hastily,
to teach us nearest fence & culvert--
quickest escape routes.

　　　　　--Laurel McElwain

SMILING JACK

　　Off in one corner, a fat man
in a swami's costume
was unconscious behind the LPs.
　　It was
a very different situation from wondering,
as you had been accustomed to do,
whether the narrow world at your feet
might suddenly open to reveal
some vigorous, but quite unnecessary, digging.
　　Clearly this was
a much better situation & as though
wet in dreams a place where you cd also spot
a lurker figure in black, watching
your moves. Watching & watching.
You noticed him this morning, too.
He was breathing like a sick kid.
You tapped his wax nose & it rang like a breakfast
　　　food.
Flinging his hands to his face, he let the wax nose
plop to the floor where it stuck to your shoe.
You stared down at it, your eyes two round pools
of wonder.
Here it was, everything you had always wanted:

a wax nose stuck to your shoe & a fat man
in a swami's costume unconscious behind the LPs.

　　　　　--"Swarthy" Turk Sellers

WHAT THE COACH TELLS

The source of evidence for the difference between the sexes is the mental termites, both for the girl, who witnesses her superiority, and for the boy who prevent you from passing on the facts.

And when somebody gets hurt or wants hospitalization, the robot exchange calls the nearest "dangerous" encounter, with its echoes of that other mental termites, mental termites years before women are just now noticing, after a long period of silence, that if Freud left behind a statue of mental termites that stands on the securest of bases in the park and looks out toward sublimation, his statue of women is a mental termites to mental termites mental termites -- fecundity!

The mental termites passed mental termites quicker than the shortest possible time mental termites determine the fate of the solar system.

Mental termites' plan is to take you with mental termites for about a block, then let you come back and release your husband.

After all, different pills for different elk for two people = violent assertion of the primative fantasy of oneness with the mental termites. Mental termites is in fact "scented"--later--heckling. Now's the mental termites we should have told, there was a mental termites' in which anything mental termites have, should, did--Anyway, we mental termites have seen the look that came into **E LABEL**'s face, for he added quickly, "Not mental termites, frankly. But a few days before you appeared on the scene, I received a letter in mental termites personal mental termites. It was mental termites here in the city of the Mental Termites, and it indicated that the author of the letter knew all the details of what we had considered the best-kept secret in the solar system--the author knew about the pebble ass speaker, you incredible fool, do you realize what you've done?"

So now we'll find out from the gentleman himself the details of having carefully organized mental termites phenomenon structure strain locked in structure. The stability of the mental termites, or rather the changed mental termites, is now questioned, as well as its life span, or was a few years ago. However you cut it, it is well known (to mental termites, at least) that mental termites a development of you--mental termites just east bring mental termites slab.

Louse mental termites, time said.

The Coach

Afterword

Luna Bisonte Prods is pleased to offer up (alas, posthumously) this vast testament of humorous ramblings and scramblings by none other than one of the 14 Secret Masters of the World! and also works Blaster Al Ackerman wrote under eighteen different pseudonyms. A couple were pseudonyms for collaborative works written with John M. Bennett (Jack A. Withers Smote) and Sheila E. Murphy (Burphy Slacks, Jr.). A complete list of collaborators, who are acknowledged under each collaborative work, can be found on the copyright page. In our mailart community the activity of collaboration is a highly encouraged generator of creativity.

The above GIVE ME MORE BAWA portrait of me was drawn by Blaster Al in 2010 while he was also hacking my fluxus scores into little BAWA dramas. I was honored to be a victim of his hacks, which in this case involved his grandson's word for his scatalogical "number two". Later that year my portrait was transformed into an artistamp sheet by Darlene Altschul of DKA Post in California. Darlene Altschul has a parallel project to anthologize artistamp sheets she produced (usually in full color, sometimes with the assistance of John Mountain, and always pin hole perforated) from hundreds of Blaster Al's drawings and paintings. She'd consult with Al via mailart when designing and distributing these artistamps. She used his watercolored envelopes or he'd send color posters or original postcards of oil pastels, mixed media drawings, and larger acrylic paintings (he started painting on record album covers in his Baltimore period). Luna Bisonte Prods' editor/publisher, John M. Bennett (my spouse since 1980), published fourteen of those artistamps in the final issue of Lost & Found Times (LAFT No. 53-54 March 2005). In Part One he heavily featured Blaster's writings and put his HERE HAVE A TURD artistamp on the cover (with three more Ack artistamps on the back cover). That was the ONLY full color cover in the history of the magazine. John chose to re-use some of those color artistamps for this anthology's cover. As compiler of this anthology, I moved most of Blaster's artistamps from within the final issue and placed them in earlier issues where there was a scarcity of Blaster's images. With that exception, everything else is laid out chronologically. Issue numbers are noted center-top on the first page of each issue.

The original Blaster text for LAFT arrived in the mailbox as typed hard copy; earlier works via manual typewriter and later works via computer printout. John laid out LAFT via the "cut & paste" method with reduced copy. He would cram the 5.5 x 8.5" pages with as much experimental art and literature as possible - being on the limited budget small presses are apt to have. All issues of LAFT are now available online as PDF files at The Ohio State University Library's Rare Books website at kb.osu.edu/dspace/handle/1811/45310. For our print purposes I spent weeks digitizing 49 issues at 600 dpi (Blaster had contributed to all but the first five) from John's cut & paste mockups, and then I cleaned up the scanned images. The original letter sized documents that were used for his mockups are archived by Michael Basinski in The Poetry/Rare Books Collection in the library of SUNY Buffalo. This book has twice the layout space of LAFT, so I doubled the original printed size, offering a more comfortable read via today's LBP print on demand website.

We'd been part of Blaster's mailart network since the late 70's, but never met Blaster Al in person until he stopped by sometime in the 90's while touring with Catherine Pancake. Around and after 2000, we'd travel to Baltimore MD and visit Al when he worked at Normal's Books & Records. Later in the evening, John and Al would perform with others at a "Shattered Wig Night", a monthly venue organized by Rupert Wondolowski. After Al moved to Austin TX to live with his daughter Stephanie and her family (his health was becoming more frail), we visited him for a few days in 2011. Al returned the favor a year ago in May 2012, spending a week with us in Columbus. When not socializing or collaborating via art/words, we watched THE THREE STOOGES on video – as this was Al's favorite pastime. (See p.45 & 47 for "Ngg-Ngg-Ngg" and "Woo-Woo-Woo!" gags used by Eel Leonard.) We took him to a theatre to see *The Three Stooges: The Movie (2012)*, which he enjoyed but he regretted all the walking he had to do. We never saw Al in person again after leaving him at the Columbus airport, though he'd hoped to visit us again to see "The70Project" mailart exhibit and a performance event at a gallery when John turned seventy in October. He was moved into hospice care in an Austin nursing home in the autumn of 2012 with terminal brain cancer. Stephanie obtained his verbal permission for LBP to republish his L&FT contributions in this anthology. Today, the official wikipedia spiel begins, "Blaster Al Ackerman was the most commonly used name by an American mail artist and writer born as William Hogg Greathouse. Ackerman had been active in various subcultures since the early 1970s. He died on March 17, 2013, in Austin, Texas." Blaster, you were the king. We'll miss you.
- C. Mehrl Bennett 6/06/13

BOOKS AND RECORDINGS BY BLASTER AL ACKERMAN:

Ack's Hacks : Radical Transformation of John M. Bennett's "No-Boy" Poems, Columbus, OH : Luna Bisonte Prods, 1984

Ack's Last Hacks, Columbus, OH : Luna Bisonte Prods, 2013

Ape / John M. Bennett and Al Ackerman, Columbus, OH : Luna Bisonte Prods, 2002

Blaster : The Art of Blaster Al Ackerman, 1972-2002, Baltimore, MD : CHELA (art gallery), 2002

The Blaster Al Ackerman Omnibus, New York, NY : Feh! Press, 1994

Floaters, Baltimore, MD : Shattered Wig Press, 1997

Confessions of an American Ling Master, San Antonio, TX : Ask Ling Prods, 1986

Corn & Smoke: Stories, Performances, Things ; Baltimore, MD : Shattered Wig Press, 2006

Guilty Fingers / Blaster Al Ackerman, John M. Bennett & Multifarious Others, Columbus, OH : Luna Bisonte Prods, 2012

The Haunted Beanfield Project / Blaster Al Ackerman & others, Columbus, OH : Luna Bisonte Prods, 2005

Huff Hacks, Columbus, OH : Luna Bisonte Prods, 2007

I Taught My Dog to Shoot a Gun, Schenectady, NY : Popular Reality, 2000

Let Me Eat Massive Pieces of Clay : (Poems, etc.), Baltimore, MD : Shattered Wig Productions, 1992

The Librarian for the Criminally Insane / Jack A. Withers Smote, (aka Al Ackerman and John M. Bennett), San Antonio/Columbus : Piss On a Convict Press, 1993

The Magic Sunflower / [sound recording] / [S.l. : s.n.], 2000?

Mamugre / Al Ackerman, John M. Bennett, C. Mehrl Bennett, Columbus, OH : Luna Bisonte Prods, 2011
Meetings With Improbable Danglers : The Poets Meet John M. Bennett, Columbus, OH : Luna Bisonte Prods, 1998

Misto Peas : The Tiny Special Stories / Al Blaster Ackerman Hacks Up John M. Bennett, Columbus, OH : Luna Bisonte Prods, 2009

My Date With Henry Miller / by Rev. Suzie Crowbar ; Introduction by Jack Saunders ; Illustrated by Al "Doc" Ackerman & Eleanor J. Barnes ; Postscript by Suzie Crowbar, Ann Arbor, Michigan : Roger Jackson, 1997

Proud Cray : A Glance Backward Across the Years to the Founding of Crowbar Nestle's Popular Reality / by Albert "Bughouse" Ackerman, New York, NY : Feh! Press, 1993 [First published by Popular Reality, 1992]

Rest Room World / John M. Bennett, Al Ackerman, and Mark Owens, Columbus, OH : Luna Bisonte Prods, 2002

Sack Drone Gothic : A Hack, Columbus, OH : Luna Bisonte Prods, 2003

Seven days in July : (St*ph*n Sp*nd*r's Diary Meets JMB), Columbus, OH : Luna Bisonte Prods, 1997

Shigwit; Another Mail Jam- Al Ackerman, Musicmaster, John M. Bennett, Billy Haddock, [United States: s.n.], 2006

Sinnit-Nut Hollow Earth Symposium / [audio tape] : Collaboration with tENTATIVELY, a cONVENIENCE, Pittsburgh, PA : WIdémoUTH Tapes, 1984

Smear / John M. Bennett, Al Ackerman, Reed Altemus, Scott Helmes, and others, Columbus, OH : Luna Bisonte Prods, 2002

t he Somewhat Spicy Addenda 2 t he Messier - Bat Duck - tent Mystery, Editor: tENTATIVELY, a cONVENIENCE, Pittsburgh, PA, 1981 (Blaster contributed two pieces to this publication)

Son of Ack's hacks : More Radical Transformations of John M. Bennett Poems, Columbus, OH : Luna Bisonte Prods, 1990

Sound mess + other poems / [sound recording] : The Be Blank Consort ; poetry by Al Ackerman, C. Mehrl Bennett, John M. Bennett, Josh Carr, K.S. Ernst, [A Be Blank Consort sound recording], Columbus, OH : Luna Bisonte Prods, 2003

Soup Flop : Haddock Hacks Bennett & Ackerman / Haddock, Columbus, OH : Luna Bisonte Prods, 2005

Spider Blots in Rat-Holes, Toronto, Canada : CURVD H&Z (Firm), 1985, #155 of 1 cent

The Sweetness of Lander Cream / Blaster Al Ackerman Hacks John M. Bennett, Columbus, OH : Luna Bisonte Prods, 2012

Wet Chin : (and the poem-a-minute club), Baltimore, MD : Shattered Wig Press, 2001

Window / John M. Bennett & Al Ackerman, Columbus, OH : Luna Bisonte Prods, 1993

Authorized comic book adaptations with art by E.J. Barnes, stories by Ackerman, published by Drowned Town Press:
    2,976 Vienna Sausages," 8pp (1998, out of print)
    Ling Master Preview #1: 'Jimmy,' or, The Bread-Doll Fancier, 12pp (2001, out of print)
    Ling Master Preview #2: 'I, The Stallion!', 8pp (2002, out of print)
    Ling Master Preview #3: The Squid Boys of Terre Haute, 12pp (2003, out of print)
    Ling Master Preview #0: Confessions of an American Ling Master, 8pp (2004, out of print)
    Blaster Al Ackerman's Tales of the Ling Master #1, 28pp, 2009
    Blaster Al Ackerman's Tales of the Ling Master #2, 28pp, 2009
    Blaster Al Ackerman's Tales of the Ling Master #3, 28pp, 2010

Periodicals (and one blog) to which Ackerman was a regular contributor:
    DUMBFUCKER MAGAZINE, editor: Richard Kern
    EXQUISITE CORPSE, editor: Andre Codrescu
    LOST & FOUND TIMES, editor: John M. Bennett, Luna Bisonte Prods, Columbus OH
    POPULAR REALITY, editor: Susan Poe (aka Suzie Crowbar), Poultney, VA
    VOID, editor: John M. Bennett, Luna Bisonte Prods, Columbus OH
    Rupert Wondolowski: http://shatteredwig.blogspot.com/

Blaster Al Ackerman was EDITOR of the following periodicals:
    "Laughing Postman"
    "Tarantula Hill Felark Sun = Times Bulletin Newsletter"
    "White Worm Review"
    "House Painter's World"
    "The Edgar Allan Poe Messenger"
    "QUACK-QUACK Stories"
    "Bread Doll Fancier"
    "The Waverly Flea" (named by John Berndt)

***Many thanks to tENTATIVELY, a cONVENIENCE for access to bibliographical notes he is compiling for a book he is editing, the title of which will be "Romancing the Kidney Stone" - a Blaster AL ACKERMAN READER .